MW01138697

Back When Mary Alice Was
STILL A BLONDE

Also by Robert F. Hastings

Three Grapes and a Cold Biscuit

Back When Mary Alice Was
STILL A BLONDE

ROBERT F. HASTINGS

iUniverse, Inc.
New York   Bloomington

Back When Mary Alice Was Still a Blonde

Copyright © 2010 by Robert F. Hastings

All rights reserved. No part of this book may be used or reproduced by any means, graphic, electronic, or mechanical, including photocopying, recording, taping or by any information storage retrieval system without the written permission of the publisher except in the case of brief quotations embodied in critical articles and reviews.

This is a work of fiction. All of the characters, names, incidents, organizations, and dialogue in this novel are either the products of the author's imagination or are used fictitiously.

iUniverse books may be ordered through booksellers or by contacting:

iUniverse
1663 Liberty Drive
Bloomington, IN 47403
www.iuniverse.com
1-800-Authors (1-800-288-4677)

Because of the dynamic nature of the Internet, any Web addresses or links contained in this book may have changed since publication and may no longer be valid. The views expressed in this work are solely those of the author and do not necessarily reflect the views of the publisher, and the publisher hereby disclaims any responsibility for them.

ISBN: 978-1-4502-6739-7 (sc)
ISBN: 978-1-4502-6741-0 (dj)
ISBN: 978-1-4502-6740-3 (ebook)

Printed in the United States of America

iUniverse rev. date: 11/22/2010

To Looney Smith, with gratitude for lessons learned.

Acknowledgements

The publication of this work would not have been possible without the contribution of Sarah Sakaan, whose grace, talent, and generosity always inspire me. And the invaluable skill, persistence, and patience of Jane Ellen Rawdon.

Author photo by Sheilah Lansky Photography

Elba Rae Van Oaks only had the one sister. There were eight years separating them and about the same number of pounds, and to the informal observer, the totality of those physical distinctions shouldn't have made them be so different. But they had nothing in common, and that may well have been the single fact over which the sisters had never disagreed.

There'd been lots of times when she considered herself an only child anyway, so the absence of a relationship with her sole sibling wasn't anything Elba Rae paid much attention to missing. She was polite if people asked, and when she answered it probably came across like they at least talked periodically. But really, they didn't.

For the most part, they were able to avoid each other after Lila married and moved north to Birmingham, and if avoiding wasn't exactly what they'd done, it was at least a successful series of subconscious evasions. Meanwhile, Elba Rae stayed in Buford all her life where they were reared, and she suspected that Lila sometimes thought the lesser of her because of it.

Elba Rae did try to love Lila, since that's what she was supposed to do according to their mother, and because that's what was droned in by her Sunday school teachers growing up and, ultimately, per the Bible itself. Lila probably loved Elba Rae back, Elba Rae did principally think; liking each other, however, was a challenge altogether different for which the Divine law had no bailiwick.

As far as Elba Rae Van Oaks saw it, Lila had never given her much reason to be overwhelmed with sentiment and with affection over their childhood together, and in adulthood, being related to Lila was sometimes tantamount to having one more sister than she needed. Lila seemed to pop in and out of Buford like a grasshopper trying to stay one hop ahead of a spider, but always on her terms—and never when it mattered much.

When Elba Rae's father took sick and required care—and when Elba Rae's mother relied on her children the most—Mrs. Maywood by and large only got the daughter who lived in Buford. Lila came on down when she could, which wasn't often enough to suit Elba Rae, but usually for one night or two on a weekend and then she'd be off again. Lila would snivel something about her children needing her back in Birmingham or her husband being left alone for too long, and what stirred Elba Rae Van Oaks's blood the most was the way their mother seemed to understand and excuse and practically condone Lila's absenteeism with no hint of ill will. Just because Elba Rae'd never had children didn't mean she didn't have her own life, even if it was in the comparatively less glamorous Buford.

Lila came to town the night before their father passed away. She hovered over the bedside and expelled a great burst of emotion when he died. And while Elba Rae certainly empathized—their daddy's expiration being equally her loss as well—Lila made use of her grief as the reason for deferring most all post-funeral tasks to Elba Rae and to Mrs. Maywood, such as she was able, stating it was just too painful to help sort through her daddy's things and clear up his business.

In the spring of 1983 when their mother was fading, Elba Rae Van Oaks had no expectations she'd share the aftermath of the final illness with a sister whose phone calls were rare and whose visits were even more so. It didn't matter if Lila's children were older and not as needy and Birmingham held less of a grip; it was as though the difference in their ages and the disparity of their lifestyles were by then two forks in a river no sick mother could be held responsible for merging into a single harmonious current.

Elba Rae stayed over at their momma's house when it was necessary, and took Mrs. Maywood to the hospital when she worsened, and pretty much attended to everything like the dutiful daughter she was. She anticipated Lila would be in and out of her life just one more time at the end because, surely, it wasn't like either of them was going to let a little thing like a death in the family foist a reconciliation.

That was, it seems, because Elba Rae had anticipated getting the same Lila she'd always gotten—the sister who'd had no use for Buford or anyone in it since the day she left for a better world elsewhere. As their mother lay dying, Elba Rae Van Oaks had no way of knowing the Lila about to arrive would be a vulnerable one, and as close to coming undone as Elba Rae had ever seen her.

PART ONE

The Chariot Came, Ethel Got In

Dr. Millford straightened back up and took the stethoscope out of his ears before shaking his head no, and for yet just a second, Elba Rae Van Oaks thought maybe he meant "no" she wasn't dead yet. But, of course, she was.

The doctor looked at Elba Rae first as if he expected her to cry. It would have been natural, after all, for someone who'd just watched the breath pass from her mother's surrendered body, leaving behind the frail, battered, and somewhat contorted looking remains on the hospital bed. But Elba Rae Van Oaks did not cry. She was already thinking about what needed to be done. The tears would have to wait until later.

"Thank you for everything, Dr. Bud. I know you tried."

"I'm very sorry, Elba Rae. You know if there'd been anything we could have done for her, we would have. But her heart just gave out. It was her time." He paused ever so briefly, and then said, "I don't think she ever gave up, though."

"No," Elba Rae said, dolefully, but still sans the anticipated emotion. She gazed at her mother's face and thought it bore little resemblance to the woman who'd given her life and who had been a force for so long before the fluid gathered around her heart and wrestled the strength away from her.

"Is there anything I can do for you right now?" Dr. Bud Millford asked sincerely. "Is there anything you need? Phone calls I can make?"

"Oh, no, thank you," Elba Rae said. "I'll go call Lila here in a minute and let her know. She was going to try to come to the hospital yesterday, but I told her just to wait, you know, till morning because I didn't want her leaving Birmingham so late and driving all the way down here at night. But I promised I'd call her right away if anything changed."

"I'd be glad to get in touch with her, Elba Rae. If you'd like."

"No, thank you, Dr. Bud. She'll be expecting to hear it from me."

"I understand." Dr. Millford looked down at the bed again for what would be his final observation of the patient. "I knew Ethel a long time."

"Longer than I can count, I expect," Elba Rae acknowledged.

"She was a good person," he said—which Elba Rae heard clearly—but wondered if these were his customary parting words to the family of the deceased. She looked at her watch.

"Goodness. I didn't realize it was still so early. Lila and them probably aren't even up yet."

"I'm going to step outside to the nurses' station and call the funeral home, Elba Rae. But you take all the time you need. There's no hurry."

The doctor placed his hands gently on her shoulders and patted the left one softly three times before leaving the room. It seemed to her the door took an especially long time to close behind him after he walked out. Elba Rae looked at her mother, and then slowly lowered herself into a straight back chair that had been pulled all the way to the bed rails several hours earlier. What appeared to be the first stream of sunlight was struggling to break through the mostly closed window blinds and Elba Rae Van Oaks couldn't be sure, but thought she heard the proud chirp of a robin nearby.

*   *   *

Dr. Millford was still at the nurses' station down the hall when Elba Rae gathered her pocketbook and left her mother's hospital room for the last time. She was grateful for the doctor's presence, cognizant in fact that his paternal bedside manner made her feel less alone in this most pivotal of life moments. Like everyone did at some point in time, Elba Rae surmised, she had imagined what it would feel like to lose her mother. Her last parent. And now she knew. It made her feel like a complete and absolute adult—a "grown up," she and her little sister, Lila, would have called it when they were children.

Being sixty years old seemed nothing if not irrelevant to Elba Rae's new status. When her father died, she was heartbroken; but she still had her mother. When Elba Rae's husband, the late Fettis Van Oaks, died unexpectedly, she was stunned and in shock; but Ethel Maywood was by her side.

Elba Rae stood quietly behind Dr. Millford until he noticed her. "I got in touch with Charles Robert at the funeral home, Elba Rae. They'll be here in just a little while."

"Thank you."

"I'll get an aid to pack up your mother's things from the room later. There's no need for you to have to do that now."

"Are you sure?"

"Of course. Do you want me to drive you home?"

"Oh, no, I'm fine. But maybe I will go on to the house before I call Lila. It's not like she can do anything about it now, anyway." The doctor had no response.

"Do I need to take care of anything before I go? Sign any papers?"

"No, there's nothing you need to do."

"Okay. Well, thank you again, Dr. Bud. For everything." And then they hugged before Elba Rae took the elevator down one flight to the ground level of the two-story building. The lobby was unpopulated as she walked the few steps to the double glass doors at the main entrance. She stopped on the sidewalk just outside when she realized she didn't readily recall the exact section where she'd left her pale yellow Ford the afternoon before. It wasn't like the parking lot of Litton County Memorial Hospital was so expansive she wouldn't be able to locate it—from memory or otherwise—but she just didn't remember right off.

By the 1980s, a lot of the little Alabama towns like Buford had lost their identities and their innocence and—from some accounts—their charms. It could be blamed on over-zealous developers and big chain retailers and struggling industries that could no longer support a community, but for whatever the reasons, Bufordians seemed immune.

The world waiting outside for Elba Rae Van Oaks that morning in 1983 may as easily have been one from a decade ago or even some period well before, because things didn't change too often in Litton County. The population had held steady for nearly thirty years according to the census folks, a statistic which went unchallenged by any local government officials since it made perfect sense and because they pretty much preferred it that way anyhow. Not many people moved to Buford and not many left on purpose; the populace was, instead, held in check by the natural rhythm of procreation and death.

To be certain, Buford was not completely archaic. Dr. Bud Millford had built a nice, modern clinic out on the highway, and it was less than a mile from the new funeral home that wasn't still especially so new; yet it was referred to as the "new" funeral home anyway to distinguish from the former location, which had been for years the first floor of a large residence just off the Square, the economic hub of Buford commerce. Everyone felt so much better about death in the new location with its plentiful parking, soft drink machine in the visitor's lounge, and separate restrooms for men and women.

Elba Rae stepped off the curb and stood for a moment underneath the portico that extended over the hospital's front door. It was the place where people drove their cars and parked them while they loaded up recovered relatives following discharge. When Elba Rae's mother had entered the hospital five days prior, Elba Rae had more or less expected to be parking there herself. Temporarily, of course. Just long enough to ease her mother into the seat and her suitcase into the trunk for the fifteen minute trip to Elba Rae's house out on Highway 29 where the convalescing would continue until Ethel was strong enough to go back home and stay alone. That's the way it had worked every other time they'd been there.

Sometimes Lila would have been to visit in the interim but it was not likely she'd still be in Buford by the time their mother was released. By then, usually, Lila had returned to her home and her husband and their family in Birmingham. It was Elba Rae who invariably did the local tending.

There was a light coating of dew covering the Ford when Elba Rae got in after ascertaining its location although the moisture was all but gone by the time she drove into the carport of the ranch-style home where she lived alone. The early May sun was mostly up and Elba Rae could tell it would be a pretty day.

She anticipated the parade would begin presently, as soon as word of her mother's passing was spoken. Lila would be the first to know, of course, being the only other direct next-of-kin; but right after she got that over with, Elba Rae would naturally phone her cousin, Hazel Burns, who would without need of prompting be single-handedly responsible for kicking off most of the regional notifying.

There would be a few people at the church, Elba Rae imagined, and then she suspected Hazel would call a couple of neighbors like the Maharrys who lived just down the road, and then Elba Rae felt sure Hazel would go on and call some people from work and let them know Elba Rae's momma had indeed succumbed. The favorable weather outlook gave Elba Rae a small feeling of relief because had the death occurred during a rain, the sympathetic visitors would inadvertently and well-intentioned nonetheless be tracking their water and their mud all over Elba Rae's otherwise clean linoleum floor when they came bearing their gifts. It occurred to her the deep freeze back in the utility room needed cleaning out, since surely she wouldn't be able to store all she knew she would receive. But before any food could be delivered, she had to call Lila.

The many flavors of dread leading up to the call hindered Elba Rae from dialing freely. At first instance, she had pulled the kitchen phone from its cradle on the wall and nearly twirled the first number before deciding the occasion more appropriately called for a sitting position, so she hung it up and walked into her adjoining den in the back of the house where she kept a phone on the end table next to her television-watching chair. Elba Rae took two deep breaths. And then she dialed the area code for Birmingham.

"Hello?" Lila Fessmire didn't sound at all asleep or close to it; in fact, she sounded wide awake and alert as if anticipating a phone call, and Elba Rae felt a mild pang of guilt for not having just gotten it over with from the hospital room. She could only hope the brief lapse in time since their mother had stopped breathing wouldn't become a source of contention.

"Lila Mae," Elba Rae wanted to be as delicate as possible. Yet she didn't suppose there was much of a euphemistic way to tell someone that her mother was dead.

"Yeah, Elba Rae. I was just about to call you to tell you I was heading out. I should have just come on last night because I haven't slept a wink anyway, and I may as well have been there."

"She's gone, Lila."

There was at first silence on the Birmingham end of the phone line. Then a "Huh?"

"She just stopped breathing. Dr. Bud was there, and he said she probably didn't feel any pain. She just stopped breathing. And it was over."

"What? When?"

"Just uh, just a little bit ago." By then, Elba Rae noticed, a good forty-five minutes had elapsed since Dr. Millford's pronouncement.

"Oh, Elba Rae. I should have come on last night!"

"It wouldn't have changed anything, honey. There wasn't anything you could have done."

"I could have been there! I could have seen her!"

"She wouldn't have known you were there."

"She might have."

"I doubt it. She hasn't spoken a word in two days. Dr. Bud said she was probably in something like a coma there at the end. Just not responsive at all."

"Why didn't you call me?"

"To do what?"

"To tell me she was getting worse! I thought you were going to call me if there was any change!"

"Well, Lila, she didn't really start to fail until around three this morning. And there wasn't any point in me waking up your whole house because there wasn't a thing you could have done."

"I just told you I was awake anyhow! I could have gotten in the car right then! And I could have gotten to the hospital before it was too late."

"I doubt it."

"Well, who's to say, Elba Rae?"

"Honey, I know you're upset. I am, too. I'm worn out and I know it hasn't really hit me yet that she's gone. But try to get yourself together and come on when you can. We'll need to get to the funeral home and get some things settled."

"Oh, Lord, Elba Rae, I can't believe it. And of all the times for her to go."

"What do you mean? Of all *what* times?"

"I mean, I know she was old. But somehow I just never thought she'd really die. I always thought she'd be too ornery to go."

"She was a tough one, nobody can deny that."

"She always seemed too big and full of life to be stopped by something like," Lila paused for a second. "Death."

"Well, it was her time, Lila. Just like it was Daddy's when he went and

Fettis's when he dropped dead and everybody else that's gone on before her. We're all leaving some day."

"I know," Lila agreed through a sniffle. "But she was our mom-ma." The sniffle gave way to a genuine sob while Elba Rae listened patiently.

"Is Bucky there?"

"What?" Lila said through a muted wail.

"Is he there with you?"

"Well, where else *would* he be at this god-awful hour? He's downstairs putting the coffee on."

"I just meant why don't you go tell him what's happened, and then come on when you can? I'll be here whenever you get here."

Lila sniffed a couple of times and seemed to regain her composure and, perhaps, some cognition. "You're already home?"

"Yeah."

"At the house?"

"Yes."

"Well, exactly when did Momma die, Elba Rae?"

"It was just a few minutes ago."

"A few minutes?"

"Yes."

"But long enough for you to see the doctor and take care of whatever you had to do at the hospital and then get home and then finally get around to calling me?"

"It hasn't even been an hour."

"Well, why didn't you call me when it happened, for heaven's sake?"

"Because I wanted to get home first! To have a little privacy."

"There was a phone in the hospital room, wasn't there? It's not like Momma was in any condition to eavesdrop."

"I didn't want to call that early! You know how it is when the phone rings in the middle of the night! You're liable to have thought—"

"That somebody had died?"

"Whether it was an hour or two minutes ago, it doesn't matter. The outcome is still the same. She's dead."

"Well, you could have let me know before half the town found out."

"Now you know you're the first person I've called. Nobody else knows a thing yet."

"How'd you stop Hazel from running up and down the road making an announcement?"

"Hazel doesn't even know yet. I told you—I wasn't calling anybody until I told you." Elba Rae then heard a voice in the background, for which she was appreciative, and hoped it was Lila's husband, G. Duane Fessmire, who everybody called "Bucky;" his arrival in the bedroom would be a good catalyst to end their unpleasant conversation.

"I've got to go, Elba Rae. Bucky's up here and I need to let him know."

"Okay, honey. Be careful driving down here."

"I will. I'll see you."

"All right. Bye-bye."

"Bye," Lila said and hung up. In Buford, Elba Rae Van Oaks said "whew" to herself.

*   *   *

Elba Rae Van Oaks was born in Litton County, Alabama. She was named after her great-grandmother on her mother's side because Ethel Maywood had vowed from the time she herself was but a child if she ever had a daughter she would name her Elba, which amused Ethel's grandmother Elba the First and endeared Ethel all the more to her.

Elba Rae got her middle name from her father, Raymond, who did not have a grandmother he remembered with undue fondness and who, Ethel Maywood knew outright, had spent nine months wishing for a son he didn't get. Ethel thought the compromise only fair since Raymond was willing, without debate, to accept the feminine spelling of the name and no one ever called Elba Rae Van Oaks just Elba.

When Elba Rae was eight, Raymond and Ethel Maywood welcomed their second child, Lila, who wasn't named after anybody; she'd simply gotten her own original and unique name that had not previously been used by any Maywood known to Raymond or Ethel. Mae was the baby's middle name because Ethel deemed it sounded cute and because she reasoned it would metrically match the double label affixed to the older sibling, thus connecting them indelibly as a pair.

Lila Mae Maywood did not comprehend the institution of carrying a double name until she entered high school and began to associate mostly with a crowd of girls who only used one name because—it was generally understood if not discussed—that was the more sophisticated way to be named. By the time she was a sophomore, "Mae" was pretty much dropped except on formal occasions, and in the decades following graduation, a period mainly lived out as a Fessmire of the Birmingham Fessmires, there were few persons outside Litton County to whom Lila's middle name had ever been disclosed.

Elba Rae had spent a night at the Georgian Terrace Hotel in Atlanta once, on the honeymoon she took with Fettis, but had not traveled much since that long ago trip, and when she did, it wasn't usually beyond the Alabama border. She'd held the same teaching job at the same school since earning her certificate in the early 1940s.

Hazel Burns and Elba Rae Van Oaks were first cousins on their mothers' side. Hazel was a handsome woman, if not pretty, and had the appearance of someone younger than she was. Though she never married, there had been through the years a few gentlemen with whom she'd kept company, but Elba Rae was always left with the impression the gentlemen were more serious about Hazel than she was about them.

The two women had a close relationship formed when they were children—playmates of nearly the same age, daughters of two sisters each devoted to the other. They were raised in the same Methodist church, and when it was time to go to work, they ended up together once more. Elba Rae taught fifth grade at the Homer T. Litton Grammar School while Hazel was secretary to its principal. They were "like sisters," Elba Rae had often said, although in her own sphere of comparison, she wasn't always sure what that meant.

"I'll be on in just a minute," Hazel said right after Elba Rae phoned with the news about Ethel, which didn't surprise Elba Rae in the least. The house was in its usual state of tidy but not company clean, and she welcomed the help to prepare for visitors.

"Do you want me to try and get hold of Mr. Bailey?"

"I do, Hazel. Thank you." Mr. Bailey was the principal of the Homer T. Litton Grammar School and their collective boss.

"And I'll let the preacher know."

"I appreciate it," Elba Rae said, and then they shortly said good-bye.

"All right, now then," she said to herself and out loud as she shifted into task mode. Water in the tea kettle, legal pad and pen from the drawer underneath the phone, and a can of Pledge from the cabinet above the deep freeze in the utility room. Elba Rae needed to organize her grief and make it presentable, preferably with a light lemony scent.

Within the hour, Hazel Burns let herself in through the unlocked carport door that opened into a short little hallway connecting the small laundry room to the kitchen of Elba Rae's house. Hazel heard a background of "The Today Show" on TV in the den where Elba Rae was not dusting furniture but rather was sitting in the weathered recliner once off limits to anyone except her late husband, Fettis. She was unconsciously sipping on a cup of instant coffee that still had its instant coffee foam floating on the top.

Hazel Burns had once benignly inquired of her cousin exactly why she didn't opt to replace Fettis's clunky old chair (whose origins Hazel Burns knew very well dated to the Christmas season of 1965) with something slightly less clunky and a lot less worn, especially given that any anticipated objections raised by the late Fettis Van Oaks were clearly no longer a consideration since Fettis himself had been resting in heavenly peace out at Glory Hills Cemetery for a number of years.

The chair was a medium-to-dark brown, upholstered in what Hazel had been reminded was genuine leatherette. The arms were shiny from where Fettis had rested his hands while he watched television. Elba Rae had acknowledged the chair's condition was less than pristine and certainly not something she'd ever want on display in the good living room in the front part of the house, but she'd vowed what the chair lacked in aesthetics it compensated for by offering unrivaled comfort. That is to say, when the wooden handle sticking out on the side—which, when properly engaged launched the chair into reclining mode—worked properly. Hazel knew for a fact Elba Rae on occasion had been temporarily detained in the tilted position if she had trouble returning the contraption to its upright and normal sitting posture, and had even once risked injury to climb over the side when the mechanism jammed up completely, leaving Elba Rae to an otherwise permanent state of laid out.

Hazel Burns had long suspected that Fettis's ratty old chair sat in Elba Rae's den for the same reason Fettis Van Oaks continued to receive a subscription to the *National Geographic* even though he couldn't read a magazine any more than he could fling wide open the side-mounted handle of his genuine leatherette recliner to enjoy fully the benefit of its near stretcher-like quality. But the chair's presence in the house, like the current month's issue of the magazine on the coffee table, was a remnant Elba Rae apparently was still not ready to abandon—reminders, that by 1983, were few and rare and all the less likely to be discarded.

Miss Jane Pauley was saying something about President Reagan planning a trip overseas and something else about some bad weather out in California before promising a follow-up to an earlier piece about an Irish setter named Daisy that saved a family of eight from certain death in a campsite travel trailer fire, but Elba Rae wasn't much listening to any of it.

Hazel was half way in the den before it seemed Elba Rae noticed or got up from Fettis's recliner to accept an embrace. There were no words spoken between them during what was to Elba Rae a comforting squeeze.

"It just doesn't seem real yet, does it?" Hazel asked rhetorically.

"No." And then Elba Rae realized her cheek was wet from a tear. She swiftly brushed it off with her hand as though it were an unwelcomed insect.

"It's all right to let go, Elba Rae."

"Oh, it's just that ole weatherman on there," she said, gesturing toward the television set and whereupon admitting she'd been overwhelmed by a moment of melancholy when Mr. Willard Scott had extended congratulatory wishes to Mrs. Iola Batts of Flouncy, Oklahoma on the occasion of her one hundredth birthday. Elba Rae Van Oaks bore no ill toward Mrs. Iola Batts or any of the Batts family, but it made Elba Rae cry just the same when she realized Ethel Maywood was never to be beneficiary of such a greeting—not from Mr. Willard Scott, and not from anyone.

Amid the otherwise somber mood of the visit, Hazel could not avoid acknowledging the gleeful reception she received from the little poodle, who bounced wildly up and down on his hind legs against her shin.

"Get down!" Elba Rae commanded, to no avail.

"Oh, he's all right." Hazel leaned down to smile at the dog and to pat him on his head.

"Poor Mr. Wiggles," she said, addressing him directly. "What are you going to do without Aunt Ethel?"

"Guess I just got myself a dog," Elba Rae sighed.

"He looks right at home, Elba Rae."

"He should. He's spent enough time here in the last few years. Every time Momma would go in the hospital. It's been his second home."

"Do you think Lila Mae would want to take him back to Birmingham with her?"

"I doubt it. I think Lila's got all she can say grace over up there as it is.

And besides," Elba Rae said as she reached down and picked up the animal, "having him here will be sort of like having Momma around." The dog looked up at her and gave her a quick lick on the nose.

"I 'spect he was a lot of company to Aunt Ethel."

"He was," Elba Rae agreed, as she lowered Mr. Wiggles back to the floor. "Of course, she'd never let on how crazy she was over him, but I know she was. It's all she ever wanted to know about while she was in the hospital. 'How's Mr. Wiggles getting along at your house? Did you remember to let Mr. Wiggles out to do his business before you came up here? Did you put down fresh water for Mr. Wiggles?' Honestly, Hazel, I don't ever remember her fussing over us so when we were children."

"Bless her heart," Hazel remarked, which really meant in the moment she recollected things similarly.

"Well, I got hold of Mr. Bailey before I left the house, and I called the parsonage and got Reverend Timmons."

"Good. Thank you."

"What about Lila and them?"

"She called before you got here and said she was leaving her house right then. Bucky is going to wait and drive down with the children tomorrow. Lila thought it'd be best for her to get in here and us settle a few things before we have a house full, and I think she's right."

"You know," Hazel injected, "some of them could come on over to my house and stay if need be."

"Oh, thank you, Hazel, but we'll be all right here. Lila and Bucky will be in the guest room and Charity can sleep on the day bed in my spare room. I'll put the boys on a pallet in the living room and they'll be just fine."

"Well, if you change your mind, it's no trouble. I'm over there all by myself. And I don't know when I've seen Lila's children."

"Me either," Elba Rae remarked.

Hazel Burns chuckled a little. "Aunt Ethel used to get so tickled at Charity when she was a little girl. Remember how she didn't want any of her food to touch on the plate?"

"Yeah," said Elba Rae. "Sort of."

"And Aunt Ethel had to keep a little set of individual bowls for her to eat out of when they came to visit?"

"Food touching," Elba Rae just shook her head. "I don't know why Lila let that child get away with such foolishness."

"Well," Hazel's smile slowly faded, "the offer still stands if you need the room."

"I know. Thank you."

"Okay. Now is there anybody else we need to call right away?"

Elba Rae rubbed her temple with the forefingers of her left hand. "I've already talked to Charles Robert at the funeral home. I've got an appointment this afternoon at four." She paused. "I can't really think of anybody else right off, Hazel. I thought maybe a little later in the day I'd try to call Begina."

"Oh." Hazel's enthusiasm seemed just ever so subtly diminished.

Hazel Burns knew, of course, there would have to be notification to Begina Chittum, as she was Elba Rae and Lila's first cousin on their daddy's side, and even if Begina did live all the way over in Hattiesburg they'd have to let her know the particulars of the arrangements, in the event she was to come. Hazel approached the subject delicately.

"Do you think she'll try to get here?"

"I don't know, Hazel. I doubt she can leave Aunt Laveetra alone for too long and surely she wouldn't try to bring her."

"You think?"

Elba Rae closed her eyes and shook her head from side to side. "I don't think I can face that possibility right now," she said. "Maybe I'll get Lila to call Begina after *she* gets here."

Hazel Burns smiled and began to slowly nod her head up and down in concurrence. "That sounds like a good idea to me."

*   *   *

Hazel Burns made a point to stay with Elba Rae until Lila Fessmire arrived from Birmingham, during which time Hazel kept herself busy by conducting a freshness test on the guest room and daybed linens and by giving the home's one bathroom a sprucing up in anticipation of company. Elba Rae, meanwhile—though she had every intention of participating in the cleaning process as evidenced by the fact she carried in her hand at most all times a half-full bottle of Formula 409 and one hygienic rag—was otherwise distracted and detained by the successive telephone calls being made to the house as news of Ethel Maywood's early morning death made the rounds in Buford.

Lila let herself in through the carport door while Elba Rae was on such a call, and stood tolerantly next to a small piece of luggage she'd brought with her and put on the floor. A matching garment bag was draped over one arm, and she securely held onto her purse.

"Ah hah … Well, I appreciate your calling, Martha Betty, and … ah hah … I imagine Hazel or some of them will let you know something just as soon as it's settled … Ah hah …Well, Martha Betty, Lila's just come in and I … ah hah … just now … ah hah … well, all right then, bye-bye" after which she was at last free.

"Mercy," Elba Rae remarked as she hung the receiver on its wall-mounted base. "That thing hasn't stopped ringing."

"I got here as soon as I could," Lila said.

"Oh, I know you did," Elba Rae assured, and then the sisters finally hugged. "Are you all right? You didn't have any trouble coming down, did you?"

"No. Not at all."

"You've changed your hair."

Lila reflexively ran her hand over head. "I guess I've lightened it some since I've seen you."

"Yeah," Elba Rae said. "And you've cut it."

"I was just tired of fooling with it. But you look," Lila returned, guardedly, "the same."

"I guess I'm not brave enough to go frosting my hair up. Have you had anything to eat? I've got plenty of eggs and some biscuits, and there's a good coffee cake in the icebox I got from Piggly Wiggly. They bake them fresh right there in the store."

"No, thank you. I don't want anything right now. Maybe later."

"Well, put your things down on the table. We'll get them back to the guest room later."

Lila complied just as Hazel Burns emerged from the hallway carrying a sponge and a can of cleanser.

"Elba Rae, you're near abouts out of Comet but I can pick some up this afternoon if you need me—oh, goodness! Lila Mae! I didn't even hear you come in!"

Hazel immediately discarded her cleaning tools and embraced Lila Fessmire.

"I'm so glad to see you."

"Thank you, Hazel, you too. You look good."

"Oh," Hazel snickered, "I'm sure I'm a mess right now. Did you just get here?"

"She just walked in the door," confirmed Elba Rae. "I was on the phone with Martha Betty Maharry and thought I'd never get off. I know everybody means well, but don't they know I've got a million things to do?"

"Well, I've dusted everything in the back, Elba Rae, and the bathroom's done. I just lack the living room and running the vacuum and we'll be through."

"Oh, goodness, don't worry about it, Hazel. You've already done too much already."

"It won't take me but a minute to—"

"No, no. I appreciate it," Elba Rae said as she glanced over at Lila, "but we'll get to whatever else needs doing here in a while. Let's just sit down and visit for a little first. Goodness, I don't know whether I'm coming or going."

Elba Rae walked into her den and resumed post in Fettis's chair; Hazel Burns and Lila soon followed.

"So Bucky's not with you just yet, is that right?" asked Hazel.

"No. He'll be here tomorrow afternoon with the children. He knew Elba Rae and I would be busy today making plans and I think he wanted to stay out of the way."

"How are the children doing? I know they must be upset about their grandmother."

"Well, sure," Lila said. "They were too young to have any memories of Daddy dying, so this is the first time they've actually lost anybody in the family."

"I bet your boys have really grown."

"You wouldn't believe how much. I think they're going to be taller than their daddy before they're through."

"And Charity, now let's see. Did Elba Rae tell me she'll be graduating this year?"

"That's right."

"Goodness. It doesn't seem possible, does it? That Aunt Ethel's got a granddaughter about to be through high school?" Hazel paused. "Does it, Elba Rae?"

"No," Elba Rae chorused, as Hazel continued her friendly chit chat.

"Does she know where she wants to go to college yet?"

"Well," Lila drifted. "Her plans are still up in the air right now."

Elba Rae suddenly seemed interested. "Hasn't she applied anywhere?"

"No, not yet," answered Lila.

"Really?"

"We haven't gotten around to it yet, but we will," Lila said.

"Well, it's already May," said Elba Rae, mildly exasperated. "It's not like enrolling in grammar school where you can wait till the week before."

"I understand that, Elba Rae, and I assure you Bucky and I have the situation under control."

There followed a discomfited silence that was interrupted by Hazel Burns declaring in the most understated of ways it was time for her to take her leave and relinquish the sisters to the many discussions and decisions that surely fell upon their shoulders to discuss and decide.

Elba Rae Van Oaks walked Hazel out to the carport, along the way expressing earnest thanks and gratitude for Hazel's detail to cleanliness, whereas Lila Fessmire just said "bye" from the kitchen.

"Is that a new car?" Elba Rae asked as soon as she rejoined Lila back inside the house.

Lila hesitated for a couple of seconds. "It's not *brand* new," she said. "I've had it a few months. It was my Christmas present from Bucky."

Elba Rae stared at it through the carport door.

"It looks like—is that a Cadillac?"

"Yes.

"Bucky's business must be good."

"It is," Lila confirmed with confidence.

"Does it have push-button windows?"

Lila let out a sort of chuckle, but not necessarily the kind born of humor.

"It has everything that comes on a Cadillac."

Elba Rae continued her assessment. "That's an unusual shade of gray. I don't believe I've seen it before."

"It's called Oyster Shale."

"Hmm," remarked Elba Rae, as she finally stepped away from the door. "It's pretty."

"Thank you. So, what do we need to do first?"

"Oh, well, I've started trying to write some things down. You know, just mainly making lists of what we've got to decide about." Elba Rae went to the kitchen table where her legal pad and pen were resting. "I'm gonna fix another cup of coffee, do you want one?"

"Yeah. Sure," Lila said.

Lila Fessmire went to the table and sat down while Elba Rae went about dispensing instant coffee powder into two cups that she rested on saucers from her everyday dishes. After delivering the steaming beverages to the table, she made a trip to the refrigerator for a carton of half and half. A sugar bowl that matched the dishes was already out in the middle of the table. Elba Rae sat down at the opposite end while Lila perused the tablet at Elba Rae's organization thus far.

"You know, I still can't believe we're actually sitting here getting ready to do this," Lila said. "It just doesn't seem possible."

"I know it's a shock but we should also be thankful we had a little notice," remarked Elba Rae.

"What?" Lila seemed confused and un-consoled.

"She could have gone like that," Elba Rae snapped her fingers. "Without any warning. At least we had a little time to prepare."

"Elba Rae, right now that doesn't make me a feel a bit better."

"Well, it should."

"It doesn't. Our momma is dead, for God's sake."

"Momma wouldn't want us taking the Lord's name in vain, and it would have been a worse shock if you hadn't had any warning—that's all I'm saying. Momma was sick and in the hospital and we knew to expect the worst. At least it wasn't like what I went through with Fettis."

"Oh, Lord," Lila sighed, as she put her cup down on its saucer while gently massaging the bridge of her nose with the thumb and forefinger of her other hand. Lila Fessmire had always tried to maintain the appropriate level of sympathy for her sister, whose marriage to a somewhat older man had resulted in Elba Rae being widowed at a relatively young age. But she nonetheless dreaded the recitation of facts she feared was forthcoming based on the phrasing Elba Rae customarily used as a way of introduction to the story, no matter who had just died. It was always the same theme centering on the fragility of life and the uncertainty of death.

"You just can't imagine that shock," Elba Rae carried forth.

"I'm sure it was, Elba Rae." Lila used both hands to cover her face but kept her eyes open, and her eyelashes tickled her palms when she blinked.

"And I hope you never have to go through it."

"I do too, Elba Rae," Lila said, but her voice was somewhat muffled through her cusped hands.

"I'll never forget it as long as I live."

By then, Lila knew there was no stopping Elba Rae because once she declared she'd never forget it as long as she lived, the story was officially launched. Lila Fessmire did not mean to belittle the tragedy of her brother-in-law Fettis Van Oaks's death, because—Fettis or not—it was a tragedy; he was, after all, the only man Elba Rae'd ever had. But the story of his last day had taken on a life of its own over time, and it seemed with each passing year, Elba Rae's version became all the more dramatic and purposeful.

It was a Sunday, as Lila was about to be reminded, and Elba Rae had gone to church. Fettis Van Oaks had not attended services with Elba Rae at the First Avenue United Methodist because, according to Elba Rae and to Fettis, his back could not endure the suffering of prolonged sitting in the unforgiving wooden pews due to a disabling injury sustained years earlier at the Buford Slaughter and Packaging plant, an injury that had served, coincidentally, to also end Fettis Van Oaks's ability to be employed. Lila Fessmire suspected Fettis Van Oaks did not attend church because he was a heathen, but that theory was never publicly entertained.

Elba Rae had not lingered any longer or any shorter than usual after preaching that Sunday, visiting with her regular circle of friends and acquaintances on the lawn of the church. She had shaken hands with Reverend Bishop, whose pulpit tenure immediately preceded that of Reverend Timmons, and had complimented his wife, Edith, on the delicious pea salad she'd brought to the circle meeting pot luck the Thursday evening prior. Elba Rae told her she was going to have to write down the recipe one day and Edith Bishop had said she'd be glad to and of course she never did.

Elba Rae had made a point to palaver with Martha Betty Maharry's mother, Mrs. Nita Perrymore, and had let Miss Nita know how good it was to see her at services, since she was rarely seen in public by then due to obvious frailty and just a smidge of senility that became evident if the conversation went on very long about anything more cognitive than the weather or the color of her dress, which was almost always a hue involving pink. And the last person Elba Rae had spoken to had been her cousin, Hazel Burns, who'd said, "See you at school tomorrow." But it was not to be.

Elba Rae Van Oaks had driven her Ford Galaxie into the carport at home around twelve-thirty that afternoon to find it perfectly ordinary that Fettis's truck was parked over to the left side. Fettis didn't typically venture out on Sunday mornings like he was wont to do during the week when he'd head to the Square early and partake of coffee and his own version of fellowship with the men who congregated at the Moss Hardware & Supply, preferring instead to relish the quiet and the solitude of home on Sundays while Elba Rae worshiped and then visited and palavered and talked about delicious pea salads and pretty pink dresses.

The door leading from the carport into the house and the little hallway off the kitchen was open, just as Elba Rae had left it, and the storm door was unlatched. She'd put her purse down on the kitchen table and gone directly to the oven to check on the status of a chuck roast she'd slid in right before leaving for Sunday school. It smelled good, she recalled in most versions of the story, and the onions had given it an especially sweet aroma.

On top of the stove had been a large saucepan with a lid, already full of water and potatoes peeled that morning after breakfast. Elba Rae had turned the electric burner on high and set the lid to the side to wait until the water boiled. The biscuits she'd planned to serve would come from a can but she wouldn't get those from the refrigerator until the roast came out of the oven.

Elba Rae had paused for only a few seconds, long enough to take in a deliberate whiff of what she'd known would be a tender, gooey roast. And then she'd walked out of the kitchen, through her den, and down the hallway leading to her bedroom where she intended to change clothes but which that day led—instead—to the body of her husband, Fettis Van Oaks, who was dead on the floor.

"Fettis?" She'd called out to him, expecting him at first to rise up from the crumpled heap into which he'd come to rest face down in the hallway. She had wondered in that very first flash of recognition why he'd chosen to take a nap in the floor instead of the big reclining chair in the den that habitually was his non-nocturnal bed of choice.

"Fettis!" The flashes and the impulses had flooded her brain at that point, as Elba Rae had somehow rationalized that it made no sense to assume Fettis was merely sleeping and that, therefore, the site before her must not bode well.

She'd dropped to the floor and rolled Fettis over, and even in her state of shock, had known the second the light illuminated his chin and mouth she was not looking at the face of a man who'd been recently breathing. But she had shaken him for several minutes anyway and had continued shouting his name. Half scolding, half pleading; either way, just wanting some semblance of an answer.

Fettis Van Oaks had not responded. The closest telephone was the extension in their bedroom, to which Elba Rae had walked with resolve. After dialing the zero for an operator and getting connected, Elba Rae had calmly asked for an ambulance but offered to the operator she believed her husband had passed away in the hall. She'd returned to Fettis to wait for the ambulance, and even though she'd held his head in her lap the entire time, she'd stopped her shaking and her scolding and even calling out his name by the time the siren was within earshot.

"And there he was," Elba Rae said to Lila, who by then had lowered the hands from her face only at the point her own breathing was labored from the self-induced suffocation.

During the dramatic height of the story, Elba Rae had gotten up from the table and walked to the stove and back more than once, and now stood looking out the bay window of the breakfast nook. "There wasn't a thing I could do," she said while staring without purpose out the window.

"You know, I don't have a thing in the world against George Timmons. He does a good job preaching. But you just couldn't beat Reverend Bishop at a funeral. Especially when he'd go to quoting. I'll never forget what he said at Fettis's service because it's made me appreciate having a little warning with Momma."

"What's that?" Lila felt foolish for even asking because she knew the answer. She'd memorized the denouement of Elba Rae's parable just as well as she knew the introductory part that always led to it.

"He said we've all got to be prepared because life can change in the twinkling of an eye. Just like it did for me and Fettis. Doesn't matter if *you're* ready or not. When the Lord's ready, he'll send the chariot. And He was ready for Fettis that Sunday morning. The chariot of God swooped down and took Fettis home. Without warning to any of us." Elba Rae paused. "In the twinkling of an eye."

Lila Fessmire especially remembered that part and found it terribly ironic since absent from Elba Rae's usual chronicle was the reality that immediately prior to boarding the chariot, Fettis Van Oaks had, from all appearances, just exited the hall bathroom from what he called his private time—evidenced, clearly, by the fact his poor dead hand continued to clutch an issue of the *National Geographic* even as the ambulance attendants attempted resuscitation before loading his body onto the stretcher.

Lila respected Reverend Bishop and had always held his ability to console in high regard, and she knew the imagery in his words had been intended to comfort. But she couldn't help but assume if Fettis Van Oaks had known the chariot of God was hovering outside in the hallway that morning, he surely would have just as well stayed in the bathroom with the door closed.

"How's he doing?" Lila asked, hoping to navigate the subject away from painful memories of Fettis's untimely ride in the chariot.

"Who?"

"Reverend Bishop. Does anybody ever hear from them?"

"Oh," Elba Rae sighed, as she sat down and joined Lila at the table. "Martha Betty and some of them tried to keep up after he retired. But you know he and Edith had to move to North Carolina to be near the children and we don't get much news anymore. They're in some kind of elderly care place."

"A nursing home? That's sad."

"Well, I didn't understand it to be a nursing home, exactly. I think they have their own little apartment. But somebody fixes all their meals and everybody eats together in a big dining room. And there's a beauty parlor right there at the place. An operator comes in once or twice a week so Edith can get her hair done. But …"

"What?"

"They say Edith doesn't have much mind anymore."

"Oh. That's too bad. I remember her being sweet. And Momma was always real fond of her."

"Yeah, Momma loved her. Everybody did. She was such a lady. And not that I've got anything against Lorraine Timmons, because I don't, but Lorraine can come across as timid and shy sometimes, and Edith Bishop was always so outgoing. She never missed one Sunday at that church, and she helped out with everything. It's right pitiful now, though. Last time I asked Martha Betty about them she said Reverend Bishop had a hard way to go with Edith."

"Why's that?"

"Martha Betty said Edith had gotten bad to just want to strip her clothes off, and that Reverend Bishop and the nurses had an awful time trying to keep her covered. They'll be eating supper and having a conversation like she's all there, and then she'll go to pulling her dress up over her head. Right there in the dining room. Martha Betty said they'd just about taken to eating all their meals in their little apartment, unless it's an occasion or a holiday or something."

"Poor Reverend Bishop," Lila sympathized.

"One night Edith got up from the bed, stripped off her gown, and got out of their room without him even knowing. By the time he came to, she'd managed to get all the way down the hall and through the lobby. They like to have never found her."

Lila burrowed her brow. "That sounds dangerous."

"I know," Elba Rae nodded. "They looked and called for thirty minutes, Martha Betty said. Reverend Bishop was beside himself before they finally found her."

"Where was she?"

"Down in the beauty parlor. Can you imagine?"

Lila Fessmire could not.

"Sitting under the hairdryer like she had an appointment. Naked as a jaybird. And you know, that's just not Edith."

"No," Lila agreed. "I don't recall ever having run into her buck naked at a beauty parlor."

"Oh hush," Elba Rae scoffed, as she sat back down at the table. "You know what I mean."

"Yes, I do, but you know all this talk about Fettis passing away and Edith Bishop taking her clothes off isn't getting us anywhere. Now, you've got 'flowers' written here at the top of this page."

"Oh, yeah," Elba Rae said. "I meant to cross that off."

"Did you order something already?"

Elba Rae shook her head yes. "Before you got here, I talked to Pearl over at the florist, and she said they could do a nice spring mix for the casket piece."

"Well, what would it have in it?"

"Just a mix, you know. Lilies, daisies—spring flowers. Maybe some tulips if she can get them. She said she'd have to check on the tulips."

"What about carnations?"

"I didn't specify any carnations."

"That's not what I mean. I meant what if there are carnations in the spring mix?"

"What about them?"

"Momma hated carnations," Lila stated matter-of-factly, with an inflection suggesting the reminder was unnecessary.

"No she didn't."

"Yes. She did."

"Why do you say that?" Elba Rae asked.

"Because she said it a thousand times. Every time we'd go to a funeral and see a spray of carnations, Momma would make a point of saying how much she hated them and to make sure we didn't have any for her. She said carnations were nothing but mortuary flowers."

"I don't remember her ever saying that."

"I can't help it, it's what Momma said."

"Well, that must have been a long time ago if it was some time when you were going with Momma to a funeral. When's the last time you and Momma went to a funeral together?"

"I don't know, Elba Rae. I must have forgotten to write it down in my diary."

"I'm just saying I don't imagine Momma would care one way or another if there are a couple of little carnations mixed in with the other flowers. Pearl said it would be a nice variety and they'd all be real fresh."

"Where's the phone book?" Lila asked.

"What do you need the phone book for?"

"Where is it?"

"It's in the far-right drawer in the kitchen. The drawer underneath the phone."

Lila immediately went toward the wall-mounted telephone and pulled open the drawer directly below. The book was thin, quickly facilitating her purpose. She removed the receiver from its cradle and began to dial.

"Who are you calling?"

"The florist," Lila announced, as she watched the dial methodically retreat in a counter-clockwise direction after each digit was engaged.

"You do know there's such a thing as a push-button phone now, don't you?" Lila remarked, as she completed another numeral—a nine—which perhaps aggravated the situation more so than, say, a two would have at that moment.

"My bill's high enough as it is without adding any fancy phones I don't need," Elba Rae defended. And then, "If I haven't got time to dial the number, I don't need to be trying to talk—"

"I need to speak with Pearl, please," Lila said into the mouthpiece before lowering it for a second and saying to Elba Rae "I hope I can get her to the phone," before, in fact, hearing florist Pearl's voice in the receiver.

Elba Rae listened to one side of the succinct conversation.

"Pearl, this is Lila Maywood. Ethel Maywood's daughter … Hey … Thank you, I appreciate it. Listen, I need to ask you about the spray Elba Rae phoned in for the casket. Are there carnations in there?" Lila held the phone down again and put her hand over the mouthpiece. "She's checking."

Elba Rae Van Oaks tried to contain her irritation. She knew of no such pall piece discussion in which Ethel Maywood had ever participated, be it with Lila or some other relative or a neighbor or merely a fellow shopper randomly encountered at the drugstore. Elba Rae even entertained, briefly, the notion Lila was doing more than exaggerating and may have just been out and out fabricating the whole carnation aversion. She even felt herself scooting her chair away from the table as if she were going to go to the telephone and Lila—to do what, she didn't know—before the talk resumed.

"Take them out," Lila said to the phone. "Yes. All of them. My momma hated carnations and I don't want there to be any in her spray. Elba Rae just didn't think to ask … Yeah, I know she's had a lot on her mind … Thank you. I sure appreciate it."

Lila hung up the phone. "She's gonna take them out," she proclaimed smugly as she closed back the drawer with the phone book in it. "Now what about the pallbearers?"

Elba Rae didn't answer at first, but within a minute or so, her annoyance over the flower faux pas subsided and she resumed the proceedings. By then, Lila had rejoined her at the table.

"I'll get Reverend Timmons to ask the Elders. If he can't get up enough of them, we can use some Deacons."

"What Elders are there to get?"

"Dr. Bud is an Elder. Ned Maharry is an Elder. There's—"

"Ned Maharry?" Lila interrupted.

"Yeah."

"Is he still able to pick up a casket?"

"Well, not on his own, but I imagine he can with five others helping him."

"He's got to be eighty by now."

"He's not but seventy-eight."

"Eighty, seventy-eight, what's the difference? Is that the best we can do? Are there not any younger ones up there who are a little stronger, and less feeble?"

"Ned Maharry's not feeble. He comes to church every Sunday and he's still working a garden that would make a man half his age take pause!"

"Well, just because he can still pick up a watermelon doesn't mean he should be trying to hoist our momma in and out of the church, not to mention out to the cemetery where the ground's not level."

"Then who do you want to ask, Lila?"

"Just somebody that'll give me a reasonable assurance he's not gonna drop her!"

"Nobody's gonna drop her! I've seen Ned Maharry carry a dozen caskets in the church and out of the church and through the cemetery—and all the way back to the old part, too—and he's never dropped one!"

Lila looked at her sister with no expression one way or the other. "What about the Deacons?"

"Fine," Elba Rae snapped. "I'll just tell Reverend Timmons when he gets here we don't want anything but a Deacon carrying Momma. And if he can't get up enough of them to get the job done, I guess we can pick up the slack!"

"Oh, Elba Rae, really—"

"Bucky's stout! And Nick and Heath are strong boys! Maybe Hazel will help, too! That makes six, counting you and me!" Elba Rae scooted her chair back and it made a rough-sounding scrape on her linoleum floor. She walked over to the stove and cautiously patted the tea kettle resting on one of the back burners in order to gauge the water temperature within.

"Do you want some more coffee while the water's hot?" Elba Rae asked.

"No," Lila answered, in a tone obvious to both sisters her decline of refreshment was much more a commentary on the state of the funeral proceedings thus far and scantly related to Lila Fessmire's desire for another cup of instant Folgers. Elba Rae didn't repeat the offer as she went about preparing her own beverage while Lila stared out the bay window of the kitchen's breakfast area, which Elba Rae had always referred to as the nook because that's what it had been called on the house plans she and the late Fettis had picked out so many years earlier before the chariot snatched him out of the hall.

Lila was still looking out the window that offered no more of a view than a neatly mowed yard with an aging tool shed in the distance when Elba Rae returned to the table carrying a full coffee cup in one hand and two books in the other. She deposited them on the table and pulled the yellow legal pad and pen back toward her.

"We need to pick out some songs," Elba Rae announced as she slid a book toward Lila. "I thought we could go through these hymnals and look for something."

"What are you doing with these?" Lila asked, as she obediently opened the book and began slowly scanning the titles.

"They're from when I was still in the choir. I should have taken them back to the church, but I'm kind of glad I've got them because now we can at least get this part settled before Reverend Timmons gets here," a less than subtle reference to the still incomplete pallbearer list.

They each turned pages of their books for a few minutes, although it was only Lila who would occasionally call out a title and it was Elba Rae who would say nay in between precise slurps of hot Folgers.

"What about 'Nearer My God to Thee?'" Lila suggested, as though she'd given the selection sincere premeditation.

"Momma wasn't necessarily too fond of it for some reason." So they looked some more.

"Well," Lila said, pausing on a page, "here's 'In the Garden' and it's always a good one."

"Oh, no," Elba Rae said, dismissively.

"Why not?"

"Because everybody and their cousin has that played at a funeral. I've heard it at the last three I've been to at the church. Not to mention the piped in version they use in the chapel at the funeral home sometimes."

"Okay," Lila relented, and turned several more pages. "What about 'A Mighty Fortress' along with—"

"Oh," Elba Rae said quickly, "that's worse than 'In the Garden.'"

Elba Rae didn't notice Lila's mild case of teeth grinding and, in fact, hadn't even taken her eyes off her songbook. She had a persistent grip on the ball point pen, ready to create yet another of her many lists as soon as she deemed a selection worthy. Lila flipped through a few more pages of the hymnal, but at a somewhat faster pace, while Elba Rae perused at a slower tempo and occasionally paused for more tepid sips of coffee.

"Here's 'The Old Rugged Cross,'" said Lila, pleasantly, in what was to be her final recommendation.

"'The Old Rugged Cross?'" Elba Rae exclaimed.

"Yeah. 'The Old Rugged Cross,'" Lila repeated. "I like that one. I remember it from when we were kids."

"It's an Easter song."

"So?"

"We can't play that at a funeral."

"Why not?"

"Because it wouldn't be appropriate."

"Says who?"

"Nobody *has* to say because everybody knows you don't play Easter songs at a funeral."

"Who says it's just about Easter? It could also be about hope and life after death and resurrection."

"It is about all that," Elba Rae conferred, "and if we were trying to get up the music for an Easter sunrise service, it might be a good one. But for Momma, it's not the right thing."

"I think it would be a message about what Momma believed all her life. And where she thought she was going after she died."

Elba Rae Van Oaks stared across the table at her sister. "I'm not having it."

"Okay then," Lila Fessmire said as she closed the songbook with enough force to produce a light snapping effect when the pages met. "Why don't we just take some of Momma's old Bing Crosby records up to the church and they can play them for the funeral?"

"What?"

"You know how much she loved Bing Crosby! We can forget the hymns altogether!"

"What are you talking about?"

"Or how about Perry Como? She always did look forward to those old Christmas specials on TV! We could make up a little medley!"

"This is not helping."

"Better yet, is he still alive? Maybe we could get him to come sing in person!"

"Don't be absurd."

"Who's being absurd? I've read out every song title in this hymnbook and you've said 'no' to every one of them. Either Momma didn't like it or you don't like it or it's too common or not appropriate enough! I give up." Lila slammed the book on the table and stood up.

"I'm just trying to put some thought into it," Elba Rae reasoned, "and not pick the first song I come to!"

"Good. You do that. I'm sure whatever you decide will be fine with me."

"Where are you going?"

"Outside," Lila said, and indeed she went. Elba Rae watched her exit through the carport door, whereupon Elba Rae gathered her legal pad and began to jot down a couple of song titles she apparently already had in mind before Lila resigned from the process.

"Suit yourself," Elba Rae said out loud, though with no intention of being heard. She completed the list in its entirely before her coffee went completely cold.

*   *   *

By the time Elba Rae heard the kitchen door open again, she was surprised by more than one pair of footsteps before realizing Lila was escorting the pastor of the First Avenue United Methodist Church, Reverend George Timmons, who had apparently arrived during Lila's pouting session in the carport.

"Elba Rae, Mr. Timmons is here."

"I see," she said, as she fumbled to get up from the table and gather herself.

The pastor extended a sensitive and sympathetic few words right away that to Elba Rae sounded like something he was at ease reciting as a habit of his work.

"Let's go in the front room and sit down," said Elba Rae, and the others complied accordingly, including Mr. Wiggles who'd awakened from a nap upon hearing the unfamiliar voice.

The living room of the Van Oaks home was generally reserved for ministerial visits or for those guests who made their entrance by means of the front door, or in extreme circumstances, the room was utilized when its floor was needed for pallet placement to accommodate the Fessmire twins who would be arriving the next day from Birmingham with their father and sister.

Reverend Timmons carried a Bible in his hand; Elba Rae Van Oaks had her legal pad and a ballpoint pen. Mr. Wiggles brought the tattered remains of a rawhide chew toy in his mouth and that seemed to excite him about the whole visit all the more, and he promptly delivered it to the pastor as soon as Mr. Timmons took his place in an arm chair near the front door. George Timmons leaned over and gave the dog a rewarding pat on the head.

"Mr. Wiggles, come over here and leave him alone!"

"He's all right, Elba Rae." The minister looked down at the dog once more and addressed him personally.

"It's all right, isn't it, Mr. Wiggles? We go way back, don't we?" He gave the poodle a few more pats, and Mr. Wiggles indicated his gratitude by shaking his behind rapidly in nearly one hundred and eighty degree sweeps.

Lila Fessmire and Elba Rae sat on a long sofa against the wall facing the front door. They perched at mostly opposite ends of it, leaving space for at least two adults between them.

"I guess he does know you from your visiting Momma at her house," Elba Rae said.

"I'm sure he does. I know he was a lot of company to Miss Ethel in the last few years."

"Oh, she was just crazy about that dog."

"I remember," he said in agreement.

"I never would have thought I'd live to see the day my momma would let a dog inside her house, much less let one sleep on the bed with her."

"It is kind of ironic," Lila contributed, "especially since she never even let us have a dog when we were growing up."

"And giving him all kinds of things from the table. Why, she'd have never admitted it, but I know for a fact she used to boil up chicken gizzards just to feed to Mr. Wiggles. She fussed over him way more than she ever did us."

George Timmons listened patiently to the exchange and given his perspective, wondered if the women didn't have something of a valid argument. Whether the degree of devotion Ethel Maywood had showed her poodle exceeded that previously afforded her two daughters—and, perhaps, it was debatable—the fact was Ethel had also dispensed discipline upon Mr. Wiggles plenty of times, especially when she'd felt his behavior inappropriate and socially repulsive. Historically, however, those occurrences had been few and mostly the consequence of a nearby female dog's wafting scent, which had what was only biologically a natural effect on Mr. Wiggles. But Ethel Maywood had never wanted to see even occasional evidence of Mr. Wiggles's manhood and had usually taken action to discourage him, her tool most commonly being a rolled up newspaper that was a weapon of opportunity more so than it had ever been a deliberate choice. Ethel had been particularly mortified one afternoon two winters prior when Reverend and Mrs. Timmons from the First Avenue United Methodist Church had come by to deliver the weekly bulletin and a packaged fruit basket beautifully wrapped in lavender-tinted Saran Wrap as a good will gesture following Ethel's influenza-induced absence from church.

At first, Mr. Wiggles had appeared with his customarily friendly demeanor, wagging his entire back end profusely as the Timmons said their greetings—to Ethel Maywood and to him—before taking their positions on Ethel's good settee. Even several minutes into the visit, no one had especially noticed anything strange in the dog's behavior. It was Mrs. Timmons, though, who'd first been distracted by the amorous gesture Mr. Wiggles directed toward her lower leg.

Lorraine Timmons was generally a quiet woman and reserved, as members of the congregation expected their minister's wife to be. She had never been known to cause unnecessary commotion and she had not, under any circumstances, ever wanted to embarrass a host. So it was understandable when she'd simply crossed her legs at the ankle as a deterrent to Mr. Wiggles and hadn't ever diverted her glances away from Ethel Maywood or her husband, depending upon which one of them had been speaking at the time.

"I'll tell you the truth, George. It really knocked me down for a while. Along about that first week of it, I thought I'd have to get better to die," Ethel Maywood had said.

Reverend Timmons had chuckled. He'd always appreciated Ethel Maywood's wry wit.

"You know, we still have several members out sick with it, don't we, Lorraine?"

As George Timmons had turned to look at his wife, he'd been immediately drawn to the little teacup poodle on the floor who had been silently—yet persistently—humping Mrs. Timmons's leg.

"Oh. My," he'd said, which had caused Lorraine Timmons to look down.

"Goodness," Mrs. Timmons had remarked, as she'd noted for the first time the advanced stage of Mr. Wiggles's erection which was, teacup breed or not, unavoidably impressive.

"Mr. Wiggles!" Ethel Maywood had screeched. "Stop that!" She'd looked to the left and to the right and had quickly grabbed the first thing she could reach, which was the church bulletin the Timmons had been so thoughtful to bring as an accompaniment to the purple-shaded fruit. She'd rolled it up with precision and swiftly applied it to Mr. Wiggles's rear end.

"Stop that! Stop it this minute," Ethel Maywood had yelled.

Mrs. Timmons had shifted nervously, although Mr. Wiggles, whose determination far outweighed his physical size, had not yet been willing to give up.

"Stop it, I said!" Ethel Maywood had continued to swat him with the bulletin. Defeated and—quite as likely—no longer in the mood, Mr. Wiggles had retreated and cowered with his head down.

"You get to the kitchen!" As Mr. Wiggles obediently turned and trotted toward the door, his human mother's scolding had continued.

"You think you're so sexy! Well, you're not! Nobody wants to see that!" Ethel had casually unrolled the bulletin and placed it back on the side table.

"I'm sorry, Lorraine. I hope he didn't get your slacks dirty."

Lorraine Timmons, unsure exactly what she meant by dirty, had just smiled and said "No," and looked at her husband as a hint for him to resume the conversation they'd been conducting prior to the awkward disruption.

Reverend George Timmons didn't suppose the two daughters sitting across from him like bookends on the long sofa knew of the incident but reasoned it would not lessen their inferred resentment of the dog's preferential treatment, nor would it, from strictly a condolence and comforting element, soothe the pain of their mother's passing that was in the greater scheme of things the purpose of his visit, along with gathering as was necessary their preference of song choices, scripture readings, and pallbearers needed for the funeral.

Elba Rae Van Oaks proceeded orderly through her lists while Lila Fessmire offered no protest, not during the musical selections and not even as Elba Rae indicated to George Timmons how much it would mean to them both if the Elders would serve as pallbearers. She'd glanced quickly at Lila when she did—perhaps expecting her to stand up, yell "Objection!" in pure Perry Mason fashion, and counter with evidence of their frailties. But Lila refrained from interrupting. The remainder of the details was shared with Reverend Timmons, in fact, without a single mention of casket-carrying abilities, Mr. Bing Crosby, or an old rugged cross.

*   *   *

The next few hours passed without incident. Elba Rae puttered around the house and mostly answered the door or the phone while Lila Fessmire did some pacing but disappeared periodically to the carport or the little patio off the back door of the house where she could indulge a recently resumed tobacco habit she had no desire to discuss with her older sister.

Lila wanted to be of help but found it difficult in an environment so firmly controlled by Elba Rae. Inside the house, Lila gave a cursory look at a list of names and noted checkmarks by a majority of the designees.

"Is there anybody else we need to call right away?"

"Well," Elba Rae paused. "I've gotten in touch with most all the ones out of town and the ones that won't have heard it already from somebody at the church."

"Then is there anything else we need to—"

"But," Elba Rae interrupted," I don't think I ever got around to calling Begina."

Lila's shoulders suddenly slumped and her head tilted way back, and she emitted a faint sigh. Then she looked at her watch.

"Are you sure we have time for that now?" Lila asked. "Don't we have to go by Momma's house on the way to the funeral home?"

"Yes, we do. The list of what we need to pick up is on that next page there. But I've got to get changed first. Do you remember their number? If not, it's written inside the cover of my phonebook you were using earlier when you called—"

"You want *me* to call her?"

"Would you? And then by the time I get my clothes on, we'll need to get off to Momma's house and—"

"Can't it wait until we get back from the funeral home?"

"Well, I hate to put it off so long until they hear it from somebody else."

"What if Begina's not there? And I get stuck on the phone trying to talk to Aunt Laveetra? You know that'll just be a waste of time."

Elba Rae was getting frustrated and it began to show, outwardly so at Lila for her seeming reluctance to execute one simple task of all the ones Elba Rae had already organized, completed, and checked off the list, and inwardly so because the mini plot she and her cousin, Hazel Burns, had subliminally agreed upon that morning—to defer the phone call to Hattiesburg until such time as it could be delegated to Lila—was not hatching so smoothly.

"If you don't want to have to make a call, that's fine. I'll get to it just as soon as I can. Hazel said she'd come over and stay while we went to the funeral home, so there'll be somebody here to take in the food—maybe I'll ask her if she wouldn't mind doing it."

"Oh, all right!" Lila accepted the challenge. "Where's the number?"

"Written inside my phone book in the drawer."

Lila Fessmire unenthusiastically retrieved the book for the second time since she'd arrived at Elba Rae's house, and located several rows of handwritten names and telephone numbers on the inside cover of the *Buford and Greater Litton County Directory*. Some of the numbers were also supplemented with a mailing address if the party lived out of town, and Lila easily found the entry for "Aunt Laveetra and Begina."

Laveetra Chittum was the elderly and only surviving sibling of Elba Rae and Lila's late father, Raymond Maywood. Laveetra and Ethel Maywood had not, through the years, ever forged a particularly close relationship, but there was no malice between them to deflect Laveetra's sense of obligation to attend her sister-in-law's funeral or her daughter Begina's determination to transport her as the token representation of their branch of the family.

Laveetra's own health was in and of itself practically a textbook of geriatric clichés—from loss of hearing to mid-level stages of dementia—and Elba Rae did not realistically anticipate nor relish the possibility of her presence at the funeral. Most any reasonable person would accept the fact Laveetra was in no shape for travel or public appearances. Laveetra's daughter, Begina, however, was less predictable than reasonable people.

Even when Lila and Elba Rae were still children, their mother had been known to refer to Begina Marie Chittum as simple. No more, no less, just simple. Elba Rae hadn't understood exactly what that meant when she was a little girl, but after she grew older the definition became clearer. Begina was not handicapped in any medical sense of the word, and she was completely capable of functioning as it were, but she did lack some of the conversational and social skills most normal adults took for granted.

Begina had never lived away from home nor held down much of a real job other than a short stint as a clerk in a dry cleaners or the occasional fill-in work cashiering at a cafeteria in Hattiesburg whenever the regular cashier wanted to take some time off. Of late, however, Laveetra's care had become a full time commitment but at least, her relatives assumed, Begina would inherit the roof over her head once Laveetra was gone.

Pondering what actually would be the sad finale of the Chittum family, Elba Rae suddenly felt a little guilty watching Lila take the phone. She did need, as had been pointed out during the debate over who should bear responsibility for placing the call, to change her clothes if they were to accomplish all that was necessary before meeting the four o'clock appointment with Mr. Charles Robert Tully at Buford Memorial Funeral Home.

Yet she stood in the den and watched Lila dial the number, put the receiver to her ear, and then close her eyes as though she were transmitting a silent prayer the ring would go unanswered.

"Hello? Aunt Laveetra? It's Lila … Lila … I said it's Lila! … Maywood … Lila Maywood! … Calling from Buford … Yes, it's Ray and Ethel's daughter! … That's right—Lila! … I'm fine, Aunt Laveetra, how are you?"

Elba Rae Van Oaks stood perfectly still; too ashamed to skulk out of the room, too curious to want to.

"I said I'm fine. How are you? … That's good. I have some bad news."

Raising her voice, Lila continued. "I said I have some bad news! Momma passed away this morning in the hospital … I said, Momma passed away this morning—in the hospital … No, she's not *in* the hospital, she passed away … Passed away! She died … No, died … Died! Dead! That's right—dead! Momma is dead!"

Lila held the phone down to her side for a few seconds, as she genuinely did not want to lose her composure with a deaf and seriously senile old woman who surely didn't intend to provoke such exasperation.

"Yes … Ethel … She died … Yes, it was this morning … Aunt Laveetra, is Begina there with you? … Begina? … Yes, is she there? … Is she where I can talk to her? … Oh, I see."

There then passed a period of several minutes when Lila appeared to be on the receiving end of valid information into which she injected an "ah hah" every so often, and when Elba Rae strained enough, she could almost catch some of the monolog emanating from the Hattiesburg point of origin.

"Yes," Lila said. "Please tell her I called … I said, please tell her I called and to call me back at Elba Rae's … Call me back at Elba Rae's! Elba Rae's house! Yes, that's right … Okay … Bye-bye … I said, bye-bye … Bye!" She practically screamed as she hung up the phone.

"Good Lord! Now I know why her name didn't have a checkmark by it!"

"Was Begina not there?" asked Elba Rae innocently.

"Apparently not. Aunt Laveetra said their tub drain was clogged up because she'd been taking some kind of oatmeal baths for a rash that helped the rash but clogged up the drain, and Begina had gone to the drugstore to try to find something to unstop it."

"Well then, that's probably the truth. From what I can get from Begina every once in a while, Aunt Laveetra still has her days when she's just as clear as a bell. And you know, I've used those oatmeal baths myself when I had the poison oak, and they'll for sure stop up a drain if you're not careful."

"Maybe so, but Aunt Laveetra's no more in her right mind than a Betsy Bug."

"How can you be sure?"

"Because right after she got through describing the particulars of her rash, including exactly where on her body she has it, she proceeded to tell me Uncle Sammy was out fishing with W'lynn and she didn't expect them back before supper."

"Oh," Elba Rae said with an allusion of disenchantment, knowing as Lila did that Laveetra's husband, the late Uncle Sammy, had been dead for years as had his cousin and frequent fishing partner, Mr. Willie Lynn Chittum, who everybody had just called W'lynn. "Well, hopefully she'll at least have enough sense to tell Begina to call us when she gets back home."

"Unless Begina's out fishing, too. With W'lynn and Uncle Sammy."

"Oh, goodness," Elba Rae exhaled. "I've got to get ready or we'll be late." She began to almost scurry toward the bedroom.

"If Begina calls back," Lila yelled out after her, "I'll tell her to hold on for you."

Elba Rae Van Oaks just waved her hand in a dismissive fashion and kept going.

*   *   *

Ethel Maywood's house stood right around a big bend in the road. The gravel driveway was easily passed up by a motorist unaccustomed to its placement, as it seemed to come out of nowhere after traveling the mile or so beyond the next nearest neighbor.

Raymond and Ethel Maywood were only the second owners of the place and had occupied it since before Elba Rae's birth. The house was old but still adequately maintained, even if it did sorely lack any recent modernization.

Elba Rae stopped the car and turned off the motor. She and Lila both sat silently for a few minutes and stared at the house.

"When's the last time you were here?" Elba Rae asked.

"That week between Christmas and New Year's."

"I thought it was Thanksgiving."

"No," Lila corrected. "I came and spent a night between Christmas and New Year's and brought the boys while they were still out of school."

"Oh."

Neither of them seemed to want to open her car door first. It was if staying ensconced in the big yellow Ford would shelter them from the unpleasant task that waited inside the house.

"Well," Elba Rae finally said, "this isn't getting us anywhere." She opened her door and stepped outside. Lila hesitated a few seconds longer, but followed Elba Rae's lead.

Elba Rae went in first since she was in possession of the key. The back door led them directly into the kitchen. Lila stopped and took in the lingering aroma, which was not one of food since the stove had obviously been idle of late, but rather a scent of familiarity as unduplicated and unique to her childhood home as a fingerprint. She thought, simply, the house smelled like her mother and it was a comforting sensation.

Elba Rae turned on an overhead light before situating her legal pad on the Formica table that rested in the center in the room. She flipped over several pages before reaching the sheet titled "Momma's House."

"All right, now then. I guess we need to just get in the bedroom and start looking."

Lila Fessmire offered no commentary. She just walked in the direction of her mother's room with Elba Rae behind her.

Once inside, Elba Rae went immediately to the double windows on the west side of the house and opened the venetian blinds, allowing a sudden flood of natural light.

"These blinds look like they haven't been washed since we were kids," she remarked while walking across the room to a closed closet. "But I guess we've got plenty of time to worry about that later."

Lila stood aside as Elba Rae opened the closet door and illuminated the inside by pulling a string attached to its single-bulb fixture in the ceiling. She pensively looked at the clothes and seemed hesitant to disturb them at first but after subtly taking in a deep breath, launched the search. Lila watched as a spectator for a full minute.

"Wait," Elba Rae said subconsciously as she slid occupied hangers down the slick, wooden clothes rod. "It's got to be in here somewhere."

"Are you sure it's in this closet?"

"I know it is, because Momma said—oh, yeah, here it is." Elba Rae parted the clothing on either side to expose solely the hanger holding the navy blue skirt with the matching blazer. "This is it."

"Are you sure that's the one?"

"It's the only navy blue suit Momma had and—and see," she said, noting the next item in sequence to the left of the blue suit, "here's the top she meant to go with it." Elba Rae took down the blue suit and a cream-colored blouse. She laid them gingerly across the foot of Ethel Maywood's bed and then rearranged them such that the blazer was on the same hanger with the blouse, which were then on top of the skirt in the manner they would have been worn. The women both stared in reverent silence at the configuration as though it were Ethel Maywood herself draped across the bed, taking a peaceful—albeit formal—nap.

"Well," Lila spoke up, "what about her under things?"

"She always said they were in a box in her dresser. Already picked out." Elba Rae crossed the room to an antique highboy dresser that, per Maywood family lore, had belonged to the girls' grandmother on their father's side. For the moment, Lila was content to let Elba Rae do the searching solo; meanwhile she gazed around their mother's bedroom nostalgically.

The rose-patterned wallpaper with the light blue background had been there as far back as Lila could remember, and she felt an immediate wave pass over her body with the sudden recollection of how soothing the first sight of flowers had been when she would awaken in her parents' room on a Sunday morning after they'd let her crawl in their big bed with them on Saturday night. She glanced up at the ceiling for a minute and even chuckled once, audibly, thinking about how hard she'd tried not to giggle out loud when her daddy started his snoring. It had been more like a game Lila and her mother routinely played on those special nights as soon as they realized her daddy was asleep.

First, they would wait to see how long it took him to start and, as though catering to the natural impatience of a child, he had usually obliged them quickly. Ethel would pretend at first not to notice and then after Lila's sniggering became apparent, she would perpetuate the fun by pretending to evoke Lila's silence by shaking her head back and forth and making a "quiet" gesture by putting her forefinger up to her tightly closed lips. The process would continue for several minutes until the snoring reached an inevitable and theatrical crescendo that usually caused both Lila and Ethel to burst into laughter and stirred Raymond Maywood to say, "What are you two hens cackling about?" before he rolled over on his side to face the wall.

When she'd been a little girl, it hadn't crossed Lila's mind to muse where Elba Rae was on those special nights, but she did wonder a little right then while watching her older sister pull open the dresser drawers.

"Elba Rae, do you remember when we were little and—or when I was little, at least—and Momma and Daddy would let me get in bed with them and—"

"Well, would you look at this?" Elba Rae obviously was going to ignore any impromptu reminiscence in favor of completing her task.

"What is it?"

Elba Rae removed an item from the drawer and placed it on the bed, whereupon she returned to the drawer and repeated the action several more times in silence.

"Those look like gowns," Lila observed. "Why are you dragging all that out?"

"They *are* gowns," Elba Rae said, crossing to the dresser one more time before returning to the bed with a robe. "They're gowns and pajamas and at least two housecoats."

Lila leaned over the bed and fingered a light pink bathrobe. "They look new."

"They ought to," Elba Rae declared. "I don't think any of them have ever been worn!"

Lila investigated further and pulled from the collection a white satin gown. She held it up by the shoulders out in front of her so that the hem barely touched the floor.

"I recognize this one. I gave it to her a few Christmases ago. I remember, because for years she said she'd always wanted just one satin gown to see what it felt like and, well, look. She never even cut off the tag."

"She was probably saving it for the hospital."

"Why?" Lila asked.

"Because that's what she always said. Every time she'd open one of these housecoats or pairs of pajamas. She'd say 'oh, that's so nice, I'd better save it in case I have to go the hospital' and then she'd never have them on. Well, little good any of them will do her now!"

"You know how Momma was, Elba Rae. Always saving and putting back. She'd hold on to a nickel till the eagle squeaked."

"I don't care," Elba said in a semi-fume. "When I think of how many times I pulled all the way to Montgomery just to go to the Penney's to get her something nice for her birthday or Mother's Day! Gowns and new house shoes and look at all this." She surveyed the warehoused bounty of the late Ethel Maywood. "And gloves to boot!"

"What?"

"Gloves!" said Elba Rae. "She was always fussing about not having one, good, warm pair of gloves. And look at these—still bound together and never worn! You know, it's not like we wouldn't have ever gotten her another new thing if she'd actually worn out some of these!"

"It's nothing we can do about it now!"

"I know," said Elba Rae. "But still. It makes me mad. Good money, down the drain."

"I can't help it, but unless we're going to bury her in one of these gowns and a pair of gloves, you'd better keep looking for what we need."

"Well," Elba Rae muttered, still teetering on the mad side of resignation.

"Do you want me to look?" offered Lila.

"No," Elba Rae said and then turned back around to the dresser. "It's got to be in here somewhere."

The bottom drawer did, indeed, house a white gift box with a JCPenney logo embossed on its top lid, no doubt having once born a thoughtful present delegated to a stockpile of nocturnal wear not intended to be squandered in days of good health. Elba Rae gently extracted the box and placed it on the bed alongside the exterior components of Ethel Maywood's assembled outfit.

"This must be it," she said before removing the lid. "Yeah. This is it."

Elba Rae delicately removed and unfolded the box's contents and wondered to herself exactly how long the articles had been stored undisturbed. She felt a fluttery sensation in her stomach as she tried to imagine what it must have been like for her mother to go about the task of selecting her own burial clothes, and she felt terribly guilty for the fact Ethel likely had done it alone.

Lila simply watched the process as an observer and didn't say anything until it appeared Elba Rae was through. "Is that everything?"

Elba Rae looked at the collection of clothing on the bed and alternately at the then empty box. "Well, we've got underpants, a brassiere, and a slip. Were you thinking we needed a girdle?"

"Not a girdle, but what about her stockings?"

"What?"

"Are there any stockings in there? If not, we'll have to look for some."

"We don't need stockings," Elba Rae said authoritatively, as she—now undistracted by morose regret—started to repack the box.

"We do, too," Lila Fessmire decreed as she walked toward the dresser for herself. She started at the top opening drawers.

"Lila," Elba Rae injected, patiently, "they don't put stockings on at the funeral home."

"Well, they won't if we don't take some."

"We're not going to take them," Elba Rae replied but a degree less tolerantly. She was surprised to observe Lila continuing the search, now into the second drawer.

"Where does she keep them?"

"Lila, we are not taking stockings. They don't put stockings on the body because nobody sees that part!"

"Momma wanted her stockings."

"Oh, that's the silliest thing I ever heard!"

Lila temporarily suspended the hunt, turning to face Elba Rae. "It is *not* silly, considering the occasion."

"If Momma had wanted to wear stockings, she would have put them in the box with the rest of the things she picked out."

"It doesn't matter if they were in the damn box or not, Elba Rae, I know good and well Momma wouldn't darken the doors of that church without wearing her stockings and her high heels! Ever!"

"Well, maybe she did wear them to church every Sunday, but she's not going to church! And nobody is going to see her legs! Much less her feet!"

"I'll see them!"

"No, you won't!"

"Doesn't matter. At least I'll know she's got them on, and I'll know we did what she wanted."

"When in the world did Momma ever say she wanted to be buried with her stockings on, Lila Mae?"

"She told me one time when we were discussing it."

"When? The same day she was worrying about those carnations?"

"I don't know when. I didn't write down the date."

"How come I didn't hear her?"

"Elba Rae, it may surprise you to know that you haven't been privy to every talk Momma and I ever had. There is such a thing as a telephone, you know. Remember that big black thing you've got stuck on your kitchen wall that looks like it came from the Smithsonian Institute? Now since Momma had one here, and I had one in Birmingham, we were able to talk just about whenever we wanted to! And unless you had the lines tapped, there's no reason you'd know everything we ever said!"

"I know Momma wasn't about to run up any big phone bill making long-distance calls," Elba Rae rebutted.

"She didn't have to, because I did the calling. Honestly—you think just because Momma didn't relay the content and the frequency of every conversation we ever had they must not have happened!"

"That's not what I said. I just meant—"

"And it just so happens, one time we got on the subject of some of Momma's preferences and she told me to make sure she was properly dressed when it was her time to be laid out. Specifically, with all of her undergarments, her stockings, and her good Sunday shoes!"

"Fine," Elba Rae Van Oaks resolved, before joining her sister in the exploration which soon rendered an unworn pair of panty hose still in the package. Lila placed them on the bed in the growing pile and then flitted toward the closet.

"Now what are you looking for?" Elba Rae asked.

"The shoes."

"Oh, Lord, you're not really gonna take shoes up there, are you?"

Lila Fessmire rose up from the bent position she'd been in searching the closet floor for just the right pair, and looked at Elba Rae with a blatant glare. Elba Rae, though pent up with plenty of things she wanted to say, deferred and decided just to keep quiet and let her younger sister have her way. It wasn't like she surmised anyone but Charles Robert Tully and perhaps a member of his staff would ever know they'd buried their momma with stockings and shoes on, and Elba Rae was optimistic there was probably some kind of confidentiality clause in their business that would ensure it remained a private detail, unlike the public nature "The Old Rugged Cross" debacle would surely have taken on had Elba Rae compromised on Lila's song submission.

Lila rummaged about the unorganized shoe collection before finally emerging with a pair of navy blue, high-heeled pumps.

"You're picking those?"

Lila didn't stop on her way over to the bed. "They're blue, and they match the suit."

"She never liked those."

"Why?"

"They hurt her feet."

Lila put the shoes down on the floor at the end of the bed before turning around and facing Elba Rae. "Really?" she remarked, sarcastically.

"And she hasn't had heels on that high in ten years. She just wasn't steady on them."

"She's not gonna be walking in them, Elba Rae."

"What about—"

"Is that it?" asked Lila, clearly indicating a conclusion to her participation in the costuming phase of the preparations. Elba Rae surveyed the room, the attire on the bed, and the still-open closet.

"I guess we've got everything." Elba Rae went to the closet, pulled the string to cut off the light, and closed the door. "Come on," she said, while beginning to re-stuff the Penney's box with the undergarments in such a way so the box could also accommodate the addition of panty hose, which she certainly meant to remain concealed until time to put them on Ethel Maywood. "Grab the suit and … the shoes. We'll be late for the appointment."

*   *   *

Charles Robert Tully was a third-generation undertaker, having learned from the watchful auspices of his father, Charles Robert Tully Senior, who just went by Charles whereas Charles Robert Tully Junior went full out by Charles Robert. Both had ultimately inherited their devotion to the craft from Charles Robert's grandfather, Mr. Charles Victor Tully, who'd founded the Buford Memorial Funeral Home business in the 1920s and had long since himself been one of its customers.

People in Litton County had occasion to share with Charles Robert Tully intimacies they never would have confided to their less casual acquaintances or even some family members, because Charles Robert Tully saw people at what was the most delicate of hours—the resolution of the departed's final arrangements. It was a trust and a responsibility he regarded as sacred.

Sporadically, Charles Robert Tully met with a family he did not know particularly well nor with whom he shared any previous history, but more often he was at least familiar with the deceased and sometimes many of the relatives, as was the case with the appointment he prepared for on a clear May afternoon in 1983.

He'd handled arrangements for Mr. Raymond Maywood when he

passed away, and he'd personally prepared Mr. Fettis Van Oaks for viewing after patiently assisting Mr. Fettis's widow, Miss Elba Rae, with the casket selection—a steel model in Radiant Silver with the Ivory Drexel Crepe interior and plain head panel that yet remained one of Buford Memorial Funeral Home's most popular sellers. Charles Robert Tully recalled these details without need of research; he just remembered. It was a skill shared and ingrained by previous Tullys.

The funeral home was quiet that afternoon save for the presence of Mrs. Imogene Winnegar, who served as receptionist as well as part time secretary to Charles Robert Tully. She was positioned at the receptionist desk just inside the lobby at the front entrance since they were expecting a family, although her presence there was redundant on the days that Mr. Charles Robert was also standing guard practically on the front door himself, reducing her role to no more than a superfluous desk sitter. Imogene Winnegar had been known to grouse about such relegation.

They both observed the car slowly enter the parking lot and make what appeared to be a deliberate selection of a space on the otherwise empty expanse of pavement. Imogene Winnegar may not have been descended from a lineage of funeral directors but she'd been around enough years to respect that a grieving family never got in a hurry when exiting the vehicle and approaching the funeral home. The movement was, instead, always tempered against a push of apprehension that seemed to permeate from the very front door of the building. She had long since learned from the Tullys never to appear in a rush when dealing with the relatives; they had to be given free and unencumbered rein to process the professional side of death at their own pace.

Elba Rae Van Oaks gently opened the front door of the funeral home and entered the lobby carrying the navy suit and the cream blouse on hangers, followed by Lila Fessmire into whose charge the JCPenney box bearing the eternal undergarment ensemble of Ethel Maywood had been placed. Mrs. Imogene Winnegar stood up from her desk but scarcely dispensed two hellos before Charles Robert Tully took command of the visit.

"You remember my sister, Lila," offered Elba Rae.

"I do," Charles Robert Tully confirmed. "It's been a long time."

"Yes, fortunately for us I guess it has," Lila replied nervously.

"Are we expecting anyone else?"

"No, Charles Robert," Elba Rae answered. "It'll be just us."

"All right, then. Let's first go down to my office and we'll begin discussing the arrangements." Upon his own direction Charles Robert Tully then turned and walked down a corridor that led to several offices as well as a door ominously adorned with a brass plaque that said "Showroom." Neither Lila nor Elba Rae was looking forward to that one.

His office was large and well-appointed, more so than the offices occupied by his ancestors in what had been the original location of the business, a home right off the Square Mr. Charles Victor Tully had purchased in 1922 with the express purpose of housing his family in the second floor quarters while utilizing the first floor and basement space for the funeral business he planned to launch. By the time the enterprise passed to the third generation Tully, the decision had already been made to build a newer, bigger, better testament to death on the highway leading into Buford proper.

Facing the desk were two leather chairs of the office variety but comfortable just the same, and against the wall underneath the window overlooking the parking lot there was a sofa in the event a larger group of planners should need to be accommodated. Elba Rae Van Oaks was at once grateful she only had one relative accompanying her.

A hook on the back of the office door made for a tactful hanging location for the clothing, which Charles Robert instinctively took from Elba Rae's hand before she sat down. Lila held onto to her pieces of the burial gear, resting them on her lap. A bulge in the lid of the Penney's box cloaked a pair of navy blue pumps.

The director and the two women conducted the meeting without noticeable emotion and in, as Charles Robert Tully categorized the likes of it, business-like fashion. He made note of their reservation of the parlor for the following evening's visitation, confirmed the exact location of the grave site, took down the germane information to forward for publication in the *Litton Times*, and then let them know it was time to adjourn to the showroom. Elba Rae promptly stood up and walked out into the hallway first, while Charles Robert Tully politely waited behind his desk for Lila to put the Penney's box in the floor, stand, and join Elba Rae in the hall.

"Do you know of any preferences Miss Ethel may have had?" Charles Robert asked once they were fully inside the adjacent room.

Elba Rae decided to remain silent for an amount of time sufficient to show deference to Lila, who ever since arriving in Buford that morning seemed to be the world's leading authority on all things relevant to their mother's funeral wishes.

"Lila?" she finally said.

"I never really heard Momma say anything about a casket."

Elba Rae seemed to glare at her. "Are you sure?"

By then Lila was positive Elba Rae was releasing a bit of hostility. "I'm sure," Lila said with her teeth somewhat clinched.

"Well," Elba Rae appeared satisfied, "knowing Momma, she wouldn't want anything fancy, Charles Robert. It should just be something simple."

"All right," he understood, and led them past a short row of mahogany and cherry wood models. Lila couldn't help but admire the beautiful, hand-crafted finishes on them. Were they pieces of antique furniture, she surmised, they would have commanded a handsome price whereupon she then noticed the discreetly printed price list resting on the pillow of each coffin and realized they, in fact, did.

Elba Rae Van Oaks, meanwhile, had navigated toward the metal versions and was standing beside a plain enough looking sample in battleship gray. She glanced across the room at Lila as if she expected her to quit her browsing and come forthwith.

"This is a very fine model, Elba Rae," Charles Robert Tully said as Lila rejoined them. "And, of course, it carries the full guarantee from the manufacturer."

Lila Fessmire wondered exactly what that meant, and to what value she should, as the daughter of the deceased, place on such a benefit. "Guarantee against what?" she asked.

"Leakage," he answered matter-of-factly and with no hesitation.

Lila Fessmire contemplated about how exactly anyone would reasonably know when a claim against such a guarantee was warranted, and while it seemed silly to her such a thing should even be mentioned, it appeared obvious Elba Rae wasn't going to take up the questioning.

"How's this one?" Elba Rae asked.

"Well," Lila waffled. "If you think it's okay, it's fine with me. I don't really care."

Charles Robert Tully looked back at Elba Rae to render a decision.

She stared into the empty casket for a moment and then said, "Okay. Let's just get this one."

"All right," Charles Robert Tully said. "Now, I'd like to also mention there are a number of head panel options available with this model."

"What?" Lila Fessmire inquired.

"Head panels," he replied, as he made a sweeping gesture with his hand up and down the inside of the upper portion of the casket's lid.

"This, obviously, is the plain panel, but if you'd like to consider an alternative—something, perhaps, that captures a preference of your mother's or speaks to her essence—we have several from which to choose. All in the matching fabric, of course."

Elba Rae Van Oaks, clearly disinterested in accessorizing her mother's coffin, attempted to draw their selection to an unambiguous conclusion but was thwarted by Lila.

"Let's just—"

"Such as?" asked Lila.

"Well, for instance," Charles Robert Tully said, "there's one that features a beautiful cross. It's prominent enough to be noticeable, but not so large that it overwhelms."

Lila looked at Elba Rae to determine her opinion, but Elba Rae gave no indication she was moved by the idea.

"We also offer a pair of hands. They're quite lovely, really. Delicately embroidered and positioned in a prayerful manner."

"Oh, no," Elba Rae quickly volunteered. "Momma always hated those old praying hands."

"She did?" Lila seemed unconvinced.

"Lands, yes. Don't you remember? Aunt Laveetra was always making up a pair in ceramics and giving them as gifts. Momma detested them. She was forever trying to pawn them off on me."

"Well," the director said.

"We don't need anything fancy, Charles Robert. I think Momma would be just fine with the plain one."

Most likely because she'd been the one to initially express an interest, Charles Robert Tully looked toward Lila to concur.

"Yeah," concluded Lila, unenthusiastically. "Whatever. We should probably skip the hands."

*　　　*　　　*

Lila Fessmire sat unwearyingly in the funeral director's office while he went over the itemization of charges with Elba Rae, who had pulled from her pocketbook a pair of reading glasses in order to study each line in earnest before, as a gesture of good will, passing the paper over to Lila for her secondary review.

"Is there anything we're forgetting?"

Lila skimmed the bill. "I can't think of anything."

"All right," Elba Rae said as she retrieved the document from Lila and handed it to Charles Robert Tully. "Then I guess we just need her clothes."

"Oh," said Lila, who bent down and carefully raised the Penney's box from the floor. She placed it on the desk in front of her.

"Everything is in there, Charles Robert," Elba Rae assured him.

"Of course. Now try not to worry about anything here, but if you need me before tomorrow evening, please don't hesitate to call me directly, or Imogene if I'm not available." He stood from his chair to signify the conclusion of the business portion of their transaction.

"Well," Elba Rae hesitated.

He tenderly smiled at her and waited, obviously offering his utmost attention until every possible apprehension was alleviated to the best of his ability and resources.

"It's just …"

"What?" Lila asked, which came out sounding as though she did not share the quantity of patience afforded by Mr. Charles Robert Tully.

"Well, Charles Robert, we, uh—"

"What's wrong, Elba Rae? Have we overlooked something?" he asked, as he resumed his seat.

"No—you haven't. But I just want to make sure, well, Charles Robert," she leaned in closer over the desk, as if she intended to speak only to him. "We brought shoes for Momma."

He said nothing. It took a lot to shock Charles Robert Tully, his somewhat ghoulish line of work notwithstanding. Lila Fessmire rested her head completely back and stared straight up at the ceiling.

"That's perfectly fine, Elba Rae," he assured.

Elba Rae lowered her voice. "They're high heels."

He retained his unflappable expression.

"Would you imagine they'll be any problem getting her all fitted in? With the shoes on, I mean?"

During the pause before his reply, Elba Rae Van Oaks sincerely believed Charles Robert Tully was taking the situation under advisement and that he was pondering genuinely the potential for trouble, and just maybe Lila's insistence on high heel pumps their mother had no use for alive much less dead and in a casket might pose a dilemma worthy of reconsidering footwear altogether.

Instead, Charles Robert Tully just said, "I don't believe that will be a problem," which made Lila Fessmire straighten her head right back up and smile at him directly.

*   *   *

Both women were markedly drained when they at last walked in through the carport door of Elba Rae's house. Whether they were in fact cognizant of it or not, Hazel Burns detected their exhaustion right away even though she herself had been quite the busy one minding things at Elba Rae's house as first one and then another stopped by to deliver a dish of some variety. Elba Rae noticed the teeming counter top and the near-covered surface of the harvest table in the nook right away.

"My goodness. Will you look at all this food?"

"I know it! I haven't hit a chair since ya'll left," Hazel said, and then seemed to suddenly regret the unintentional temperament of her tone. "But you know I was glad to do it," she assured.

"Were you able to get them all written down?"

"I was sure to do that. They're all on your pad over there."

"Thank you," said Elba Rae.

"Oh, and before I forget—Begina called back while ya'll were gone and said to tell you she wouldn't be able to make it for the visitation, but to let her know about the arrangements anyway because she did want to try to get here for the funeral, just depending on Laveetra and all."

"Good Lord, she's not gonna try to drag Aunt Laveetra, is she?" asked Elba Rae.

"Well," Hazel said, "she didn't precisely say what she was doing about Laveetra and I didn't think to ask her."

"Surely not," Lila remarked.

"And you know she'll be driving over here on a wing and a prayer in some old piece of car," Elba Rae said. "But that's just gonna have to be her problem. I've got more than I can worry with as it is."

"So many have asked about the arrangements, Elba Rae, but I told them I just couldn't promise anything for certain until you and Lila got home."

"Well, I think it's all worked out, Hazel," Elba Rae said as she looked askance at her sister.

"Yeah," Lila Fessmire replied.

"The visitation is set for tomorrow at five, and we'll have the funeral day after tomorrow at eleven," Elba Rae stated.

Lila turned to Hazel. "Now all we have to do is live through it."

In Loving Remembrance

"And she said to tell you she was thinking about you, but she just didn't 'spect she'd better try to get out."

They stood facing one another, barely inside the kitchen and nowhere close to an area of the house suggesting the visit would be anything but brief—just long enough to deliver the dish, express the condolence, extend the offer of assistance, and move on.

"Well, poor thing, Ned. She's sure had a go with her stomach, hasn't she?"

"She has, I tell you. And we never know what's going to set her off."

"Is that right?" Elba Rae was genuinely engaged in the matter. Martha Betty Maharry had been a faithful friend and neighbor for years, and Elba Rae knew for a fact she was not one to use feeble excuses to neglect others and certainly not at a time of death. If Ned Maharry declared his wife's absence was the byproduct of gastric distress, Elba Rae didn't doubt it in the least.

Whatever the ailment, at any rate, it had not rendered Martha Betty unable to bake what Elba Rae knew would be—without need of peeking under the foil that securely covered it—a pecan pie. Elba Rae knew positively as sure as she and Ned Maharry were standing in her kitchen discussing his wife's condition that he held in his hands a pecan pie. Martha Betty Maharry was just predictable that way.

But then, so many people in Buford were. And when it came right down to it, Elba Rae was of the conviction the content of the dish wasn't really the focus so much as it was about caring for friends and neighbors and loved ones and being there for them in the bad times, which sooner or later everyone in Buford was going to have.

That was not to infer it was acceptable to make a call on the family of the deceased without putting a little thought into it first. Elba Rae Van Oaks had always prided herself in the fact she gave as good as—if not sometimes better than—she received. Her own condolence food of record, Chicken Florentine casserole, as a rule was not duplicated, either because it typically required more preparation than those items provided by others who didn't go to the trouble, or just because everyone knew in general and accepted as fact that if there was going to be a Chicken Florentine casserole presented, it would be provided by Elba Rae Van Oaks, it being more or less her signature dish.

"She'll be fine for the longest," Ned Maharry continued while still perfectly balancing the covered pie, "and then she'll eat something that goes to telling on her. And she'll need to get out and go somewhere, but she's so afraid she won't be able to hold her wind."

Maybe because she'd known him for so long—the physicality of his face so familiar—Elba Rae still saw some patches of red hair on top of Ned Maharry's follicle-challenged head when they talked, whereas to the naked and uninformed eye, what remained were merely a few wispy odds and ends of mostly gray.

"I'm so sorry, Ned, but you tell her don't worry about coming to anything unless she feels like it." She paused, reflectively. "You know, Fettis was the same way."

"Is that so?"

"His system could hardly tolerate a thing after he got older. There were days he couldn't take on a cup of broth without getting gas on his stomach."

"Yeah," Ned Maharry studied. "I do sort of recall that about Fettis now that you mention it."

"His momma was the same way," Elba Rae nodded. "Bless her heart. They just inherited some kind of bad gene that naturally gave them problems with their digestion."

Ned Maharry may have audibly replied, but if he did it was no more than a "yeah" and it made Elba Rae realize she'd never taken the pie from his hand.

"I'm sorry, Ned, the least I could do is set that down for you," she said, taking the pastry and walking it over to the harvest table and confirming, based merely on weight, her assessment of the dish was correct. "Come on in here and sit down."

"Oh, Elba Rae, I guess I better get on back and see about Martha Betty."

"Well, thank you so much for coming. We appreciate the pie and we appreciate everybody thinking about us."

Ned Maharry was, at that point, already turned around and headed toward the door. "You call us if there's anything we can do," he remarked.

"I sure will, Ned, and thank you for coming." Elba Rae watched him cautiously open the aluminum storm door and take the first step down into the carport. She couldn't help but notice the firm hold he took of the door's small knob in order to steady himself, not letting loose of it until he'd cleared the bottom step. Elba Rae quickly surveyed the kitchen and then looked over her shoulder into the den, and was relieved Lila was nowhere in sight to make ado of Ned Maharry's minor but apparent unsteadiness. The pallbearer list was complete, and Elba Rae had neither the time nor the patience to revisit it.

When Lila did enter the kitchen, having obviously bathed, applied fresh makeup, and perfumed herself with the subtlest hint of fragrance, Elba Rae's head was fully immersed in the refrigerator.

"Oh," Elba Rae remarked as she pulled herself up. "There you are."

"What are you doing?"

"Trying to rearrange this icebox best I can, but we're already running out of room. People are still stopping by in droves and every one bringing a dish."

Lila noticed the notepad on the counter and stepped over to survey the growing list of visitors and the corresponding food item to which each belonged.

"Oh, great," she said. "Just what we needed. Another pecan pie."

"I know it," Elba Rae agreed. "I bet the Piggly Wiggly hasn't got a bottle of Karo syrup left on the shelf. But at least if Martha Betty made it, we'll be able to eat it."

"What about the rest of them?"

"Well," Elba Rae said, "I can tell you right now we'll have to give that one Willadean Hendrix brought a sling in the big gully before it's over."

"How come?"

"I don't know. Ordinarily, Willadean is a good cook. And she puts up her own pecans from all those trees they've got on their place. But I think the settings must be off on her oven."

"What's wrong with it?"

"Uncover it and see for yourself. Looks like she put it in to bake and forgot about it. I bet we couldn't slice it with a hatchet."

"Well, there're plenty of backups," Lila observed, as she almost involuntary raised the corner of the aluminum foil covering a rectangular glass casserole dish before leaning in to take a whiff, from which she immediately retracted.

"What's this?"

"It's the one," said Elba Rae with her voice once again emitting from inside the refrigerator, "that I'm trying to get stuffed in here."

"It smells awful. What is it?"

"Chili Mac."

Lila quickly resealed the foil around the corner of the dish and she did it tightly. "If I wasn't already upset, I would be if I had to eat that."

"I don't imagine I'm going to be wanting any over engorgement of it either, but I've still got to cram it in here somehow," Elba Rae said as she emerged long enough to extract Florine Moss's thoughtful chili macaroni casserole from the counter and wedge it into the refrigerator next to a congealed salad.

"Florine has always been bad about wanting to try out something different, but you know, a death is no time to experiment with new recipes." Elba Rae glanced at the clock hanging on the wall in the breakfast nook.

"Goodness, I've got to start getting ready. It'll be five o'clock before you know it."

"Well, go on. I can man the list until you get back. Bucky and the children ought to be getting here any minute. And—speaking of which, was that a car door?"

Lila walked around the corner to the little hallway so she could see out the storm door through the carport. "Yep. And she's got a bowl of something."

Elba Rae stuck her head around the corner as well, just enough to identify the next guest.

"Potato salad," Elba Rae said.

"How do you know?"

"Cause it's Ulgine Babcock and that's all she ever knows to bring. To every circle meeting, to every covered dish at the church, and any time somebody passes. She probably started peeling the potatoes when she heard Momma had gone in the hospital."

"Well," Lila reasoned, "doesn't look like we've got any yet so it least it'll be something to get the pecan pie taste out of our mouth."

"If you want some potato salad, you better hope somebody else has the same thought."

"Why?"

"Because she never uses more than a teaspoon of mayonnaise. It's always so choky. And if there's one thing I can't stand, it's choky potato salad. I feel like telling her some time I'd be glad to give her a dollar if she'd just go buy a jar of mayonnaise. Oh, and I haven't got time now to get hung up in a long conversation with her. Tell her I'm taking my bath and thank you for coming."

"All right."

Elba Rae was halfway through the adjoining den on the way to her bedroom when she quickly added, "As soon as you write it down, get my jar of mayonnaise out of the icebox and stir some into that potato salad."

As irritating as her sister could be, Lila Fessmire couldn't help but sometimes marvel at Elba Rae's prophetic proclamations. Mrs. Ulgine Babcock had, indeed just as Elba Rae swept through the den and disappeared down the hallway, reached the carport door bearing a large plastic wrap-covered pottery serving bowl that obviously contained the declared potato salad.

Lila courteously entertained Ulgine Babcock as best she could, answering each of her polite questions revolving around Lila's children, their ages, their scholastic and extracurricular interests, Lila's husband, his business affiliations, and—in summation—the general whereabouts of all of them—to which Lila explained she was expecting them just any minute, and that seemed to help serve as Mrs. Ulgine Babcock's notice to conclude her visit.

And just as Elba Rae had also predicted, Lila Fessmire peeled off the plastic wrap as soon as Ulgine Babcock left and gave the potato salad a perfunctory taste—quickly determining it was distinctly prepared with a deficit quantity of any nature of lubricating condiment. Lila obliged Elba

Rae's request and enhanced it with two heaping wooden spoon wallops' worth of mayonnaise before covering it back up and stuffing into the already over burdened refrigerator.

*   *   *

Lila Fessmire had not cried since arriving in Buford the morning before—not upon greeting her sister, and not when they faced the depressing duty of selecting burial clothing; she maintained equanimity throughout the heartbreaking ordeal of funeral planning and sales pitches for embroidered praying hands. But at the sight of her children—and more so her husband—who walked through the door of Elba Rae's house just minutes after Ulgine Babcock had departed, she broke down and nearly sobbed. Buford was Lila's home as far as most people knew. But she'd felt anything but at home since leaving Birmingham.

Bucky Fessmire stood about five feet ten inches tall with thinning hair that had once been dark blonde but that he still managed to present as more voluminous than it was through use of some products Lila made sure he always had in stock in their bathroom back home. The once stocky and athletic football star who'd played offensive guard in his Tuscaloosa college days moved a little slower due to a deteriorating knee he refused surgery for and a waistline that —while still socially acceptable—concerned his more aesthetically conscious wife. He made a point not to leave the house without at least two rolls of Tums in his pocket at all times.

Bucky held his wife tightly for about half a minute, but it was solace enough for Lila to recapture her composure. She cleared her nose quickly with one strong sniff and walked over to embrace her two sons. Neither of them seemed disturbed by their mother's display of emotion.

Nick and Heath Fessmire were only fourteen years old, yet they already matched Lila in height and—to her chagrin—could probably have passed for eighteen barring their too-often lack of maturity. Looking at them as they stood shoulder to shoulder in Elba Rae's kitchen, however, Lila still saw the red, puffy faces of the two tiny babies the doctor and his delivery room nurse had placed in her arms in the predawn hours of a Tuesday in 1969, and when she did, there were never any residual hard feelings toward the boys over the fact they'd chosen a Monday—of all the days of the week—to initiate their entrance into the Fessmire family.

Monday nights had been special to Lila Fessmire back then. She never publicly admitted to having a crush on Mr. Lee Majors, the dashing young actor who'd once appeared every week as a character named Heath Barkley on her favorite television program, but neither had she ever renounced it. She'd not previously been unduly drawn to period westerns before the discovery of Mr. Majors, favoring comedies and not sharing her husband's devotion to Mr. James Arness who starred on the show Bucky Fessmire preferred, but she made it a ritual every Monday night to watch the sweeping saga of the rich and powerful family of California ranchers in which the object of her affection would ride to the rescue on a horse named Charger.

Oddly, however, and never serving to dilute her loyalty to Mr. Lee Majors, Lila Fessmire had noted as the series evolved of just how striking a pose was cast by another of the male leads, especially when he was just about to embark upon a provoked brawl with one of the town's many ne'er-do-wells. And so powerful had the influence of this second character been that barely into season two, Lila had resolved that as much of a problem as was presented by the unpleasant lack of amenities available in the 1870s, she decided she could have suffered through it as long as she got to do her suffering with Heath Barkley's brother, Nick.

Bucky Fessmire had not understood Lila's enthusiasm for the Barkley brothers in the least, and had apparently been too naïve to ponder that his wife might have anything of a prurient interest in the attractive men who were paid to portray improbably valiant heroes. He accepted without prejudice her choice of names for the twin boys born to the couple the same year the final episode of the show was broadcast. And as tacky as Elba Rae Van Oaks had thought it was to name children after fictitious characters on a western, she'd long since decided that fretting over her nephews' given names was futile and, more to the point, genuinely reckoned (given what she knew to be Lila's taste in popular television programs of the era) the boys should just consider themselves lucky they hadn't ended up being named Skipper and Gilligan Fessmire.

Charity Fessmire was eighteen but bore more of her mother's petite build than what her brothers had obviously inherited from their father's side of the pool. She was a pretty girl with auburn hair that hung below her shoulders and parted on one side. Lila hugged her.

"Are you all right, baby? You look pale."

"I'm fine, Mom. How are you?"

"Well," Lila took a few seconds to survey her family. "I'm glad ya'll are here."

"Where's Aunt Elba Rae?" asked Charity.

"Getting ready to go to the visitation."

Bucky Fessmire walked into the den and gave it a look over, as though testing its degree of familiarity to him, and Lila momentarily followed.

"You two making out okay?" he asked.

"Me and Elba Rae? Oh, yeah, we're getting along great—as long as I don't dare question anything she says."

"Well, it's probably better if you just try to keep the peace."

"I'm trying," she said.

"I know it's a bad time for your sister, too. But it'll be over soon."

"You got that right," Lila Fessmire assured. "Because I don't plan to spend one more minute here than I have to."

"She Looks So Natural"

Charles Robert Tully was waiting for the family in the small but well-appointed lobby area of Buford Memorial Funeral Home as they somberly filed in the door, with Elba Rae and Lila in front, followed by the Fessmire children, Hazel Burns, and finally Bucky. Imogene Winnegar was on duty at her desk to receive and direct visitors, and stood at attention as the processional went by.

The director once again extended his sincerest of condolences and expressed to Elba Rae and Lila that he hoped they'd be pleased with the work the staff had done on their dear mother.

"You know," he said to them both, "some cases pose more of a challenge than others. And while we strive to present the best appearance possible every time, sometimes the family has," he chose his verbiage carefully, "unfulfilled expectations."

"I know you did the best you could, Charles Robert," Elba Rae replied in a strange sort of reverse solace. "But she was just so sick there at the end. I know her body was in bad shape."

"All right, then," Charles Robert Tully said. "She's right this way."

He led them a short distance off the lobby in the direction opposite the office and showroom they'd visited the afternoon prior until they reached a pair of closed double doors.

"I'll let you have a few minutes to yourselves. But if you need anything, I'll be in the office."

"Thank you, Charles Robert," Elba Rae said. Then without visible signs of trepidation, she opened the door to the visitation parlor.

The sisters walked in unison. Not too fast, but with determination and resolve. Bucky Fessmire stayed several paces behind nearer to Hazel Burns, who had already surreptitiously confided to Elba Rae that she'd keep a watch on the Fessmire children in the event one of them went to crying or falling out, because the reaction people had at the instant they saw a loved one displayed in the casket for the first time was always unpredictable.

Sometimes it was a peaceful transition—especially if the deceased had, like Ethel Maywood, been as poorly sick and wretched-looking right at the end—for the next of kin to see a relative dressed and made up and coifed once more, and looking as close to normal as was possible given the reclined pose and unnatural lighting. But it could also be a shock to the system, as Hazel had pointed out to Elba Rae before volunteering to assume the honorable duty of being on standby for shoulder patting, tissue passing, and emergency consoling in general to whoever might need it. She had even reasoned to Elba Rae that strife was all the more looming in the case of the Fessmire family in particular since none of them had seen Ethel Maywood right at her own wretched end, a situation apparently at the crux of a new rift between Lila and Elba Rae that Hazel didn't want stirred up.

At some point in the march, Hazel Burns, Bucky Fessmire, and all Fessmire children broke rank and fell back, and let Lila and Elba Rae initially approach the pall by themselves. The women stood completely still and quiet for a full minute and possibly longer, absorbing the dreamlike scene before them in which their mother lay serenely and calmly in a navy blue suit and a cream-colored blouse with just the slenderest hint of a smile on her otherwise paralyzed face. It was Lila who finally broke the silence.

"That lipstick is awful."

Elba Rae looked down and seemed to study it for herself. "It's too heavy, isn't it?"

"Too heavy," Lila concurred, "and she wouldn't have been caught dead in that shade of red."

Elba Rae suddenly began riffling through her pocketbook.

"What are you doing?"

"Have you got a Kleenex?" Elba Rae asked, while continuing to fumble.

"Probably," replied Lila, after which she momentarily began fumbling outright through her own purse although before she could conduct the search in earnest, Elba Rae said "never mind" and walked on over to a well-polished Queen Anne reproduction side table where a complimentary box of tissues was out for the taking. The table, besides being a logical place to present Kleenex, was also serving to segregate two sprays of flowers. One was a plentiful arrangement of yellow roses, while the other was a less fortunate and sparse sampling of blue carnations. Elba Rae was momentarily distracted by the temptation to begin opening the attached cards and find out who had sent what but realized attending to Ethel was the more pressing of concerns.

She extracted a tissue and returned promptly to the casket, waiting until she was directly over the body to give the tissue a generous lick. Without hesitation, which could have possibly drawn attention and also allowed the saliva due time to dry, she reached down toward Ethel Maywood and gave her crimson lips a quick wipe—making sure the one swab was sufficient because, red or no, she didn't really intend to re-lick a Kleenex that had already been used for such a purpose.

"Is that better?" Elba Rae asked.

Lila studied the lips and agreed the lesser quantity was more befitting.

"Yeah. That's better," she said but stopped short of suggesting the lips now looked somewhat smeared because she feared Elba Rae might take reciprocal action to remedy them.

"Except," Elba Rae observed "they didn't get her hair exactly right."

"What's wrong with it?" Lila whispered.

"The way it's pulled behind her ear."

"What about it?"

"Well, she never wore it pulled behind her ears like that. It looks silly."

"I think it looks nice," Lila said. "It's sort of flattering."

"It doesn't look like her," and with that, Elba Rae reached inside the casket yet again and delicately loosened the tufts of hair that had been tucked behind Ethel Maywood's right ear. She gingerly fluffed them a few times with her fingers until the ear was mostly covered.

"How's the other side look?"

Lila leaned slightly over the casket to check. "I can't see that ear. It's too far into the pillow."

"Well, then I guess it's all right."

They continued to scrutinize for another minute or two and were oblivious to the fact Bucky Fessmire had taken a seat on a dark leather sofa while his children sat down in various chairs toward the back of the room.

"They did a good job with her under the circumstances, don't you think?" Elba Rae said to Lila although she was almost talking to herself.

"Do you?" questioned Lila.

"Oh, Lord, yes. She was so sick there at the end. She didn't look a thing like herself in the hospital."

"I didn't see her in the hospital," Lila reminded, curtly.

"Well, if you had, you'd know what I'm talking about. I'm sure Charles Robert did the best he could with what he had to work with."

Lila suddenly realized Hazel was standing closely behind them. "Oh, Hazel, I'm sorry," she said as she stepped to the side. "Come on up here."

"That's okay, Lila, you take as long as you want."

"No," she insisted. "Come on."

Hazel Burns tentatively approached and looked down at her deceased aunt. Within seconds, she was fraught with emotion.

"Oh, Elba Rae," Hazel sobbed. "She looks so pretty."

Elba Rae put her arm around Hazel and patted her on the shoulder—a gesture Lila immediately noted wasn't offered during the first view the sisters had shared.

"I know," Elba Rae said to Hazel. "I hope she's up there with Aunt Ruby right now and they're getting all caught up on everything."

Hazel sort of laughed through her sniffle. "I hope they are too."

Though her own purse was adequately stocked, Hazel Burns—in the throes of her spontaneous wave of grief—did not reach for a tissue, and that prompted Elba Rae to reflexively give her the crumpled one she held in her own hand. Hazel was tenderly dabbing at the tip of her nose before Elba Rae even thought to notice the trace evidence of Ethel Maywood's red lipstick on the impromptu hankie, and she was grateful Lila seemed unaware.

"Momma and Aunt Ethel are probably talking about everybody in Litton County," Hazel continued, "and who's done what to who, whether they know the facts or not. You know it never stopped them before."

Lila Fessmire obliviously rolled her eyes just for a second and turned around. As she walked toward her family at the back of the parlor, Bucky rose from the sofa and gave her a hug.

"Do you want to look?" she said to her husband.

"I'll go in a minute," he said. "Let your sister and Hazel get their fill."

Lila turned around to observe Elba Rae holding Hazel's hand. "I don't know when that will be," she remarked.

Charity Fessmire abruptly stood from her chair. "Mom, where's the restroom?"

"It's out the door and to the right, Sweetheart," after which the girl wasted no time exiting.

"Is she okay?"

"Seemed okay in the car on the way over here," Bucky replied, as he pulled a roll of Tums out of his pocket and tore away enough of the paper wrapper to extract two.

"I hope she's not having a sick spell."

"Could just be her nerves," Bucky said, trying to sound reassuring through the crunch of chewing antacid.

"I hope it's just that and not … I better go see about her." Lila left the room momentarily and Bucky Fessmire hunched his shoulders once when the boys looked over at him for direction.

Rather than continue to stand around in the rear of the parlor, Bucky decided to use the calm as opportunity to get his looking over and done with. He'd never been much for the public viewing aspect of the funeral process— and had expressed as much to his wife when discussing his personal wishes on any number of occasions, which were usually immediately following the gesture he was about to make. However, in the interest of being polite, he would force himself to walk by for a quick glance whenever the situation warranted so as to avoid offending the loved ones. So he walked to the pall where Elba Rae and Hazel were still gathered.

Elba Rae turned around when she felt his approach. "Oh, hey, Bucky." He put his arm around Elba Rae.

"She looks mighty pretty, Elba Rae. Just like she's resting."

"I hope she is now." The three of them stared at Ethel Maywood.

"Where's Lila?" Elba Rae asked.

"Oh, she just went to the ladies room, I think."

Bucky stood for a couple of minutes more before the door in the rear of the room opened and Charity Fessmire returned, followed by her mother. "Excuse me," Bucky said before he went to them.

"Everything okay?"

"Everything's fine," Lila said to him. "Just nerves, I think." Bucky Fessmire gave his daughter a big hug and it seemed she didn't want him to let go.

Lila looked at her watch. "Have Heath and Nick gone up to see yet?"

"No," Bucky confirmed. "But I have."

"Well," Lila lamented as she looked toward the boys, who were by then each slumped deeply into wingback chairs, appearing to be unconcerned. "We're running out of time if they want any privacy." Lila crossed the room to them.

"Do you want to see your grandmother before all the people get in here?" She got no immediate response from either son.

"Huh?" Nick?"

Nick Fessmire shrugged his shoulders but otherwise exerted no communication.

"Heath? Do you want to see?"

"Do we have to?" he asked.

"What do you mean, do you have to? Don't you want a chance to say good-bye to your grandmother? This is the last time you'll ever get to see her."

"I don't want to," Nick Fessmire replied.

Lila leaned in and simultaneously took both boys by their arms. "I think you should," she said, pulling them to their feet. "Before it's crowded in here. You can have a little time by yourselves."

She managed to walk them almost all the way to the casket before they capriciously stopped.

"I don't want to!" Heath protested.

"Why not?"

"I don't know. It's just," he said without finishing.

Lila seemed indifferent to debating the point and certainly not for the first time in the twins' lives, she bet to herself Miss Barbara Stanwyck never had to suffer such insubordination from the namesake sons.

"There's nothing to be afraid of. This is just a natural part of life we all have to go through. And ya'll are both old enough to stand up in here and act like you've got some sense. It's the least you can do."

They heard, but did not move.

"Now come on over here and look at your mammaw before they fling those doors open!"

Though Elba Rae did not necessarily condone Lila's insistence that her boys absorb the view of their deceased grandmother from a vantage point closer than their comfort obviously allowed, she did not impose and, rather, stood aside to give them ample berth as Lila ushered them directly to the coffin, one on each side of her. There the trio stood and for once, Elba Rae thought, her nephews exhibited authentic reverence through their calm and stillness.

"See," Lila said. "It's just your mammaw."

They all looked down at about the same time. The boys were stoic at first, but recoiled when they observed their mother's hand reach into the casket and rearrange Ethel Maywood's hair ever so slightly such that it was tucked behind her right ear once more.

"There," Lila said.

"Why is she blue?" asked Nick Fessmire.

"She's not blue," Lila corrected.

"She looks blue to me," he insisted.

"It's just those bulbs they use," explained Lila, gesturing toward the ceiling at the strangely-hued spotlights that were trained on the casket. There was a soft rose-colored one also, but the blue seemed to be packing more wattage and, for better or worse, was pointed right on Ethel Maywood's face.

"She looks creepy," Nick opined.

"She does not," assured Lila. "She looks peaceful. It's just like she's asleep."

In spite of his mother's best euphemistic commentary, Heath Fessmire was having none of it, either.

"She looks dead," he said.

"Hush!"

"Can we sit down now?" pleaded Nick Fessmire.

"Yes," his mother said. "Please do. Both of you. Just sit down back there and don't talk unless someone speaks to you first." The boys turned without need of further inducement and did not, for the rest of that evening, get within ten feet of the late Ethel Maywood.

Based upon her sons' inapt manners with regard to the viewing process overall, and as much upon her daughter's uncertain nervous state, Lila decided to forgo a personal escort to the casket with Charity Fessmire and let her look—or not—on her own. In the ensuing lull, Lila was afforded opportunity to join Elba Rae and Hazel Burns in the inventory of the floral arrangements, a sport involving removal of the card from a small envelope discretely attached to each item in order to identify the sender. She approached Hazel and Elba Rae already in progress and standing in front of a tasteful offering of lilies and other seasonal blooms that were engulfed by greenery Lila suspected was enhanced with some manner of oil-based product to give it such an impressive gleam.

"Who are those from?" Lila asked.

Elba Rae handed the card to Lila, but told her anyway as she did. "They're from Mary Alice."

"Oh, Elba Rae," Hazel perked up, "I was meaning to ask if you'd heard from Mary Alice."

"I did," interjected Lila. "She's been keeping up with Momma since she went in the hospital this last time, so she knew to be on standby."

"She's been calling you?" asked Elba Rae.

"She calls me, or I call her every once in a while. But we try to stay in touch with more than just a Christmas card here and there."

Elba Rae Van Oaks was not necessarily shocked by the casual nature with which Mary Alice's contact was disclosed, but neither was she unaffected by the revelation that Lila's allegiance with her apparently remained intact to some degree, defying decades of geographical separation. Elba Rae felt oddly unsettled all of a sudden.

"Is she coming from Colorado?" Hazel asked.

"No. She said they really wanted to get back for the funeral but it wasn't going to be possible. Her husband just had gall bladder surgery and can't travel—and Mary Alice didn't feel comfortable leaving him."

"Husband?" asked Hazel. "I guess I didn't realize she'd married again."

"Yeah," Elba Rae said. "Number three." As soon as the words came out, she wished she'd kept her mouth shut, since there was nothing to gain by inferring moral infractions over the quantity of marriage licenses Mary Alice had collected; Elba Rae doubted it made much difference in Lila's eyes.

"Well," Hazel lamented, "I guess Butch and them will come over from Montgomery."

"Yes," said Elba Rae. "I imagine we'll see them tomorrow." Elba Rae Van Oaks looked at her sister, then focused attention on the lush display of yellow roses she'd briefly observed on the earlier Kleenex hunt necessitated for the modifying of Ethel Maywood's lipstick.

"Those are beautiful," Elba Rae continued, as a means to change the subject.

"Aren't they, though?" agreed Hazel, as they waited for Elba Rae to open the card.

"They're from Dr. Bud and Virginia Millford," she reported. "Just beautiful. I'm almost ashamed people spend so much money for these flowers."

"Momma loved flowers," Lila remarked. "I'm glad she's got a good stand of them tonight."

"There are some pretty plants here too, Lila, and I think several of them are from Birmingham."

"Really?"

"That one," Elba Rae said, pointing across the room "is from the staff at Bucky's office. And that schefflera next to it has got some women's names on it I don't recognize so they must be some of your friends."

"And I believe that spray yonder might be from Bucky's family," Hazel Burns offered.

"Oh," said Lila. "I'll go check in a minute."

One spray over on the other side of the Kleenex-holding table, however, Lila was unavoidably drawn to a suddenly contrasting arrangement of blue carnations. A strange sort of lump began to form in her throat; not so much one spawned by sorrow or angst, but rather disappointment. Disappointment that as hard as she'd tried to create a carnation-free viewing for Ethel Maywood, she ultimately couldn't control the ill-conceived intentions of others.

In the case of the blue carnations, it was not necessary to extract a card to determine the responsible party, since before Lila could even situate herself within card-snatching proximity, Elba Rae took closer note of the blooms herself and just said it aloud for the benefit of all.

"Oh, good Lord."

Hazel Burns stepped over to observe what the other two already knew. Draped diagonally across the economical arrangement was a matching sash cut of six-inch wide blue ribbon with the words "Goodbye, Sweetie" spelled out in silver glitter, a calling card that could belong to no other than simple Begina from Hattiesburg.

Elba Rae obligatorily removed the card, though with a complete absence of suspense, and read it to the group.

"We will always miss our Sweetie. Love, Aunt Laveetra and Begina."

Lila gazed at the sash. "That's the tackiest thing I've ever seen."

"Bless their hearts," Hazel Burns nodded.

Lila subconsciously twiddled with the cut end of the ribbon which hung over a carnation bloom that was already turning brown at the tips. "Can't we just take this out before anybody comes in?"

"We're not taking anything out," Elba Rae ruled.

"Why not? If we get it out now, no one will ever have to see it."

"It's the thought that counts."

"Exactly when did you go to championing Begina so? You know as well as I do Momma hated being called Sweetie. Hated it with a passion. And Begina and Laveetra were the only ones who ever did it."

"I don't care," Elba Rae continued. "I don't want to have to lie if Aunt Laveetra or Begina were to ask how their flowers looked. What am I supposed to say? That we threw them out the back door before the visitation started?"

Lila rolled her head back and forth with frustration. "Aunt Laveetra hasn't got mind enough to dial the telephone, much less ever remember what kind of flowers Begina put her name on! For heaven's sake! She probably won't even remember that Momma died!"

"I don't care! I'm not throwing anybody's flowers out and that's that. This time tomorrow they'll be dumped on the grave along with the rest of these and—"

The sound of a single door opening in the back of the room distracted Elba Rae and when she turned around, she observed Charles Robert Tully approaching.

"Do you ladies need some more time?" he asked. Lila and Elba Rae exchanged glances.

"No, Charles Robert. I don't think so," Elba Rae replied. "Are you ready?"

"Yeah," Lila said. "As ready as I'm ever going to be," and then she took in a deep breath.

"It's just," he explained, "we already have a few guests waiting in the lobby. They were a little early, I imagine, but if you're okay, I'll go ahead and let them in."

Elba Rae nodded affirmatively. "We're ready, Charles Robert." He smiled and nodded once before returning to the back of the room, whereupon he opened both doors to their widest capacity.

"Here we go," Lila Fessmire mumbled to herself as the first assemblage of guests stepped forth.

*   *   *

Initially there were those who Elba Rae Van Oaks knew had come to the visitation out of respect and concern for her, such as Mr. Bailey and some of the faculty from the Homer T. Litton Grammar School, as well as a few assorted and distant cousins somehow connected by blood or marriage to the late Ethel Maywood and even some who were related on Elba Rae's daddy's side.

There were also the familiar and comforting faces belonging to members of the First Avenue United Methodist Church, including Reverend and Mrs. George Timmons. And then there were those present for whom Elba Rae Van Oaks knew attendance was something they did out of habit and from boredom and, quite possibly, as a hobby—perhaps a combination of all three. This segment was the contingency seen at most any visitation in and around Buford due to a lack of other alternatives that might purge them of the need to see and be seen. Elba Rae even recognized a couple of her mother's contemporaries who, in fact, had often attempted to solicit Ethel when they went calling even though Ethel had, as a rule, declined most invitations to the viewings she'd judged to be nothing more than recreational. Regardless, Elba Rae and Lila received each person sincerely.

Among the peripheral visitors was Mrs. Virginia Millford, the wife of Dr. Bud Millford who had treated Ethel Maywood—as well as most everyone else in Buford—over the years via his medical practice. Dr. Bud had long since attained as near about sainthood as would ever be bestowed in Litton County while as a couple, he and his wife were likely the region's most wealthy and socially prominent.

Virginia Millford hugged Elba Rae and Lila tightly. "Bud's sorry he couldn't be here, Elba Rae, but he got called to the hospital just as we were getting ready to come."

"Oh, goodness, I understand, Virginia. I know he must never get a minute to sit down."

"But he wanted me to let you know how much we're thinking about you. And the family," Virginia said, as if to emphasize recognition of Lila and the Fessmire federation.

"Thank you," Lila replied. "And the flowers you sent are just beautiful."

"Were they?"

"They are," Elba Rae joined in. "They're over there." The three women looked in the direction of the previously admired yellow roses.

"Good," Virginia Millford concluded. "I hate it when they skimp."

There followed several seconds of awkward silence.

"Well, you all take care and know you're in our thoughts."

"Thank you, Virginia," Elba Rae said, which prompted a repeat of the hugs.

"I think I'll look around at some of these pretty arrangements," she said, and then walked away.

Elba Rae and Lila were immediately engaged by the next visitor, with whom they mingled pleasantly. The conversations were already becoming repetitive, as could be expected since there were only so many words and phrases in the comfort catalog from which to choose and because of the recurring euphemisms guests used to describe Ethel Maywood's appearance. There were some, however, who took advantage of the societal nature of the setting to convey the status of their own ailments, illnesses, and general miseries including—but not limited to—Mabel Moss's herniated disc, her sister-in-law Florine's vertigo, and the lingering cough afflicting Florine's husband, Jack, who indeed did sound burdened with an unhealthy build-up of phlegm. After a while, it collectively began to feel to Elba Rae like some kind of contest whereby the winner of the worst malady would be announced at the conclusion of the visitation even though it should have been obvious that trophy already belonged to Ethel Maywood. For the benefit of their mother's caring friends and relations, however, Elba Rae and Lila maintained the demeanor of having heard each consolation and compliment and complaint for the very first time.

"Miss Marjorie," Elba Rae said.

"Oh, Elba Rae," returned a matronly looking woman who struggled to be five feet tall and, without heels and the contribution of an indefatigable hairdresser who believed in adding height through teasing, really was not.

"I'm just so sorry about your momma," the diminutive woman allowed, as she casually glanced at Ethel Maywood. "We were friends for a long time."

"Thank you, Miss Marjorie," Elba Rae said methodically.

"We're sure gonna miss her in the garden club. Even though she hasn't been able to be there lately, her chair was always empty and waiting."

"Well," Elba Rae Van Oaks affirmed politely. "Miss Marjorie, do you remember my sister, Lila?"

"Hello, Miss Marjorie," Lila said convincingly, as though she knew to whom she was speaking.

"Why, Lila Mae. It sure is," she said, as she reached out with both hands and took hold of Lila's arms at the elbow in a firm clutch. "It's so good to see you. I'm sorry it has to be under these circumstances."

Though Lila Fessmire's visits to Buford had been sporadic and sometimes far apart over the years and she often did not readily recognize her mother's occasional acquaintances they might encounter when out and about in town, Lila was skilled, nonetheless, in carrying forth with the pretense that she did. Her mother's friends were never any the wiser for it. Elba Rae suspected immediately Lila did not recognize Marjorie Whittlehurst.

"Thank you, Miss Marjorie. It's so good to see you, too. How have you been? You're looking mighty well."

"Oh, thank you, hon. I'm guess I'm doing okay for eighty-five. Up and going, so I won't complain."

"Well, you're still just as pretty as ever and we so appreciate you coming tonight." And among her other talents, Lila Fessmire was advanced in the art of benign dismissal.

Miss Marjorie smiled and reflexively let loose of Lila's arms, and turned her attention over to Ethel Maywood for a final glimpse. "We'll see ya'll tomorrow, Elba Rae." And then she shuffled away.

"Did you not know who that was?" asked Elba Rae, somewhat glibly. "She and Momma have been friends since before we were born."

"Of course I knew who she was, but Good Lord, Elba Rae, I probably haven't seen her in twenty years."

Elba Rae gave her sister a quick look up and down, as though there was no excuse for unfamiliarity with their mother's surroundings—including her friends and acquaintances.

"And maybe even longer than that. Probably not since Momma tried to make me take piano lessons from her when I was eight. For heaven's sake."

"S-h-h-h-h."

"It's the truth," Lila protested. "Plus she looks like she's shrunk a foot since we were little."

"She has not," contradicted Elba Rae. "She's never been any taller than a good-sized midget in the circus. None of those Whittlehursts ever were."

"I'll never forget the day she took me home after my lesson when Momma couldn't pick me up for some reason. Scared me to death. There's no way she could see over the hood of the car." Lila paused just for a few seconds to reflect.

"I think the only reason Momma let me stop taking lessons from her is because I convinced her I could already ping out a tune better than Miss Marjorie could. Is she still trying to play at the Baptist church?"

"Lands no," Elba Rae answered quickly but quietly. "I think she finally knew it was time to get in home and sit down. Oh—Willadean," Elba Rae acknowledged, in a more audible tone to signify the arrival of a new guest to the casket as well as to denote the conclusion of what might be misinterpreted as disparaging commentary about Miss Marjorie Whittlehurst.

Mrs. Willadean Hendrix politely gave Elba Rae a hug, after which she spoke to Lila but without physical contact.

"It's good to see you," Elba Rae said to her.

"Well," Willadean Hendrix said, "it's a sad time for ya'll, I know."

"It is," Elba Rae said. "But Momma had a good, long life and we just have to remember all the good times."

Willadean Hendrix made sort of an 'um-hum' gesture to signify agreement. "How are you, Lila?"

"I'm fine, Miss Willadean." In the deepest recessions of Lila Fessmire's subconscious she wanted to ask Willadean Hendrix if she'd checked the thermostat on her oven lately, and then follow with the recommendation she either seek the services of a skilled appliance repair technician or begin offering a complimentary hatchet with the next pecan pie she delivered to a poor grieving family.

"I saw that pretty young lady in the back as we were coming in and knew she must be your daughter."

"Thank you. Yes, that's Charity."

"And then the twins?"

"They're back there, too. Somewhere," Lila said.

"Ethel was always so proud of her grandchildren," to which Lila said, "Yes, she was."

"I saw those flowers over there were from Laveetra and them in Hattiesburg."

Elba Rae Van Oaks sort of nodded in an affirmative action but felt no need to infer responsibility by specifically looking in the direction of the glitzy carnation spectacle, as there clearly could be no feigning uncertainty over which arrangement was about to get discussed.

"For some reason," Willadean Hendrix continued, "I didn't realize Laveetra was still living."

"Oh, yeah," Elba Rae confirmed, almost sympathetically. "Of course, she doesn't have a lick of mind. And she can't hear thunder. But Gabriel will have to knock her in the head with the trumpet to get her to go."

"Is that right?"

Elba Rae just shook her head.

"Well, for goodness' sake. And I guess Begina looks after her."

"She does the best she can, Willadean."

"Bless her heart," Willadean Hendrix said. "Well, I'd better see about Miss Marjorie."

"Is she with you?" inquired Elba Rae.

"I called her this morning and told her I'd be happy to pick her up if she wanted to come, and of course she did. She and your momma were together in the garden club for so long."

"She still looks pretty spry," Lila remarked.

"She is," Willadean Hendrix said. "Always has been, you know."

"Hey, Miss Elba Rae!" A lanky young man approached her, seemingly unconcerned that he might be interrupting Elba Rae and Mrs. Willadean Hendrix in the midst of a poignant moment taking place right there in the very shadow of the casket. Willadean Hendrix turned around briefly to look at him and then continued her exit by hugging Elba Rae.

"Take care, hon."

"I will, Willadean, and thank you for coming."

With that, Mrs. Hendrix filed out of the way, pausing to pat Lila Fessmire on the shoulder twice as she went by.

"Well, Ronny Lee," Elba Rae said. "Aren't you sweet to come?"

"Yes, ma'am. We're sorry about your momma and all."

"Thank you," said Elba Rae. "Ronny Lee, this is my sister, Lila. Lila, this is one of my pupils from way back, Ronny Lee Fowinkle. His momma and daddy used to go to the church before they moved to Louisiana. How *is* your grandmother, Ronny Lee?"

"She's doing okay, Miss Elba Rae, but they still can't let her stay by herself."

"Well, that's a shame. And this is Ronny's wife."

Ronny Lee Fowinkle's spouse, who had until that moment remained silent and secondary, nodded her head collectively at Lila and Elba Rae.

"And I'm sorry, honey, but I'm bad with names," Elba Rae stalled.

"Dawn," the young Mrs. Fowinkle spoke up.

"Dawn," Elba Rae repeated.

"Well," Ronny Lee Fowinkle said, stepping aside such that the women had a completely unobstructed view of his wife. "I've done it again."

Dawn Fowinkle looked down at the floor and was notably embarrassed by what passed as an announcement that— afforded by his stepping aside—was unnecessary from purely a visual standpoint for the purpose of declaring her pregnancy; it would have been obvious to anyone.

Lila Fessmire stared with no discernible expression one way or the other.

"My," Elba Rae Van Oaks offered. "You're having another baby."

"This one makes four," Ronny Lee Fowinkle beamed with pride. Although Lila accepted the fact she was removed from the whole history of the connections between her sister, the pupil, his parents and his conspicuously fertile bride, she still found the venue for which he'd chosen to make the broadcast to be in unquestionably poor taste. This was a visitation to pay respects for the deceased, not a class reunion.

"I'm happy for you, Ronny Lee," offered Elba Rae. "You too, Dawn."

"Thank you, Miss Elba Rae," Dawn Fowinkle said.

"Yep," Ronny continued. "I guess I just point 'em good," he crowed, in front of what looked like an appreciative wife. "Never had no trouble. Despite what they all said."

"No, I guess you haven't," Elba Rae agreed. "Well, good for you."

There were smiles all around that did not, even so, displace the unease.

"Thank you for coming, Ronny Lee. It was mighty sweet of you."

"Yes, ma'am," he said, and off he went leading his expectant wife by the hand, with neither of them the least intent on viewing the late Ethel Maywood.

Lila Fessmire was unclear at that point whether to be happy, confused, appalled, or none of the above, but waited until the couple had safely moved on before she raised her eyebrow.

"What did he mean by that, Elba Rae? He just points 'em good?"

"Well," Elba Rae said, "there was a mishap at school. It was when he was in my room."

Elba Rae went silent as if it were all she had to offer on the subject.

"And?"

"They thought he might not be able to have children. But obviously, he hasn't had a bit of trouble. Four, indeed."

"What kind of mishap?" Lila wanted to know.

"Oh, I don't remember all of it, but they were worried for a while. Guess it doesn't matter now."

Elba Rae took immediate note of Lila's skeptical glance in the direction of the tall lanky boy and his once again pregnant wife, and could tell Lila doubted Elba Rae's ignorance of the situation. As it turned out, Elba Rae Van Oaks did have additional information about Ronny Lee's "mishap," as it had become known, but the somber setting of the Buford Memorial Funeral Home was no place to be gossiping about Ronny Lee Fowinkle and more to the point, Elba Rae considered it a private matter that shouldn't be frivolously repeated—not even to family.

Watching the blithe young man put his arm around his wife, Elba Rae felt protective of him, just as she had the day of the mishap; responsible for him, in fact. Because what happened to Ronny Lee Fowinkle had occurred on one of the days Elba Rae dreaded more than most during the month when with special education teacher Irma Young, it was her turn in the faculty rotation to serve as playground steward during the recess for grades four through six.

Ronny Lee Fowinkle had always been a showoff. In the first and second grades he'd do childish and sometimes foolish things to get the attention of anyone who'd look. By third and fourth, he'd realized select adults were intermittently impressed by a few of his more practiced stunts and routines, even if they discouraged activity they deemed unsafe or judged to be inappropriate in public settings.

In the fifth grade, as would be Elba Rae Van Oaks's luck, Ronny Lee Fowinkle had discovered girls. He seemed to revel in the epiphany that the attention he drew from them was different from the kind theretofore gleaned from a more general audience, and it had served to encourage him all the more.

When she called on him during lessons—about any of their subjects, it had never really matter which to Ronny Lee—Elba Rae had come to expect what passed for a fifth grade standard of pre-pubescent comedy in his one-liner of an answer. There'd been days when Elba Rae had guessed she knew exactly what Mr. Peter Marshall went through on the "Hollywood Squares" when all he really wanted was a simple answer to a problem but had to endure first the glib and borderline vulgar remark he was likely to get from one of those actors or entertainers, especially that silly one that sat in the center box.

Ronny Lee was, Elba Rae always had to admit, however, a fairly good student despite his insatiable need for acceptance, and there had even been a couple of instances when Ronny Lee Fowinkle had come close to making Elba Rae laugh aloud from either the originality of his answers or the mere slapstick value of his playground antics, though she had never let on in his presence. Such had definitely not been the case on the day of the mishap.

It had been the first genuinely warm week of March, and the children were feeling the effects of spring whether they knew what was affecting them or not; the adults recognized the physiological signs. Elba Rae Van Oaks was just glad the wind wasn't in the north and she didn't have to huddle against the exterior wall of the gymnasium with Irma Young to keep from having rigors.

The children had been running and being boisterous, as usual, with some participating in organized games of sport while others enjoyed the various equipment available on the playground, including a slide Elba Rae thought entirely too tall for young children, two sets of monkey bars to accommodate a range of ages, a swing set that seated eight at a time, and a contraption called the Roundabout that most kids had just called the merry-go-round.

Of all the recreational apparatus installed on the playground of the Homer T. Litton Grammar School, the Roundabout had been if not the most vintage, the least durable. The monkey bars were nothing more than welded steel that had well endured the elements for many, many years; the slide pretty much the same. The seat components on the swing set had to be replaced every now and again, but it too had been a permanent fixture enjoyed by a generation of children.

Accidents were rare. When they had occurred, recovery was usually noted before the bell rang to signify the conclusion of recess. There'd been an arm broken once when a sixth grader had taken a tumble off the slide, but for the peace of mind of Elba Rae Van Oaks, the plunge had not taken place during her watch. And for two decades, kids had managed successful play on the frail metal and splintery wood circular bench of the Roundabout with no more serious an injury than a scraped knee or elbow when some of the bigger students would get it to spinning so fast that an unsuspecting smaller one would at last lose his or her desperate grip and propel freely into the grass which was, for the most part, absent of gravel, debris, or other threatening abrasives. It had been a safety record maintained in part because no child had ever attempted to stand upright on the Roundabout's axle which rose at its epicenter while the device was in use. Ronny Lee Fowinkle had been the first to try that.

It had all happened so fast that neither Elba Rae Van Oaks nor Irma Young had time to take any sort of preventive action. By the time they'd witnessed Ronny Lee clinging to the support rods that connected the bench at the outer edge to the axis in the center—on his way to the middle—it had been too late, really, despite their later remorse.

He'd managed to rest on his knees fairly easily through six or seven successively slow spins before rising up and attempting to stand like the materialization of some kind of Roundabout flagpole. Despite his best effort to amuse the legions of playground children who otherwise would have been his captive audience for the production, however, Ronny Lee Fowinkle's thirst to entertain had been no match for centrifugal force, a concept his fifth-grade mind apparently hadn't yet understood in the least, and he'd quickly twirled off his would-be perch as soon as the merry-go-round picked up some speed. He'd screamed so loudly when he straddled the support rod those children who were not even at recess had run to the windows of their classroom to see what the matter was.

The hollering had continued all the way inside the gymnasium building where Elba Rae sought refuge in order to remove Ronny Lee from the general population of the playground, even though the gym did not house the school infirmary. He'd walked inside unaided but remained stooped over, clutching his groin with both hands, and before Irma Young had returned with the school nurse, Elba Rae had known funny little clown Ronny Lee Fowinkle would need a level of medical evaluation she had no intention of conducting.

The results of the x-ray taken by Dr. Bud Millford that afternoon at the Buford Clinic remained, for legal purposes, confidential, but because she'd been witness to the accident, Elba Rae Van Oaks was privy to certain information not commonly shared. It had been bad enough, she thought, that the fall had resulted in the child suffering a compressed testicle without it being known and repeated by untold correspondents. But by the time the complications that followed into middle school warranted its removal all together, Elba Rae had been sure the young man would be mortified if word had gotten out and he'd inadvertently fallen victim to some manner of merciless nickname that crudely referred to his unique number of testicles which was, by then, just the one.

That his absence of a full complement of genitalia would later prove to be a badge of merit born as proudly as any Boy Scout in Litton County had not been a phase through which Elba Rae Van Oaks ever anticipated the youngest Fowinkle boy would pass. She'd been shocked enough when news spread of his wife's first impending motherhood. By the time Ronny Lee stood before her at the Buford Memorial Funeral Home just feet from her mother's body and confidently proclaimed the gestation of baby number four, Elba Rae accepted that what he lacked in quantity he more than compensated for in concentration, although she had been relieved, nonetheless, when the school board had eventually voted to allocate funds for select replacement of playground equipment, after which the particular type of mishap that befell Ronny Lee Fowinkle was not known to have reoccurred.

While Elba Rae Van Oaks had no intention of discussing Ronny Lee Fowinkle's private area with Lila, she did not, however, feel as duty bound to withhold commentary about any of his other parts that were out in the open and clearly visible to the public at large.

"And you know," Elba Rae said discretely to Lila, "his arms just never were right either."

"What do you mean?"

"They just weren't. Look in a minute when nobody's watching. That left one is way longer than the right. He tried to play baseball in high school, but they said he never could get a good hold on the bat. Cause his arms just weren't right."

"Maybe it was some kind of birth defect."

"I don't know if it was a birth defect but he definitely had something. Of course, I had his older brother in my room, too. He had all kinds of colon trouble when he was young but his arms hung just as even as you please. He's a deputy sheriff now. Anyway, their momma had a time keeping that one," nodding toward Ronny Lee, "in clothes. She was always having to buy a coat with the sleeves long enough to fit his left arm, and then she'd hem up the right sleeve to match. Because otherwise it looked like he didn't even have a right hand."

Before Lila Fessmire could fully absorb the ramifications of unbalanced limbs, she and Elba Rae were alerted to a commotion generated by a flower arrangement tumbling to the floor. When Elba Rae looked to the source, she observed Mrs. Lorraine Timmons attempting to steady an apparently off-balance Virginia Millford who had, in the course of her trip around the room, somehow managed to entwine her foot with the insubstantial tripod supporting a spray of white gladiolas. And although Virginia Millford recovered quickly from her stumble, the arrangement of lovely flowers delivered in sincerest sympathy from Ned and Martha Betty Maharry had unfortunately during their descent brushed against the neighboring display of blue carnations chosen by Laveetra and simple Begina Chittum from Hattiesburg, just enough to cross-pollinate in several areas with some genuine Sweetie glitter such that when up righted, the gladiolas sparkled like a thousand tiny crystals.

"Oh, for heaven's sake," Elba Rae said with irritation in her voice. "That's all we need is for her to fall out in here."

"Virginia Millford?"

"Yes."

"Do you think she's been drinking?" Lila asked, dubiously.

"Lands yes. I smelled her before she ever got close to the casket."

Lila stared across the room at what appeared to be a recomposed Virginia

Millford, who was, by that time, enjoying carefree conversation with another guest. "I thought Dr. Bud sent her off to dry out."

"He did send her way back when. And this has never been repeated as fact, but Mabel Moss told me she'd been two more times since then—to two different places. Hadn't any cure ever taken with her, though. And it's a wonder she hasn't killed somebody in that car the way she gets a snoot full and then takes out driving all over the place."

"Didn't she get on a toot once and drive her car up on the Square?"

"She did. Ran right over the statue of old man Litton in front of the courthouse. Drunk as Cooter Brown. That's when Dr. Bud packed her off the first time, but she hadn't any more gotten home good before …" Elba Rae's disbursement of information unexpectedly stopped.

They had each noticed the unaccompanied woman in the back of the room who took pause just a few steps inside the door, and her entry distracted Elba Rae in an odd way. It first appeared the woman might be waiting for someone to join her, but then she started slowly to make her way directly toward Elba Rae and Lila, who discretely whispered, "Who is that?"

"I don't know," Elba Rae softly replied. "I can't tell from here."

The woman didn't stop to speak to any other guests on the approach, nor did anyone else in the room seem to recognize or detain her with a greeting.

"Guess we'll find out," Lila said, as she prepared to begin a conversation with yet another stranger.

"Miss Elba Rae." The woman extended her arms and hugged Elba Rae before she had any chance to react but let go before Elba Rae had time to consider returning the gesture, which she would have, she supposed, just to be polite.

The woman's hair was light on the ends—not blonde, exactly, but just somewhat streaked—while the roots were a mix of dark brown and more than a few hints of silver. And Elba Rae was positive the woman had extinguished a cigarette in the parking lot on the way to the front entrance; she had detected as much before the onset of the awkward embrace.

"I was so sorry to hear about your momma."

"Thank you," said Elba Rae, though she was at a loss for what to utter next.

"Had she been sick for a long time?"

"Uh, no. Not really. Well, not this last time in the hospital, anyway."

Elba Rae found it particularly peculiar that the visitor had arrived profoundly uninformed of the underlying circumstances that had claimed Ethel Maywood. The woman then seemed to notice Lila Fessmire for the first time since approaching the casket.

"Hello."

"Hello," Lila said back.

Elba Rae sensed an obligatory introduction to Lila was required but before she could do so, the woman stepped to the casket and looked down at Ethel Maywood. Elba Rae decided to leave her to the moment.

"I'm sure you took good care of her," the woman said, turning back around slightly to face Elba Rae. "Just like you always took care of me."

"Well," Elba Rae didn't know what to make of what was, she supposed, some type of compliment.

"I don't want to keep you. I just wanted you to know I was sorry about your momma and," she hesitated, "and you've always meant so much to me. I just never had the chance to tell you."

The woman repeated the hug she'd instigated a few minutes earlier, and this time Elba Rae was quick to return it, patting her on the back a couple of times for good measure.

"That's so sweet of you," Elba Rae said as they released. "And it was so nice of you to come."

The woman quickly dabbed her eye of what appeared to be a tear.

"Bye, now," she said. She looked at Lila and smiled.

"Thank you for coming," Lila returned. And then Lila and Elba Rae watched her gradual but direct exit toward the back of the room and out the door without so much as a look to either side.

"Who was that?" Lila asked, but in no longer so much of a whisper.

"I have no idea," confessed Elba Rae.

"No idea?"

"She doesn't look a bit familiar."

"Well, she obviously knows us. What was all that about you meaning so much to her?"

"I don't know."

"And you don't even recognize her?"

"Well, I probably will when I see her name in the guest book. Hopefully she signed it before she came in. If you get a chance, give it a look next time you're out there."

Lila cut her eyes slightly at the thought of another command from Elba Rae, and decided short of a forced evacuation, she wouldn't leave her post at the casket again that night if her life depended on it.

*   *   *

It was nearly eight thirty by the time the family settled back in for the night at Elba Rae's house. Charity Fessmire quickly retreated to her allocated quarters and Bucky momentarily drifted as well. The Fessmire twins hovered over Elba Rae's television in the den, continuously turning the dial that repeatedly rotated the same sequence of three broadcast channels yet settling on none of them.

"Let me do it," Heath Fessmire said.

"There's nothing on!" his brother replied.

"Let go of it!"

It was not so much the way both boys had their hands on the knob at the same time so much as it was the fact they were each trying to turn it in different directions that made it eventually detach from the set completely. Nick Fessmire was left holding it.

"Mom," he said, "Heath broke the TV."

"What?" Lila Fessmire glanced in their direction and noticed a television screen full of static offered by the off-channel they'd unfortunately been on when the selector popped out. She rolled her eyes and marched into the den.

"What did I tell ya'll before I left home the other day about being on good behavior when you got here? Huh?"

"*He* did it," Nick inferred.

"Then why's it in your hand?" Heath pointed out. They were soon joined by Elba Rae.

"What's going on?"

"Heath broke your TV, Aunt Elba Rae."

"I did not!"

"Did too, freak!"

"You're the freak, freak!"

"At least I'm not the dumb ass that broke the TV, dumb ass!"

"Stop it!" Lila screamed, before forcefully extracting the selector knob from Nick Fessmire's hand.

"Give me that, and get out of here. Both of you. Go."

"Where?" Nick asked. "There's nowhere *to* go here."

"Go in the living room."

"There's no TV in the living room."

"Well, there's no TV in here either now that you've broken it. So go, or I'm going to get your father and you can show him what you've done. Where'd he go? Bucky?" she called out.

"Forget it," Heath said, and walked away in the direction of the living room, followed thereafter by his brother.

"Elba Rae, I'm sorry about the TV. Some days, they're just more than I can deal with."

"They seem a little high strung."

"They—" Lila suddenly stopped in what appeared to Elba Rae an instant of self-censorship. "They're just a little too rambunctious for their own good sometimes."

"I guess boys will be boys," Elba Rae said, as she then took possession of the knob and tenderly reattached it to her television set before successfully utilizing it to get on a legitimate station. "But they're a little disrespectful, too."

Lila Fessmire took in a deep breath and let it out. Elba Rae got the impression there was something she was about to tell her, but as before, Lila was mindful of her words.

"I'm sorry. I know you're not used to a house full of people. Especially teenagers."

"It's not that. For goodness sake, I've been around children day in and day out ever since I first got hired at the school. It's just some of them act out when they get the chance."

"I'm glad the TV's not broken," Lila said. "I'm hungry."

She walked away from Elba Rae and into the adjoining kitchen. "Do you want anything?"

"No," Elba Rae answered before stepping over to the old recliner. She sank into it with a near thud while Lila went about rustling through the refrigerator as well as a few non-perishable items left out on the counter. Whatever was playing on the restored television set was of no interest, and it was obvious that any discussion of how to introduce etiquette to boys who were otherwise devoid was over.

"You know, I forgot to look in the book before we left the funeral home."

"You mean to see who that woman was? I did, on the way out," Lila said, unconcerned and still fumbling with a couple of containers.

"Well, who was it?"

"If it's the right one that belonged to her, it wasn't anybody I recognized. The last name was Mhoon."

Elba Rae Van Oaks was taken somewhat aghast by the reveal. "Mhoon?"

"Yeah. But I still don't know exactly who she was. The only Mhoons I remember were those that lived back up in the woods off the road going toward Alexander City."

"Well," Elba Rae said slowly, "it had to be some of them."

Lila rattled a plate from the stack inside the cabinet. "I think her first name was Celeste."

"That's it," Elba Rae said, just as she reclined slightly in the chair. "Celeste Mhoon. I had her in my room at school. But I wouldn't have recognized her in a million years."

"What's wrong?"

"Nothing, I guess," Elba Rae resigned. "I just hadn't heard anybody say she was back in Buford."

"Where's she been?"

"Lord, I have no idea."

"Wait a minute. Was she that Mhoon girl that ran off?"

"Ran off and I don't think anyone's known for years whether she was living or dead."

"Well, obviously she's living."

"I know. But I just can't get over it." By then Elba Rae was mostly talking to herself because Lila was too engaged in the slicing of a piece of pie—chosen carefully from the available selections so as to avoid dryness, excessive sweetness, or choky-ness.

"Of all the places for her to show up, wonder why in the world Celeste Mhoon would come to the funeral home to see Momma?"

"Is there any more Cool Whip?" Lila asked from the kitchen, ignoring Elba Rae and most assuredly not giving another thought that night to Celeste Mhoon.

Dust to Dust, and
Pass the Fried Chicken

Elba Rae Van Oaks gave the door key one hard jerk to remove it from the lock before loading into the house with Lila Fessmire behind her.

"I don't care *who* it was. I thought if he pulled that thing out and pointed it at me one more time, I was going to slap it out of his hand!"

"Oh, he probably meant well. Some people just do that," offered Lila, defensively.

"I don't care what he meant," Elba Rae protested. "A cemetery is no place to be packing a camera. It's a funeral for heaven's sake, not a picnic!"

Heath and Nick Fessmire finally plunked into the kitchen behind their father.

"You boys go change out of those suits right now," their mother said. "Before you slop something on them that won't come out," and they sloughed out of the room without argument. Charity Fessmire and Bucky drifted out of the kitchen together of their own free will sans any directives from Lila.

"It'd be bad enough if he were just taking pictures of some people standing around. But to be snapping all the flowers, and getting right up there at the grave. Now who wants to see all that later?"

"Apparently Mary Alice wants to," Lila replied. "I heard Butch tell somebody that he wanted to send his sister some pictures since she couldn't come back to Buford for the funeral."

"Well, it's just tacky."

"I can't help it, Elba Rae, I'm just glad it's over."

"Me, too, I guess. I think everything turned out real nice, though. Don't you?"

On some level—and now that the plans had been fully carried out—Elba Rae Van Oaks did want the approval of Ethel Maywood's only other next of kin as it would, perhaps, offer her some degree of closure. In hindsight, Elba Rae didn't suppose the alleged preference for hosiery and pumps mattered much since no one outside a very small circle knew about it. The organ solos she'd selected were pleasant enough, but she did wonder had she not felt as rushed and under pressure whether she and Lila would have eventually compromised on some mutually agreeable tunes. And though she had no intention of bringing it up, on the way from the hearse to the grave Elba Rae Van Oaks was pretty sure even the most casual of observers would have noted the casket listing to one side due to an obvious breach at the corner manned by Ned Maharry.

It had been gratifying and comforting that the service was well-attended by Ethel Maywood's living contemporaries, sparse though their number was by the time Ethel left them, as well as a majority of the active members of the First Avenue United Methodist Church. Even Martha Betty Maharry had risen above the gastric distress plaguing her only one day prior to attend both the funeral and the graveside service, although it hadn't escaped Elba Rae Van Oaks—not even in the open air—that poor Martha Betty was still suffering some residual effects of whatever had compromised her stomach in the first place since Elba Rae was certain she'd pooted a little right outside the church.

Lila hesitated before answering but decided her relief at having arrived at the conclusion of the public events commemorating her mother's death overshadowed what was likely to be a lingering irritation over Elba Rae's sledgehammer tactics.

"It was all fine, Elba Rae. Like I said, I'm just glad we're through it. But Dear God, I thought if Begina didn't stop squeezing me I was going to pass out right there on top of a tombstone."

"I know. She did the same thing to me. Bless her heart. She got up this morning and drove all the way over here. And you know it's more than two hundred miles."

"I was afraid to ask what she did with Aunt Laveetra."

"Begina said one of the ladies from their church had come to sit with her for the day. I told her to try to stop by the house for a minute if she could. I hate that she's got to turn around and drive all the way back to Hattiesburg this afternoon, but at least we don't have to worry about her wanting to spend the night. I just don't think I could stand it."

"Me either," Lila agreed. "And did you see her once she spied Butch with the camera around his neck? She couldn't wait to drag him over to those gaudy flowers they sent so she could get her picture taken next to them. Made him promise he'd mail her some copies so she could show Aunt Laveetra how pretty the sash turned out!"

"Well, then, I guess it's a good thing we didn't give them a sling at the funeral home last night because I would have been mortified if she'd come to the cemetery today and not been able to find them," Elba Rae said, coyly. Lila stared at her and made no attempt to reply.

The house was soon swarming with visitors who reflexively followed the ritual of stopping by the home of the deceased (or as was the case with the late Ethel Maywood, the home of the next of kin of the deceased) to offer an epilogue to the passing and an endorsement of the service and likewise to partake of a post funeral buffet which, from the standpoint of sheer quantity and variety, served as the climax of the food offerings. By the day of the funeral, everything that was going to be brought had been brought and was put out on display even if it took the kitchen table, the good dining room table, and a tablecloth spread over the top of the washing machine to hold it all.

There were several new entrées that afternoon, including a generous portion of barbecued pork shoulder with all the expected accompaniments, and two platters of chicken—one fried in a Buford home, and one Mabel Moss had dropped off that Elba Rae Van Oaks knew good and well had been fried in the deli at the Piggly Wiggly and then carefully arranged on Mabel Moss's own silver tray as if Elba Rae was to assume Mabel had cooked it herself.

With due caution in the case of the pink-colored one and near about dread when it came to the vivid green one, Elba Rae also set out a pair of congealed salads delivered separately by members of the First Avenue United Methodist Church. Elba Rae Van Oaks had nothing against congealed salads as a whole, provided the bearer didn't suffer from the condition known to unfortunately afflict so many congealed salad enthusiasts who were wont to be overly ambitious when it came to discerning the additional ingredients that reasonably should—and should not—be expected to harmoniously coexist in gelled suspension. Canned fruit cocktail was predictable, for certain, as were the little miniature marshmallows Elba Rae readily observed to have floated to the top of the pink version she'd received; nuts were a staple for those inclined to embellish, and she'd bit into plenty of salads laden with liberal quantities of coconut.

But as was the case with the darker shades of congealed salad like the lime, where mere visual scrutiny was insufficient and particularly so if the components were more dense and likely to be settled on the bottom, daring to indulge a bite could become an audacious game of chance. Such had surely been the situation several Thanksgivings prior when Virginia Millford had brought to the covered dish supper in the fellowship hall a congealed salad that looked for the entire world to be lime Jell-O with small chunks of pear but that had instead turned out to be lime Jell-O with bits of cucumber. Elba Rae Van Oaks had been awfully sorry she'd heaped such a conspicuous helping of it on her plate but guessed she was just glad Virginia had dissolved the gelatin in water and not in hot gin.

For serving purposes, Elba Rae initially fretted over placement of the pecan pies, of which there were nine by the day of the funeral, and finally settled on them being together at one end of the dining room table. Finding that the more she fussed over them the more the formation looked like the ever-changing view through a kaleidoscope, she decided to simplify and to be merciful to any unsuspecting guest by removing the over-baked Willadean Hendrix entry because eight pies were plenty and lent themselves better to an orderly display anyway, symmetry having always been important to Elba Rae Van Oaks.

All in all—and except for the sad occasion precipitating the gathering at Elba Rae's house—it was an uneventfully pleasurable finale to Ethel Maywood's formal farewell. Elba Rae didn't even seem to mind when her cousin from Montgomery, Butch Hornbuckle, began wandering the rooms taking random as well as some posed photographs of the company because, after all, despite the best intentions and sincere declarations from first one and then another that surely they shouldn't wait until someone else passed before they got together and congregated again, Elba Rae knew as well as they did someone else dying would most likely be the catalyst.

The refreshments were plentiful and the tension with Lila appeared to have subsided, and not a single of the more lingering guests even seemed to notice when Mr. Wiggles discretely entered the dining room and quietly began humping simple Begina's leg while she obliviously sat in the corner chewing on a piece of Mabel Moss's counterfeit Piggly Wiggly fried chicken.

Bucky Fessmire endured the crowd and made every effort to be polite to the relatives and the acquaintances who, in turn, attempted to be pleasant back by making cursory conversation with him about his insurance business although by the end of the day he was quite weary with—and frankly irritated by—the sheer quantity of people who inquired of his best auto rates when, had they been listening in the least to Bucky Fessmire, would have realized his family enterprise was engaged strictly in the commercial underwriting of insurance and didn't have a diddly damn thing to do with individual automobile policies. At the peak of his frustration he'd even said to his wife in an aside, "For God's sake, Lila, I wish you'd explain to that cousin for the last time I can't insure her car!" He plucked the last Tums from a roll and wadded the empty wrapper in his hand. And then he crunched on it like a crouton.

"What cousin? Lila inquired.

"That one!" Bucky gestured, with a head nod toward the dining room.

"Oh," she said. "Begina. Bless her heart. I can't imagine she's got a car worth insuring."

"It doesn't matter! I tried to tell her—nicely—I don't write policies on vehicles! But it was like she didn't hear me! She just kept on and on and on about how her momma doesn't drive anymore and she has to keep up the car and maybe the house doesn't have enough coverage and what happens if there's a tornado? What is wrong with these people?"

"They mean well, Bucky, and they're probably just trying to make conversation."

"I don't care! For the last time, can you just let them all know? I can't insure their car! I can't insure their chicken coops or their outhouses or their riding lawnmowers, and I don't care if they do come with the cute little trailers that hitch on behind to carry the leaves!"

"It's probably good you're going home in the morning," Lila said to him before looking away. "Good Lord. What is Mr. Wiggles doing in there?"

Charity Fessmire stayed mostly in the background unless summoned by her mother for an introduction to a distant cousin or one of Lila's childhood friends, who typically followed with a barrage of compliments centering on Charity's prettiness and what they believed to be charming shyness. As the afternoon went by, that shyness seemed to Elba Rae to be more of an unmistakable aloofness.

Elba Rae did not readily know the whereabouts of her two nephews for most of the afternoon and felt a twinge of guilt over the fact she was just glad they were wherever they were and not engaging in one of their vulgar scuffles in her house, but decided surely between their two parents one of them was occasionally offering some adult supervision. Had she known the details of their effort to start a brush fire out back by rubbing sticks together in the pile of limbs Elba Rae had picked up over the spring and thrown together in a heap, she might have preferred they'd been in the house scuffling because at least they would have been restrained from attempting to wreak devastation.

The swarm eventually thinned until at last only the family remained. Even Hazel Burns was gone and Lila and Elba Rae were once again packing and shuffling remnants of leftovers, cognizant the final event was over.

"I thought Begina was going to sit here till dark," Elba Rae remarked.

"You were right to sort of herd her out."

"Well, it's not that I wasn't enjoying visiting with her, but I just hated to think of her being out on the road late."

"I know it. And she would have stayed all night if we hadn't. But did you get a chance to study her outfit? I swear she had on one brown shoe and one blue."

"Oh, she did not," protested Elba Rae.

"Well, it's possible cause I know once she stands up she can't see her feet. She must be pushing two hundred and seventy five."

"I know it—and it's no wonder, either, the way she eats. She had everything but a spool of barbed wire. I've just never seen anybody who could take on a meal like she does."

"I know she tried at least one of every dessert," Lila agreed.

"I'm not surprised. She caught me on one trip and asked if I had any vanilla ice cream in the deep freeze because she wanted to dob it on top of her pecan pie! She is going to have to reduce, bless her heart. I wonder if she doesn't just have some sort of glandular problem."

"Oh, for goodness sake. You sound like Momma—trying to get us not to stare at some fat stranger."

"Well," Elba Rae muttered as she picked up a platter onto which she'd consolidated fried chicken, barbeque, and slices of clove-encrusted ham underneath a swatch of plastic wrap and began walking toward the refrigerator.

"You make sure Bucky takes some of this food back with him. It's no sense in him and the children being up there trying to scramble for something to eat when we've still got all this here."

Lila hesitated when she noticed Bucky standing in the doorway, having obviously overheard. "I will," she said.

"Whew," Elba Rae said as she closed the refrigerator door. "I think I'll go get out of these good clothes and just try to take it easy for a few minutes."

She left the kitchen, smiling at Bucky Fessmire as she passed. He waited until Elba Rae was through the den and down the hall.

"Have you told her?" asked Bucky

"No," Lila replied quickly. "I'll wait until tomorrow morning."

"What are you going to say?"

"I don't know. I haven't thought about that yet."

"What if she puts up a fuss?"

"Let her," Lila said.

*   *   *

Bucky Fessmire gathered his children and their belongings, and hastened his leave just as soon as breakfast was served the next morning. He didn't mean to be rude, he assured Elba Rae, but the children needed to be back in Birmingham for school, and he thought it best under the circumstances to return them to their customary habitat. Elba Rae Van Oaks told him and Lila she understood completely, and hugged all three of the children earnestly before they climbed into the car, even as their mother stood by to prompt Nick and Heath to thank their aunt for her hospitality. At least Lila tried to instill some manners in them, Elba Rae thought, even if it was obviously sporadic and unheeded.

Within the hour Elba Rae Van Oaks was busy drying the underside of a casserole dish when Lila came into the kitchen carrying her suitcase and garment bag, a not so subtle indication of her own eminent departure that initially went unnoticed by Elba Rae.

"I didn't realize how many dishes we've got to return until I started washing up all of them. It's liable to take two trips," Elba Rae said without turning around from the sink.

"I went ahead and threw out that ole Chili Mac casserole. You were right. I took one bite of it and shoo law, I wouldn't feed that to a dog."

Elba Rae put the clean and dried dish on the counter and turned around then to face Lila while wiping her hands on the small towel. The sight of Lila standing next to luggage was startling.

"What in the world? You're not getting ready to leave, are you?"

"I'm afraid I'm gonna have to for now. But I'll be back as soon as I can to take care of whatever we need to do."

"But," Elba Rae stuttered, "There's *everything* to do."

"I'm sorry. But I can't help it."

"What's the matter?"

"Well, I didn't want to bring it up while we were all involved in making the funeral arrangements, but some of the girls from our club are planning a big fiftieth birthday party for me and it's this coming weekend. I know it's awful soon after Momma passing away and all, but they've been getting it ready for a month. The party was supposed to be a surprise, but you know how that goes. Like Daddy used to say, just tell a woman. Anyway, the room is reserved at the club and I can't not show up."

"A what?!"

"A surprise party."

"I heard that part—but did you say fiftieth?"

"Oh, don't start with me, Elba Rae."

"As I recall, I was eight years old when you were born. And I'm sixty now. So for you to just now be having a fiftieth defies all rules of arithmetic!"

"I know, but it's an honest mistake that started with a little misunderstanding years ago when we first joined the club and they somehow got my date of birth mixed up on our membership information, so all our friends think I'm forty-nine."

"I can't believe a grown woman—a middle-aged one, at that—would still be lying about her age."

"I'm not lying about it! I just never corrected them when they got it wrong! People have always assumed I'm younger than I am since Bucky and I waited so long to have the children. And what's the difference? They still would have planned a party—it just would have been two years ago."

"Well, at least if it'd been two years ago you wouldn't have any excuse to rush back to Birmingham now and leave me with all this."

"Elba Rae, I'm sorry. I'm not trying to leave you with anything. I'll call you next week and we can go over the names for the thank you notes. I can write those from my house, you know. It's not like we've got to be sitting side by side in the same room."

"The notes are only the beginning of what it's gonna take to settle Momma's things. I don't mind running all these dishes back to where they belong but we've got to get her will to the lawyer's office, and what about the house?"

"You said yourself you didn't want to think about that until school was out, didn't you?"

"Yes, but that'll be here before we know it."

"Then we'll talk about it then. For goodness sake, it's not like the house is going to get up and walk off if we don't start going through it right away."

Elba Rae wiped her hands one more time on the dish towel she was still holding before folding it neatly and draping over the handle of her oven door. Lila Fessmire, meanwhile, made for the exit.

The conversation thereafter was scant as Elba Rae obligatorily walked her sister toward the car. They said goodbyes to one another, and they hugged tepidly, and then Elba Rae watched Lila turn the Cadillac around in the driveway and slowly pull out onto Highway 29 in a northerly direction toward Birmingham. Lila had said she'd call in a few days to coordinate the thank you note writing—and implied she'd come back to Buford as soon as she could to facilitate other issues regarding the business of their mother's affairs. As Elba Rae Van Oaks stood in her carport and watched the big Cadillac disappear down the road into a final faint blur of Oyster Shale, she began to wonder if she'd ever see her sister again.

PART TWO

Elba Rae and the Grasshopper

Elba Rae Van Oaks returned to her classroom at the Homer T. Litton Grammar School the next week amid consolatory salutations from members of the faculty, the majority of whom had already expressed as much during their funeral home visitations or outside the church following Ethel Maywood's service. The routine of being in front of the children again was a therapeutic distraction from the stage of grief that only managed to slip in once the flurry of activity following a death had passed and everyone else was already going about their business as usual.

In the evenings, Elba Rae sat at the kitchen table in the nook and methodically went down the list of recipients due a written appreciation for their sundry kind expressions of sympathy, systematically drawing a line through the names as she addressed each note. She did so with determination and before she was through with bitterness—not because she was doing it alone, but because she'd allowed herself to believe she wouldn't have to. Yet there'd been no conversation with Lila since the day she left Buford the morning after the funeral.

When she went to the post office to mail the notes, Elba Rae extracted from the stack of thank-yous an envelope addressed to Lila Fessmire and stuffed it back down into her purse. What should Lila care about receiving a birthday card from her only sister, Elba Rae mused, when she had big parties at the country club instead?

The last day of classes was on a Friday. Elba Rae Van Oaks always looked forward to the end of the school year and her much needed break but oddly wished that year it could have been delayed a bit longer, since she already knew the summer would offer another phase of challenges to her physical and emotional resilience. She intended to relax over the Memorial Day weekend but was determined thereafter to get back on task.

Following Sunday services at First Avenue United Methodist Church, Elba Rae and her first cousin Hazel Burns kept to their routine of lunch at the All Seasons restaurant located just off the Square whereupon they would (during the academic year) recap the particulars of events and personnel at the Homer T. Litton Grammar School or (being as it was then considered off-season) adapt their discussion to domestic matters that might encompass other members of First Avenue United Methodist or neighbors whose activities might warrant some mention. Or the cousins might just fall into general dialogue inspired by the arbitrary meeting of a rumor-worthy fellow patron of All Seasons.

"The crowd's kind of scarce in here today," Elba Rae observed while looking around after their orders were placed.

"The church wasn't very full either," said Hazel. "I imagine a lot of people have headed out for the long weekend."

"Well, I'm just glad it's more than a long weekend for us."

"Me, too."

"Not that I won't have a monkey on my back all summer."

"Oh—that reminds me," Hazel announced before reaching into her purse and removing a small piece of newsprint that was neatly folded in half.

"Before I forget, here's the extra copy of the obituary I saved from the paper."

She handed it across the table to Elba Rae. Elba Rae unfolded it, briefly, but closed it after a quick glance.

"Thank you for saving it."

"You're welcome."

"But it still makes me mad every time I read it."

"Oh, Elba Rae, I doubt anybody else even paid attention to that."

"I don't care. That's still no excuse. If I didn't have at least one person up there on that staff who could spell, I wouldn't even be trying to put out a newspaper every week. It's just ridiculous."

"Well, everybody knows who you are."

Elba Rae shook her head from side to side and unfolded the article again. "You notice they didn't have any trouble with Lila's information. 'She leaves two daughters, Mrs. Bucky Fessmire of Birmingham, and Mrs. Elba Mae Van Oaks of Buford.' The very idea. Elba *Mae*." She folded the clipping back up and stuffed it into her pocketbook.

"Speaking of Lila, have you heard from her since she went back home?"

"No," Elba Rae answered bluntly. "Not a peep. But unless she's in a better humor than she was before the funeral, it's just as well with me."

"What do you mean?"

"Well, I told you—during the whole time we were making the arrangements she was as cross as a sore-tailed cat in a room full of rockers. Just wanted to argue over every little detail we had to settle on. And when she wasn't fussing at me about Momma's clothes or something else, she was worrying Charles Robert Tully about putting some praying hands on the casket."

Hazel contemplated for a few seconds. "I didn't notice any hands on the casket."

"That's because I finally had to put my foot down about it."

"Still. I know you need her to be here to start going through Aunt Ethel's things."

"We'll see," Elba Rae said matter-of-factly. "But I went ahead and got you that plunger cover."

"Oh, Elba Rae, now I didn't mean for you to be taking anything out of the house before you and Lila had a chance to decide what to do with it."

"Lila's not here and I can't wait on her to make every single decision. Momma would have wanted you to have it and enjoy anyway."

"Are you sure you don't want it?"

"Lands no. Momma crocheted two of them for me and I just don't need another."

"Well, you know I've always admired the one you have in your bathroom. If you didn't know any better, you'd never know the plunger was in there."

"Just enjoy it and you can think about Momma when you clog the bowl."

"I sure will."

Hazel meticulously dispensed two droplets of Fast Sweet into a glass of iced tea their waitress had just refilled, and gave it a quick stir.

"What are you going to do, Elba Rae?"

"About what?"

"The house. Will you go ahead and start trying to clean out? Because if you are, you know I'd be glad to help you do whatever I can."

"I know you would, Hazel, but digging through Momma's house is not your problem."

"But what will you do? I mean, if Lila …"

Elba Rae Van Oaks just shook her head slowly from side to side, with her eyes mostly closed.

*   *   *

On Monday afternoon while the families in Buford and surrounding Litton County were leisurely frolicking about their patios attending to the barbeque grills and dishing up heaping piles of potato salad on paper plates, Elba Rae Van Oaks was sitting at the kitchen table with her yellow legal pad and her ballpoint pen reviewing a list. Ethel Maywood's will was already in the hands of the proper authorities—check. The Social Security Administration was automatically notified of Ethel's death—check. All dishes had been returned—check. All thank you cards had been mailed. Pause.

There remained still a few odd names for which Elba Rae did not have the proper mailing address, and it was because they were from Birmingham or somehow otherwise affiliated exclusively with Lila, including employees at the Fessmire Insurance Group. She stared at the list debating the lesser of irritants, ultimately deciding that letting the list go unchecked was more worrisome than having to talk to her sister.

She gazed out the window over her kitchen sink after dialing Lila's number and was temporarily diverted by an odious splatter of bird excrement on the roof of her car.

"Poke berries," she said under her breath before being joggled by Lila's voice on the other end of the phone.

"Hello."

"Uh Lila?"

"Yeah, it's me. Hey, Elba Rae."

"I didn't really expect to get anyone at your house today."

"Why not?"

"Because of the holiday. I guess I just figured you'd all be at your club or some other party somewhere celebrating."

"Well, we're not, obviously. How are you?"

"I'm fine." Elba Rae hesitated. "How was the party?"

"What?"

"The surprise party for your birthday."

"Oh. Yeah. It was fine."

"Good," said Elba Rae.

Silence.

"I wanted to let you know I've mailed off all the thank you notes except for—"

"Oh, Elba Rae, I'm sorry. I know I was supposed to call you before now so we could get together on that. We've just been so, uh, busy up here, I can't tell you."

"Well, it's all right," Elba Rae said in a tone that even she knew sounded insincere. "All I wanted to say was I've sent them except for a few that I still need addresses for. They're all in Birmingham, I imagine."

"Oh. Well, just give me the names and I'll take care of it."

"I don't mind. I can just as easily do it, if you'll just get me the addresses."

"No, really, Elba Rae. I'll take care of it."

Based on the near-conciliatory sound in Lila's voice, Elba Rae took no time to ponder the repercussions of expanding the topic of their conversation.

"Why don't you just bring the addresses with you when you come?"

"What?" Lila asked, almost surprised.

"When you come down here."

"Oh. Well, I should probably go ahead and get them in the mail, don't you think? I mean, it's already been over two weeks since Momma died."

Elba Rae turned away from the view of her mauve stained Ford and let out the combination of a sigh and a puff.

"Are you not planning to come down here, Lila?"

"What? Yes—of course I am. I told you I was coming."

"Well, I'm ready to get started. Momma's got sixty years' worth of clutter packed up in that house and it's going to be the devil trying to go through all of it."

"I know it. And I have every intention of being there. Why don't I get my calendar right now and we can go ahead and settle on a date?"

"A date?"

"Yeah. Hold on while I get my book out and—"

"I don't need to study any calendar, Lila, I just need to get started."

"When?"

"Now!"

"Elba Rae, I can't do it right now."

"Why not?"

"I just can't."

"Aren't Heath and Nick out of school yet?"

"Yes, their last day was Friday, but—"

"Are you worried about leaving them up there? Surely Charity can keep an eye on them. If not, bring them with you. If you have to," she sort of mumbled.

"It's just going to have to be a little later."

"How much later?"

"Not long. Just a month or so."

"Lila, I've only got three months off. I can't sit around lollygagging until the summer's nearly over before we even get started. Now I'm going over there tomorrow just to look around so I can begin to get organized. If you want to come, fine. If you want to stay out of it, that's all right with me, too!"

"Oh, Elba Rae, just hush!"

"I will *not* hush!"

"There's a reason I can't leave Birmingham right now! There's a reason I have to wait."

Elba Rae leaned against the counter and cradled the phone receiver between her ear and her shoulder so that her arms were free to cross.

"What?" she asked.

"Well, I didn't want to say anything yet because we haven't told anybody outside the immediate family. But …"

Elba Rae waited patiently for the revelation and based on Lila's hesitation, suddenly feared unpleasant news. She unfolded her arms and took the phone back in her left hand.

"What is it? Is somebody sick?"

"Oh—no, it's not that. It's good news, actually."

"Well?"

"It's Charity. She and her boyfriend … are engaged."

"Engaged? Are you joking?"

"Well, certainly I wouldn't kid about something like this, Elba Rae. But we've been keeping it sort of quiet."

"When did *that* happen?"

"It's been a little while ago."

"Well, why didn't you say something?"

"Because they wanted to keep it to themselves, at first. And then Momma went in the hospital, and it just didn't seem right to be making an announcement in the middle of her dying and having the funeral and all. We wanted to wait a respectable amount of time."

"She's so young, Lila."

"I know," Lila sighed. "But she's eighteen years old and they both think they're grown, and Bucky and I have accepted we've got to let her make her own decisions."

"Well, are they at least going to wait until she's through school?"

"You mean finished?"

"Yes—until she's gotten her education."

"That's four years from now!"

"I know that, but she's still a child. She's got all the time in the world to wait."

"That's easy for us to say, but they're young and in love and they're anxious to be married."

"Have they already got a date in mind?"

"Yes," Lila said nervously. "And that's part of my predicament. I need to be here to help Charity with all the planning. She may be old enough to get married, but she doesn't have the first clue about what it takes to put on a wedding, and of course the groom's no help."

"Is it that soon?"

"Yes," said Lila. "It's the last Saturday in June."

"Last Saturday in June?!" Elba Rae screeched. "That's hardly a month off!"

"I know. So you see why I can't be in Buford? We've been addressing invitations like mad because they've got to go out this week."

Elba Rae was quiet on her end of the phone, momentarily overwhelmed by the magnitude of information her sister had just shared.

"Are you there?"

"Yeah," Elba Rae answered softly. "I'm here."

"Is there not anybody in Buford we could hire to do some of this?"

"Well, you know I've never had a cleaning woman, Lila, and I don't know many people who do. And the ones that do, I don't know them myself. And I'm not about to turn loose some stranger in Momma's house."

Elba Rae went on to expound on "all kind of valuables" waiting to be discovered in the late Ethel Maywood's house that would, no doubt, be unavoidably tempting to a mere stranger even if he or she initially entered the dwelling with the purest of intent.

There was a pocket watch once carried by the women's father, Raymond Maywood, and an opal broach originally belonging to their grandmother. A silver-plated chafing dish Ethel had procured with her S & H trading stamps was stowed inside the china closet in the dining room, and those prizes seemed only to scratch the surface of possible bounty.

"And there's all the good crystal and the china. Why, somebody could just back a truck up to the door and make off like bandits," Elba Rae said with a fret. Lila Fessmire, meanwhile, just rolled her eyes; it was a bad habit once nearly broken, reborn since she'd been in the company of her sister once more.

"Well, what's the big rush, Elba Rae? After the end of June I won't have anything pressing in Birmingham and I can come stay as long as I need to."

"Because it's not safe, Lila. Like I said—Momma's house is full of everything she's ever owned and it doesn't take long for word to get around to the wrong kinds that the house is just sitting unoccupied."

"It's Buford, for heaven's sake, Elba Rae—not New York City! Are you expecting a crime wave?"

Elba Rae's fortitude was fading. "You know what? Never mind. School is out, and I can just spend every day over there until I get it finished. I've got all summer before I'll have to go back to work. And Hazel's already said she'd pitch in."

"Now don't go acting like I'm not willing to help!"

"I'm not. It's okay. Really. I'm sure you've got your hands full."

"I'll come later in the summer, I promise."

"It's all right. I'll just make the decisions as best I can about what to keep and what I get rid of, and then later in the summer we can talk about getting the house sold. Willadean Hendrix has already been sniffing around a little. I think they want it for rental, which is fine with me. They rent to half of Litton County as it is and—"

"Oh, Elba Rae, why do you always have to make everything so difficult?"

"I'm not trying to make anything difficult on you, Lila. To the contrary—I just said I'd take care of everything."

"What you just said is you'll go through everything in Momma's house before I even have a chance to get down there, and you'll parcel out all of her things and the deed will be signed over to Willadean Hendrix without me there to even have a say!"

"Well, you can't expect to have it both ways, Lila."

"Fine!"

"What does that mean?"

"If you're in such an all fired hurry, I'll try to get down there for a couple of days this week."

"Well, you don't have to on my account."

"No, I don't," Lila said. "But I'm sure I need to do it for my own."

*   *   *

Two mornings later, Elba Rae Van Oaks was dressed and ready to go by ten o'clock although she knew it was foolish since she had no delusions Lila would make an effort to depart from Birmingham especially early. The house was clean, and the bed in the guest room was freshly made up; the kitchen floor had been swept, and she'd even taken a broom to the sidewalk leading to the seldom-used front door. There was nothing left to do but wait.

It was nearly noon before the gray Cadillac arrived. Elba Rae immediately noted Lila's use of what amounted to no more than an overnight bag for her belongings but restrained herself from commentary, and decided any attempt at cooperation would suffer if she challenged Lila's commitment to their duties before she'd even gotten in the door good.

"Well," Elba Rae said while glancing at the wall clock, "we may as well get us a bite to eat before we get started."

"I'm sorry I couldn't get here any earlier, Elba Rae, but I've got a million things going on at the house, and Charity, she's … she's starting to get a case of the jitters about this wedding, and—"

"Do you think she's having second thoughts about it?"

"What? No—oh, no. She's definitely going to go through with it. It's just, there's so much to do and she tends to get overwhelmed easily."

"I hope she knows what she's doing."

"She knows," said Lila. "Anyway, if you want to go straight to the house it's okay with me. I'm not that hungry anyway."

"Well, I am," Elba Rae decreed. "And maybe it'd be a good idea for us to sit down and decide what we're going to do anyhow before we get started. Let's go by the All Seasons and we can talk while we eat."

Lila sighed. "Okay. Whatever you say."

Elba Rae Van Oaks collected her pocketbook from the kitchen table and pulled keys from it.

"I'll drive," she said.

Being a life-long Bufordian such as she was, Elba Rae Van Oaks was well beyond any lingering apprehension over dining in a restaurant occupying an early-century residence that had for years actually been site of the Buford Memorial Funeral Home. Admittedly, awkward moments may have intruded upon the first meal or two she'd tried there, but Elba Rae barely gave a thought to the building's previous usage by the day she and Lila strolled in for a meal.

"Doesn't it give you the creeps to eat in here?" Lila Fessmire remarked, as the two women seated themselves at a centrally located table.

"You mean because of the funeral home?"

"Well, yeah. I would hope that's the only reason."

"No, I guess I don't think about it anymore," Elba Rae said. Lila gazed unconsciously around the room, recalling the last embalmed loved one she'd seen lying in state at just about the location of the All Seasons self-serve salad bar.

"Oh, good!" Elba Rae exclaimed, as she folded the menu and set it aside on the table before Lila had even unrolled her mummified cutlery from the thin paper napkin. "They've got the sweet and sour catfish on the special today."

"Huh?"

"The catfish," Elba Rae clarified. "Look at that little extra page in your menu. They don't fix it all the time so it's just lucky we're here today."

Lila opened her menu whereupon, indeed, a small but neatly presented insert with barely two typographical errors fell out. She studied it briefly and put it down. "I'll just have a chef salad. Do you think it's fresh?"

"Everything's good here, but don't you want the catfish? They don't fix it all the time. They cut the fish up into little nuggets before they roll it in the meal, and after they fry it, it's all mixed up good with the pineapple and the sweet and sour sauce. I've always wondered what's in that sweet and sour sauce. I bought some in a jar at the Piggly Wiggly once but it was so sour it would have made a pig squeal and run up the hill backwards. But it's so good here. Why don't you try it?"

"Because it sounds like it would gag a maggot," Lila snapped before placing her own menu to the side."

"Well, suit yourself. But you don't know what you're missing."

"To the contrary, I think I know exactly what I'm missing which is why—"

At about that minute a starchy-uniformed waitress approached bearing two glasses of water, the arrival of which likely served to prevent any superfluous hard feelings being created over the difference of opinion regarding the culinary merit of Wednesday's lunch special at the All Seasons Restaurant. Lila Fessmire ordered the chef salad without hesitation and Elba Rae Van Oaks requested the sweet and sour catfish with equal determination, while not being able to resist saying to the waitress as she gestured toward Lila "she doesn't know what she's missing" as a concluding editorial to her selection. Lila rolled her eyes and took a sip of water.

"And what to drink, hon?"

"I'll have tea," said Elba Rae.

"Tea," Lila repeated.

"All righty. We'll get that right out," the waitress promised as she took the menus off the table and walked away.

Elba Rae discretely inventoried the room. "I don't see a soul I know in here. There's usually somebody from the church, or school, or Book Club eating in here. Wonder where everybody is?"

"They must have heard about the special." Lila couldn't help but laugh aloud.

"This may not be fancy, but I'm telling you the food is good."

"I'm sure it is, Elba Rae. I was just kidding. The fact is I don't happen to care for catfish. Doesn't matter if it's sweet and soured or fried or baked in a pie, I wouldn't like it."

"Momma used to fry catfish for us all the time when we were growing up."

"And don't you remember what Daddy told me when I asked him what a catfish was?"

"No. I don't," said Elba Rae.

"He told me they were from the little cats that lived underwater in the pond. It gave me the willies. And I haven't been able to tolerate the sight of a catfish since."

"Well, it sure didn't stop Momma from making us eat it."

"She used to make us eat a lot of things I couldn't stand, but now I'm grown and I don't have to eat them anymore!"

Elba Rae was actually amused by the remark and it made her smile.

"I know what you mean. To this day I can't look a beet in the face and I know it's because Momma tried to force us to eat them when we were little."

"Beets, and that nasty old calf liver. Just the thought of liver gives me the chills."

The women laughed together.

"Oh, I hated those liver nights, too," Elba Rae giggled, "but it wasn't because I disliked what we were eating. It was because I knew you and Momma would eventually get in a standoff when she'd say you couldn't leave the table until you cleaned your plate. And I knew you'd never back down."

"She could be stubborn as a mule sometimes."

"And you know she had to have figured out you were just chewing it up a little and then spitting it out in your napkin to make it disappear off the plate."

"But she never let on."

"No," Elba Rae agreed, "but I imagine she got a surprise when she shook the napkins out after supper."

"She was a mess," Lila said with a grin.

"Yes, she was."

The women gaped around the room again but in a manner more reflective than in search of recognizable patrons.

"So who is this boy Charity's engaged to?"

Elba Rae's question was an abrupt turnover from the giddy reminiscing about their late mother's supper regimens, and it seemed to catch Lila unprepared.

"What?"

"Charity's fiancé—do you like him?"

"Well …" Lila cautiously chose her words. "Yes, we like him."

"How long have they been going together?"

"Uh, since last fall, actually."

"Did he go to her school?"

"No, he's wasn't at the academy."

"What about his people?"

"They're …" Lila's sentenced went unfinished. "You know, while we're sitting here going down memory lane about Momma we should probably be getting organized. Now I'm sure you've made some lists already."

Elba Rae's smile retracted slowly.

"Not really," she replied. "Just a shopping list."

"But you were saying something about the clothes on the way over here."

"Oh, yeah. Well, if there's anything you want and can—or *would*—wear, then you should certainly take it. But for everything else, I thought we'd just as well donate it all to that store the Buford Baptist people run."

"What did you say it was called?"

"The Buford Baptist Benevolence Boutique. They take in donations and then resell them for next to nothing in a little store they keep up over on Geeter Street. Clothes, shoes, coats—anything. They'll even take furniture. Mabel Moss told me someone had even offered them a billiard table once but I don't believe they actually took it in on account of it'd been in that old pool hall the sheriff busted up down there around Mitchell Dam. Anyway, somebody told me the money goes to their mission fund. Personally, I don't know what they think the Chinese are going to do with all those Catechisms they pack over there, but I guess that's their business."

"That sounds fine with me. I doubt Momma's got anything either one of us would wear."

"We'll see," Elba Rae said.

A waitress arrived at the table bearing two glasses of iced tea. Before they'd either had time to sufficiently sweeten them, she was back with a chef salad in one hand and a steaming plate of the day's special in the other.

"Do ya'll need anything else right now?" she asked.

"No, I think we're all right," confirmed Elba Rae.

"All righty. Ya'll enjoy."

The server hurried off to the next table of freshly arrived guests as Lila looked over at Elba Rae's plate of breaded and browned chunks of what could have been anything underneath a bright reddish-orange glazed sauce, and when she merely shook her head from side to side in an obviously negative direction, Elba Rae was too enticed by the entrée to notice.

*   *   *

It was Elba Rae Van Oaks's first order of business after the conclusion of lunch and as soon as the ladies re-boarded the Ford to announce a stop would be necessary on the way to Ethel Maywood's house to procure an appropriate variety of cleaning products and trash bags for the task she anticipated awaited the women once inside their mother's former residence, which—aside from a few cursory visits of a custodial nature by Elba Rae—had stood vacant since the late Ethel's last entrance into Litton County Memorial Hospital. On the way to the Highway 29 Plaza, featuring as its anchor tenant the Friendly Dollar Store, Elba Rae made a point to remind Lila to remind her to buy at least two sponges because she had forgotten to put sponges on the list.

Lila held the list as Elba Rae drove the car. "Is all this really necessary?"

"Well," Elba Rae said, "I don't know what Momma's got over there and what she hasn't. And I don't want to get in the middle of trying to clean something and run out of anything."

Lila studied the list. "Scouring pads, rubber gloves, ammonia. I thought we were just trying to start going through the clothes and some of the closets."

"We are. But we'll likely need all of that eventually." Elba Rae, mildly weary at being challenged about a list of supplies she knew full well would be utilized and then some, turned the LTD into the parking area of the Highway 29 Plaza and drove into a parking space more or less straddling her intended target of the Friendly Dollar store and its immediate next door neighbor business, the Buford Wash-a-Teria—one of only two coin-operated Laundromat facilities in Litton County.

Elba Rae stopped the car and turned off the motor. "Now what did I say," she mumbled to herself while situating the car keys just so inside her pocketbook. "Oh, yeah. Sponges."

"I got it. Sponges," Lila said. "Sounds like we need to add industrial overalls and goggles for all you've got in mind."

Elba Rae stopped her car key fumbling and looked across the seat at her sister, and although she knew she'd probably regret whatever words were about to escape her, she was still prone to continue. Except Lila wasn't looking back at her. Lila wasn't paying attention at all, having been distracted by a woman who was walking down the sidewalk.

"Who in the world is that?" Lila asked, apparently unconcerned with the undelivered lecture Elba Rae had planned. They both stared through the windshield of the car and observed the older woman who carried a neatly stacked but obviously dirty bundle of clothing in a large wicker basket.

"That's Eleanor Mhoon," said Elba Rae.

"What's she got on her feet?"

Elba Rae peered just ever so more intently to be sure. "Galoshes."

Lila Fessmire looked upward through the car window to observe a near azure sky but that did offer an occasional patch of white fluffy clouds.

"Is it supposed to rain?"

Elba Rae looked out her own window to judge for herself. "No. But this time of year, you never know when a thunderstorm will blow up. Especially late in the evenings, right before supper."

"Well, why wouldn't she just carry them in a bag or something? Why put them on when the sun's still out?"

"I don't know, but she's always worn them," Elba Rae observed, as she nodded toward the door of the Buford Wash-a-Teria, into which Eleanor Mhoon had already disappeared.

"I don't imagine she's got any choice if she were to get caught out in the rain. She'd never be able to wade up through the woods to that house they live in."

"They don't have any kind of road to get to the house?"

"Oh, I think they used to have an old piece of road. But you know, you've got to have a load of gravel put down on it every once in a while or it'll just go right back to mud. In the winter when the weather really sets in, the only way they get out is on the tractor. And I imagine they stay eaten up with chiggers during the summer tromping back and forth to the mailbox."

"And she has to wag the laundry all the way down here to wash?"

"Oh, you remember those Mhoons, Lila. Leland Mhoon dairy farms. They never did have a pot to pee in nor a window to throw it out. Those girls used to come to school wearing the worst old worn-out clothes. Of course, you'd think by now Leland would have tried to save up enough money to get poor Eleanor a washing machine so she didn't have to go clumping in there in her galoshes carrying it like a pack mule."

"She's obviously been willing to put up with it all these years."

"Well," Elba Rae lamented, "maybe Celeste can be some help to her now that she's back."

"I don't see any sign of her helping right now."

Elba Rae Van Oaks took pause for a moment. "No," she said. "Neither do I."

"I wonder if she sleeps in them," Lila muttered more or less to herself.

"They were always a peculiar bunch. Kept to themselves, and minded their own business mostly. Mabel Moss goes to church with them and she told me one time they never mentioned Celeste. Their older girl is married with children that are nearly grown, I think, but Mabel said Eleanor never breathed a word about Celeste and Mabel nor anybody else ever dared ask. She said Leland wouldn't even come back to church for the longest."

"Well, it wasn't their fault."

"I know. But they still had to bear the brunt of it after Celeste took off."

The women stared thoughtfully straight ahead into the windows of the laundry facility.

"I remember Celeste being a sweet little girl. And shy as a mouse," remarked Elba Rae.

"Well, she got over being shy according to the story I remember Momma telling."

Elba Rae briefly took Lila's comment under consideration. "Maybe. But there's something about that whole thing with her that hasn't been told."

"What do you mean?"

"I don't know," Elba Rae answered. "And it may never get out. But there's just something about her that hasn't been told."

And with that, Elba Rae opened the car door and promptly stepped out. Lila Fessmire passively followed into the Friendly Dollar Store, carrying the list.

*   *   *

They arrived at Ethel Maywood's house with three full bags of supplies, and before unpacking any of them, Elba Rae Van Oaks went to the living room and switched on the air conditioner that was mounted in a window.

"Do you want to start in the bedroom?" she asked.

"I guess." Lila looked around the kitchen. "But what about in here?"

"I cleaned the refrigerator out last weekend," Elba Rae said. "Most everything in there was spoiled anyway."

"Okay."

Elba Rae led the way, stopping to turn on the ceiling fan as they entered the bedroom.

"Why didn't Momma ever put an air conditioner in here?" asked Lila.

"She never wanted one. She said the one in the front room kept it cool enough for her in here, but you know how cold-natured she was. She liked to have burned me up whenever we were in the car. Fussed any time I tried to turn up the air conditioning."

"Well, it doesn't feel very cool to me."

Elba Rae inferred agreement and raised both windows letting in a soft but refreshing breeze through the screens.

"I'm going to go up in the attic and get the suitcases. I thought we'd just pack the clothes in them to take over to the boutique."

"Do you need me to help?" Lila asked.

"No," Elba Rae said on her way out the door. "They're not heavy when they're empty."

Lila Fessmire stood still in the bedroom by herself for a moment, looking around but not moving. It seemed to her it had been months rather than just weeks since she'd last been in the room having a contentious debate with Elba Rae over stockings and navy blue pumps, making the parallel worlds she'd been in of late even more bewildering.

She opened the closet door and pulled the string to turn on the light. Her eyes instantly focused on the unoccupied gap on the clothes rod where the burial outfit had been removed. She reached out and gently rubbed the shiny wooden pole with her hand.

"If we fill these up," Elba Rae announced upon re-entering the bedroom carrying a piece of Ethel Maywood's vintage luggage in each hand, "we can just stuff some things in garbage bags. Mabel said they clean all the clothes before putting them out anyway so I don't guess it'll matter if something gets wrinkled."

"Are those all the suitcases Momma had?"

"There's another old one up there but it's got a dirt dauber nest on it the size of my hand. We'd be better off with the garbage bags."

Elba Rae put one of the cases on the bed and opened it fully.

"Shoo!" exclaimed Lila. "It stinks!"

"Well, she probably hasn't had it out of the attic since we were grown."

Lila waved her hand back and forth under her nose. "Yeah, maybe garbage bags would be better."

Elba Rae went over to the dresser from which the JCPenney box bearing undergarments had been procured before the funeral.

"I'm going to start over here. Do you want to get in the closet and see if there's anything you want?"

"I guess so," said Lila. "But I already know there's not."

Elba Rae opened the top drawer and began while Lila carefully examined the closet once more. She initially took no time to scrutinize the clothing, but rather removed five hangers at the time and tidily folded and packed the garments in the dirt dauber-free luggage. Elba Rae more or less did the same with the contents of the dresser drawers.

During one such traverse, however, Lila Fessmire hesitated at the sight of a dress that appeared to be especially vintage. It was a burgundy and lavender floral print over white with half length sleeves and a delicate looking collar of faux lace. She separated the dress from the bundle and held it up in front of her.

"For heaven's sake …" Lila said.

"What?" Elba Rae asked, without really looking.

"This old dress."

Elba Rae turned around to see for herself but was not otherwise impressed one way or the other. "That looks as old as Momma."

"Not exactly," Lila said while continuing to hold it up. "It's the dress she wore for my wedding."

Elba Rae stopped to take a closer look.

"I don't remember it."

"Well, you should. She's wearing it in every one of our wedding pictures."

Elba Rae stepped toward the dress and briefly touched the shoulder.

"I didn't really remember the dress," she said, "but I do remember having to drag her in F & F three times before she'd finally settle on one. You'd a thought she was going to meet the Queen of England."

"It was important. She was the mother of the bride."

"She was the mother of the bride when I married, too, but I don't think she bothered to buy anything new to put on."

"Well," Lila said, defensively, "maybe it was because you had a smaller wedding."

"Yeah," Elba Rae Van Oaks said, upon which she returned to the dresser and with her back to Lila, resolved not to allow herself to be distracted by dormant hard feelings. Smaller wedding, indeed, she thought.

The fact was, Lila—although younger—had married first. Her engagement and wedding and all the festivities in between were a spanking new experience for the Maywoods, and much of the fanfare was predicated by the fact Lila was marrying into a somewhat prominently established Birmingham family.

By the time Fettis Van Oaks had come courting Elba Rae some years later, well after she'd earned a teaching certificate and entrenched herself at the Homer T. Litton Grammar School, it was easy to dismiss the notion of another big put-on wedding because Elba Rae was somewhat past the standard age for a Buford bride and Fettis was even older. The Maywoods had done little of nothing to dissuade the couple from a simple ceremony at the First Avenue United Methodist Church.

Fettis Van Oaks had not descended from a prominently established Litton County family or one that was ever known to be prominent in any region they'd previously settled, and some of his people were, in fact, of questionable breeding. Ethel Maywood had gone so far as to proclaim outright from the beginning she thought them to be common. Elba Rae had condemned her mother's hastening to judgment and vowed she would be receptive toward the new family she was about to join, a pledge she managed to keep up until the first time she met Fettis Van Oaks's mother, Miss Helma.

It had come about as a rather spontaneous get-together since the declared itinerary of their date that Friday evening when Fettis picked Elba Rae up at her momma and daddy's house had only included driving over to Alexander

City for an early supper so they could catch the seven twenty-five showing of the new John Wayne picture Fettis was dying to see. The plans had not specified anything about what they'd do after the movie let out—certainly nothing about going visiting for the purposes of making introduction—because Elba Rae surely would have taken more time to work with her hair before leaving home, having already spent the day teaching a room of raucous fifth graders.

"And maybe if you're not too tired after the picture show, we could stop off and say hidey to my folks," Fettis had said to her at the Three Plates Diner across the street from the theatre in Alexander City.

"Tonight?" Elba Rae said, in a mixture of surprise, excitement, and apprehension.

"Yeah. Momma's awful anxious to meet you. Daddy, too."

"Well, Fettis, if I'd known you were wanting to introduce me to your family tonight, I would have fixed up a little."

"Fixed up? What's wrong with the way you look?"

"Nothing, I guess. For a movie, anyway. But, I don't know about meeting people for the first time."

"You look just fine."

Elba Rae smiled, sort of, at her beau and assumed he meant to sweet-talk.

"Besides," he said, "there's no need to put on for my momma and daddy. They're just simple folk, Elba Rae."

"Well," she hesitated. "If you don't think they'll mind …"

She had returned to her meal and felt the butterflies flutter in her stomach, even as they had to share the space with her meal of country fried steak and mashed potatoes that were equally submerged in a sea of brown gravy. What must it mean, she couldn't help but ask herself, that Fettis wanted to introduce her to his mother and father? And that his mother was apparently eager to be introduced? They'd already been on three dates, and he was obviously pushing their relationship to the next level. That night at the theatre, Elba Rae Maywood paid scant attention to Mr. John Wayne—as if she would have anyway.

She had been unusually quiet on the short car ride back to Buford and concentrated on not letting her nerves get the best of her. Elba Rae's father, Raymond Maywood, had recollected making the acquaintance of the Van

Oakses at some point but Elba Rae's mother, Ethel, seemed only to know them by reputation and had not been unduly flattering when sharing what she knew to be their manner. But Elba Rae knew her mother could be unnecessarily critical sometimes and consequently thought better of being predisposed to an unfavorable opinion about a family of people she'd not even had the pleasure of meeting for herself.

The Van Oakses lived on a blacktop off the road that went to Weoka. The house had a tin roof that expanded over an apparently sizeable front porch although as she and Fettis approached it in the dark, Elba Rae hadn't been able to distinguish much about the place. Fettis parked his truck in the grass and said, "Well, here we are" to Elba Rae while she stared at the unlit front door. On what was probably one end of the porch, she had been momentarily distracted by a tiny light that seem to fly steadily back and forth—a lightning bug, possibly, although April was a bit early for lightning bugs and the bug's glow wasn't the usual yellow green nor did it ever extinguish. She was startled when as they'd exited the truck, the lightning bug had spoken to them.

"That you, Fettis?"

"Yeah, Momma. It's us."

"Us who?"

"Me and somebody I brought to meet you and daddy."

As soon as they reached the steps to the porch, it had been obvious to Elba Rae that the lightning bug squeaked a bit, as well, with the squeaking somewhat synchronized to its flight pattern. It was only when they'd got a little closer and Elba Rae's eyes had become accustomed to the dark that she'd seen for the first time Helma Van Oaks rocking herself gently back and forth in a bedraggled swing, with a lit cigarette dangling from her mouth.

She had worn a simple sleeveless housedress that buttoned up the front, and in her hair was a nest of rollers, each one so tightly engaged Elba Rae had been certain it was the cause of both eyebrows appearing to be unnaturally raised. She'd worn no shoes.

"What are you doing out here?" asked Fettis.

"I had to come out for a minute to get away from your daddy," Helma Van Oaks replied after a substantial drag on the cigarette.

"How come?"

"He went to sleep on the settee in there right after supper and he's been snoring like a gaggle of geese ever since. I'm surprised you can't hear him. I just had to get away from it for a minute."

"Oh," Fettis said, after which Helma took in another quick puff. "I was hoping he'd still be up."

Elba Rae, in fact, had heard the rather strident noise coming through the screen door that was intermittent with some very loud whistling, and wondered how anyone else would possibly expect to rest under the same roof with such a disturbance going on.

"Well, I'm up. So are you gonna introduce me to your young lady?"

"Oh—yeah. Sorry." He tried subtly to clear his throat.

"Momma, this is Elba Rae Maywood. She's the girl I told you about. Elba Rae, this is my momma."

"It's very nice to meet you, Ms. Van Oaks," Elba Rae said first.

"It's nice to meet you, too, honey. Come over here and sit down for a minute," she said, lightly slapping the slats of the swing's bench seat beside her.

"Oh. All right. Thank you."

"If you wait on Fettis to get you a chair, you'll be standing up all night."

Helma Van Oaks had paused her swinging long enough to accommodate Elba Rae's boarding and then promptly resumed. Fettis pulled over a metal chair for himself and so it was that the three of them sat and swung and visited and became generally introduced for the first time.

Elba Rae had considered avoiding the topic the following morning with her own mother when they'd sat down to breakfast, but decided to go ahead and plant the seed in the event the detour by the Van Oaks homestead really did have significance.

"I didn't hear you come in last night," Ethel Maywood said while salting some scrambled eggs on her plate. Elba Rae was holding a coffee cup to her mouth with both hands.

"It was late."

"Did the movie run long?"

"No, it wasn't the movie. But Fettis took me by his momma and daddy's house on the way home. You know—to meet them."

Ethel stopped her salting. "Why?"

"Why? Because I guess he just wanted to introduce me to them."

"Just how serious are you and this boy, Elba Rae?"

"Oh, Momma, don't be silly. I'm hardly a teenager, and Fettis is ..."

"Yeah, I know. Fettis is hardly a spring chicken himself. But, are ya'll really that serious?"

"Well," Elba Rae hesitated, but elected to disclose as much as she reasonably knew of their status. "I guess maybe we are."

Ethel took a few bites of egg and then began buttering a slice of toasted white bread.

"What are his momma and daddy like?"

"I didn't get to meet his daddy."

"Why not?"

"Because he was—he'd already gone to bed."

"Gone to bed? When Fettis was bringing you by there for the first time?!"

"He didn't know Fettis was going to bring me by there last night, it was just sort of a spur of the moment thing."

"Well, that doesn't sound very proper."

"It was fine. Anyway, his mother was still up and we got to visit for quite a while."

"You know," Ethel said, crunching some toast, "I mentioned to your aunt Ruby the other day that you'd been going out with a Van Oaks and she reminded me that Dorothy Willard was in her graduating class, and you know Dorothy married Helma Van Oaks's younger brother, Stooks—the one that works for the power company—and Dorothy told Ruby one time she didn't have a thing in the world against any of Stooks's family, except for his sister was just about the worst housekeeper she'd ever seen in her life. Dorothy said their house was nasty as buzzards."

"Well, I don't know anything about that because we sat outside on the front porch the whole time and I'm not going to believe every bit of gossip you and Aunt Ruby spread."

"I'm not gossiping, Elba Rae. I'm just repeating what I heard."

"I don't care. She seemed like a nice woman to me."

Ethel Maywood snapped a strip of bacon in half and bit into one end.

"I don't know about Fettis, Elba Rae."

"What do you mean, you don't know?"

"Well, what is he doing with himself? What are his plans?"

"Why does he have to have plans?"

"Every man needs to have plans. Take your sister's husband, for instance."

"Oh, here we go," Elba Rae said with exasperation before getting up from the table. She took her coffee cup to the sink and rinsed it out.

"I'm not trying to compare the two, Elba Rae, but just think about it. Bucky's got a good job and he's learning a trade he'll have with him for the rest of his life."

"That's because his daddy already had an insurance company and handed him a job!"

"Maybe he had an advantage, but he works hard. And he's providing for your sister pretty well."

Elba Rae turned the coffee cup upside down in the metal dish drainer that sat next to the sink before rejoining her mother at the table.

"I know you think Fettis isn't as good as Bucky, but it's not fair to compare the two of them. They're different—as well they should be! Lord knows, Lila and I couldn't be any less alike if we tried!"

"Well, maybe this is one time you ought to think about following your sister's example."

"She is *no* example for me!" Elba Rae exclaimed, and when she got up from the table that second time, she didn't come back. It infuriated her to be compared with her sister and what Lila had done, and who Lila had chosen to marry bore no connection to the outcome of anything concerning Elba Rae in Buford. Bucky Fessmire did come from a nice family, but Fettis was earnest and he had a steady job working on a crew with the road department and it was pointless for mothers to presume they could influence the outcome of true love if, Elba Rae surmised, that's what it was.

One week later, Fettis Van Oaks proposed. Elba Rae had said yes and assumed things were working out just about the way they were supposed to.

*   *   *

"I need something to stand on to reach this shelf," Lila Fessmire said the next afternoon when the sisters resumed excavation in the late Ethel Maywood's bedroom. They'd spent the morning unloading the linen closet and bathroom vanity, the contents of which went almost exclusively into a large capacity garbage bag save for one set of sheets Elba Rae thought might fit her daybed in the spare room; the various ointments, creams, gardenia-scented lotions, and out-dated medicine bottles were discarded without the burden of sentiment.

"There's a little stepladder in the pantry," replied Elba Rae without turning around. One old suitcase had been filled with clothes, closed, and carried to the back door. The second piece was well on its way.

Lila momentarily returned with a small wooden ladder and unfolded it inside the closet whereupon she assessed that Ethel Maywood had not been to the top shelf anytime recently since among its other as yet undiscovered treasures, the shelf was obviously the final resting place for items that had been segregated from their mainstream counterparts on the floor or still hanging on the clothes rod. There were mainly old shoes inside old shoe boxes that had apparently been put there to make room for the newer pairs that got to live on the ground level. Lila methodically stepped down with the boxes two at a time and put them by the door of the bedroom.

"I don't know if we need to bother packing these up for the boutique or whether we should just throw them away," Lila remarked as she climbed back to the shelf.

Elba Rae Van Oaks, meanwhile, had already become distracted by a generous bundle of rubber-banded mail she'd discovered in the second drawer of a nightstand table and didn't appear to pay attention to Lila's suggestion. The rubber band snapped from dry rot when Elba Rae attempted to remove it, causing her to drop several envelopes. She picked one up from the floor, a greeting card of sorts with a postmark too faded to make out. She sat down on the edge of the bed with the bundle before opening it.

"For heaven's sake," Elba Rae said out loud.

"What?" Lila asked, as she set another box of ancient footwear in the rising stack by the door.

"It's a card Miss Nita Perrymore sent Momma when Daddy died. She wrote the sweetest note in it, talking about how she suffered when Mr. Perrymore passed but how time would eventually heal her grief."

"She always did palaver," Lila said.

Elba Rae sorted through several more. "Momma must have saved every sympathy card she got."

She randomly opened several more and then noticed a smaller piece of mail with a Hattiesburg return address. She removed the note and read the brief message.

"And get a load of this one."

"Another sympathy card?" Lila asked.

"No," Elba Rae said tersely. "It's a thank you note. To Momma, from Begina."

Lila had ascended the stepladder inside the closet by then such that her head was no longer visible through the door opening, and when she said "Yeah?" back to Elba Rae, it was muted.

"Begina's thanking Momma for the pretty gown she sent for her birthday!"

"What's wrong with that?"

"What'd you say?"

Lila briefly squatted on the ladder low enough for her head to emerge through the doorway. "I said, what's wrong with that?"

"Because the way she's describing the gown in this note, it sounds exactly like one I got Momma for Christmas!"

Lila rolled her eyes and rose back up to reach the remaining contents of the closet shelf, leaving Elba Rae to fume.

"When I think of the trouble it was to make sure she had some kind of present at every holiday and occasion, and all the while she was just parceling them out to Begina and Lord only knows who else!"

"Oh, Elba Rae—look what I found!"

"Huh? I can't hear you in there."

Lila descended the ladder with another shoebox in her hand.

"What's that?"

"It's pictures," said Lila, who went immediately to the bed and overturned the box. "Come look."

"Pictures of what?"

"Looks like a little of everything. And everybody. Come look."

"We'll never get anything cleaned out if you're gonna stop and go down memory lane with all of it first," Elba Rae protested, even as she was on her way around to the side of the bed Lila was utilizing.

"Here's one of Momma and Daddy. Looks like it was taken in front of the house." Lila handed the photograph to Elba Rae. She studied it for a few seconds.

"Look how young they were."

"And here's one of Daddy standing next to the car." After Lila handed that one to Elba Rae, she unconsciously sat down on the bed and joined Lila.

"I don't think that was Daddy's car. I think it was Uncle Sammy's."

"Well, it looks like our yard in the background," Lila contended.

"It is our yard. But that's Uncle Sammy's car. Must have been some holiday when they were over here."

"That could have been just about any of them because I don't ever remember us going to Hattiesburg to see them. Seems like they were always over here."

"They were," Elba Rae said in agreement. "Momma used to fuss for two weeks before they came and for a week after they were gone. Aunt Laveetra and Uncle Sammy would drag over here with Begina, and Aunt Laveetra never offered to help Momma with anything. And she never brought so much as a dish. Not even the relish tray."

"Oh, yeah, look," Lila said as she handed off another slightly crinkled photo. "Here's one of Aunt Laveetra and Begina standing next to the same car."

Elba Rae tilted the picture forward slightly to catch more light on its subjects. "And just look at Begina, poor thing. Looks like she got caught in the barbed wire fence. Aunt Laveetra must have never so much as run a comb through that poor girl's hair."

"Good thing Begina was too off to know the difference."

"That's not nice."

"Nice or no, it's not like I never heard Momma and Daddy saying Begina was simple."

"Who is that?" Elba Rae asked, as she picked up a picture of a group posed in front of the fireplace mantle of someone's long-ago living room before realizing she was in it.

"Good Lord, that's us over at Aunt Sister's house. I look like I've been sent for and couldn't go."

"Let me see," Lila said while simultaneously taking the photograph from Elba Rae. "Oh, that's a good one of you."

Elba Rae promptly retrieved it and returned it to the discard pile. "Aunt Sister was the worst about having that camera out every time we got together for anything. You couldn't stop to say 'how do' without her wanting to line you up and strike a pose. I guess that's where Butch gets it from."

"Well, think about it this way, Elba Rae—if she hadn't, we wouldn't have any of these to look at now."

"Some of them wouldn't be any great loss."

"Maybe, but I'm glad we've got these with Momma in them. Wonder how she ended up with so many."

"Because that's what Aunt Sister did. She wagged that old camera with her everywhere she went, and then she'd give all the pictures away for Christmas and birthdays. Momma was forever getting a card from her with a picture falling out. Eventually Momma would just shake out the card first before she even opened it good when the return address was from Aunt Sister, because she knew a picture was going to fall out."

Lila Fessmire flipped in quick succession through a series of apparently un-captivating prints before another pause.

"Oh, look," Lila said. "Here's one of Mary Alice. It was when she was going with that Crutcher boy." Lila held the photo out and away from her a bit further, as if to savor more from a distance. "And she's all dressed up. Wonder where they were going." Although Elba Rae hadn't asked, Lila handed it to her for inspection.

Elba Rae studied the faded color image for a moment. "Well, how do you know that was when she was going with the Crutcher boy? He's not even in the picture."

"Because I just remember," Lila replied.

Elba Rae tossed the picture on the bed and resumed the review she was conducting of her own mini pile. "No telling who she was going out with when *that* was taken."

"It was the Crutcher boy," Lila repeated.

"Okay."

"It was!" Lila put down the group of as yet unviewed pictures she held in her hand, and reclaimed the slightly creased likeness of Aunt Sister's only daughter, Mary Alice. "I know, because her hair is blonde in the picture."

Elba Rae stared across the bed at her sister. "What's that got to do with it?"

"Oh, Elba Rae, don't you remember anything? Aunt Sister liked to have had a fit when Mary Alice came out of the bathroom with her hair dyed. They got in such a fight she stayed over at our house for two days until Momma made her go home and make up."

"Well, now, I do remember when she blondined her hair but I don't recall her staying away from home any two days."

"It was two days," Lila insisted. "Momma finally had to call Aunt Sister on the phone and remind her that Mary Alice was sixteen years old and making her own money at the Ben Franklin's, and if she was a mind to spend it on hair color there wasn't a thing anybody could do about it."

"What does that have to do with the Crutcher boy?"

"Because that's the only reason she wanted to dye her hair blonde in the first place! Have you really forgotten all that? Mary Alice went from one phase to the next, depending on which movie star she was trying to imitate. And I distinctly remember that Crutcher boy came along right about the middle of her Veronica Lake time."

"Veronica Lake?" Elba Rae squealed.

"Yes, Veronica Lake. Mary Alice used to cut all her pictures out of the magazines and keep them in a suitcase under her bed so Aunt Sister wouldn't find out. Aunt Sister didn't want any of those movie magazines in her house because she thought they were a bad influence on Mary Alice."

"Which they were," Elba Rae said with a hint of condemnation.

"Well, it didn't matter because Mary Alice was working at Ben Franklin's after school and she could buy whatever she wanted up there and bring it home in a Ben Franklin's sack and tell Aunt Sister it was a sewing pattern or a songbook for the piano, and Aunt Sister never knew the difference."

"Sounds like you and Mary Alice were more in cahoots than any of us ever gave you credit for."

"Oh, for heaven's sake, Elba Rae, you sound just like Momma. We were kids."

"How do you remember so much from back then, anyhow?"

Lila Fessmire laughed. "I just do. Mary Alice was crazy about that Crutcher boy but he was going with a girl from down around Prattville. So Mary Alice decided she'd have to do something drastic to get his attention. And that just happened to be when she was going through her Veronica Lake phase." Lila paused briefly but still held on to the photograph. "But Lord, was Aunt Sister ever mad."

Aunt Sister was neither an aunt to Elba Rae Van Oaks and Lila Fessmire nor was she, as a point of reference, even anybody's sister. Aunt Sister had a real name, Wilella Hornbuckle, and strictly from a biological standpoint she was a cousin of Elba Rae and Lila's father, Raymond Maywood. Because Wilella had for all intent and purposes been reared in the same household by Raymond's mother and father, Ray had taken to calling her Sister at a very early age when he still didn't grasp the technicalities of her lineage. The name stuck somehow, making for a natural progression when Raymond's children were born to consider her an aunt, even if she wasn't.

Little Wilella had been only three years old when her own mother succumbed to pneumonia after suffering for but a week. Wilella's father worked as a hand on one of the larger cotton concerns in Crenshaw County, and although his parenting skills had to that point not been called into judgment, Raymond Maywood's mother and father had suspected just from word of mouth and from general observation it would not have been in Wilella's best interest for her to remain in the tenant house the family occupied, as there was no one to care for the child. And, it had been obvious even on the day of the funeral that Wilella's father had cultivated a faithful relationship with the whiskey.

The child's belongings, which had barely added weight to the cotton sack into which they got packed, were gathered without debate the morning after the burial. Even though he hadn't offered resistance to the child's relocation, little Wilella's father had still cried out loud as her new parents prepared to leave with her, vowing through his sobs he'd come for her just as soon as he could get his own place and arrange for the feminine presence of a caregiver. Raymond Maywood's mother, especially, eventually conveyed that scene to Wilella when she had deemed Wilella old enough to know, even though Wilella's father had left Crenshaw County three months after his wife's death and was never heard from again.

Wilella had lived in Buford for the rest of her life. She'd married Morris Hornbuckle right after they graduated from high school and given birth to their only son, Butch. A daughter, Mary Alice, had come later, and while occasionally serving as a source of bemusement to others, Mary Alice's sense of nonconformity had produced plenty of strife for Wilella and for Morris but especially for Wilella, who outlived Morris long enough to see Mary Alice through two of her eventual three marriages.

"We thought Mary Alice was going to pine over that Crutcher boy for the rest of her life," Lila said. "And then she saw that movie. Oh, what was it?"

"I don't know what you're talking about it."

"The one with Rita Hayworth. *Gilda*! That's when she got obsessed with being a redhead and finally got over Veronica Lake."

"Well, now I do remember her being redheaded for a long time," Elba Rae said.

"She was. But we laughed about that Crutcher boy for years. Except we never could mention him by name, cause we were always afraid she'd get upset all over again. So if we ever wanted to refer to him, or to something that happened along about that time, we just said it was when Mary Alice was a blonde. That was the code." Lila laughed out loud, recollecting a relaxed and frivolous youth perhaps not shared by her sister.

Lila continued her picture flipping through an apparent patch she deemed would be of no particular interest to Elba Rae or that did not warrant any special mention, the flipping accompanied only by an intermittent titter but absent verbal commentary. Elba Rae quickly grew restless and was about to resume her purging of the nightstand drawers when Lila came about another notable photograph.

"Oh, look, Elba Rae. It's Mary Alice and Aunt Sister." She handed it to Elba Rae, who studied it as well. "That was taken right before Mary Alice got married."

"Which time?" Elba Rae asked, while handing the picture back to Lila.

"The *first* time," said Lila sharply.

"Well, I'm just asking. It's not like she stayed with any of them."

"Oh, you're so cynical." Lila was gathering the assortment of variously shaped photographs and stacking them in a pile as best she could to return them to the shoebox when she noticed one lone image left in the box. She put the big pile down on the bed and removed the single picture, studying it in silence before carrying it over to the window and tilting it just so to catch some natural light.

"What's that one?" Elba Rae seemed once again curious.

"It's me and Mary Alice."

Elba Rae joined Lila at the window for a look, peeking over her shoulder while Lila held onto the picture.

"What color is she in that one?"

"She was still blonde."

"You look like you're in some kind of formals."

"We were," Lila said. "This was taken in the dressing room at the VFW

Hall. Course it really wasn't a dressing room—it was just a big walk-in storage room they let us use for a dressing room." Lila had yet not taken her eyes off the photograph.

"Dressing room for what?"

"The contest," answered Lila.

"What contest?"

"That contest we were in," Lila said before promptly returning to gather the remaining photos out on the bed and dropping them back in the shoebox. "Now, what else have we got to do here?"

"What contest?" Elba Rae persisted.

Lila walked over to Ethel Maywood's dresser and pulled open a drawer. "I think we should just sack up most of these underclothes and take them over to that charity store you were talking about. Don't you? I mean, I don't want any of these things. They won't fit *me*, and even if they did—"

"Are you talking about the time you and Mary Alice were in the Miss Honeysuckle pageant?"

Lila Fessmire said "yes" but otherwise didn't turn around from her drawer fumbling.

"Lord, what a bunch of hullaballoo that was."

"It was fun," Lila said, with a smile still on her face. "And you know, I'm sure it was Mary Alice's blonde hair that helped her win. Maybe if Momma had let me dye mine, I wouldn't have just been runner up."

"At least you got to be in it in the first place," Elba Rae said in somewhat of a mumble.

"Now, you know you were past the age cutoff by the time Mary Alice and I entered."

"Well, sure I was by then. But I could have been in it when I was younger. Except Momma never wanted to fool with it back then. The one time Miss Printup said anything to her about filling out the entry, Momma said she didn't have time to mess with me being in any pageant. Said we couldn't afford all the costumes and she didn't have time to make them herself—like she did for you when you got in it."

"Elba Rae, you know good and well you never wanted to be in that pageant."

"How do you know?"

"Because I know!"

"You were a child during the years I could have been in it!"

"So what if I was?" Lila protested. "I still know you'd have never been in it! You had to be a little outgoing to participate in those things! You had to get up on a stage—in front of people! Now, you know you were too shy back then. You know you'd have never been able to do it when the time came. And Momma probably knew it, too. That's why she wasn't about to go to the trouble of stitching up three different outfits just to have you come down with the stage fright the night of the pageant."

"I seem to recall her having to do plenty of coaxing to get you to be in it."

Lila was furiously folding a petticoat, anxious for the discussion to end. "She was just helping me with my talent."

Elba Rae let her tense shoulders relax and fall to their at-ease posture. "Talent. I should say so."

"What does that mean?" Lila turned around, and was suddenly less intently interested in preparing Ethel Maywood's delicates for resale at the Buford Baptist Benevolence Boutique.

"She had to force you outside with the yardstick every day to get you to practice that baton twirling."

"She did not."

"Did so. And where did you ever get the idea you could twirl a baton?"

"Well, I had to do something different. Mary Alice had already said she was going to sing, and three of the other girls were singing, too. And Janie Hendrix was playing the piano—I couldn't do that."

"You couldn't do that because you couldn't play the piano."

"Well, how could I, with nobody but Miss Marjorie Whittlehurst to give us lessons?"

"She never gave *me* lessons. Because I never took piano. Momma said it was a waste of money."

"Trust me. It was. I'm not sure Miss Marjorie could even read the notes herself."

"That's not the point."

"Then, what is, Elba Rae?"

Elba Rae had no explanation.

"I can't believe I'm having to stand here nearly forty years later and listen to you being bitter because I was in a silly beauty pageant and you weren't! Honestly, Elba Rae—how petty can you get?"

"I'm not being petty! But maybe I don't enjoy you rubbing all this in my face!"

"Rubbing what in your face?"

"Pulling out all these pictures of you and Mary Alice and laughing and giggling about her blondined hair and how much fun ya'll used to have sneaking around and cutting up and being in your beauty contests together!"

"We were kids! We were having fun! Why does that bother you so much?"

"Because Momma and Daddy never let me be in the damn Miss Honeysuckle contest, that's why! They never pushed me, or encouraged me, or said 'go on, honey, it'll be fun for you' like they did with you!"

"Well, if they didn't ever encourage you to be in it, it's probably because they knew you didn't have a snowball's chance in hell of winning! And maybe they were just trying to spare your feelings!"

Elba Rae stood with her mouth slightly open and her shoulders once again raised. Lila put her hand to her own mouth and watched Elba Rae slowly turn around and walk out of the bedroom. Momentarily, Lila heard a clang in the kitchen, followed by another and then a series of clangs in rapid succession. With reservation, she left the temporary safety of her late mother's bedroom to investigate.

In the kitchen, Lila found Elba Rae had opened several cabinet doors and was removing the pots, pans, and skillets—and sometimes all three at once.

"What are you doing?"

"What does it look like I'm doing?" Elba Rae said in a duet with the clank of a saucepan. "I'm cleaning out this kitchen."

"Why—"

"I found that little set of individual serving dishes Momma used to keep for Charity so her food wouldn't touch. Do you want them? If not, I'm throwing them out."

"I thought we were just going to finish up in the bedroom today before we started anything else. Why do you want to drag out all this stuff?"

"Because I feel like doing it now!" Elba Rae said, right before whamming an iron skillet onto an eye of Ethel Maywood's stove with such considerable force the electric coil came loose from its socket.

"Sounds like all you're doing is tearing up Momma's stove!"

"If you want to finish the bedroom," Elba Rae said without turning around, "then go on back in there and do it! And leave me alone!"

"No," Lila screamed. "I am not gonna be bossed around by you just because you're older! And you're not going to do it just because you're mad about a silly old beauty pageant nobody even remembers!"

"I'm not mad, Lila, just go on! Go to the bedroom, or go back to my house, or better yet," she turned around to face her sister, "go back to Birmingham! I don't need you here."

Lila Fessmire was momentarily stunned. Shocked at the specific words, perhaps, but more so by the venomous tone Elba Rae made no attempt to conceal. It was blatantly obvious to Lila that Elba Rae was beyond mad; she had struck, like a wounded animal.

"You'd like that, wouldn't you? Well, I'm not falling for it."

"Falling for what?"

"You'd like it if I just tucked and turned and walked out on all this, because then you could do it all yourself—which is probably what you want anyway—and then play the martyr. Poor Elba Rae that has to do all the work because Lila won't help. Well, forget it."

"No, Lila," Elba Rae said after finally ceasing her pot banging. "The truth is, I *don't* want to have to do all of this by myself. But forgive me for wanting to be organized and for just wanting to get on with it and get something accomplished without having to dig through a bunch of old pictures and waste time indulging your glory days with Mary Alice."

"It shouldn't be this hard, Elba Rae. And what's wrong with having a little fun while we're doing it? I mean, why are you so critical of me?"

"I'm not being critical of you! I just don't have time for all this."

Lila Fessmire paused, and let out a deep breath. It seemed to her the gale might have passed.

"I'm sorry for what I said about the pageant. Momma should have let you be in it the same as she did me. It wasn't fair."

"Forget about that silly beauty contest. I don't care about it, and I certainly don't need to know about any of the other shenanigans you and Mary Alice were up to."

"Well, for heaven's sake, Elba Rae, it's not like we were a couple of juvenile delinquents or something."

"Momma and Aunt Sister might have begged to differ if they'd ever known some of the things ya'll were pulling."

"Well, if I had Mary Alice to get into things with growing up, then you had Hazel. You two always were thick as thieves. Still are."

Elba Rae Van Oaks took exception to the characterization of the cousins' adolescent activities. "I bet Hazel and I never got into the likes of things you and Mary Alice were up to. We would have never gotten away with it. As if Momma and Daddy weren't bad enough, Aunt Ruby was worse when it came to making sure our wings stayed clipped."

Elba Rae took only a brief pause with her reflection. "Can you even imagine what Momma would have done to me if I'd dyed my hair a different color every two weeks like Mary Alice?"

"Well, don't you wish now you'd tried it?"

"No! I don't!"

"Then how about something else?"

"What are you talking about?"

"Don't you ever regret now you didn't at least try a few new things when you were growing up? Even if there was a chance you would have gotten in trouble for them?"

"No. Trying new things—whether you ever got caught or not—was your department."

"And I think that's always been part of your problem, Elba Rae. You were jealous of me and Mary Alice. Not just because we were close girlfriends and confided everything in each other, but because you thought we were getting by with all sorts of things you thought you'd missed out on. And you've resented me for it ever since."

"That's ridiculous. I was so much older than the two of ya'll I didn't care what you were doing, and I never resented you for anything."

"How can you stand there and say that to me—with a straight face, no less?"

"Because it's the truth, Lila. You're just over dramatizing things."

"You have always resented me! I know it, you know it, Bucky knows it—hell, everybody knows it!"

"That's crazy, Lila! What reason would I have to resent you?"

Lila Fessmire was completely exasperated, and it was beginning to unnerve Elba Rae.

"You said it yourself! Right here, just a few minutes ago! Because Momma let me do things she never let you do. Because she … because she let me be in the Miss Honeysuckle contest and—if I had to venture a guess—because I came in second place!"

"None of that amounts to a hill of beans now. And you want to know something else? It's never crossed my mind during what I've had to go through the last few years."

"What do you mean, what you've had to go through?"

"Momma hasn't been able to go and do for herself in ages, Lila. Who do you think made sure she got to every doctor's appointment? And who do you think got her to the drug store regular to keep her prescriptions filled?"

"I told Momma this myself—and I know I told you plenty of times, too—all you ever had to do was let me know when Momma had doctors scheduled and I would have made a point to come stay. All you had to do was let me know."

"It wasn't just the doctors she needed help getting to! Do you realize she hasn't driven that old car out there in five years? Did you not even notice three of the tires are flat? Who do you think carried her to church every Sunday and to the beauty parlor and the post office and made sure she always had a stock of groceries in the house? And, Lord, don't even get me started on what we had to go through when she knew you *were* coming!"

"What are you talking about?" Lila was uncomfortable at what she felt the launch of a new unfair confrontation.

"The carrying on that woman would do." Elba Rae let out a faint laugh and shook her head from side to side. "'We've got to get to the store, Elba Rae—Lila's coming. I've got to cook a ham, Elba Rae—Lila's coming. I need to bake a cake, Elba Rae—Lila's coming.' Of course she did! Lila's coming, so let's break out the champagne!"

"This is just your usual, typical pettiness, Elba Rae, and I—"

"Do you know she never baked a cake for me after my thirteenth birthday?"

Lila Fessmire found herself without words but did make note she had never brooded over the history of her mother's cake baking.

"What am I supposed to do about that? Apologize because my own mother acted like she was glad to see me?"

"Of course not. But you needn't think anybody's got time now to waste indulging foolishness about some old beauty contest. Nobody's going to be throwing a parade this time, Lila, just because you've shown up for a minute to finally do some of the dirty work."

"What more do you want me to do?" screamed Lila, at a decibel that alarmed even her. "I'm here, aren't I? I'm at your command! Whatever you want! But you're still finding a way to complain and be miserable!"

"It would have been nice," Elba Rae's retort began, "if you'd wanted to come on your own and not because I twisted your arm."

"Oh, good Lord, Elba Rae, what difference does it make?"

"Because I didn't want to feel like I had to force you to come this time. I wanted you to come on your own—because you wanted to. But all you can do is worry about getting back to Birmingham so you can plan a wedding! Of all the insensitive and selfish things you've done in your life, Lila Mae Maywood, I believe this about takes the prize!"

"My daughter didn't decide to get engaged just to spite you, Elba Rae! In fact, I can pretty much promise she didn't give you a thought!"

"Charity might not have, but our momma isn't even cold in her grave yet and all you can think about is putting on in front of your friends! Well, go! Go on, and good riddance!"

"Oh for God's sake, Elba Rae, I don't want to have to go back to Birmingham to plan a wedding! I don't even want there to *be* a wedding!"

"Why not? Are you afraid you'll have to share the spotlight with the groom's family? Huh? Is that it? What's the matter? Aren't they from the right side of the tracks to suit you? Or are you afraid the boy's not good enough for your precious daughter?!"

"Charity's getting married because she has to! Don't you get it? We don't have any choice!"

Elba Rae was at once unsure how to react.

"What?"

"She's pregnant! My daughter is pregnant."

Lila seemed to have stunned even her own self with the announcement. Without a further word, she calmly retrieved her purse that was on the counter top next to the mismatched lid of a frying pan, and walked out the back door of the house. Elba Rae Van Oak stood completely speechless, with her mouth agape.

Charity Fessmire

The old picnic table on the patio outside Elba Rae's back door was faded, with its color bearing little resemblance to the barn-red paint once applied by Fettis Van Oaks. The legs on the benches were somewhat wobbly which necessitated being seated in due center to diminish the threat of collapse.

Lila Fessmire sat with her back to the house and didn't react when she heard the screen door open and close behind her. Elba Rae reached across Lila's shoulder and set the glass of iced tea down on the table before going around to the other side to be seated in a facing position. They each took one full, satisfying swallow of the cold tea before Elba Rae sensed Lila was ready.

"How far along is she?"

"Almost ten weeks, we think." Whether it was the trickle of cold tea down her throat, the fresh air, or the present physical distance between herself and the situation, Lila said it with remarkable calm.

"How long have you known?"

"I knew something was bothering her. Bucky thought it was just anxiety about graduating and thinking about going off to school in the fall—you know, worry over being away from home and from us for the first time. But I could tell it was more. One morning about a month ago I heard her in the bathroom. Sick as a dog. And it just all started to make sense."

"What did you do?"

Lila Fessmire took another long drink of iced tea. "I just went in the bathroom with her. Without thinking first, I guess. And the look on her face. Well, whatever I might have thought about saying went right out the window when I saw her. I could tell she was petrified. And all I wanted to do was hug her and tell her everything was going to be all right."

"I imagine she felt a relief to get it out in the open," offered Elba Rae.

"Probably. But then all I could do was think about what I was going to tell Bucky when he got home."

"How is he taking it?"

"He was shocked, at first—like I was. Then he got mad. Not at Charity so much as he was at the boy. It's a good thing he'd never heard of the family because I'm afraid of what he might have done that first night, if he'd known where to find him."

"Well, what about the boy?"

"His name is Skippy. Skippy Grinbar."

Lila Fessmire shook a cigarette free from its mostly empty pack and ignited it with a lighter she no longer had motive to conceal from Elba Rae.

"He didn't even go to the Academy; he went to public school. But apparently one of his friends had a cousin at the Academy who's the same age as Charity, and somehow they all met up after a football game last fall. Bucky and I weren't even aware she knew the boy, much less that they'd been sneaking around dating behind our backs."

"Well, honey, I may never have had any of my own, but one thing I've learned about kids—especially once they get to be teenagers—is there's no controlling them. Not really. You can try. And they may even let you think you're good at it. But the truth is, kids grow up and eventually they're gonna have wills of their own. Just like they did when we were coming up."

Elba Rae made a point to smile at her sister. "Just like when you and Mary Alice were sneaking movie magazines and hair dye in the house under Aunt Sister's nose."

The memory made Lila smile back, but it was short lived. "I wish all I had to worry about was some magazines. Things are different now, Elba Rae. Times are different. It's not like when we were growing up in Buford." Lila took an extended drag on her cigarette.

"Well, what can you do about it now, huh? The damage is done, and the boy's obviously doing right by her. They'll get married, and they'll do the best they can. And I'm sure you and Bucky will be there to help."

Lila rolled her head back and exhaled a billow of smoke.

"It'll be all right. People will talk, I'm sure. At first. But you know how these things are, Lila. Something else will eventually come along and they'll go to talking about that and forget about Charity. Especially once the baby comes."

"Oh, it's not just Charity, Elba Rae."

"Well, what else is the matter?"

"It's everything."

"What?"

"Well, Bucky for one thing."

"What's wrong with Bucky?"

"I don't know if you noticed when he was here for the funeral, but Bucky's gaining weight and his hair is thinning. I've been on him for a year to go see about his knee, but he's convinced they'll want to operate so he just tries to ignore it."

"I did notice him favoring his right side a little."

"He's letting himself go," continued Lila. "I don't think he even cares anymore. But if he won't take care of himself for his own benefit, the least he could do is think about me."

"Husbands are just like that after awhile, Lila. You can't expect the honeymoon to last forever."

"Oh yeah? Well, I bet it'd be a different story if the shoe were on the other foot. If I didn't watch my figure every day and if I let my hair go and just showed up at things wearing any old kind of outfit. I bet he'd have plenty to say."

"Well …" Elba Rae restrained herself.

"What?"

"Well, it's none of my business, but are you and Bucky all right? As a couple, I mean."

Lila looked perplexed at first but then understood the nature of Elba Rae's inquiry.

"If you mean how's our marriage, I guess it's fine. I mean, Bucky works all the time, and when he's not working he's playing golf or hanging around that silly gentlemen's lounge at the club. But he's never been unfaithful as far as I know. And if he had, I'm not sure I'd want to know."

"Doesn't he ever want to do things with the boys? Take them on a camping trip, or to a ballgame?"

"Oh!" Lila let out a tremendous sigh. "The boys! My God, don't even get me started on them."

"Don't tell me they're in some kind of trouble, too."

For the first time since they'd arrived back at Elba Rae's house, having spent the ride in the car in complete silence and ignorance of each other, Lila couldn't contain her emotion and she pursed her lips together in a way such that Elba Rae knew she was trying to ward off a cry.

"They're going to be the death of me, Elba Rae," she said, shaking her head but staving the tears. "The absolute death."

"Are they not doing well in school?"

"They're lucky they're still *in* school and not expelled from the Academy."

"I can tell they've got a rowdy side."

"I could handle a little rowdy every once in a while," Lila said. "They're still kids, after all, and I'd expect it."

Elba Rae wanted to get to the bottom of her sister's woes but was careful to temper her questioning. "Have they been in any sort of bad trouble?"

"Well, just to give you an idea, they're banned from the country club. Do you know how embarrassing that is?"

Elba Rae Van Oaks didn't suppose it was an appropriate moment to point out what a foolish question it was to ask of her since Lila obviously knew full well Litton County, no matter its other facilities, was home to no sign of a country club, and even it had been and even if Elba Rae Van Oaks had been a member of such a place—the joining of which she would have never considered—it was ridiculous to infer she'd do anything to become acquainted with the shame of being thrown out of it. The very idea.

"The president of the club had to meet with us personally, to tell us. I was mortified. Of course, Bucky just sat there and nodded his head a few times and tried to laugh it off like it was just something we should expect from a couple of teenage boys. But I don't expect it, Elba Rae. My boys weren't raised to go around trying to blow up things! I don't care what Pig thinks!"

"Pig? Who's Pig?"

"He's the head groundskeeper at the club. He used to be in charge of maintaining the golf course until he got too old to walk it anymore. They tried to teach him to drive a cart but he's half blind and he kept running it off in the traps and getting it mired up in sand, and they were afraid he'd eventually go off into one of the lakes and drown. Poor old thing. Never learned to swim."

"What's he doing still working there?"

"It's an understood agreement the Board has with him. He's worked there since he was in his thirties and they just feel obligated to take care of him so they keep him on the payroll. Anyway, the boys got caught playing with some firecrackers in the maintenance shed where Pig has his little office. It didn't hurt him any, but I guess it scared him half to death. And of course my two boys just thought that was hilarious!"

"Well, for heaven's sake, what were they even doing prowling around in a shed where they had no business?"

"Trying to scare the daylights out of Pig! Which, apparently, they did. He came running out of the shed hollering and screaming that someone was shooting at him and bless his old heart, I guess that's what it must have sounded like. But he managed to get all the way inside the club and into the main dining room where the Vonderbrandts were hosting a ninetieth birthday party for Mr. Vonderbrandt's mother. And when Pig busted in there screaming about somebody shooting, Mr. Vonderbrandt pushed his mother down and got on top of her to protect her, but he knocked her to the floor so hard it dislocated her shoulder and they had to take her to the hospital."

Elba Rae took a minute to let it all soak in. "You're lucky they weren't arrested."

"Oh, Pig was all right once he got calmed down and realized he wasn't under attack. And he didn't want to press any charges. But the Board didn't take too kindly to it and the boys have been temporarily banned until they're eighteen years old, and even then we're not sure they'll let them back in. They can't even go if they're with me and Bucky. We had to sign a special one-time only waiver for them to be able to attend Charity's wedding reception, which we're lucky to even get to have at the club because of them, and make a promise either Bucky or I would have them under constant surveillance the entire evening. The membership committee had to convene a special meeting just to vote on it."

"Well," Elba Rae said as she braced herself to harvest a positive outcome from the situation, "hopefully it's taught them a lesson. That there are consequences to your actions."

"That's the thing, Elba Rae. I don't think they have learned. Or if they have, they just don't care. Getting caught means nothing to them. It just means they have to try harder to come up with something different."

Lila Fessmire at once lit a new Salem, having barely extinguished the previous one. Elba Rae did not approve of smoking, partly because the patrolling of it was, among other disciplinary obligations, a byproduct of her duties at the Homer T. Litton Grammar School.

"I imagine they've wanted to take up smoking, too," she said to Lila and not in the form of a question.

"Of course they've tried it. Fortunately it made Heath sick and it made Nick so dizzy he fell off the tree limb they'd been sitting in out back where they'd snuck off to try it. I might never have known if he hadn't come whining to me for a Band-Aid."

Lila inhaled and held it in as long as possible. "It's the drinking that was the real rude awakening."

"Are you serious?"

"I'm afraid so."

"They're fourteen years old!"

"I can't help it, Elba Rae. They don't fear anything."

"Well, obviously they got caught with that too."

"Oh, yeah," Lila said. "And in a way, I'm glad it happened. Because at least it finally got Bucky's attention. For the time being, anyway."

"What happened?"

"The Fessmires were hosting their big Christmas party like they do every year for the agency. Charity was out with some of her friends, or so she said. Probably sneaking around with that Grinbar boy now that I think about it. Anyway, we left the boys at home by themselves. And apparently they thought it'd be fun to see what beer tasted like, so they went out in the garage where Bucky keeps it in the other refrigerator and proceeded to drink themselves into a stupor. By the time we got home from the party, Heath was in the middle of the front yard straddling one of my good plastic reindeer, throwing up all over it. And Nick had cranked up the lawnmower and was racing it back and forth across the backyard! It's a wonder my neighbors didn't call the police."

"Merciful heavens," Elba Rae finally replied.

"Every time Bucky buys beer now, he has to count how many are in the refrigerator. Same when he drinks one. He has to pull out his clipboard and check it off the inventory. And we had to threaten Nick and Heath within an inch of their lives if we find out so much as one can is unaccounted for. We even put a lock on the liquor cabinet in the house, just to be on the safe side."

"Sounds like you've got your hands full."

Lila Fessmire readily nodded in agreement. "So whatever you think about me—and my life—well, it's no bed of roses, Elba Rae."

"Nobody's is, Lila. But ..."

"But what?"

Elba Rae smiled. "You're going to be a grandmother," and as soon as she said it, she could tell Lila was not amused. "Aren't you and Bucky at least a little bit happy about that?"

"No one knows about the baby, Elba Rae. We weren't about to tell the twins. Bucky's parents don't even know. Although I'm sure they suspect something is up by now."

"What about the boy's mother and father?"

"Oh, I don't know. He's told them, and Bucky had a talk with his daddy, but I certainly haven't discussed it with them. I don't care about them anyway."

"You mean ..." Elba Rae seemed unsettled by her revelation. "You mean I'm the only person you've told?"

"Yes," Lila said.

They each raised their glasses slowly and sipped some tea, as a means to process the particular relevance of that confidence.

*   *   *

Lila Fessmire stayed in Buford exactly two more days following the afternoon she and Elba Rae disagreed over the history of who was allowed and encouraged and who was not allowed or encouraged to enter the Miss Honeysuckle Pageant, during which discussion Lila Fessmire had disclosed instead that her daughter was in the family way and that Lila could not be expected to devote fulltime her attention to the matters of sorting out Ethel Maywood's belongings since she was desperately trying to get the announcement of a forthcoming wedding initiated.

Elba Rae Van Oaks empathized with the dilemma her sister faced and agreed with all sincerity that a wedding was called for under the circumstances, and she concurred the situation did not warrant a prolonged engagement. But even though she finally understood the reasons behind Lila's neglect of her responsibilities in Buford since the late Ethel had surrendered, she couldn't help but feel she was getting the short end of the stick.

A tangible reminder arrived in the mailbox three days after Lila left, the formal invitation letting Elba Rae know that Mr. and Mrs. G. Duane Fessmire were requesting the honor of her presence at the marriage of their daughter, Charity Luanne, to Mr. Skippy Grinbar. Elba Rae Van Oaks wondered to herself what kind of young man presumably old enough to take on a wife and father a child would still be going by the name "Skippy," especially on something as important and everlasting as a wedding invitation. Perhaps, she thought, Lila was justified in some of her disparaging comments about the groom.

Due to the time constraints under which the wedding party was operating, Elba Rae had been informed the event would be small. Tasteful, Lila said—and appropriate, she was assured—but not at all the large scale, full out spectacle Lila's own wedding to Bucky had been. Consequently, it was up to Elba Rae to do any local announcing, and Lila had been adamant that any such announcing was to be followed by a disclaimer that the couple had opted for an intimate event to which only immediate family and just a scant few others would be invited to attend. It was within the set parameters of this makeshift script that Elba Rae Van Oaks let her first cousin and closest confidant, Hazel Burns, know not to be waiting by the mailbox for any invitation to the wedding because she wasn't getting one.

Hazel assured Elba Rae she understood and she told Elba Rae to be sure and tell Lila and Bucky she understood but decided the exclusion of an invitation to witness the actual nuptials did not excuse her from properly gifting the couple. So Elba Rae said she'd make a point to find out the name of the store hosting young Charity's bridal registry while being careful not to give even the slightest hint to the fact the bride would just as well make better use of a bassinette as she would worrying about tea cups and hand towel sets. Hazel Burns, meanwhile, had again offered to assist Elba Rae in some of the sorting and the cleaning at the late Ethel Maywood's house, and given what Elba Rae knew about the state of affairs in Birmingham, she gratefully accepted the help without the smallest dose of hesitation.

On a Wednesday in the third week of June, Elba Rae Van Oaks—as a diversion to the tediousness which had befallen the house cleaning project—decided she would instead enjoy a day of leisure and browse for a new outfit to wear to her niece's wedding that was by then mere days away. Her subconscious initially had told her it was foolish to spend good money on new clothes for the event, and if she went to the trouble to fuss over her own appearance, it was just out and out pandering to an annoying situation since the hurried up wedding represented Lila's excuse for ditching her responsibilities. A quick inventory of her closet, however, was enough to subdue her subconscious and rationalize the purchase—practical though she intended it to be—of something new to wear.

She was able to park on the Square practically in the front door of F & F Fashions. It was the middle of the day, it was hot, and Elba Rae surmised the shop might be hers alone, thereby facilitating a quick trip.

Inside, she was greeted by the shop's owner and one "F" of the F & F—Mrs. Kathleen Fike—who assured Elba Rae they'd be able to efficiently locate the perfect ensemble for the upcoming nuptials of her only niece, and would accomplish such while also promising Elba Rae's dollars would not be squandered on something she wouldn't feel appropriate to wear again to a less formal event. After a mere fifteen minutes, Elba Rae Van Oaks did, in fact, believe she was near about through. Kathleen Fike excused herself to the stock room to check the availability of a different size in the dress Elba Rae had already selected, and Elba Rae casually passed the time looking at some sleeveless blouses she'd no intention of leaving with. She looked up when she heard the jingle of the bell that hung on a string off the front door's handle, and waved at Mabel Moss.

"Kathleen will be out in a minute," Elba Rae said to her.

"No bother. I didn't really come in for anything in particular. I was on my way over to the post office and mainly just wanted to get in out of the heat for a minute. Whew!" Mabel Moss said, accompanied by a symbolic wipe of her brow.

"I know it. I heard the weatherman on TV say last night we're likely to not get a break from this for another week."

"Summer's definitely here," said Mabel. She strolled carelessly around a rack of dresses before suddenly surveying the store for other customers.

"Oh, Elba Rae, there's something I've been meaning to call you about."

Elba Rae stopped shuffling blouses to give Mabel Moss her attention, even though—because it was Mabel Moss—she felt both her legs stiffen just a bit because it would not be unheard of for Mabel Moss to have been meaning to call and ask something that wasn't necessarily any of Mabel Moss's business.

"Was that the Mhoon girl we saw talking to you at your momma's visitation?"

The seemingly unobtrusive question gave way to one leg's relaxing while the other remained stiff in case the question was merely an introduction to something else.

"It was," Elba Rae said. "It was Celeste."

"Well, I thought that's who it might be, but then Florine and I got to talking about it and we couldn't decide."

"To tell you the truth, Mabel, I didn't have any idea who she was until we went and read her name in the book. There was something a little familiar about her, but you know I've taught so many children over the years, and after I got to thinking about it, Celeste must be at least forty by now. And goodness, I don't know when it would have been that I'd seen her last."

"We were sure surprised—to see her, too. Especially at the funeral home. I wouldn't have guessed she knew Miss Ethel."

"I didn't realize she knew Momma either," replied Elba Rae as the relaxed leg got back in formation. "But then, I didn't know she'd come back to Buford for that matter. The last I ever heard of Celeste, her own momma and daddy didn't even know where she was."

Mabel Moss looked around the store again carefully as though ensuring the two of them were still alone, and she even took a step closer toward Elba Rae before speaking.

"As far as I can tell," Mabel Moss allowed, "they still don't."

Celeste Mhoon

Celeste Mhoon was never particularly photogenic, a deficiency for which no photographer could plausibly be assigned liability. It had not mattered necessarily whether the image of her was made from the miraculous kind of film where the paper peeled off a minute after exposure to reveal an instant picture, or whether the pose had been capably assembled in a controlled environment with Celeste Mhoon perched on an adjustable height stool in front of a pretty blue swirl-painted background or scene of a bucolic meadow with a distant stream—like the kinds of background customarily featured in the Member Directory of the Buford Baptist Church, the publication of which being the only occasion the adult Celeste Mhoon ever had to be professionally photographed.

Prior to distribution of the first Member Directory, the Mhoons were known to have saved and preserved all twelve pictures taken during Celeste's enrollment in the Litton County public school system, and featured prominently her framed twelfth-grade portrait with Celeste donning her graduation robe and tassel-adorned cap on the wall of their living room, circumspectly hung right over the television between the expanse of the set's v-shaped antenna that was angled so as not to block the view of Celeste while also ensuring optimal reception of their programs.

There were other assorted family mementos about the Mhoon home including, as was common among members of Buford Baptist, said photos collected via sittings arranged for purposes of publication in the directory that was updated about every seven to eight years even if the successive books mostly varied due to existing members' ages rather than from the addition of new people. The last directory Celeste Mhoon appeared in had featured her for the first time in her new contact lenses instead of the glasses with the copiously sized frames that had for so long given the young woman an unflattering aviatrix-like appearance. Celeste's father had questioned her, at first, since his knowledge of contact lenses was exclusive to their recurring expense; her mother, however, understood. Celeste was a young woman struggling to overcome plain.

The old eyeglasses went in a drawer but not much else changed. In the Young Adults Sunday school class at Buford Baptist Church, Celeste Mhoon was a spare. It hadn't been so bad when she'd first transitioned from the Senior Youth because, after all, that's what happened once you passed seventeen and became eighteen; it was the Buford Baptist way, the church's sanctified endorsement of maturity. It hadn't particularly weighed on Celeste's mind heavily when she turned twenty-five and most all in her group had achieved married couple status and started families of their own.

But when Celeste Mhoon turned thirty-one years old, she felt like the most conspicuous spare in all of Litton County, Sunday school enrollee or otherwise. She had never moved out of the house she'd grown up in, choosing instead to live with her mother and father and go diligently each morning to her teller job at the Litton County Farmers & Merchants Bank. And it wasn't as if Mr. and Mrs. Mhoon minded in the least since Celeste had always been such a good child. Never a bit of trouble out of her, they would later lament to one another and to only a few close relatives.

Celeste's sister, Cheryl Jean, didn't live in Buford because she'd married her high school sweetheart a week before he was drafted into the Army, and they lived wherever he was stationed at the time. Cheryl Jean seemed happy when they visited but looked aged beyond her years, and Celeste pretty much thought that was what having four children in six years would do to you, coupled with all the packing and unpacking they were always having to do.

Celeste dated a few times in her early twenties but never lingered in a serious involvement. Most of the boys she'd known growing up had become husbands and fathers, and the ones who hadn't just didn't seem to be interested even though she still painfully longed for a beau who would eventually indulge her wedding plans and surprise her with the plot of land he'd saved for where they'd build a brick house with a big kitchen and a stainless steel sink. It never happened for Celeste Mhoon.

She was still the same sweet child at thirty-one she'd been at eleven, but her loneliness caused the ache to intensify more and more. And even though her parents had not been completely unmindful, it was nonetheless a devastating blow to Leland and Eleanor Mhoon when their daughter teetered on fulfilling her fantasies in the most unforgiving of ways.

*   *   *

The fifth grade was a hard transition for Celeste Mhoon. She was not yet a teenager but she was old enough to experience the first phases of awareness— of how the real world could be and what it meant to be different. And it wasn't so much a feeling of being different on the inside; rather, she discovered her differences to be mostly on the outside.

Most of Celeste Mhoon's clothes had been worn originally by her older sister, Cheryl Jean—and many of those, Celeste would deduce some years later, had not exactly been new when Cheryl Jean came to possess them. It was a testament to Eleanor Mhoon's talent as a seamstress, as well as her unfailing devotion to cleanliness, that most of the wardrobe endured as long as it did. Because no matter how tatty Celeste's little dresses might have been, never were they dirty.

Not all her classmates in fifth grade that year at the Homer T. Litton Grammar School, however, marveled at Eleanor Mhoon's commitment to making certain Celeste didn't look any scruffier than she might have otherwise, given the fiscal constraints in the Mhoon household during the mid 1950s. Some of the children, in fact, thought it amusing and intermittently downright funny when Celeste Mhoon showed up at school on Thursday in the identical ensemble she'd been known to sport on Monday of the same week. Celeste's teacher observed such things as well but with the eye of a trained professional and the heart of a compassionate protector, and as one who understood there came a point in the natural life of a little girl's saddle oxford when polish should no longer be expected to triumph over scuffs.

Through the decades in her classroom at Homer T. Litton Grammar School, Elba Rae Van Oaks didn't envision she'd missed much. She'd seen bright articulate girls she imagined would be nurses and future teachers, and smart boys she confidently knew would reach greatness in life. And she'd wrestled to teach the less shining ones she reluctantly but surely knew would work the fields when they graduated, if not before, married to young women to whom motherhood would come way too soon.

She'd seen shy children who quivered when called upon and boisterous ones who never seemed to lose their enthusiasm, even if she did some days just wish they'd be quiet. Or absent.

A few children of means (such as that was) in Buford attended Homer T. Litton Grammar School but Elba Rae was well aware others went home in the afternoon to hardship and perhaps even squalor. It wasn't that hard to figure out even if clothing wasn't clue enough; Elba Rae could tell right off during the first few weeks of the school year, just after she'd had sufficient time to observe the children in the cafeteria.

Elba Rae wasn't sure exactly where the Mhoon family fit into to the Buford standard of the monetary spectrum but knew it was obviously toward the bottom. She knew of no one who'd been inside the Mhoon home, which was remote and invisible from the gravel road even in the winter—much less in the summer when the area immediately beyond the battered mailbox where the school bus stopped looked like nothing more than a mosquito-inhabited thicket shared with ticks and other untold vermin.

It was barely into the first month of school the year Celeste Mhoon was in the fifth grade when Elba Rae Van Oaks observed the child to be sitting at the lunchroom table one day without a napkin. Without her cutlery, and without her tray. Without a lunch.

"What's the matter, honey? Where's your lunch?" she asked Celeste.

Elba Rae assumed the reason and had no desire to embarrass the child, but needed to confirm. So when the little girl told her teacher she'd forgotten her lunch money, her teacher gingerly took her by the arm and led her to the line where the other children were in formation. Elba Rae nodded to the cashier at the end of the modest row of steam tables and stainless steel railings, then said to the child, "It's okay, honey. You can bring extra tomorrow."

Into the third month of the school year, Elba Rae had forgone the nodding gesture in lieu of discretely handing Celeste Mhoon the necessary coins once inside in the cafeteria on days Elba Rae suspected the child was again without her lunch money, though by then it was obvious there was less wrong with the child's memory than was amiss with the Mhoons' finances.

By the first week of January and until the end of the school year when thereafter the girl would pass down the hall and into the care of a sixth grade teacher, Elba Rae Van Oaks maintained and funded a separate coin purse within her own pocketbook of which Celeste Mhoon was sole beneficiary. It haunted Elba Rae at night that year—most often while she was frying a chicken for Fettis or slicing him a second piece of chess pie—to imagine there wasn't anyone standing off to the side of the Mhoons' kitchen table poised and ready to hand little Celeste the coins she needed to have supper.

As sincere and genuine as was Elba Rae's concern, however, it was inevitable the subsequent crops of students occupying the desks in her classroom—each with their own set of quirks and needs and circumstances—would lessen the worry Elba Rae Van Oaks had about one little girl among them. She knew, without doubt, that despite what might pass as tribulation to adults, the children somehow mostly overcame and turned out all right; people had been doing it for decades, and without the benefit of her intervention.

Sometimes when the high school students would pass her elsewhere on the shared campus, they'd say, "Hey, Miss Elba Rae" and Elba Rae would simply say "Hey, now" back because more times than not, even when she could mentally connect them to a particular family of students she'd taught in the past, she didn't always remember their precise first names. And there eventually came a time when "Hey, now" was all Elba Rae had to offer Celeste Mhoon.

*　　　*　　　*

In the winter of 1974, Elba Rae Van Oaks was still teaching fifth grade in the same room at Homer T. Litton Grammar School (and still occasionally sponsoring someone's lunch) while Celeste Mhoon went to work every day at the Farmers & Merchants Bank. The mud still kept most outsiders from reaching the Mhoons' house way up in the woods, and young people at Buford Baptist Church were still turning eighteen and being automatically enrolled in the Young Adults class Celeste Mhoon attended on Sunday mornings, unpaired and vulnerable.

She was sitting to her mother's right on the fifth pew on the east side of the sanctuary that February, which is where she'd sat every Sunday since being old enough to leave the nursery, when Brother Lumpkin announced from the pulpit there would be a brief reception in the fellowship hall after evening services to welcome Mr. Dudley Potts as their new choir director.

Eleanor Mhoon seemed to smile slightly, and Celeste observed the wrinkles around the mouth and eyes of her mother's unmade face were becoming more pronounced. The wrinkles matched the spreading gray in her shoulder length hair that no one else sitting in the sanctuary of Buford Baptist Church with the exception of her husband and daughter necessarily knew was shoulder length because they'd never seen it down. They just saw the disappearing suggestions of brown at the peak of Eleanor's bun.

Leland Mhoon had no visible reaction to Brother Lumpkin's news and there was no reason he should have since Leland Mhoon did not attend the evening services. Eight o'clock was entirely too late to be getting in home from church when he had cows expecting to be milked at four on Monday mornings just like they did any other day of the week. Cows were just like that, he'd often told Eleanor. They didn't know a thing about the Sabbath. Celeste gazed past her mother's accepting expression and noted her daddy was stoic as usual. His beard was snow white except for a small splattering of gray at the sideburns, which he trimmed every Sunday morning before putting on the same brown suit.

The Pottses were not native Bufordians. They had migrated to Litton County two years prior when the school board hired Mr. Dudley Wayne Potts to teach music history and appreciation at the Walnut Hills High School. Donna Potts was a housewife and took care of the couple's two little girls, ages eleven and seven.

They had joined Buford Baptist Church through transfer of letter and were unassuming members save for Dudley Potts's participation in the choir. He was extraordinarily musically inclined, the rest of the choir observed right off, and his sturdy tenor voice—which seemed to defy his barely five foot six inch frame—lent itself well to the special solos he was allowed from time to time.

Brother Lumpkin made the announcement of Dudley Wayne Potts's acceptance of the choir director duties with enthusiasm albeit with sensitivity toward Miss Marjorie Whittlehurst. Miss Marjorie had only recently stepped down from serving as organist and choir director herself, a position she'd held at Buford Baptist for just one month shy of thirty-five years. Brother Lumpkin had wanted to combine the reception celebrating Mr. Potts's appointment with an official retirement gathering to thank Miss Marjorie for her selfless decades of devotion and service. But she'd declined. Brother Lumpkin proclaimed she was being modest as had always been her demeanor. Marjorie Whittlehurst, on the other hand, just preferred not to dwell on the events which predicated her sudden decision to abdicate.

The evolution had come just two weeks earlier and only hours after church was over that Sunday. Until then, Marjorie Whittlehurst had not let herself think her age was a factor in effectively producing single-handedly all special music provided at Buford Baptist Church. No one had complained, after all. Not that she knew of. The choir loft had a few vacant spaces and she wished more members would commit the time and their talents to singing, but she had never entertained the notion their lack of participation bore any connection to her diminishing capacity to play the organ and lead the music.

That revelation had sadly come to her right there in front of the congregation she so loved, perched as she always was atop a green velveteen pillow with the tie straps that kept it from sliding off the organ bench when she mounted it to play—adding just enough height to enhance her overall view of the choir loft while still enabling her feet to reach the organ's pedals. To the untrained observer, Marjorie Whittlehurst had been the epitome of calm and grace when she played. She had never appeared nervous, and no one had ever seen her flinch in the latter years when sometimes the keys she struck weren't necessarily the same ones intended by the composer, even when the blunders caused others to cringe.

She'd begun to feel nervous, however, and especially in that last year of directing. Between the medication she took for her high blood pressure and the pill she had to remember for her thyroid, not to mention the one the doctor gave her at his suggestion to help sleep through the night, Marjorie Whittlehurst had worried some Sunday mornings that she might make a mistake.

That late January morning she'd not eaten much of her breakfast because her stomach was just too upset. She hadn't slept well even though she'd lately taken to doubling the dose of her sleep medicine, and right before preaching she'd begun to feel fluttery. It was just her nerves acting up, she had decided— something they'd done more and more by then. Once she sat down on the bench and began the organ prelude, she'd told herself, she'd get so involved in her duties she wouldn't have time to think about being fluttery.

That strategy had worked a long time for Miss Marjorie Whittlehurst.

It had even worked that January Sunday in 1974, through the prelude, the "Call to Worship," and the opening hymn. And even though she had still felt decidedly light headed all the way through the second hymn, she'd managed to faultlessly perform the music as written.

But at the point in the service when it was time for the choir to sing forth their previously rehearsed and rather placid arrangement of "For the Beauty of the Earth," Miss Marjorie Whittlehurst had unfortunately instead with open throttle impelled the organ full of "O God Our Help in Ages Past" with near about furor, in as much as Miss Marjorie Whittlehurst still had it in her at that point to do anything with furor. For an agonizing thirty seconds neither choir members nor choir director had known exactly what was going on or how best to proceed, but then each faction had chosen what they thought to be in the best interest of the other and reversed course, with Miss Marjorie fumbling to open up and play the "For the Beauty of the Earth" music while the choir had altered the program and begun spontaneously singing "O God Our Help in Ages Past," a considerable feat since Miss Marjorie Whittlehurst had been the only person in the loft with an actual copy of that sheet music. The choir had been in tune and Marjorie Whittlehurst never missed a note, yet the overall cacophony generated by the debacle was completely and totally horrid. Into the first verse, Miss Marjorie had stopped playing the organ all together and just given the choir their familiar nod, directing them to sit down.

By the time evening services dismissed that night, everyone had pretty much known Miss Marjorie Whittlehurst had played her last service and directed her last choir although she didn't officially notify Brother Lumpkin until the next morning after she'd slept on the decision.

Dudley Wayne Potts had been the obvious choice to replace the retiring septuagenarian. He was already a member of the church choir, had a beautiful voice himself, was trained in music appreciation, and benefited from youth and vigor—two qualities the former director had decidedly been lacking for quite the while. And it hadn't impeded the selection process any that Dudley Wayne Potts had begun putting the bug in Brother Lumpkin's ear the day he joined the church.

Celeste and Eleanor Mhoon mingled with the congregation that Sunday evening in the fellowship hall to formally welcome Mr. Dudley Potts as their church's new choir director. The refreshment committee had put out a delightful variety of store-bought cookies and cupcakes, complemented by the contents of a family-sized can of mixed nuts for those who desired to get the sweet out before dispensing from the big silver urns either a cup of full strength Folgers or decaffeinated Sanka. Eleanor Mhoon opted for the Sanka since even though she was used to staying up a little later than Leland, she still made a habit of retiring fairly early since she was expected in the kitchen to serve breakfast upon his return from milking. Celeste Mhoon didn't care for coffee, regardless of bedtime considerations, and chose to nibble on a Pecan Sandie without benefit of a beverage.

"We're looking forward to hearing your music, Dudley," Eleanor Mhoon said politely, even though change was not necessarily welcomed or embraced by most members of Buford Baptist Church. But since Eleanor Mhoon couldn't exactly tell the new choir director she was still distressed over the pitiful conclusion to Miss Marjorie Whittlehurst's thirty-five years of devotion, she just sipped on her Sanka and delivered a justifiable fib.

"Thank you, Miss Eleanor. I appreciate your support. I know it's going to be a big adjustment for most folks to look up in the choir loft on Sunday mornings and not see Miss Marjorie sitting at that organ bench, but I'm going to do everything I can to carry on her good work."

Whether due to apparent humility and graciousness, or more just the elegant speaking manner he possessed, Dudley Potts sounded sincere. Eleanor smiled back at him. He then directed his attention toward Celeste, who was trying discretely to brush some Pecan Sandie crumbs from her blouse.

"One of the things I've been thinking about since Brother Lumpkin asked me to take this on," he said, "is how I might encourage more people to join the choir. Our numbers have kind of dwindled since I've been at the church, and we could use some new voices."

Celeste Mhoon swallowed the last of her cookie and gave her blouse one more quick brush.

"Have you ever considered joining the choir, Celeste?"

"Me?"

"Yes. Do you like to sing?"

"Well ..." His question suddenly made her nervous, which prompted her to begin the brushing again although, clearly, all traces of Sandie dust had been knocked to the floor.

"I sang in the youth choir when I was a kid."

"Was that fun for you?"

"Well," Celeste reflexively looked at her mother before answering. "Yeah. It was fun."

"They were so sweet," Eleanor Mhoon said. "One of my favorite pictures of Celeste from when she was a little girl is one they took at the rehearsal for their Bible School program. Back then they wore little white robes—not those light blue ones they're wearing now—and I used to keep them all washed and ironed."

"Well, we don't have little white robes in the adult choir but I imagine we have a black one that'll fit you. What do you say?"

"Oh, I don't know, Mr. Potts. I haven't sung in years."

"And we won't even make your momma wash the choir robes this time."

Eleanor Mhoon laughed out loud. The abrupt conclusion of Marjorie Whittlehurst's tenure notwithstanding, the new choir director was witty if not just out and out charming.

"How about this?" Dudley Potts continued. "Brother Lumpkin didn't mention it yet, but I want to present a cantata for Easter service this year."

"A cantata?" asked Eleanor.

"Yes, ma'am. You know, it's an extensive piece of music with multiple movements. The one I'm thinking about for Easter will take about forty-five minutes to perform. But more importantly, it'll take quite a few additional voices from what we currently have as choir members if we want to do it justice. So I'm going to invite—and hopefully not have to beg—people who aren't in the regular choir to consider joining just for the cantata. Would you do that, Celeste?"

"Just for the cantata?"

"For the cantata, but hopefully after it's over, you'll decide you want to be a full time member of the choir."

"That sounds nice, Celeste," her mother said as an endorsement.

"Just think about it," he said. "Brother Lumpkin will make an announcement from the pulpit next Sunday so we can begin to weigh interest and participation. But be thinking about it."

"Okay," Celeste said with a smile. "I will."

"Good," he said. "Now I'd better get over here and speak to some more potential members." He nodded politely at the women and walked away.

"He seems like a nice young man," Eleanor Mhoon remarked, as she sipped the last drop of coffee from a thick ceramic cup. "I'm glad you told him you'd sing in the choir."

"Well, just the cantata."

"It wouldn't hurt you to sing in the regular choir, too, Celeste. It's a way to serve the Lord."

Celeste Mhoon watched Mr. Dudley Wayne Potts repeat his campaign to a group of two men and one woman across the room. "Maybe," she said.

Marjorie Whittlehurst did not attend the reception for her replacement at Buford Baptist Church, choosing instead to stay home and watch the "Columbo" movie on TV although she dozed off before Mr. Peter Falk ever got his chance to unravel the crime and expose the culprit. Celeste Mhoon, on the other hand, had a difficult time waiting for sleep to come that evening. She didn't know exactly why, then. But the revelation was not long coming.

*　　　*　　　*

Celeste Mhoon could never deny the attraction between them had been strong and it had been instant, born though it was of an innocent encounter in the fellowship hall over a Pecan Sandie and simple chitchat. Perhaps it was the intense and prolonged rehearsals necessitated by the Easter cantata or an eventuality that would have come to fruition regardless; no one really ever knew. But by the time it was over, the relationship between choir director and singer was undeniable—even if still unspoken.

Reviews for the Easter cantata were overwhelmingly glowing after it was finally presented on the fourteenth of April, and even Marjorie Whittlehurst was quite moved by the enhanced choir's performance under the direction of Mr. Dudley Potts, so much so she nearly offered him praise directly. It was obvious the congregation had accepted the transition, and their acceptance, in turn, gave her a sense of peace she'd not known since the morning "For the Beauty of the Earth" got tangled up with "O God Our Help in Ages Past."

Dudley Potts, meanwhile, seemed to revel in the fact that some of the temporary cantata recruits chose to upgrade their status to permanent choir members, a net gain of five; Celeste Mhoon, however, was not among them. She didn't know then hers was an absence that distracted Dudley more than the rest of the post-cantata defectors combined.

He approached her after services on the first Sunday in May as she stood on the lawn in conversation with her mother, Eleanor, and Mrs. Mabel Moss, making it mainly just a listening on Celeste's part since Eleanor and Mabel were doing plenty of talking.

"Ladies," he said to the group as soon as he'd sufficiently encroached.

"Hello, Dudley," said Eleanor Mhoon.

"Dudley, that was a beautiful piece the choir did this morning."

"Thank you, Miss Mabel."

"Wasn't it though?" Eleanor agreed. "I don't when I've heard the choir sound as good."

There was at once a suggestion of discomfort among the group.

"Oh, I don't mean that the way it sounds," Eleanor said. "I just meant, well, since you've gotten so many new people to join."

"Yes, ma'am, I understand. Each individual voice helps." Everyone smiled in relief and seemed to accept Eleanor Mhoon's statement in appropriate context.

"But you know, that doesn't mean I wouldn't still welcome more people in the choir." He looked directly at Celeste Mhoon.

"I was kind of hoping you would have stayed with us after the cantata."

"You know, I said the same thing, Dudley."

"Oh, Momma, I told you I just needed to take a little break and then I'd think about it."

That was what Celeste Mhoon said to her mother in front of Mabel Moss and Mr. Dudley Wayne Potts that Sunday afternoon standing on the lawn of the Buford Baptist Church, because she'd not even allowed herself—not while alone in the break room of the Farmers & Merchants Bank or while driving to and from work nor even while lying in the dark at night in the isolated privacy of her own bedroom—to admit she'd found it increasingly unsettling to attend cantata practice by the time the music was performed on Easter. She was a grown woman and too old to succumb to the upsetting commotion of a crush, but that didn't begin to compare with the shame of allowing herself to have adulterated thoughts about a man who could never know the effect he'd had upon her.

"I was afraid you might still feel that way," Dudley Potts said to her. "Which is why I was wondering if there's any way I could enlist you to help with a new music ministry I want to start."

"A what?" asked Celeste, completely unprepared for any repeat of their association.

"It would be working with the children," he continued.

"The children!" Mabel Moss and Eleanor Mhoon exclaimed simultaneously.

"Children?" Celeste Mhoon chorused.

"Yes, well, Brother Lumpkin and I have been talking about what kind of activities we might be able to come up with for them now that summer vacation is about here—which means I'll have more time too of course while I'm not teaching—and I told him I wanted to do something they'd really want to participate in. You know, something we could all have fun with."

"Like children's choir?"

"Well, not exactly. Something with music, certainly, but not just gathering the children together in a rote assemblage of another youth choir."

Dudley Wayne Potts then began to expound upon the concept he'd already shared with Brother Lumpkin wherein he intended to incorporate musical selections about biblical characters with his personal love of hand puppetry to create Buford Baptist's own Puppets of Praise. The innovative program would involve the children singing but would also certainly necessitate adult participation to prepare for and stage the productions.

Brother Lumpkin, Dudley told Celeste just so she'd know, was absolutely delighted with the idea and was confident Dudley would be able to solicit enough cooperation to make it a success, much as he had with the Easter cantata. In fact, he already had aspirations of expanding the ministry beyond the campus of Buford Baptist to patients in the sick children's ward of Litton County Memorial Hospital, the long-term and oft-forgotten residents of the Restful Haven Care Home, and possibly even some neighboring congregations, if a puppet show could be integrated into their preference of services of course.

"For some reason," Dudley said, "the first idea that came to mind was the story of Zacchaeus."

"Climbing the tree?" mused Celeste.

"Right. We can act out the entire scene of him trying to see Jesus in the crowd, and then the children could sing the song. You know—I'm sure you must have sung it as a child. 'Zacchaeus was a wee little man and a wee little man was he. He climbed up in the sycamore tree for the Lord he wanted to see.'"

Celeste Mhoon broke out in a big grin. "Oh, sure. We used to sing it in Sunday school."

"Well, that's just one of them. We can have an Adam and Eve, and Noah, and Jonah, and even a whale. But that might take two hands!"

They both laughed together.

"That's such an interesting hobby," Mabel Moss said with regard to Dudley Potts's theretofore undisclosed affinity for spiritual hand puppetry before ultimately excusing herself from the group under the guise of attending to a slow-roasting chicken in her range at home. Celeste Mhoon felt a mild shock at the realization she'd for a moment forgotten her mother and Mabel Moss were even still standing there.

*   *   *

Eleanor Mhoon told her husband Leland all about the Puppets of Praise in the truck on the way home from church before Celeste had the notion to mention it, endorsing the project wholeheartedly because, as it turned out, Eleanor Mhoon had every intention of volunteering to help sew up the puppets on her machine and offer whatever hand stitching might be necessary, for which it was known she had quite the flair.

It delighted Celeste to witness her mother's enthusiasm since there was not anything outwardly envious about Eleanor Mhoon's life, yet Celeste knew Eleanor's gusto would compromise any potential resistance she might have thought about to offer as an excuse not to join the troupe. Dudley Potts made Celeste tense in a manner no man ever had. But she had genuinely enjoyed singing in the cantata, and coaching the children and helping to put on puppet shows sounded like fun, especially if her own mother was going to be involved. Before the truck carrying the three together in its cab got all the way up the dirt path to the house, Celeste Mhoon dismissed any contemplation of declining.

Within weeks Eleanor Mhoon was busy sewing, and Leland Mhoon allowed as to wouldn't it be helpful if he were to construct pieces for the puppet stage in an easy-to-assemble fashion out in the barn, and when everyone agreed it would, he, too, had a Puppets of Praise related job.

Celeste helped the children practice their songs while also honing the skills necessary to effectively operate not just one but sometimes two active puppets at a time, depending upon the demands of the particular story being told. During the lesson of the Garden of Eden, Celeste was both Adam and

Eve while Dudley Potts's hand gave life to the serpent—a bit of staging that necessitated their being on their knees together behind the plywood wall Leland Mhoon had sawed and painted in his barn. But after several rehearsals and two presentations at the Bible School program and to the patients at the Restful Haven Care Home, Celeste was decidedly more comfortable with Dudley Potts and much less concerned about any repercussions from her infatuation with him.

Most of the old people at Restful Haven Care Home seemed to like the puppets as much as the children did when they were utilized in the youth ministry, and the fact they were singing puppets always created a special element of surprise, which generally invoked delight with the occasional exception of a patient who just didn't think it was a puppet's prerogative to sing—even if it generally was about Jesus. But the troupe's popularity soon spread throughout Litton County, and barely a week went by absent an invitation from another congregation or at least the parents of a child planning a birthday party with a theme more righteous than the average cartoon character or clown had to offer. Celeste Mhoon found herself engrossed.

Celeste's mood at the bank noticeably changed. Though always cheerful and thoughtful with her clients at the teller window, she became more outgoing and confident—a manner which didn't escape the bank manager, who in July promoted Celeste to a customer service position in the lobby. It perhaps wasn't a monumental decision on the part of an unsuspecting manager. But for the little girl within still hiding the scars of an impoverished childhood and living in the disappointments of unrealized womanhood, it was yet another awakening.

Leland Mhoon's routine was generally undisturbed by anything except weather or a sick cow, but Eleanor Mhoon noticed a change in their daughter that summer as well. Celeste had always been frugal with her money; her parents had taught her to be, and there wasn't much in Buford proper to squander money on anyhow. Celeste had saved up nearly half the price of the used Ford Pinto she drove to work before taking advantage of a small employee discount at the Farmers & Merchants to borrow the balance, which she'd paid on time and early most of the time. But Eleanor quickly recognized when Celeste began to expand her wardrobe. Not with anything flashy or bordering on suggestive, but certainly conspicuous enough to a mother who decided it was to be expected due to Celeste's new position at work. When

Eleanor mentioned it in passing to her husband, Leland Mhoon said he was proud of Celeste and quickly left the room because he feared getting choked up and showing emotion in front of his wife.

One night following a telephone call Dudley Potts placed to the Mhoon home—the purpose of which was expressed as exploratory as Dudley Potts was considering introduction of a new sequence he feared might be controversial whereby the Puppets of Praise would depict The Last Supper—Celeste Mhoon was especially restless.

She discussed the proposal with Eleanor, whose buy-in was crucial considering the number of new puppets to sew, but she knew her mother's passion for the undertaking would not match her own. Leland Mhoon had retired at his normal hour and Eleanor soon turned out the lights in the living room and retreated to the bedroom as well. But Celeste was anxious, and the thought of sleep seemed farfetched.

Quietly and without bothering to leave a note, she eased the front door closed behind her and got into the car. She drove slowly down the path and to the gravel road before eventually maneuvering over to Highway 53 with no destination in mind.

Celeste rolled the window all the way down so that her hair blew wildly, and when she recognized the song playing on the Prattville station the Pinto's AM radio picked up on clear nights, she increased the volume and sang along with Miss Helen Reddy in her cantata-best soprano voice the lyrics she could almost allow herself to believe were written for her.

"I am strong," Celeste Mhoon sang out. "I am invincible. I am woman!"

* * *

Miss Marjorie Whittlehurst had tried many things over the years to aid her vision while driving, which was made unduly challenging by the low-sitting nature of the bench seat in her Dodge Polara. She had discretely purchased from Buford Furniture Sales two throw pillows that offered comfort but compressed too much under her weight to serve a purpose. She then switched to the prior year and out-of-date *Buford and Greater Litton County* telephone directory but discovered that while the book did elevate her on the Polara's seat to a level unattainable by the two throw pillows combined, its inflexible firmness usually resulted in a soreness if the trip was of any significant duration.

The compromise was more or less a solution stumbled upon strictly by accident, because it was pure happenstance that led Marjorie Whittlehurst to her treasure on a Monday afternoon when all she'd set out to do was pay her bill at the Litton County Power & Light out on the highway—near but on the opposite side about a third of a mile down from Buford Memorial Funeral Home. The utility company serving the entire community was thoughtful enough every month when they sent the bill to include an envelope with their address already printed on it to facilitate remittance of payment through the postal service, but since their generosity stopped with the envelope and did not also include a stamp, Marjorie Whittlehurst found it economically negligent to mail her check when she and the Dodge were both willing and able to present it to them in person.

The Power & Light facility was constructed in the mid 1960s and contained adequate parking on any average day of the week, and there were many times when Marjorie Whittlehurst was able to land in the space adjacent to the front door where nothing more than a hedge of neatly trimmed boxwood separated her from the customer service entrance. Perhaps spoiled, in fact, by the usual ease of paying her bill in person, Miss Marjorie was perturbed upon approach that Monday when she observed the customer parking lot was completely blocked off by a congruent row of bright orange cones, and that the only vehicle moving about in front of the building was some nature of a steamroller smoothing out what appeared to be new asphalt. Frustrated and somewhat grumpy as a result, Miss Marjorie obediently complied with the temporary signage pointing patrons to the parking area of the business next door.

Buford Tractor Sales was set back from the highway a little further than the utility company, allowing for use of its ample road frontage to display an assortment of what looked to Marjorie Whittlehurst to be all shiny new machinery, even though it would have been obvious to any legitimate consumer—farmer or not—that one of the combines and two of the tractors were refurbished models.

She managed to park the Dodge in a space that would have been most convenient had she set out that afternoon to shop for a tractor or a riding lawnmower or maybe a plow, as she found herself facing the tall front window of the showroom. Marjorie Whittlehurst had never paid much attention to the business before and perhaps until then not even cared that Buford Tractor Sales was, in fact, Litton County's only authorized John Deere dealer; yet, that day it was impossible not to notice the big vinyl banner hanging in the window advertising twenty percent off on accessories because the ad featured a proportionately sized image of a yellow seat cushion trimmed in green piping with a graceful green deer in its center. Miss Marjorie did not readily make the connection between the sensation of the phonebook suddenly feeling as much like concrete under her posterior as it ever had. She knew later, however, the unforeseen detour to the panorama of the window was intervention of a divine nature.

She sat in her car and studied the banner for a few minutes, trying to imagine the actual size of the cushion, and when her curiosity could stand it no longer, she took a deep breath, picked up her pocketbook, and strolled into the store.

The showroom housed a much greater variety of products than Marjorie Whittlehurst would have ever guessed from just driving by the outside on occasion to pay her light bill or go to a visitation at the funeral home. The remainder of vehicles and major equipment inventory not parked out front was lined up in the couple of acres behind the building, but inside a customer would find all sorts of things to maintain his machinery or, as she was about to find out, make it more pleasant to operate.

The young man noticed Miss Marjorie right away and although he recognized her, assumed she was probably there to seek directions or perhaps to use the telephone, because he did not suspect she was there to look at fan motors or test drive a cotton picker. Miss Marjorie, likewise, knew the young man to be Mr. Doug Simpson, who had once worked the fields himself before the Farmers & Merchants Bank relieved him of his land after a succession of unfortunately unproductive growing seasons rendered him unable to satisfy the mortgage.

"Afternoon, Miss Marjorie," Doug Simpson said to her cheerfully while standing with his hands clasped behind his back.

"Hello, Doug."

"How are you doing today?"

"I'm just fine, thank you for asking. And you?"

"Couldn't be any better," he said with conviction.

"Well, I wonder if you could help me with something."

"Absolutely. You in the market for a tractor are you?" He laughed out loud and looked at her as if he'd expected at the least a smile in return, but

Marjorie Whittlehurst had never had much patience for sarcasm, nor was she especially renowned for witty banter.

"Heavens no," she said without a hint of appreciation. Doug Simpson's grin quickly disappeared.

"Yes, ma'am. What can I do for you today?"

So she told him—how she'd just been trying to get next door to pay her bill at the Litton County Power & Light but how their parking lot was such a mess and Doug Simpson said, "Yes, ma'am" in agreement because of course he knew what was going on next door since he'd been there all day and all, and then she told him how she'd noticed the big sign in the window and asked if he could approximate the measurements of the yellow cushion because she'd reckoned since it was made to fit a tractor it most likely would overwhelm the seat of her Dodge, but she was so anxious to know for sure.

When he finally got the chance, Doug Simpson said, "Well, why don't we just take one out there and try it on for size, Miss Marjorie?" He left her briefly to go pull one of the seat cushions from the stockroom.

It was evident from the look on her face as soon as she got up in the car that the sale was as much as complete. She gripped the steering wheel with both hands and methodically moved her right foot from the accelerator to the brake pedal and back again. Only then did Marjorie Whittlehurst smile at Doug Simpson. She was so excited, in fact, the original destination of her trip that day completely slipped her mind until she reached her home and discovered the Litton County Power & Light envelope still resting on the front seat beside her. The oversight had made for just the right excuse to break in the new cushion the next morning when Miss Marjorie sat tall and proud as she drove her Dodge to a reopened parking lot next door to Buford Tractor Sales, where she finally delivered her utility payment.

At Buford Styles, it was generally understood without need of any written notice in the scheduling book that Miss Marjorie Whittlehurst had a standing appointment each Saturday morning at nine o'clock because she had, after all, been in the chair of her regular operator every Saturday morning at nine o'clock for more years than some of the younger operators even knew. The resulting style of Miss Marjorie Whittlehurst's hairdo had varied over the years no more than the day of the week or the time of day of her appointment; that, also, was understood.

Buford Styles was located on the east side of the Square within easy walking distance of the Ben Franklin's dime store (should Marjorie Whittlehurst need any incidentals after getting her hair done), as well as F & F Fashions (should she have wardrobe needs). Some Saturdays she drifted into both, and some weeks she went to just one or neither.

Without fail, however, Miss Marjorie's Saturday routine had for years definitely included a stop by Buford Baptist Church on her way home from the beauty parlor. The church was quiet on Saturday mornings; Brother Lumpkin was never in his study then, and events were rare, save for the preparations of an occasional wedding. The privacy had afforded Miss Marjorie opportunity to practice on the organ straight through the following day's worship service sections—as well as the special choir music—enough times until she felt comfortable with the arrangements.

That custom had been a hard one to give up during the weeks following Marjorie Whittlehurst's resignation as organist and choir director in early 1974. She had tried lingering longer at F & F a few times, though rarely purchasing anything of note. One week she'd even wandered into Moss Hardware & Supply on the south side of the Square to look at a new deep freeze she'd considered installing in her garage before concluding such an investment was unquestionably foolish since she'd no sincere intention of stocking food in such magnitude as would overburden the freezer capacity provided by the side-by-side model she already had in the kitchen. But at least it had taken her mind off the fact she had no selections to practice and no unfamiliar song arrangements to interpret.

Along about May of that year, however, a revelation came to Marjorie Whittlehurst on a Saturday morning as her rinse-tinted hair was being teased with a comb and hand-shaped into what appeared to the other, newer operators as some type of cone structure. The epiphany startled her somewhat, to the degree her operator apologized for pulling her hair too tightly.

"Oh …" Miss Marjorie said. "You didn't pull. I was just thinking about something, hon."

A broad and satisfying beam came over her face when she realized maybe it wasn't the practicing she missed so much as it was just the playing part and hearing the sound of the music filling and echoing in the solitude of the empty sanctuary. Because in that one hour on Saturdays, Marjorie Whittlehurst's world had been reduced to nothing more than heavenly melodies and a marvelous closeness to God that was definitely diluted by the presence of a full congregation on Sunday mornings.

To that end, Marjorie Whittlehurst decided right there in her chair at Buford Styles that nothing was to stop her from taking her former seat on the organ bench, assuming the Potts boy hadn't out and out done away with the green velveteen pillow, and playing at will on Saturdays just as she'd done for years. It would, after all, also serve to keep her technical skills intact should Dudley Potts have an emergency or—at the special request of a member's family—she be asked to play for a funeral service once more. Thereafter, Miss Marjorie's Saturday visits to F & F were fewer; she didn't walk through the Ben Franklin's unless she wanted something specific, and she was not known to have ever been seen again at Moss Hardware & Supply on the south side of the Square.

There was never any pretense that Marjorie Whittlehurst was sneaking into her church on Saturdays to play the organ. She parked the big Dodge in plain sight at the side door and as a courtesy, she had even mentioned to Brother Lumpkin how much it meant to her to have access to the organ, although she insinuated his discretion would be appreciated and he had obliged her request. Eventually, she even secretly delighted in the infrequent times a member of the flower committee might drop by to place an arrangement at the altar for Sunday services as it was, albeit brief and small, an audience once more. But more often than not, the church was hers.

She rarely played more than five or six hymns although the number of verses of each sometimes varied and tended to be more if one of the committee members did just happen to be there delivering some ferns or a vase full of roses. When it was over she'd untie the green cushion and return it to what she liked to think was its secret hiding place inside the organ bench, a haven obviously not breached by her successor. And then she would happily motor home in a cloud of contentment.

Once resumed, the return of the Saturday schedule satisfied Miss Marjorie for months. On Sunday mornings, she sat in her pew with the rest of the civilians and listened to the choir as a spectator, hoping the coy grin that occasionally came over her face when she looked at the organ wasn't suspect.

The sun was still strong and warming on the mid-October Saturday when Marjorie Whittlehurst, perched regally on the green deer, taxied across the empty parking lot of Buford Baptist Church—empty, that was, save for the vehicle resting in the spot usually awaiting Miss Marjorie and the Polara. Had it been unfamiliar to her, she likely would have gone on home to return later or perhaps not at all that day, but because she recognized the little light blue car as the one driven by the young Mhoon girl, she did not consider it intrusive to enter the church as usual and proceed with her organ playing. Hopefully, the Mhoon girl was helping out on the flower committee and would soon be gone. She pulled up next to the Pinto and got out.

*   *   *

Celeste Mhoon had not come to the church that Saturday in her occasional capacity as helper on the flower committee, and Dudley Wayne Potts, certainly, had no horticultural purpose for being there either. They stood inside together in conversation that was, by then, natural to Celeste. Her confusion and angst had somehow managed to balance itself with an acceptance of her circumstances, and she was able to take pleasure in her puppet work and simply enjoy it for what it was.

"All clean," she said ever so softly, yet clearly audible within the acoustics of the empty choir loft. She'd been holding a box that she then bent down to place on the floor. "I didn't think you were here."

"I parked my truck around at the kitchen door."

"Why?" she asked.

"I," he sort of stuttered, "I just did. People are so …"

"What?"

He seemed uncertain of continuing. "Interested is the word, if I'm being polite about it."

Celeste looked at him doubtfully. "You mean like nosey?"

"Yes," Dudley Potts agreed. "Nosey about things they don't understand and would be better off leaving alone."

"Then," Celeste's pause was more than hesitation. It was as though to continue would have been opening a door and exposing a truth that could never again be concealed and put out of plain view.

"Go on," he said. "What were you going to say?"

She turned away from him, and looked toward the back of the choir loft and the lifeless organ.

"Tell me, Celeste." Dudley put his hand to her chin and tenderly turned her head so she was looking at him.

"No one else is coming to rehearse today, are they?"

"No," he confirmed. "Did you really think they were?"

"I …"

"What, Celeste? Just say it. Say it!"

"Oh, Dudley. I hoped they weren't! Is that what you want to hear?"

"I want you to speak your heart."

"Then it's true!" she said with a release of exasperation. "I didn't want to let myself think it, or hope it was true. But I wanted it to just be you when I got here today. I wanted us to be alone!"

"Oh, Celeste, I want it too!" His attempt to kiss her was met with immediate opposition.

"But Dudley, how can we? It's wrong."

"Why is it wrong, Celeste? If it's what we both want."

"Because of her. Donna. What about her?"

"Celeste," he said, lowering his voice to the decibel of a near whisper. "I can't even force myself to feel like this has anything to do with Donna. Okay, maybe it should—but all I can think about is you. You're all I've been able to think about since the first night of cantata practice. I know it's wrong. I know it is. But I can't help it. God help me," he said while looking up, as if to infer God was standing on a rafter overlooking the choir loft. "But it's true. And I don't know what that means for Donna."

"How, how," Celeste stammered, "how can we be together like this?"

Dudley Potts slowly framed Celeste's face with the palms of his hands and held her still without resistance. "I don't know what the future holds, Celeste. I only know now. You, and I. And I know one thing."

He stopped and they stared at one another as intently as Celeste Mhoon had ever been stared at.

"What?" she asked.

"I'm a man, Celeste. I have my needs."

She offered no repeat of the previous opposition when he grabbed her and pulled her into a tight embrace, so quickly and forcefully she unconsciously kicked over the small cardboard box where the Puppets of Praise lived when their insides weren't inhabited by a hand. Over time, the little creations had become dirty from use and in a couple of instances were missing a button or other adornment comprising the individual costume. Eleanor Mhoon had spent the better part of a week's spare time painstakingly hand cleaning and repairing all the characters in preparation for the choir's upcoming visit scheduled at the Presbyterian church over in the Walnut Hills community.

When Dudley Potts had planned the rehearsal, his heart had told him to notify all members of the Puppets of Praise troupe. But after telephoning the Mhoon house and leaving the message with Miss Eleanor, who had gladly assured him she'd let Celeste know about the practice on Saturday right before letting him know she'd managed to get the Kool-Aid stain out of Jonah's hair and that maybe it wasn't the best idea to let the children actually play with the puppets themselves, Dudley Potts had been absolutely stricken—with doubt and with guilt, and with a desire for Celeste Mhoon that when combined resolved him unwilling to stop the events he was possibly and secretly hoping to set in motion.

In the cool of the choir loft his heart pounded as it seemed irrefutable that Celeste Mhoon reciprocated his feelings. He kissed her like she had never been kissed, and when she kissed him back she felt fire race through her veins for the first time in her life. She kept her eyes closed as he slowly led her through the door in the back of the choir loft.

*   *   *

As a rule, Marjorie Whittlehurst let herself in through the door that opened into a small vestibule at the rear of the sanctuary. It was there that the week's designated greeter passed out the official program with announcements and the order of service to regular members and guests on Sunday mornings, and it was in the vestibule that Brother Lumpkin stood at the conclusion of the service to shake hands with and grin at those members and guests that didn't take advantage of a side door near the altar as an expedited means of exiting without having to shake and grin.

She looked around upon entering and expected to find the sanctuary area occupied—by the Mhoon girl or maybe by her and her mother together—and found it odd to see no one. She subconsciously touched the back of each pew on the right side of the aisle as she approached and then cautiously went up the four wide steps into the choir loft at the front of the church.

The overturned cardboard box in the floor was obviously out of place and the disorder disturbed Miss Marjorie, but before she could see to the box's content, she'd practically stepped on the lifeless figure that had been ejected. She bent over with a slight grunt and picked Zacchaeus up off the floor. It made no sense, she thought. Not any of it. But when she was suddenly distracted by a noise, she put Zacchaeus back down without even thinking.

The door in the back of the loft led to a small gathering room where the choir assembled on Sunday mornings. It was there the choir members would slip into their robes and get into the correct formation to enter the sanctuary just as the service officially began. Afterward, they filed back into the room, removed the robes, and hung them in the spacious closet built especially for their storage but that was also used to stockpile extra folding chairs utilized in the fellowship hall for special occasions like wedding receptions or Sunday school parties.

Whoever was in the church that afternoon, Marjorie Whittlehurst surmised by the sound, was in the choir room, and she would not be comfortable playing the organ unless she knew who it was. She warily stepped through the doorway.

She saw no one in the room and entertained briefly the idea that the sound she thought she'd heard was but her imagination, and she turned around to walk back out to the sanctuary. But then she heard the noise again and knew it was not of her own invention.

The door to the robe closet was open. Marjorie Whittlehurst let out a little sigh that was almost involuntary as she realized someone was obviously looking for something. Relieved, she intended just to let them know she was there as she could imagine how startling it would be to think you were alone in the church only to suddenly hear a thunderous burst of melodious air discharge from the splendid pipe organ.

So she walked over to the closet door and guardedly peeked inside. And there underneath the neatly hung choir robes in the glorious splendor of consummation lay Celeste Mhoon and Mr. Dudley Wayne Potts, the man who'd presumed to take Marjorie Whittlehurst's seat on the organ bench and lead her choir in the special music each Sabbath.

She wanted to gasp. She wanted to scream. But Marjorie Whittlehurst's throat was as devoid of moisture as the driest riverbed in all the deserts of Africa, and although her mouth was clearly gaping, no sound emitted there forth.

She instinctively clutched her heart, even if later she would not recall that she had, and took several steps backward before turning around to walk in a forwardly direction in time to narrowly avoid tripping over a music stand.

She took pause just long enough to grab hold of the door frame leading back to the sanctuary, steadying herself as her rapid breathing was already causing a mild dizziness. But the sound of commotion in the robe closet behind her—a scrambling of sorts accompanied by some muffled shrieking—jolted her into retreat.

She staggered through the door and stumbled past the cardboard box, unwittingly kicking Zacchaeus in the head so hard it popped out his left eye, which was really a recycled cuff button from an old shirt once worn by Leland Mhoon. She tottered and swaggered and clutched her heart and made little guttural sounds in her throat all the way out of the church and to the Dodge, where she climbed aboard the John Deere cushion and drove off, leaving Dudley Potts, Celeste Mhoon and one-eyed Zacchaeus in her wake.

*   *   *

Given the technology of the day, the general population of Litton County was remarkably well-informed of events taking place in their community, effected by a relay system relying on no more than chance contact in the grocery store or other random public place, and that at best required no more than use of a telephone but served to ensure that most everyone who cared to know would find out about any noteworthy incident, and they'd indeed find out quickly.

Information deemed especially significant easily transcended denominational boundaries, and it was not at all unusual that a member of the First Avenue United Methodist would know—and convey—a bulletin about a member of Buford Baptist before even all their own members had been duly notified.

Such was the case on an October afternoon in 1974 when Hazel Burns had gone into F & F Fashions on the Square in search of a new all weather coat and had immediately run into Mrs. Imogene Winnegar, whose sister Doris was a nurse out at the hospital, and had mentioned to Imogene during a brief telephone call while in the lounge on her break that she'd just encountered Marjorie Whittlehurst. Hazel Burns, in her own right, was an inexorable vessel of communication.

"Well, I don't know much news," Hazel said to her cousin Elba Rae Van Oaks on the telephone that evening. "Except they said Miss Marjorie Whittlehurst had some kind of spell this afternoon and had to go to the hospital."

"With her heart?" asked Elba Rae.

"I don't know," Hazel said. "I ran into Imogene at F & F's, and she just said Doris had seen Marjorie out at the hospital."

"Well …" Elba Rae deduced, "if she'd passed, I guess we would have heard about it."

"Yeah," agreed Hazel. "I expect you're right."

Marjorie Whittlehurst, even in her physically distressed and emotionally frenzied state after staggering, stumbling, tottering and swaggering her way out of the church, had mustered the fortitude to drive herself to the emergency entrance of Litton County Memorial Hospital whereupon she'd parked in a handicapped designated space and walked inside of her own volition. Thereafter, especially as she attempted to impart to the nurse working in the admissions window how she'd come to be feeling so compromised in the first place, Miss Marjorie had become weak, and it appeared to the nurse that collapse was imminent. So Imogene Winnegar's sister Doris personally went around to the other side of the counter and assisted Miss Marjorie to a chair until an attendant could be summoned to help hoist her onto a gurney.

Miss Marjorie frantically clawed at the oxygen-dispensing mask covering her face even as the attendant wheeling the gurney down the hall implored her to leave it on.

"I need to make a call!" she hollered at him right before the mask was repositioned over her mouth and nose.

"Just take it easy, Miss Marjorie. There'll be time to call whoever you want to just as soon as we get you checked out."

The second time she removed the mask she crumpled it up inside an impressive fist. "You need to get my preacher on the phone. Brother Lumpkin at the Baptist church parsonage. Tell him I'm here!"

Upon entering an examination room the attendant wrested the oxygen mask from Marjorie Whittlehurst's hand, straightened out the tubing, and reaffixed it to his patient.

"Tell you what I'll do," he said to her, using his most reassuring approach. "I'll go out there and let the nurse know we need to contact your clergy. But you've got to leave the oxygen on. Do we have a deal?"

Marjorie Whittlehurst nodded and eased back just slightly onto the gurney's inferior pillow. The attendant left the examination room and did indeed inform the nearest nurse he believed the patient would be much less agitated and likely more agreeable to treatment if someone could place a call to Brother Lumpkin at the Baptist church parsonage and inform him of Miss Whittlehurst's arrival at the hospital.

And so it was that an otherwise disinterested party became the conduit who within the hour brought the preacher directly to the Litton County Memorial Hospital emergency room and to the waiting bedside of Marjorie Whittlehurst. By the time Miss Marjorie concluded the report of what she'd unwittingly chanced upon in the choir robe closet, she was voluntarily installing the oxygen mask on her own face, and even asked Brother Lumpkin if he wouldn't mind helping her turn it up a little.

Bucky and Them

Garland Fessmire was in the men's room of the Sinclair station when the tragedy occurred and it haunted him for the rest of his life. It was a detail that never became any less upsetting, even after they moved to the new house.

The truth was Lila's husband, Bucky Fessmire, had not come from money—at least not from old money—but that had never stopped Lila from perpetuating and perhaps even creating the illusion in the first place that he had. His people certainly had not come from money at all, but rather acquired a respectable sum later in life after more or less rearing Bucky and his one sister in modest surroundings.

The Fessmire children grew up outside Birmingham proper in the Trussville community in a tract house built before the town was incorporated. If Trussville, Alabama, was the "Gateway to Happy Living," then the Fessmire family pretty much complied. Garland Fessmire had become suitably successful in the insurance business by the time the children were through high school, growing a small independent shop into a medium-sized one that employed two dozen other agents. It was a long, hard, and well-executed process that served the Fessmires well—if not quite in the fashion they would adopt after Bucky was grown.

Lila and Bucky's daughter, Charity, was still a baby at the time of the tragedy. It happened on a Saturday morning in early August, and had she not been running a low grade temperature, it was generally told in the eventual lore of the events that the potential loss would likely have been magnified beyond the actual loss. That being because Bucky and Lila would not have been able to make an excuse of Charity's feverish condition as the reason they weren't in the Oldsmobile with Bucky's mother and father on the way to the family reunion outside Muscle Shoals. Otherwise, it was understood their participation was not optional.

The extended Fessmire clan supported the institution of family reunions wholeheartedly, and as far as Lila Fessmire was concerned (although she never shared the opinion with anyone except perhaps her own mother), the hotter it was the more probable a Fessmire somewhere was going to want to plan one. The reunions were almost always annual events—scheduled no later than Labor Day and no sooner than July Fourth, ensuring optimal representation from all age groups of anyone who'd ever been a Fessmire or related to one by marriage.

That August in 1966, Mr. Garland Fessmire was not yet a member of the elder generation of Fessmires, as he still had two aunts and three uncles living even as his own parents were gone to glory, they being some of the older siblings in their respective families anyway. Mrs. Geraldine Fessmire had started bringing her mother, Miss Effie, to the reunions years back when Bucky and his sister were little, and her presence was expected that year, too, right up until spring when she'd tripped over the space heater cord in her bathroom and fell backward into a filled tub, where she lay semi-submerged with a broken hip for nearly a day. And everybody said after the tragedy it was just lucky Miss Effie hadn't been in the car with Garland and Geraldine, just like they'd say the tragedy could have been so much worse if Bucky and Lila and baby Charity had been along.

Geraldine Fessmire's pre-reunion duty consisted of making pimento cheese and transporting it to the designated gathering site in a large metal cooler with sufficient loaves of white bread to accommodate the expected throng. Mr. Garland Fessmire's assignment, at least in 1966 before he became a member of the elder generation of Fessmires, was to stop off in Decatur and to pick up Uncle Hubert where he resided full time at the Loving Care Convalescent Center, and generally be his escort at the event.

Uncle Hubert's mind was still remarkably sharp in 1966 even if his bladder did seem to have shrunk to the size of a walnut. He'd excused himself in his room right before Garland and Geraldine arrived to pick him up and just to be on the safe side and as a gesture of good will, he'd veered off to the restroom near the Loving Care Convalescent Center lobby on the way out to the car. Yet despite his most earnest of intents to be fully drained before getting situated in the Oldsmobile for the ride over to Muscle Shoals, he with apologies let his nephew Garland know as soon as they saw the first "Sinclair Ahead" sign on the approach to Hillsboro that he believed he might need to make a stop.

Mrs. Geraldine Fessmire was adamant she did not need to leave the car again so soon, and in a tone of voice only her husband was used to deciphering, reminded Garland Fessmire of the enormity of their pimento cheese cargo traveling in the metal cooler in the trunk, and mentioned to him it wasn't packed in a glacier which, she guessed, apparently it needed to have been had she known it was going to take them all day to get to the campground outside Muscle Shoals.

The Sinclair station was busy with late summer travelers in station wagons and big sedans and one pickup truck that was pulling a pop-up trailer. Upon the first approach to the business, it was evident there was no parking space near the side of the building where the restroom doors were clearly marked GENTLEMEN and LADIES with metal stick-on signs just below the chain's familiar dinosaur logo, so Garland Fessmire drove the Oldsmobile back around the island housing the two gasoline pumps and stopped on the far side just next to the road.

"Sorry, Uncle Hubert, but it looks like this is as close as we're going to get right now."

"It's all right, boy. I still got two legs," Hubert Fessmire reminded as he opened the back door. "Want anything while we're here, Geraldine?"

"No, thank you, Uncle Hubert," Geraldine Fessmire replied, politely and with a smile on her face.

"You sure?"

"I'm sure."

"Pack of peanuts?"

"No, thank you."

"How about a Co-cola? There's a machine yonder."

"No. Not for me."

"All right, then," Hubert said, closing the car door behind him before heading in the direction of the GENTLEMEN dinosaur, a mild shuffle to his step.

"I guess I may as well go—long as we're here," Garland Fessmire announced, as he opened his own door.

"For goodness sake," his wife said. "If all my pimento cheese is melted and not fit to eat by the time we get to the campground, don't blame me."

"Well, look at it this way," he told her. "I'd rather get there with a puddle of pimento cheese than get there with one from Uncle Hubert."

"Oh, hush up!" Geraldine Fessmire laughed with a loud cackle. "Leave the car running so I can have some air. It must be ninety-five up here."

It was the last thing she got to say, before the tragedy.

Garland Fessmire went inside the station to get the key to the men's room and then waited outside the door while Uncle Hubert trundled in first to take care of his business. As seriously as Garland took his escort responsibilities, Uncle Hubert being childless such as he was, and as much as he believed it was an honor to be of service to his elders, in that one moment—as the late morning August sun bore down on him with the only breathable air being an egregious casserole of petroleum fumes, motor oil, and the pungent aroma of ammonia mixed with urine that had wafted out as soon as Uncle Hubert opened the restroom door—Garland Fessmire did hope thereafter his uncle would just cross his legs until they got to the campground outside Muscle Shoals.

He patiently waited until at last the toilet flushed and Uncle Hubert emerged. "I think I'll go get me a Co-cola," Uncle Hubert said. "You want one?"

"No thanks, Unk," as they basically passed one another through the doorway. Garland Fessmire closed the door behind him and unzipped his fly and wondered if it ever occurred to Uncle Hubert that the continuous introduction of fluids into his system was no way to cut down on the number of times he needed to visit the restroom. Garland assumed a stance and began to relieve himself. And then he heard it.

It began with a jolting execution of the horn that played rather like a trombone right at first until it was drowned out by the squeal of rubber burning on asphalt. The succession of even those two was in and of itself sufficient to interrupt Garland Fessmire's stream, and that was before the sounds were lost in the overall blast of reverberation that occurred when the Oldsmobile was actually struck.

Instinctively, Garland Fessmire bolted from the restroom and afterward he couldn't exactly explain how it was he'd just known whatever horror was waiting outside would be his. But there, in the daylight, the world had changed. The people running in the direction of the melee seemed to do so with restricted motion like a scene from a movie, and at the outset all Garland Fessmire could do was stand there and watch them. Out of the corner of his eye, he noticed Uncle Hubert standing in the entrance to the station with a bottle of Coke in one hand, his mouth ajar; their eyes met, and then they simultaneously rushed toward the road although, of course, Garland Fessmire was mainly the one doing the rushing since Uncle Hubert's gait never really picked up, not even with the advantage of an empty bladder.

The left-side wheels of the big delivery vehicle—the ones no longer touching the earth— were still spinning vigorously, even as the driver's head materialized through the window of the cab and he began trying to lift himself out before it became evident he was too fragile and dazed to do so unassisted. Garland Fessmire would be able to recall for the rest of his life how in that instant the gas, oil, and piss stink overwhelming him just minutes earlier gave way to a sweetened bouquet of grapefruit vapors being discharged from the hundreds of shattered Fresca bottles littering the ground in the middle of a sudden fizzy river.

The scene was too bizarre to process at once even without the audio confusion of screams and shrieks and yells to one another to call for the police and then, finally, the one yell Garland Fessmire clearly distinguished that mentioned the ambulance. He stood in shock and stared at the sight. Of his Oldsmobile and, more to the point, his wife—who were both somewhere underneath the overturned truck. Amid the smoke and chaos and what was still then a possibility of carnage before them, it was Uncle Hubert who ever so discretely leaned over to his nephew and said, "Zip up your fly, boy."

*   *   *

The Fessmire Insurance Agency may not have ever been engaged in the underwriting of individual automobile policies, but that certainly didn't exclude Garland Fessmire—or his associates in the firm—from familiarity with the litigation process often taking on a life of its own following a tragedy, as it was just a byproduct of the trade. He absolutely had the wherewithal to engage legal counsel without the unneeded advice and blatant solicitations that besieged him even before Mrs. Geraldine Fessmire was upgraded from the intensive care unit and moved to a semi-private room at the Princeton Baptist hospital.

The doctors and the nurses and even one of the women whose function it was to keep the floor of Geraldine Fessmire's room freshly mopped all remarked that it was just a miracle and a defiance of medical probability and—attributed specifically and solely to the woman whose function it was to keep the floor of Geraldine Fessmire's room freshly mopped— evidence the hand of God had reached down and touched Geraldine right there in front of the Sinclair station that she wasn't out and out squashed like a pancake underneath the Fresca truck.

To be clear, Geraldine Fessmire did suffer immensely after the tragedy. Her right leg was badly broken and no amount of casting ever got it back just so again, resulting in a limp for the rest of her life that oddly gave her the appearance of someone walking on legs that varied in length. And she sustained numerous abrasions about the face and neck as a result of at least a carton's worth of Fresca bottles that crashed through the passenger window of the Oldsmobile and pelted her about the head with considerable force. But the scarring was mercifully not permanent. Her other residual condition, however, was.

None of the family realized fully the lingering effects the tragedy would have on Geraldine Fessmire until after she'd been fully discharged from the care of the doctors and the therapists who helped her with her walking again once the last cast came off. Certainly the medical staff noticed she was an especially cheerful patient, considering the pain and suffering inflicted upon her, and friends and relatives who visited oft commented on the almost anomalous spontaneity of her laughter—in the absence, sometimes, of anything the least bit funny.

But about a month after the Fessmires were deluded into finally thinking life had returned to their normalcy of before the tragedy, Garland Fessmire was convinced things would never be the same. It was at that time he not so coincidentally gave his attorney the green light to pursue monetary compensation from the bottler employing the errant delivery driver who'd undoubtedly disregarded the posted speed limit along the stretch of road passing the Sinclair station, else it wouldn't have mattered how much he lost control when he'd swerved to avoid the young couple who'd peddled out in front of him after stopping to pump air into the front tire of their tandem bicycle.

Garland Fessmire's convincing that someone should be culpable for Geraldine's damages came two weeks before Christmas when the floor nurse who worked the midnight to eight shift at the Loving Care Convalescent Center in Decatur telephoned the Fessmire home in Trussville to notify Mr. Garland Fessmire with great sadness and sympathy that his uncle, Mr. Hubert Fessmire, had expired sometime in the night, and to further inform him, as the listed next of kin, they needed to know what to do with him.

The funeral was in Russellville, birthplace of that generation of Fessmires, at the church where Uncle Hubert had received the sacrament of baptism over eighty years earlier. All of his surviving siblings managed to be in attendance although the degree of their faculties was diverse. Nieces and nephews and cousins gathered, and Garland and Geraldine Fessmire sat on the front pew.

A few anecdotal but certainly tasteful remembrances were offered by the minister, having been derived from his preparatory visit with Garland Fessmire, and the stories elicited smiles and subdued chuckles where appropriate. Geraldine Fessmire laughed aloud and louder than most and it occurred to the minister that perhaps his delivery was better than the credit to which he'd ever been given by members of his own congregation when he'd attempted the introduction of light humor into his sermons. Garland Fessmire, meanwhile, suspected all was not well with Geraldine and was relieved when the service concluded.

The family walked across the church yard and into the adjoining cemetery. After they'd all gathered and Uncle Hubert was placed at the grave, the minister recited a few concluding verses of scripture before bowing his head for the final prayer to be spoken over the remains before the burial.

"I am the resurrection and the life, says the Lord. He who believes in me, though he dies, yet shall he live, and whoever lives and believes in me will never die," the minister read, from the book of John. Geraldine Fessmire giggled.

"I know that my Redeemer lives, and that in the end he will stand upon the earth. And after my skin has been destroyed in my flesh I will see God," quoted the minister—from the book of Job. When Geraldine Fessmire laughed, her husband took her hand and nervously squeezed it in his own. But she didn't seem to notice.

The minister looked up and momentarily took his cue from Garland Fessmire that it was all right to continue. "The Lord gave and the Lord has taken away; may the name of the Lord be praised."

The minister would have then said "Amen" had the guffaw from Geraldine Fessmire not left him utterly speechless. She laughed so raucously at one point she bent over in her seat and faced the ground beneath the chair.

"Geraldine!" Garland cried out to her.

She returned her posture to an upright position. "What?" she whispered.

"What in the world has gotten into you?"

She leaned over to him so he'd hear her when she softly replied.

"What are you talking about?"

"This is embarrassing."

"I beg your pardon?"

"Amen!" the minister announced. By then, of course, word of Geraldine Fessmire's peculiar behavior was as good as out.

It was not so much she out and out denied being amused at the funeral service for Uncle Hubert as it was the fact Geraldine didn't seem to remember; not the stories in the church, the quoting at the grave—not the drive over to Russellville in the new Buick in the first place, even as much as Garland had feared her reaction when they'd passed the "Sinclair Ahead" sign.

Before the tragedy, Geraldine Fessmire had never been known to exhibit inappropriate or ill-timed behavior nor was she particularly prone to bouts of amnesia, but along with her wobbly walking she was thereafter on any given day liable to suffer from any or all. So with the sworn affidavits of medical personnel who'd been intensely involved in the case, along with those of a couple of family members and the minister from Russellville, and the photographic evidence preserved by the Hillsboro police department, there was enough momentum to convince counsel for the insurance company representing the employer of the by-then unemployed truck driver that wrecked on top of Geraldine Fessmire it would be in the best interests of all parties concerned to settle and to do so outside the presence of a seated jury.

When Garland Fessmire showed his wife the papers detailing the precise sum of money awarded to them, she laughed so hard he had to get her a Kleenex. Bucky Fessmire did not laugh, however, nor did his wife, Lila.

"Bucky, your parents are …"

"I know," Bucky said.

"I mean, now they're *really* rich."

"I know," he said again even while shaking his head slightly in disbelief.

It was following the tragedy, then, that Mr. and Mrs. Garland Fessmire moved over the hill to Mountain Brook, after which it became Lila Fessmire's urgent ambition to join them there, and several years later after giving birth to twin boys, she finally did—incorporating the young family's growing requirement for additional living space into her own need to live better than she'd previously been brought up to do.

And everyone pretty much assumed—regardless of the fact his father already owned the business—it was the outcome of the tragedy that cemented Bucky's devotion to the insurance industry where he worked hard and excelled and genuinely earned the living he made and the comfort afforded his family, which was not to say the degree of comfort they enjoyed was never enhanced over the subsequent years by the generosity of the senior Fessmires. But Mr. Garland Fessmire applied discretion when it came to his wealth, and as a rule especially with his son and daughter-in-law, directed much of their bounty through the Fessmire Insurance Agency to avoid any appearance of blatant aid.

Lila Fessmire never really minded how it was she permanently came to put the economic limitations Buford represented behind her. But the tragedy was, overall, the source of Bucky Fessmire's sensitivity toward discussing the origin of their resources, while also serving to clarify his preference for Mountain Dew.

Dearly Beloved

The last weekend in June slipped up on Elba Rae Van Oaks like an uninvited supper guest. It was an irksome interruption to the progress she and Hazel Burns had been making in the late Ethel Maywood's house, where most everything of significance had either been thrown out, packed away, given to the Benevolence Boutique, or tactically put aside for Lila to paw through whenever it was she would eventually come back to Buford.

Elba Rae pulled her one Samsonite off the top shelf of the bedroom closet on Thursday night before the wedding and started to pack for the trip, and shortly into the preparations realized the relative briefness of the excursion would not necessarily lighten her load. She was expected at Lila's house by early the next afternoon whereupon she'd need her rehearsal dinner outfit, sleepwear, an afternoon getup for the bridesmaids luncheon to which Lila insisted she be included, the brand new dress and accessories for the wedding, more sleepwear, and then just something—she didn't care what—to put on for the drive back to Buford Sunday morning, a time she felt sure wouldn't roll around soon enough.

When Elba Rae was through gathering the total of her own belongings, she pulled out a shopping bag saved from F & F Fashions because it had little handles on it and was just the right sized luggage to hold the supplies necessary to sustain Mr. Wiggles during what likewise was to be his weekend away at the home of his temporary guardian, Hazel Burns.

Hazel told Elba Rae to "have a safe trip" and to "tell everybody I said hello," as well as "I like your permanent," when Elba Rae dropped off her adopted poodle and Elba Rae said "I'll try" and "I will," as well as "I'm just glad Sylvia could work me in," but it was decidedly absent enthusiasm because the whole thing just felt strange to her, and she thought it must be because Ethel Maywood wasn't in the passenger seat where she rightly should have been. Elba Rae was at once cognizant of the fact she'd never been her sister's houseguest as a party of one, and it had been so long since she'd traveled with Ethel up for a visit it might have been awkward still, even if they had been together at the wedding.

The drive to Birmingham was uneventful in and of itself, and it was only after she'd gotten close to the city limits proper that the traffic made Elba Rae somewhat nervous. Too many people, in too many cars, all trying to go too many places and too fast all the while, she thought.

She cautiously motored off the interstate at the Highway 149 exit and headed toward the narrow, tree-lined lane where Bucky and Lila lived just minutes away from his parents. It was, aesthetically, a beautiful community and she guessed she could see why people wanted to live there. Many of the homes were quite large and Lila had never been remiss to point out that some of the wealthiest families in the Birmingham area lived in her little suburb. The lawns were perfect and it didn't look like anybody needed to mow.

Lila and Bucky's house fit the surroundings completely with its two-story colonial columns stretching the entire width of the elevation. A magnolia tree that Elba Rae barely recalled in the front yard had matured and was loaded with sweet summer blooms.

Whatever dread and despair Elba Rae suspected might continue to linger over the weekend due to the genesis of the engagement had, apparently, at least momentarily dissipated because Lila Fessmire was nothing if not exuding hospitality when Elba Rae got inside. She seemed genuinely glad to see Elba Rae and Elba Rae wondered if perhaps Lila was just lonesome for a relative of her own.

Charity Fessmire was not home and was said to be visiting with the mother of the bridegroom-elect over some last minute rehearsal dinner details, the one aspect of the entire function Lila by tradition was not allowed to control, and Bucky was said to be finishing up a few things at his office. Heath and Nick Fessmire were present and seemed to be in particularly good moods as they cheerfully transported Elba Rae's belongings from the LTD to her guest room after only one request from their mother.

It was not long, however, before Lila's facade of calm and goodwill gave way to what Elba Rae accepted to be natural mother of the bride jitters when, innocently yet regrettably, Elba Rae as a means of making conversation mentioned the wedding rehearsal dinner scheduled for that evening. It was instantly clear that Lila took umbrage to its delegation to the Grinbars.

"There's nothing you can do about it, Lila. It's the groom's family that's responsible so you may as well just try to enjoy it. You don't want to be fussing over it so you ruin it for Charity."

"I won't be the one ruining it for Charity, Elba Rae. It's those hillbillies she's marrying into that'll take the trophy for that. Can you imagine? Cooking all that food at their house and then packing it up to the church like some kind of gypsies in a chuck wagon?"

"Well, now, I don't see anything wrong with having the rehearsal dinner at the church. You don't have to go out somewhere fancy to have a nice meal. Why, we've had plenty of them in the fellowship hall up at our church and I've never heard anybody complain."

"Of course not," Lila said, condescendingly. "If people don't know any different, what is there to complain about?"

"What is that supposed to mean?"

"Oh, Elba Rae, don't start on me with the finger-wagging and telling me Bucky and I are snobs. I just don't have the energy."

"I'm sure the Grinbars don't mean you any harm."

"Really? Then don't even get me started on what passes for his mother's idea of decorating. I'm not supposed to know, but she's apparently having trouble coming up with enough tablecloths and linens and was wondering if she could just use paper. I've never heard of anything so tacky."

"Then it's a good thing everybody knows you're not responsible for any of it!"

"Well …" Lila relented, just slightly. "I'm trying not to think about it."

"Is there anything we need to be doing?" Elba Rae Van Oaks thought it wise to change the subject.

"Surprisingly," Lila said, "I believe everything is under about as much control as it possibly can be."

"Do the boys have all their clothes in place?"

"They do, and—oh, I almost forgot to show you. Come upstairs and see my dress."

Elba Rae Van Oaks smiled. Not so much because she anticipated pleasure out of fawning over another example of her sister's expensive couturiere clothes, but because she'd gotten Lila's mind off the apparent disparity which existed between the Fessmires and the soon-to-be in-laws.

Elba Rae sat down on the foot of a chaise lounge in Lila Fessmire's bedroom. The drapes were open in the large bay window and the room was drenched in sunlight. Lila made her entrance from the walk-in closet holding the formal gown in front of her as though wearing it, and Elba Rae dutifully extended what she hoped to be a sufficient quantity of praise for the garment.

"And it's *very* similar to one Nancy Reagan wore at a big dinner they had at the White House last year to welcome some foreign leader or dignitary or somebody," Lila couldn't help but point out, and Elba Rae suspected it wouldn't be the last time she'd hear the comparison made before the wedding was over.

"I don't know why you'd want to mimic her," said Elba Rae, dismissively.

"I happen to like her. She's done a lot to bring some style and class back to the White House!"

"Style and class … there wasn't anything wrong with it before she got there!"

"Oh, don't get your dander up, Elba Rae. I'm not saying anything against the Carters. But you know how Rosalyn was."

Elba Rae Van Oaks did not know Mrs. Rosalyn Carter. Not personally. But it made every nerve ending in her body stand at attention to await further instruction just the same when she heard a completely unjustified swipe taken at the former first lady from their neighboring state of Georgia, and especially since Elba Rae knew full well her sister's embrace of all things Reagan was influenced more by the company she kept in Birmingham than by any perceived fashion deficiencies—real or imagined—suffered by an otherwise gracious and lovely woman.

"To each his own," concluded Elba Rae. "You're the mother of the bride."

"Well, Charity happens to approve in this case. She was with me when I bought it."

Elba Rae's nerve endings were waving and fluttering by then, and they wanted to say "like mother, like daughter," but for the greater good of peace in the family she suppressed them.

"But wait until you see what Miss Geraldine bought. She found it in Atlanta—somewhere in Phipps Plaza, I think—a couple of weekends ago. It's a really pretty shade of pink. It flatters her."

"How is she doing?"

"Oh, she has her bad days every now and again. But she's mostly just," Lila thought for a second before finishing, "happy."

"How's her walking?"

"Well," Lila began, before tenderly re-hanging her Nancy Reagan-inspired mother of the bride dress back in the spacious closet. "It probably hurts her more than she lets on. By the wedding tomorrow night, we'll have to get somebody to help hobble her into the church and then somebody to help hobble her in and out of the reception."

"Now, you know she can't help it, Lila."

"I know she can't help it, but we've still got to get her hobbled in and out of there without too much of a spectacle."

"Can Bucky's father not manage her anymore?"

"Well, he still thinks he can, bless his heart. But the combination of the two of them together is just another disaster waiting to happen."

"Poor old thing. It's a wonder there's still a piece of her left to hobble after what happened at that gas station."

"I know ..." Lila momentarily slowed her pace as she thought about her mother-in-law, Mrs. Geraldine Fessmire. "I guess it's always been a blessing she doesn't remember a thing about it. But that doesn't mean we won't all have to be on pins and needles during the entire ceremony."

"Does she still have those cackling spells every once in a while?"

"Not as often as she used to the first few years after the wreck. But you still never can be sure what might set her off."

"That's right pitiful," Elba Rae sympathized.

"I know she can't help it. But just a few months ago, Mr. Garland took her to the hospital with him to visit one of the retired secretaries who was with him forever at the agency. She's just about on her last leg. Heart's bad, she's had emphysema forever, and anyway, while they were visiting, she mentioned to Mr. Garland that her kidneys were failing and they were going to have to put her on dialysis."

"Bless her heart."

"Yeah, well, Miss Geraldine—and I know she can't help it—got so tickled Mr. Garland had to just make their excuses and practically pull her out of the room! That old lady was near about crying, but it was Miss Geraldine that had the tears running down her face. From laughing!"

"You don't think she'll disrupt the wedding, do you?"

"We *were* sort of worried about it at first. But Bucky had a little talk with his daddy, and Mr. Garland agreed to double up on her pills tomorrow so she'll be extra calm by the time they get to the church."

"Won't she know what he's up to?"

"No. He does it all the time. Just crushes them up in her oatmeal and she never knows the difference. But then if she should have one of her spells and go to laughing, we've actually got her seated in an alcove off the sanctuary so she won't be as conspicuous."

"Alcove?"

"Yeah. That way it won't be so noticeable if Mr. Garland has to start squeezing her hand like he does."

"I thought you said the wedding was going to be in that little chapel."

Lila Fessmire suddenly tensed.

"Oh. Well, we thought it'd be best if we went ahead and moved into the big sanctuary."

"Just how many people are you expecting at this wedding?" Elba Rae Van Oaks was suddenly much more interested in the venue for the nuptials than she was the seating chart, who'd outfitted each member of the wedding party, or whose hand might likely get squeezed during the vows.

"Based on the RSVPs and allowing for a few last minute changes of plans, we've designed for no more than three hundred."

"Three hundred?!"

"As best we can estimate," Lila said, calmly, without revealing apprehension to what she might be unleashing.

"Well, what was all that story about being in such a hurry you didn't have time to plan for very many guests, and ya'll just wanted to keep it small under the circumstances, and you probably wouldn't even invite any of the relatives in Litton County?"

"Of course we've been in a hurry! And," Lila continued, after lowering her voice, "you know very well why."

"So I do. But three hundred guests is no small little family wedding."

"Well, maybe it grew a little from what we'd first envisioned when we started. To be honest, I was probably still in shock then and didn't know what I was saying. I just knew we had to get them married. But once we sat down and started thinking about who we absolutely *needed* to put on the guest list—Bucky's associates, and our friends from the club, and, well, don't even get me started on everybody the Fessmires wanted to include—it just multiplied."

"Obviously," Elba Rae observed.

"And the other thing, after she got over being so upset, Charity actually started to get excited about the plans and the prospect of having her friends there, and regardless of the fact we all wish she were older and more settled it's her wedding day. Think about it, Elba Rae."

Elba Rae's stare didn't indicate to Lila she was thinking about anything other than the demographics of the guests.

"Oh, for heaven's sake, Elba Rae, we had to cut it off somewhere! If we'd invited all the cousins in Litton County we may as well have opened it up to everybody we've ever known, and the next thing you know we'd have had Begina sending in an RSVP for her and Aunt Laveetra. And I'm not going to be responsible for ruining what better be my daughter's only wedding!"

The eight chimes of the Fessmire doorbell served as conclusion to the conversation.

"That's probably another delivery. I'll be right back," Lila said hurriedly as she left the bedroom. Elba Rae Van Oaks leaned back on the chaise lounge until she was looking straight up at the ceiling. She closed her eyes and wished she could go to sleep.

*   *   *

The wedding rehearsal took place that evening with the bride, groom, the sundry attendants, and the parents of the couple in attendance. Elba Rae Van Oaks sat in the back pew of the very formal sanctuary and watched. While she had no intention of saying one inflammatory word to her sister, she did hope the woman introduced to her as Skippy Grinbar's mother would start early the next day trying to do something with her hair, as Elba Rae was most confident it would warrant extra time to corral. Likewise, she hoped the shoes Skippy Grinbar's father had on were not representative of his best pairs.

It took but one glance inside the entrance of the reception hall for Elba Rae to know there would be no redeeming the Grinbar-sponsored dinner in the eyes of Lila Fessmire. While Elba Rae didn't necessarily take personal offense to the choice of a western motif, she was sure her sister would scowl at the first sight of the decorations, which included paper tablecloths with a wagon wheel and spurs design, paper napkins rolled up inside green plastic napkin rings made, apparently, to simulate a cactus, and centerpieces on each table consisting of some matching and some not vases that sported the ever-popular carnation Lila Fessmire so despised. The flowers were red and not blue, but Elba Rae held no hope it would make a difference.

Surprisingly, there was little commentary about the evening on the return to the Fessmire residence, but since Charity was in the car Elba Rae assumed Lila was exercising a little restraint by not being completely insulting.

Bucky Fessmire temporarily disappeared to his refrigerator in the garage when they got to the house before returning with a bottle of imported amber-colored beer.

"Did you remember to check it off?" asked Lila.

Bucky stopped in his tracks and dropped his head. "Shit," he said and back out the door he went.

"We can't afford to let our guard down," Lila said to Elba Rae. "Especially not until we get through this weekend."

"I thought the boys were very well behaved tonight at the dinner."

"Yeah, well, that's when they worry me the most. When they're behaving. Makes me thinking they're plotting something."

"They'll grow out of this, Lila," Elba Rae laughed.

Lila sat down at the end of a long sofa in the family den and let out a sigh. "I'm glad this is over with."

"Everything turned out all right," said Elba Rae, as she joined Lila on the sofa. "Don't you think?"

Lila turned and gave her a serious glare. "Baked beans?"

"Well, they tasted fine. I don't know that I would put that much

Worcestershire sauce in mine, but then everybody makes beans a little different."

"I would have spit mine in my napkin if I'd thought no one was looking at me."

"I did think the fried chicken was a little on the greasy side, though," Elba Rae lamented. "I imagine she just doesn't let her skillet get hot enough."

Elba Rae left open the opportunity for Lila to interject one positive comment about the event, but Lila clearly wasn't budging.

"The banana pudding was good," Elba Rae said as yet another prompt.

"Who in the world serves banana pudding at a wedding rehearsal dinner, Elba Rae?"

"Well, it *was* good."

"The vanilla wafers were stale."

"They might have been. But the bananas were nice and ripe."

"Oh, I knew the food was going to be a disaster. But I thought I'd die before Mr. Grinbar ever got through with that mess of a toast he was trying to make!"

"It was sweet."

"Using broken English isn't sweet. It's just unsophisticated," Lila barked.

"Well, the momma seemed kind of nice. What was her name again? Jane something? Jane Ellen?"

"It's June. June Helen," Lila answered.

"Oh, yeah. But I never did actually catch the daddy's first name."

"That's understandable," Lila remarked with an ease of sarcasm. "I'm not sure I know his real name myself."

"Really? You don't even know who the boy's people are or—"

"Oh, I know, but it's just so foolish. The boy's real name is Verlon. Verlon Junior, to be exact. But of course he can't be Verlon because they've always called him Skippy for some ungodly reason. And you know that'll come back to haunt him now that he's grown and out trying make a living. Skippy … for goodness sake. Sounds like something you name a Chihuahua." She took a brief pause to reflect.

"Well, anyway, of course that makes the daddy Verlon Senior I figured out. But they've never introduced him to any of us as anything but Hip."

"Hip?" Elba Rae said, in a tone indicative that clarification would be necessary.

"Hip," confirmed Lila. "Hip Grinbar. Did you ever hear a worse name? If you have, then I can top it because, as it turns out, Hip is just a shortened version of the full nickname—Hipshot."

"What kind of name is that?"

"Oh, just ask him," Lila said while nodding her head in an affirmative gesture. "He'll be happy to tell you about his glory days in high school playing basketball. And how he first started getting the attention when he was a sophomore because he was so quick to shoot the ball as soon as it was passed to him but how the nickname 'Hipshot' didn't really stick until he was a junior and, well, of course by the time he was a senior everybody'd just pretty much forgotten, for all time it seems, that his name was Verlon. And not that I ever intend to see the proof first hand for myself, but apparently that's how he's listed in his yearbook. As Hipshot Grinbar. Now isn't that tacky?"

Elba Rae Van Oaks contorted her mouth ever so slightly, just enough to make a pronounced frown. She didn't deduce the moment was quite right to point out to her sister that "Bucky" wasn't exactly a nickname suffering from an overdose of superiority; nonetheless, Elba Rae couldn't decide which of the three answers she'd received to her original question—Hip, Hipshot, or Verlon—was the more stupid.

"And Verlon or Mr. Hipshot or whatever he wants to go by never calls the boy's momma by her name, either," Lila continued. "It's always Junie or June Bug or June Babe or Junie H or sometimes just JH."

"Honestly," she sighed. "When I think of all the boys Charity could have been introduced to—our friends' sons, people we know from the club, or sons of Bucky's agents in the company even. But no. Our daughter has to take up with some lowlife she had no good reason to have ever crossed paths with in the first place."

"Well, now, maybe you're being too hard on them."

"Too hard?"

"Yeah. I mean, I met the boy. And I've got to say, he couldn't have been any more polite. He shook my hand and he said 'nice to meet you, Ms. Van Oaks' and he called me ma'am and all."

"Well, if he did, Charity must have been coaxing him."

"No, now that's what I mean about you maybe being too quick to judge.

If there's one thing I've learned in all my years of teaching, the children aren't ever going to be any better—or any worse—than what they've got showing them at home. When I think back to some of the worst pupils I've had in my room, it's no wonder they were that way because they came from bad stock to begin with. The parents were trash or they drank, and some of those kids didn't even have both parents living under the same roof."

"Is this supposed to be cheering me up?" interrupted Lila. "Because all it's doing is giving me a glimpse of what the next sixty years is going to be like for Charity."

"No, what I'm saying is, I've always been able to tell what kind of upbringing the children have had by the way they act in my room. Manners and being polite and saying 'Yes, ma'am' and 'No, ma'am' is something children either learn at home or not at all."

Lila Fessmire stared at her sister with no change of expression to suggest Elba Rae's attempt at a point was being taken.

"Well, think what you want," Elba Rae went on. "But I'm just telling you. I've met the boy. He seems like a very nice, mature, young man to me. And if he is, it's more like than not because he was raised right."

"That's easy for you to say, Elba Rae. He's not fixing to marry your daughter."

"No, he's not. But let me tell you something else I've learned over the years that I know as fact. Some of the worst ole children I've ever taught were the ones that came from the most. They were spoiled rotten from the day they were born and no teacher in that school could ever tell them a thing. But some of the very best ones I've had that I'll never forget—the smartest and the brightest ones that could go on to do whatever they wanted to do—came from the very least. They did just fine without having rich mommas and daddies handing them everything on a tray."

"Like that Mhoon girl you were remembering after Momma's funeral? Yeah. She turned out to be a real prize! Did you ask her momma and daddy if they were proud of her?"

"She was a sweet child and if she weren't, she wouldn't have bothered to show up at the funeral home! And I appreciate that from her—even if she *was* poor!"

"There you go again, Elba Rae. Trying to make out like this whole mess is just because I'm a snob! Like I wouldn't be bothered by any of this if the boy just came from money! You're missing the point!"

"Am I?"

"Yes, you are! I'd be upset about this no matter who Charity was about to marry! Because she's still too young to be somebody's wife! And, my Lord, she's way too young to be a mother! But now she's about to be both! I wish I could change all of it, but since I can't, I'm just saying things would be so much easier for her—no, that's not even what I mean because none of this is going to be easy. It would be less of a burden to her if she were going into this with somebody with a better background. That's all I'm saying. Somebody that had more advantages who we could at least expect to provide for her and the baby. Whether that's fair or not or makes me sound like a snob, I don't care. It just happens to be the truth."

Elba Rae did not respond, which seemed to further agitate Lila.

"You *do* know," Lila said, "that they're going to be living downstairs in our basement apartment until at least after the baby comes—don't you?"

"Yeah," said Elba Rae softly. "Bucky mentioned it."

"And no telling how long that could turn out to be, because what kind of job is that boy going to be able to get with no education? One that pays enough to take care of a wife and a child?"

Again, Elba Rae offered no rebuttal.

"You see, Elba Rae, it's just not as simple as you make it out."

Elba Rae Van Oaks considered Lila's case and did, in fact, begin to understand the argument she made. There were, after all, economic consequences to setting up house and welcoming a baby, especially for such young parents. And on a more practical level, Elba Rae conceded, alleviating the strain of financial challenges would seem on the surface to make the situation more palatable. But Elba Rae knew, too, that the union between the Fessmires and the Grinbars—forever solidified due to the bond of a shared grandchild—was more wounding to Lila than she'd ever let on.

To Elba Rae Van Oaks, it was obvious Lila did not hold her daughter and the expectant mother to the same standard of accountability as she did young Skippy but it didn't surprise her much. That was just Lila. And much more so since the morning Ethel Maywood died than in many, many years before, Elba Rae was getting a crystal clear picture of how her sister coped with her own life.

Charity Fessmire's future—once presumably certain to include a college education and indoctrination into whatever professional world her imagination chose to explore—was now in an unplanned upheaval. Elba Rae ached to remind Lila that Charity had evidently made the acquaintance of this young man willingly and was no more or less responsible than the baby's father for how their lives turned out, and that for the good of their new family, Lila should make peace with the situation. Lila had been supportive to her daughter, no doubt. But it was clearly not an acceptance extended to Hipshot and June Bug Grinbar, and certainly not to their little boy Verlon Junior, who everybody just called Skippy.

*   *   *

Elba Rae Van Oaks helped in any way she could the day of the wedding but mostly just tried to stay out of the way while Lila and Charity's nerves fed off each other. She especially made a point to make herself scarce when Bucky took Heath and Nick Fessmire into the garage and delivered unto them a rather stern address regarding his expectations of their behavior while they would be on the premises of the country club that evening.

At the church, Elba Rae wanted to go ahead and get settled in her seat early but Lila had apparently decided it would be more ceremonial if Elba Rae were to be escorted to her pew just prior to the seating of the mothers. So she'd bitten her lip and agreed to stay back and join Lila, Bucky, and Charity when they took their positions in the roomy foyer off the sanctuary to wait with June Helen Grinbar for the official start. Elba Rae tried to smile at June Helen Grinbar as often as possible just so she wouldn't think everyone on the bride's side of the family was coming into the union with predisposed acrimony. June Helen smiled back every time but otherwise remained silent and, if Elba Rae had to guess, deferential to the mother of the bride.

"I think it's just about time," Lila said quietly to Bucky and Charity.

Lila Fessmire at last had genuine happiness about her face, Elba Rae thought, for the first time since announcing the wedding. Though there'd been scant time to plan the kind of event Elba Rae knew Lila had probably always wanted for her only daughter, the moment had arrived and it was just as pivotal despite the abbreviated preparation.

"All right, then," Elba Rae said. "I'll go on in."

She then looked over at Charity Fessmire, who stood poised and ready at her father's side.

"Next time I see you you'll be a married woman," Elba Rae whispered. Charity didn't say anything, but her glowing aura spoke for itself.

For good measure, Elba Rae smiled at June Helen Grinbar one more time but she managed to get only three tip-toes toward the sanctuary and a waiting usher before the big wooden door pulled open from outside and a flash of late afternoon sunlight blew into the foyer.

"Oh—wait, Elba Rae," Lila said in a hushed tone. "Let whoever that is be seated so you can go in by yourself."

"What? I—"

"Obviously, there are some latecomers about to drag in!"

Elba Rae stopped and then took a few steps back to more or less huddle with the Fessmires. They could all hear the voices of whoever was attempting to get inside the church because there was unbridled conversation going on, even as one hand of the party was holding the door open. After another half minute or so, the first of the pair stepped inside.

"Dear. God. In. Heaven," Lila said out loud, enunciating each word as an individual and personal revulsion.

Standing in the doorway—practically pulling on the arm of a second party who was still outside and obviously putting up something of a resistance—was none other than Begina Marie Chittum, from Hattiesburg. Elba Rae and Lila looked on in horror, as they could only surmise the body attached to the arm Begina was persuasively tugging on would belong to Begina's mother, Laveetra.

A musical cue in the organ prelude suddenly prompted the usher previously assigned the job at rehearsal to stick his head around the corner and look for Mrs. Grinbar, because it was her time to go. June Helen stood dumbstruck in the confusion until he motioned for her to enter, and then she complied.

"Wait!" Lila said, but June Helen Grinbar was already joined to the usher and mere seconds from being visible at the rear of the aisle. "Elba Rae needs to go first!"

"Did you know they were coming?" Elba Rae demanded.

"No!" said Lila, who peered around Elba Rae's stance in disgust as June Helen disappeared from sight and onto the bridal path.

"You mean to tell me they were invited to this wedding—and you couldn't even squander one lousy invitation on Hazel?"

"I didn't send them an invitation! Because they weren't on the guest list!"

"Then what are they doing here?!"

"I don't know! I guess they heard about it somehow and just decided it was fair game! Who knows?!"

Across the foyer, Begina Chittum had braced herself and was holding onto Laveetra's arm with both hands before giving her one firm jerk.

"Come on, Mother! We're going to miss the wedding!"

"I don't need to come in there, Begina!" Laveetra Chittum protested.

"Why not?"

"Because I feel fine! There's nothing wrong with me!"

"I told you, Mother, this isn't the hospital. It's the church. It's the church where they're having the wedding. We talked about it in the car—remember?"

"I don't know, Begina."

"Come on, Mother. It'll be fine. We're just going to sit down in there and watch little Charity get married."

"I don't want to, Begina."

"It's all right, Mother. I promise."

"Mom," Charity Fessmire said from across the foyer, with her full bridal bouquet in front of her mouth to stifle the sound. "Is that your cousin, Begina?"

"Yes."

"I don't get it. I thought you said we weren't inviting them."

"We didn't," Lila said. "But that apparently means nothing to Begina."

Lila at once strode in something of a march toward the door and in the throes of the surprise, Elba Rae feared there might actually be a confrontation.

"Begina!"

"Oh, Lila Mae!" Begina exclaimed.

"Begina—what in the world?"

"Oh, Lila, it's Mother. She just got a little turned around in the car on the way over here from the motel. We passed a hospital a couple of miles back, and now she thinks that's where I'm trying to take her."

Lila looked through the open door and observed Laveetra Chittum holding onto a railing with one hand.

"Aunt Laveetra!"

"Lila Mae?" Laveetra Chittum asked, but with marked uncertainty.

"Get in here!"

"I don't need to go to the hospital, Lila, I—"

"Now!" Lila commanded, whereupon she grabbed hold of Laveetra Chittum herself and yanked her inside. "The wedding's already started!"

Laveetra's right hand, into which a mild tremor had obviously manifested, clutched the tip of a tissue that was peeking from underneath the sleeve of her dress. It was apparently the same unsteady hand she'd used to apply lipstick—miraculously mostly contained within the boundaries of her lips on the left side of her face but notably escaping the borders of the right side by about a fourth of an inch. That the lipstick was a shade of red so grotesquely similar to what Elba Rae had wiped off of Ethel Maywood at her last public appearance did nothing to assuage the blatant smears.

"Oh, I'm sorry, Lila Mae. Mother has these spells every now and then, especially in unfamiliar surroundings, and—"

"I know, Begina, I understand, but ya'll need to get to your seats so I can get Charity down the aisle. Aunt Laveetra, are you all right?"

"I'm fine, Sweetie."

"Good. Now why don't you go right inside the door there and just sit down in the first pew in the back?"

Begina took her mother's hand. "I'll get her settled, Lila," and then she winked, unaware of how much Lila hated to be winked at—especially by a middle aged woman she wanted to slap.

As Begina successfully led the suddenly docile Laveetra toward the sanctuary, she couldn't help but stop long enough to wave fervently at Elba Rae, Bucky, and Charity, who remained in position across the foyer in frozen bewilderment.

*   *   *

As Elba Rae Van Oaks witnessed her young niece being walked down the aisle on her father's arm, a peace finally came over her, and for at least the duration of the ceremony, she felt swathed in tranquility where all was well. It was a state of being cumulatively nurtured by a flawless execution of the protocol rehearsed the evening prior (save for her own out-of-order seating), the forgiving tailoring of the bride's gown that gave away no secrets, the fact Mrs. June Helen Grinbar had seen fit to address her mess of a hairdo, and—

last but not at all least—the absence of any inappropriate outbursts from Mrs. Geraldine Fessmire who, on the other hand, appeared especially groggy and inattentive during the whole event, making Elba Rae Van Oaks wonder if anyone ever especially audited Mr. Garland's loose-handed administration of her medicines.

The wedding and the reception were both well attended, and to no one's surprise, the surroundings at the country club were most opulent (and not just by Buford standards). Tables of food displayed on tiers and on mirrored glass were supplemented by neatly attired waiters who carried trays with yet more hors d'oeuvres, alternated with trays of sparkling champagne in tall fluted glasses, and Elba Rae Van Oaks couldn't remember when the last time—if ever—she'd been serenaded by live harp playing.

Bucky and Lila seemed to know everyone in the room unless, of course, their last name was Grinbar or they were otherwise an invited guest of the groom. Elba Rae was proud, nonetheless, that everyone seemed to get along and that Lila was at least outwardly affable—a pretense she maintained until pulling Elba Rae aside next to the table where the four tiers of wedding cake awaited cutting.

"Have you seen Begina?"

"Well, no, not in the last few minutes," Elba Rae replied.

"We need to find her."

"Why? What's wrong?"

"I just walked up on Aunt Laveetra. And she was having the longest discussion with Skippy's mother!"

"Oh, now, I wouldn't let myself fret about that tonight. You can explain after the wedding's all over with and things have calmed down. She'll understand."

"I don't think that'll be necessary."

"Why not?"

"Because apparently June Helen hasn't got sense enough herself to know Laveetra's not all there! She just told me she'd had the nicest conversation with my aunt and how sweet it was they'd ridden all this way on the train just to be at the wedding."

"Train?! Begina drove them up here in that old piece of car. Where'd June Helen ever get the idea they came on a train?"

"From Laveetra! She told June Helen it was such a long trip, what with them having to stop at so many stations along the way to pick up other passengers, and that the next time they came she hoped it'd be on an express straight through. Lord. Anyway, Laveetra wandered off somewhere and—well, Elba Rae, we've got to get them out of here before they start talking to somebody that matters."

Elba Rae looked around the room nervously. "I'll see if I can't find Begina somewhere and at least make sure she's keeping an eye on her momma."

"Well, just check the nearest buffet. She won't be far."

By the time Elba Rae worked her way through the host of reception guests to locate simple Begina, Laveetra had already been apprehended and all seemed to be under control. Begina held a plate onto which she'd strategically built an impressive pyramid with hors d'oeuvres. Laveetra took occasional sips of punch that jiggled in a crystal cup held by her unsteady hand and every time she did, she tattooed the rim with more of her signature red lipstick.

"Elba Rae, this is about the nicest wedding, isn't it? I'm so glad we decided to come on," Begina gushed.

"Oh, yeah. When did you get here exactly?"

"We got to the motel about two o'clock, I guess. We tried to get off from home earlier but Mother got a little dizzy after breakfast so I thought she'd better lay down for a while before we got in the car. It's a mess when we're out from home in the car and she has one of her dizzy spells. Anyway, I expect I may need to give her some rest medicine before we leave in the morning."

Laveetra Chittum took a shaky swig of punch and smiled at Elba Rae as though she knew exactly where she was and about whom her daughter was speaking, but Elba Rae doubted either.

"But isn't it just about the swankiest wedding you've ever been to, Elba Rae?" reiterated Begina.

"Yes," Laveetra said. "You're so sweet to invite us, Elba Rae. Your momma would be proud of you."

"Oh, Mother," laughed Begina and looking at Elba Rae. "I think she's a little mixed up about whose wedding it is."

Elba Rae Van Oaks—in her quest to capture the elusive Laveetra—had not entertained the possibility of a sensible conversation with her aunt, who did not appear poised to disappoint, but neither had she expected a side-handed accolade.

"Well, thank you, Aunt Laveetra."

"But where's Fettis? I don't believe I've seen him since we got here."

Begina Chittum took in a deep breath that Elba Rae interpreted as a hint of the exasperation she must have felt on a daily basis.

"Now, Mother, you know Fettis is not with us anymore. He's passed on."

Laveetra Chittum suddenly looked sad and she turned to face Elba Rae. "He is?"

"Don't you remember, Mother? He locked up while Elba Rae was at preaching one Sunday."

"What?"

"He locked up while Elba Rae was at church."

"He what?"

"Locked up!" Begina screamed, causing a nearby couple to turn their heads in curiosity.

"Oh," Laveetra said, as though she were learning the details for the first time. "I'm sorry to hear that, Elba Rae."

"It …" Elba Rae started, but trailed off. Whatever temper had been aggravated back at the church by the Hattiesburg gatecrashers was slowly melting. Elba Rae put her arm around her elderly aunt.

"That's perfectly all right, Aunt Laveetra. We're just glad you're here and having a nice time."

Begina at once slurped the tips of several fingers. "Elba Rae, have you tried these shrimps wrapped up in the bacon? They are just out of this world. I'm gonna have to get me some more!"

"Begina," Elba Rae said with a smile, "you help yourself."

*   *   *

Heath and Nick Fessmire, although under the heavy guard of their parents throughout the evening, exhibited no outward signs of mischievousness, nor did they attempt to leave the perimeter of the designated reception area except as was necessary to visit the men's room, where they were not allowed to go at the same time. The only discomfited moment attributed to them, as far as Elba Rae Van Oaks was ever aware, occurred through no direct fault of the twins who were for all intents and purposes minding their business when the family at last, after the happy couple had been photographed one more time gleefully motoring away in a car laden with all sorts of messages on the windshield and a dozen cans tied to its bumper, finally made their way out the front entrance of the country club to go home for the night.

Unbeknownst to Bucky Fessmire—into whose charge his delinquent sons had been placed—an older gentleman was assigned special duty that evening to supervise the additional valet staff required to service the many wedding guests. No introduction was necessary for Elba Rae Van Oaks to figure out the older gentleman was none other than the previously victimized Pig, who upon just the sight of the Fessmire boys, snatched a set of keys from a pegboard and told Bucky Fessmire he'd fetch his car personally before jumping over a flower bed and taking out through a grassy median toward the parking area. In a flash, the big Cadillac came whirling up the drive that circled the entrance under a large porch. Based upon what Elba Rae was quite certain to be the squeal of a tire as the vehicle came around the corner, she could concur—gentlemen's agreement notwithstanding—Pig had no business behind the wheel of a golf cart.

*   *   *

Elba Rae Van Oaks regretted that she deviated from her original departure plan—the one she'd mentally drafted before she ever pulled the Samsonite out of the closet or stuffed the F & F Fashions shopping bag with a rawhide chew toy, a quilted dog bed, and a box of Gainsburgers—because it would have had her up and gone early the Sunday morning after the ceremony.

Instead, she was apparently still under the lingering spell of the wedding night's magical ambience when she offered no objection to extending her stay long enough to enjoy a late brunch with the Fessmire family rather than just swallowing a cup of instant coffee and coating her stomach with a slice of toast before pointing her LTD toward Buford. A post-wedding meal together with Lila had sounded almost pleasant, Elba Rae thought, especially with all the hoopla behind them. The sun was proverbially shining. Lila could relax, and the weekend would be over without incident, as long as no one particularly labeled Laveetra Chittum and simple Begina's unforeseen attendance as an incident.

Around ten o'clock, Elba Rae decided to partake of more coffee as a means to curb her appetite and as a diversion to pass the time until the family was ready. In the flurry of activities since she'd arrived in Birmingham, they'd not spent much time in the kitchen. Elba Rae was drawn to an antique hutch near the table and six chairs. It was a large piece of furniture that would have likely overpowered the average kitchen, but Lila Fessmire's kitchen was not average; it was an extensive space that included an eat-in area bigger than most formal dining rooms.

She walked over to get a closer look at the various objects and decorations on the upper shelves of the hutch. There was an eclectic mix of demitasse cups and matching saucers displayed on their little stands, figurines, a few notable cookbooks, one live plant, and a framed assortment of what primarily looked to be family photographs taken during holidays and featuring the children at various ages with Bucky, Lila, and their paternal grandparents.

Elba Rae inventoried them informally, not being too interested in the sundry poses of the Fessmire in-laws, and when she heard Lila's footsteps on the kitchen's tile floor at the other end of the room, she almost turned around before seeing the one picture that stood out the most amongst the pretty statuettes and expensive bric-a-brac. Her mouth even opened slightly at the recognition. She took the photograph from the shelf to examine more closely, as confirmation.

"Is this …?" Elba started but couldn't exactly finish.

"Oh, yeah," Lila noticed. "They did a great job with it, don't you think?"

"This is that same picture?" asked Elba Rae.

"It is. I decided to bring it home with me after we found it at Momma's because I knew I could take it to this great camera store we've got here where they enlarge and restore old photographs. See how they got all the cracks out of it? And how the color isn't all faded anymore?"

"It looks like it was just taken," Elba Rae said, as she tentatively returned to its exact designated space on the hutch shelf the now five-by-seven image of her sister and their cousin, the former Mary Alice Hornbuckle, garbed in fancy gowns and standing in the improvised dressing room of the Buford VFW Hall during the period historically referred to as Mary Alice's blonde chapter.

"You know, I was thinking," Lila remarked while walking over to join Elba Rae at the collection, "we ought to go through all those old pictures of Momma's again and see if there aren't some more we'd like to have blown up and restored. It's just amazing what they can do."

Lila retrieved the frame from where Elba Rae had just put it back and held it up.

"I don't know if you remember, but the top corner of it was bent all the way down, and there was a big crease going across the whole picture," Lila said, as she turned the picture around for Elba Rae to see again. "And look—not so much as a scratch."

She handed it to Elba Rae to hold again, but having already concluded her examination, Elba Rae promptly put it back on the shelf. "It's amazing," she said unenthusiastically while walking away. Lila stood at the hutch and observed Elba Rae go toward the sink and reach to the back of the countertop for the travel-sized jar of instant Folgers she'd brought from Buford.

"I'm sorry," Lila said. She couldn't tell whether Elba Rae didn't hear her or was choosing to ignore her on purpose.

"I'm gonna make a cup of coffee—do you want one?" Elba Rae removed the lid from the jar, and opened a cabinet door housing the coffee mugs.

"Did you say yes?" asked Elba Rae, as she turned to Lila.

"No. I said I was sorry."

"About what?"

"Having this picture out. I guess I should have put it up before you got here."

"Why in the world should you have to do that?"

"Because it upsets you."

"It doesn't upset me, Lila. It's just a picture. And this is your house. You're free to put out whatever you want," assured Elba Rae as she took a spoon from the drawer.

"You know, I think that's when it all got started between you and me."

Elba Rae shoveled a generous helping of coffee powder into the cold mug. "When what got started?"

"It was back then. When Mary Alice and I were getting ready for Miss Honeysuckle."

Elba Rae bristled immediately and her respiration intensified mildly.

"I told you when we were cleaning out Momma's house I don't have any intention of talking about that stupid contest again. Now just hush and don't ever mention it to me again!"

"There! You see, Elba Rae? It just proves my point! You can't talk about the Miss Honeysuckle pageant without getting upset. And I can't even *mention* it, because it strikes such a nerve with you. You're just like Mary Alice was when we were teenagers and we had to talk in code any time we wanted to bring up the Crutcher boy."

"You and Mary Alice and that Crutcher boy and the whole lot of the rest of you were silly kids back when all that was going on. I was practically grown then, and I'm certainly too old now to still care about any of this," Elba Rae proclaimed fiercely, as she filled a tea kettle with water.

"What do you suppose I should think about when I look at this picture up here?" Lila rhetorically continued. "Just say, oh that was back when Elba Rae wasn't in the contest. Instead of what I really think—which is, that was back when my sister started to hate me."

The crash of the kettle being slammed down on the stove was piercing, and it made Lila jerk.

"That is an awful thing to say to me!"

"It's not awful if it's the truth."

"I don't hate you," Elba Rae tried to say calmly, as she slowly released her grip on the kettle's handle.

"You know," Lila said, "I used to think it really was just resentment on your part. That it really was just jealousy. Because I was more popular and—hell, because Momma and Daddy really did let me get by with so much more than they ever did you. I know they did!"

"Well, I'm glad to hear you admit that for once in your life."

"So they favored me! I don't think hearing me say it satisfies you in the least. Because during all this time since Momma died while we've had to spend so much time together, it seems obvious to me it's much more than plain ole sibling rivalry. I think you've hated me ever since I was runner up in Miss Honeysuckle."

"I wish you'd stop saying that! I don't hate you!"

"Then what would you call it?"

"If anybody hates anybody around here, it's you! You've never cared a *thing* about me! You never have!"

For all her pomposity, Lila was suddenly stunned and perhaps unprepared for what she'd finally uncapped. Yet, she sensed immediately there was no way to avoid the wave that was about to hit her as though it were being pulled in by an afternoon tide.

"You've lived up here all these years with your rich in-laws and your country club friends, and the best you could ever do was be ashamed of me—your old dowdy sister living down there teaching school in Buford! Your old sister with her husband that didn't work, living in our little tacky house and never traveling anywhere or ever knowing anybody important! You may have fooled some people over the years, Lila, but you never fooled me!"

Elba Rae was startled when out of the corner of her eye she noticed both Nick and Heath Fessmire standing in the doorway.

"What are you fighting about, Mom?" inquired Nick.

"We're not fighting."

He laughed. "Then what would you call it?"

"I'd call it none of your business. Now go outside and leave us alone."

"Why do we have to go outside?"

"Because I said so," Lila implored wearily.

"I thought you told us we were getting ready to leave for—"

"Hit the yard!" Elba Rae screamed, with such conviction, volume—and fierceness—the boys were shocked and suddenly afraid of her. They walked in single file through the kitchen and out a door that opened to a shady wooden deck.

"I never tried to fool anyone, Elba Rae," and that's when Lila's bottom lip first began to quiver.

"You'd come to Buford and visit Momma for five minutes every six months, and half the time I wouldn't even know about it until after you were gone!"

"I had small children to deal with, Elba Rae. I couldn't just stay gone for weeks at a time!"

"You could have brought the children with you or hired somebody to look after them if you'd wanted to spend any time with us! But you didn't! Because you didn't want to be in Buford! It wasn't good enough for you growing up, it certainly wasn't after you married and got up here—and neither were we! And it didn't have a damn thing to do with any foolish beauty contest or what color Mary Alice's hair was at the time!"

Lila Fessmire could hold out no longer, and she finally let go; the quivering gave way to a full-out shake and the tears came out of both eyes simultaneously in near-perfect choreography. But Elba Rae was not ready to relent.

"You never came to help Momma all the time Daddy was down sick, you hardly spent a day in the hospital with Momma in the past five years … you barely stayed long enough to get her buried before you were packing up."

"You know I had to get back up here because of Charity and the wedding," Lila sniffed.

"So you say," Elba Rae went on with undiluted persistence. "But it's not like a day was going to make a difference either way. It was like you couldn't stand to spend one more minute with me than was absolutely necessary!"

"Well, maybe I didn't feel welcomed to stay!"

"Nonsense!"

"Nonsense?" Lila attempted to ask indignantly, ineffective as it was due to the accompanying sob.

"I don't think you ever wanted me there in the first place! Every time I tried to make one suggestion about the funeral arrangements or the music or anything, you bit my head off and told me what we were and weren't going to have! I think you'd have been happier if I hadn't even come to Buford at all!"

"That's ridiculous! It was your place to be there!"

"You didn't care about my place, Elba Rae. You just did the least you could to tolerate me. And not all that well, I might add."

"You know, I've had it with this. There's no point in my staying here another minute just to fuss and fight and dredge up old stories about Mary Alice."

"And why is that, Elba Rae? I mean, why is it so difficult to imagine we could at least be civil to one another?"

"Because I guess we're just too different, you and me. Because even though we had the same mother and father and lived in the same house we weren't raised the same way. Things had changed by the time you came along. I don't know, Lila. Because we're sisters."

"And that's exactly why it shouldn't be like this."

"What do you want me to say?" Elba Rae was calming down and beginning to sound genuinely unmotivated to continue the disconcerting quarrel.

"Why can't it be like the patio?"

"The what?"

"The patio. That afternoon in Buford, at your house. The day I first told you about Charity."

Elba Rae leaned her head back slightly and nodded slowly from side to side. She discharged a heavy and rather deliberate sigh while looking at the ceiling, but offered no answer.

"The day I told you about Charity, and Heath and Nick getting thrown out of the club, and the way I felt about Bucky. You sat out there with me for hours and just let me unload without arguing, without contradicting me—without telling me I'm a snob. We were sisters then, too, Elba Rae. Only that day, we were the good kind. The kind that are friends."

Elba Rae lowered her head to look directly at Lila, and she felt the intensity of Lila's stare. But she still had no answer.

Lila Fessmire took the photograph of two long ago beauty queens and serenely returned it again to the hutch. She paused briefly, as if offering Elba Rae one final opportunity to tender any kind of conciliatory remark, but walked out of the kitchen when it became obvious Elba Rae's passive declaration of stalemate was non-negotiable. When Elba Rae was sure Lila was gone, she used a napkin she still held in her hand to wipe away the single tear that was rolling down her cheek.

Elba Rae Van Oaks left Birmingham that morning absent further contact with any member of the Fessmire family.

PART THREE

Eleanor Mhoon

Sunday afternoon when Elba Rae Van Oaks arrived in Buford to pick up Mr. Wiggles, Hazel Burns naturally greeted her with "how was the wedding" but all Elba Rae was in the mood to say was "it was fine," and even though Hazel Burns was genuinely interested in just a little more detail than that and had anticipated at least some degree of extemporaneous commentary about the attendees to include possibly relative information about the groom's people, nothing more was said about them either except "they were fine."

Hazel Burns was not unfamiliar with the sometimes difficult relations between Elba Rae and her sister, Lila Fessmire. She knew, in fact, when to ask questions and when to simply put the rawhide chew toy and the little quilted bed and the surplus Gainsburgers back in their F & F sack and bid Mr. Wiggles adieu sans further probing about the Birmingham wedding weekend.

"Your hair looks like it held up," Hazel Burns offered instead.

Elba Rae looked at her but didn't encourage additional conversation.

"Thank you for looking after Mr. Wiggles. I hope he wasn't too much trouble," said Elba Rae, and they were soon on the way home.

Thereafter, Elba Rae didn't out and out ask Hazel Burns to assume the role of primary assistant in the final disposition of Ethel Maywood's assets, but since Lila's absence in Buford was obvious, Hazel again volunteered and made no mention of the presumed estrangement. Hazel didn't even inquire as to the context of the communication they'd had that prompted Elba Rae's announcement to Hazel in about mid July that the newlyweds were expecting a baby.

Because it eventually became necessary to finalize distribution of Ethel Maywood's furniture and other keepsakes, it was Elba Rae who with trepidation wrote a letter to her sister around the first of August and requested they confirm in writing their formerly verbal agreement regarding who was going to take what.

Elba Rae nervously opened the return letter from Birmingham the next week, unsure whether she would find a detailed list of their mother's belongings on the page or whether she'd get the revised written version of a dissertation on the alleged origins of Elba Rae's unsubstantiated hatred for her sister. She was relieved to find only a list of items that didn't deviate from Elba Rae's recollection of their previous accord.

To Elba Rae's further satisfaction, Lila had even gone on to explain that she and Bucky would travel to Buford the following weekend in a rented carrier, and with the aid of their two sons, would remove said belongings and return with them to Birmingham. Lila closed the letter by saying she would leave her copy of Ethel Maywood's house key on the kitchen counter upon final departure, as she did not anticipate a return trip before sale of the real estate.

"Thank you for coming with me," Elba Rae said to Hazel Burns on the second Monday in August as they stepped out of the attorney's office and onto the sidewalk of the Square's west side. They were sure to remain under the large awning that hung over the door, offering respite from the midday sun.

"I don't know why I felt so jittery about coming just to sign my name on some papers."

"Well," Hazel comforted, "it's a big step. It's just papers to them, but you're finally having to say good-bye to Aunt Ethel's house—the house you grew up in. I know it's hard."

"It is."

"And they're just going to send the other papers to Birmingham?"

"The part Lila has to sign? Yeah. Sending them in the express that gets them up there overnight. Probably costs an arm and a leg."

"Well, it's probably safer than sending in the mail, don't you think? Since it's so important?"

"I guess, but—Merciful heavens—would you look at that?"

"What?" asked Hazel, turning her head about but recognizing nothing of particular significance.

Elba Rae employed the polite way of pointing by utilizing a nod rather than the extension of a finger to effectively single out Mrs. Eleanor Mhoon walking the distance of sidewalk between the bank and the post office.

"Oh," Hazel said. "Eleanor's not wearing her galoshes?"

"Not just the galoshes, Hazel, it's the dress."

They stood still and kept the subject of their curiosity in sight until she entered the post office.

"It looked sort of old fashioned to me. Reckon it was something she made?" asked Hazel.

"If I didn't know better, I'd swear it was the dress Momma bought to wear to Lila's wedding. It was in the things we took to Baptist church boutique."

Hazel Burns and Elba Rae gave each other a fleeting look.

"That's strange," said Hazel.

"There's something strange about that whole bunch, if you ask me. I got behind Leland on the tractor the other day just as I pulled out of the Piggly Wiggly. I nearly had the thumps before he finally turned off on their road and let me pass!"

"Oh, I do hate to get behind him when he's on the tractor," Hazel agreed.

"Just a strange bunch," said Elba Rae.

"I wouldn't mind stopping in All Seasons and getting a bite. Are you hungry?" inquired Hazel.

"No, but I hope they've got plenty of tea made up. I'm thirsty as a dog on the desert standing out here in this awful hot."

"Let's go," Hazel said.

*   *   *

Eleanor Mhoon had long since given up any semblance of embarrassment about going inside the Buford Baptist Benevolence Boutique on Geeter Street. The first time or two had been awkward, to be sure, because the ladies working that day had assumed Eleanor Mhoon was there to volunteer for a shift or perhaps make a donation of some sort, although her empty handedness should have been clue enough she wasn't there to make a bequest.

After a while, her presence in the store as a shopper no longer carried the shock value it once had, and most any of the usual volunteers just had to accept that being a regular member of Buford Baptist Church didn't automatically preclude Eleanor Mhoon from purchasing gently used clothing and accessories. The money she paid for her items, after all, eventually got all mixed in together with everyone else's money that went to the Mission Fund and ensured a little boy or girl somewhere in China wasn't missing out on contact with proper religious training, and wasn't that the benevolent purpose? That, and being of aid to people in the community deserving of decent clothing and accessories who otherwise might not be able to afford the full and undiscounted retail price for new?

Eleanor Mhoon was a wiz at taking a discarded outfit and exploiting her talent to refurbish and sometimes remake it into one unrecognizable as having once hung on a makeshift rack in a secondhand charity store, and it especially gratified Eleanor when she would come about a piece of clothing bearing the monogram of Dr. Millford's wife, Virginia, because she realized it was as close to wearing expensive clothes as she would ever know.

Mrs. Florine Moss was working alone in the store the afternoon Eleanor Mhoon came in and purchased the mother of the bride dress discarded by the daughters of the late Ethel Maywood. It was the Saturday before the July Fourth holiday. Florine and her sister-in-law, Mabel, had decorated the front windows with red, white, and blue crepe paper, and Florine had even taken some of the small flags on wooden sticks that her husband, Jack, sold at their hardware business on the Square and affixed one on each side of the cash register with some Scotch tape.

The morning sun had given way to an ominously dark afternoon sky, and for Eleanor Mhoon it was the perfect kind of galoshes-wearing atmosphere, although the clumping the overshoes made while Eleanor walked around on the store's uneven wooden floor was of no consequence to someone as familiar as Florine Moss.

"Looks like we're about to have a toad strangler," Florine commented as Eleanor browsed the aisle with the ladies' dresses. "Have you got a ride today, Eleanor?"

"I've got the truck, but thank you for asking."

"Well, I was just going to say, I'm surely not going to let you head home in this."

As if prompted, the first rumble of thunder spoke up. Florine Moss nonchalantly stood in one of the front windows looking out onto Geeter Street until a bright flash of lightning sent her scurrying to a more interior position in the store.

Eleanor carried the old dress up to the patriotic register and placed it on the counter while she retrieved a small wallet from her purse.

"Do you want to try it on, Eleanor?"

She held it up for a minute by the hanger and contemplated the possibility but then put it back down. "No, I don't believe so. I already know I'm going to have to let those sleeves out, and if it needs any other alterations I can do them."

"Well, if anyone can, I know you can." Florine Moss removed the dress from its hanger and neatly folded it before putting it inside a brown paper grocery sack.

"I'm sorry about this big bag but it's all we've got today. We never can keep enough of the smaller ones here."

"Oh, that's all right."

Florine completed the monetary portion of the transaction with a well-practiced look of empathy glued on her face. Eleanor Mhoon stood patiently, all but ready to galumph out of the store and drive herself home, where she'd likely park the truck in the gravel tracks beyond the mailbox, and trudge in her galoshes up to the house while attempting to keep the brown paper sack from dissolving in the rain that would surely be falling by the time she got there.

Florine Moss arguably meant no harm and maybe it was perfectly reasonable for her to assume Celeste's long flight was finally over, but the expression on Eleanor Mhoon's face told a different tale after Florine said, "It must be so good to have Celeste home."

Eleanor Mhoon didn't exactly drop the sack on the floor outright so much as she slowly let it slip from her fingers.

"What?"

"Celeste. I know it must be a blessing to have her back home with you again."

"I ..." Eleanor realized she'd dropped her dress on the floor and bent down to pick up the sack.

"I don't know what you're talking about."

"Oh," Florine replied. "I'm sorry, Eleanor."

"I don't understand."

"Well, it's just when I saw her at the funeral home the night they were having the viewing for Miss Ethel Maywood, I thought—well, I guess I thought maybe she was home to stay and not just visiting."

Eleanor's expression was glassy and faraway and according to Florine's later account, devoid of any observable emotion.

"Excuse me, Florine. I need to get going if I'm going to try to beat this storm home."

Eleanor Mhoon clumped out the door and left Florine Moss standing alone in the Buford Baptist Benevolence Boutique with her crepe paper and her flags, entertaining for the remainder of her afternoon shift that perhaps she'd stirred up an awful mess.

*   *   *

Leland Mhoon had maintained a rather monotone voice the last time he'd spoken to his daughter on the day after Christmas in 1974. He hadn't even gotten up from the chair he was sitting in, which had made them all know he was not speaking in anger—at least not in the essence of anger likely to retract quickly to be followed by regrets and apologies and promises that the words weren't meant. Celeste had cried but it wasn't a hard cry, and she'd been determined not to let her father believe her decision to leave was the sole result of his ruling jurisdiction, although absent his edict, she might likely have stayed in Buford.

Eleanor had wept as well—softly, at first, as she'd listened to her husband tell their daughter she was no longer welcomed in his house and that she was, in fact, no longer a daughter of his, but by the time Celeste had carried the lone suitcase out the front door and down the rain-soaked path where her dirty Pinto was parked at the road, Eleanor Mhoon's restrained tears had given way to a hysteria her husband had never witnessed during their marriage.

The rumors persisted for years—subsiding at times into a state of dormancy, perhaps, but never going away with any finality. The stories circulating around Buford never directly impacted Donna Potts or the Potts children so much; they'd moved away by the winter following Marjorie Whittlehurst's untimely

Saturday afternoon organ playing, a ritual she'd taken up again in an official capacity after Brother Lumpkin had sheepishly asked her to resume the duties of organist and choir director at Buford Baptist Church. Her vindication was bittersweet, however, when a mild stroke the week before Bible School ensured that Marjorie Whittlehurst had reveled in her last musical comeback.

The rumors were mostly a plague to Eleanor and Leland Mhoon, and the awkward vanishing of their daughter Celeste did nothing but spawn gossip and theories and reports of the occasional sighting, although none of those were ever confirmed with any reliability.

Leland Mhoon spent much of his time in the barn with his cows, while Eleanor kept busy with seamstress obligations to the degree her pace was sometimes manic. The customers who engaged her services never talked to Eleanor Mhoon about anything more than clothing and material and new patterns they'd seen somewhere or another, and if the conversation varied much from sewing it was about weather or randomly about an activity at the church. But underneath the nattering there was always a tension in Eleanor Mhoon's voice suggesting a fear the line would be crossed, that one of them would deliberately ask how Celeste was doing.

But no one ever asked. Not the co-workers and the friends left behind at the Farmers & Merchants Bank; not Brother Lumpkin, and certainly not Marjorie Whittlehurst. And also, as a point of historical reference, Leland and Eleanor Mhoon never heard from Dudley Wayne Potts again even as they understood he'd ended up somewhere in Florida near his people, and Eleanor was most grateful for the leaving alone he'd given them since she was afraid of what Leland would have done if presented with a spontaneous opportunity.

In the nine years since she'd been gone, Leland never asked Eleanor if she'd heard from Celeste. If he had asked her, she would have been truthful in answering that she had not; whether she would have qualified her answer by confessing she'd clandestinely tried to do the contacting herself was never to be known. Because he never asked.

Eleanor Mhoon managed to get the truck all the way up to the house before the large raindrops began pelting the landscape on the day she found her prize at the Buford Baptist Benevolent Boutique. She threw the sack in an old rocking chair in her bedroom and then closed the door, and she sat at the foot of the bed with her hands clasped in front of her for almost an hour.

Since spring, she'd had the feeling Celeste was close by. It wasn't because

Eleanor Mhoon was particularly clairvoyant or because she'd come to possess any conclusive physical evidence of her presence. It was mainly because the last time she'd mailed the small brown envelope to Celeste at the post office box in Monroe it had come back to her at the post office box she'd rented in Buford with messages stamped across it that said "BOX CLOSED" and "NO FWD ADDR."

Eleanor Mhoon's sister, Frieda, who lived in Monroe, Louisiana, never confirmed nor denied that Celeste had sought refuge with her after Christmas in 1974, but eventually Frieda had mailed Eleanor the number of a post office box with a note that said she thought Celeste might be receiving her mail there. It was as if everyone privy to the situation had taken vows of silence never to be breached. And the fact that Eleanor's sister Frieda never visited Buford on account of her dislike of Leland Mhoon, and Eleanor Mhoon never visited Monroe on account of visiting would just upset Leland, it had been explicably easier for all of them to avoid talking about Celeste.

The week after the last small brown envelope had been returned undeliverable to Eleanor Mhoon, she'd gotten another note from her sister in Monroe that stated simply, "Celeste wants to come home." And Eleanor Mhoon had been on edge ever since.

Leland Mhoon

Leland Mhoon said "Good morning, this morning" to everyone he met. He said it at church on Sunday mornings in response whenever someone said to him first "morning, Leland" as he went up the walk toward the sanctuary door, and when the person designated by the Hospitality Committee as that week's greeter asked "How are you this morning, Leland?" while passing out the bulletin, Leland Mhoon never exactly said "fine, thank you" but he did always say back "Good morning, this morning" as he took the bulletin in his hand and ambled to his regular pew.

Leland Mhoon said, "Good morning, this morning" to people he passed on the street and interacted with in the feed store, and he said it to his children on a daily basis until they were grown. It was his proprietary brand of salutation after which and for the remainder of most days, Leland Mhoon was generally a man who made parsimonious use of his vocabulary. He loved his daughters and he loved his wife, Eleanor, and they all knew it despite the absence of much verbal confirmation; his devotion wasn't a theory the family was prone to question.

No one save the cows knew it, but Leland Mhoon sometimes two and three times in a week gave them a collective "Good morning, this morning" upon entering their barn in preparation for milking, because to him, they were more or less an extension of his biological children.

Leland Mhoon owned two vehicles to service both his business and personal needs. The first, and the means by which his wife and family traveled on outings together, was a 1963 Ford pickup with two factory-matching hubcaps, one hubcap from a Chevrolet truck, and one bare wheel with exposed lug nuts. Leland Mhoon wasn't exactly sure of the original factory paint color of his truck since it was more or less a dull royal blue and white by the time he'd acquired it around about 1970. The previous owner had accessorized the bed with a camper top, and after some astute negotiations on Leland's part had agreed to include it in the sale, although the Mhoons were never known to camp, travel, or indulge in recreation. The covering did, however, allow for general hauling without consideration to weather conditions, and Leland seemed to appreciate that.

On the other hand, the truck was not necessarily Leland's vehicle of choice during prolonged periods of precipitation, as it tended to mire down in some of the deeper ruts that cut through what passed as a dirt driveway between the house and the gravel road going by the Mhoons' place. During long rainy spells, Leland considered himself fortunate that he'd always maintained a tractor, while in dry spells considered it a luxury, in fact, when he needed to make an impromptu trip into town on days when Eleanor was away from the place in the truck.

Rain on a Sunday posed its own variety of dilemma in the Mhoon home. Leland did not believe the Lord cared what type of transportation His flock made use of when traveling to and fro as long as an excuse was not made of weather to avoid His house of worship, but in a rare show of dissent assuredly uncommon for Eleanor Mhoon, she refused to be delivered to church on the tractor, choosing instead to don her galoshes and walk the three and a half miles there instead.

To comply with the demands of her job at the Farmers & Merchants Bank—one essential demand being that she report to work every day and by a certain hour—Celeste Mhoon had once implored of her father than he level a clearing near the road as a provisional parking space for her Pinto where she could leave it for more immediate access when conditions did not favor use of the driveway. Thereafter, Eleanor Mhoon had been able to enjoy an era of not walking to church anymore unless it was by choice.

The Mhoon house had four rooms and was constructed in the shape of a square. The front door opened into the living room, on the walls of which hung faded photographs of Celeste and her sister, Cheryl Jean, as well as one framed eight-by-ten color picture of Leland and Eleanor posed for the church directory. The home's only television sat on a portable stand with wheels but it had pretty much been stationary since they'd first plugged it in, there just not being much cause to roll it around anywhere.

Leland and Eleanor's bedroom was to the left. It did not have a closet, but Leland had built a large wardrobe from native pine and finished it off with commercial grade shellac and some door pulls he bought at the Moss Hardware & Supply.

The kitchen and a second bedroom once shared by Celeste and her sister, Cheryl Jean, were in the rear half of the square. The bathroom, an addition not planned until after both children were born, had taken in part of the back porch through which it was necessary to pass in order to use.

Leland Mhoon dressed in either a long-sleeve thermal shirt or a short-sleeve undershirt beneath one of two pairs of denim overalls that he interchanged during the week, and on Sundays he wore a dark brown suit his wife Eleanor had stitched on her automatic sewing machine using a pattern she ordered from a catalog. Every once in a while, she'd allow as to how she still had the pattern and would be pleased to create an alternate in a different fabric, but Leland Mhoon regularly declined and saw no value in wasting money on textiles just to impress people once a week because the Lord didn't care what kind of clothes he had on.

People in Buford thought Leland Mhoon was poor. Some people thought him peculiar, too—an opinion perhaps perpetuated by his unabashed use of a tractor as a perfectly acceptable mode of travel to run errands and purchase supplies—but Leland Mhoon felt blessed. He lived in a house for which he was not beholden to any individual or institution; he had a faithful wife who'd never trifled over the kinds of foolish indulgence that distracted so many of the women in Buford (some in his own congregation at Buford Baptist Church). He'd reared two mannerly daughters; and with the Lord's help he'd provided for them as best he could and to a degree for which criticism was unwarranted, whether it suited the standards others would impose or not.

Leland Mhoon's older daughter, Cheryl Jean, had gifted him with four grandchildren, and although they didn't get to live in Buford, Leland had no right to complain about geography when he'd been so blessed to have them in the first place. Celeste was still single even after turning thirty, but her father had more or less taken for granted she would stay in Buford to raise a family of her own, and it had still been feasible to think it would happen in his lifetime, God willing. He'd just always had to remember to be patient and not doubt the Lord's plan.

All that Leland Mhoon valued and relied on was irreversibly trampled one Saturday afternoon in October of 1974. In the end, he could only blame himself. He'd been impulsively quick to lay fault elsewhere, whether on the snooty people who would work in banks and wear fancy clothes and talk about things with one another that should never be talked about outside the walls of the home, or on a mother who surely should have possessed the womanly instincts to detect covetousness in her own daughter.

Leland Mhoon even questioned his very faith and his God and begged in prayer to understand how the Lord could forsake a man so ignorant of the sin he'd committed to deserve such tribulation. But in the end, Leland was Celeste's father. And her shame belonged to him.

After October 12, 1974, Leland Mhoon never said "Good morning, this morning" to anyone ever again. Not even to a cow.

Mrs. Potts

On the evening of October 12, 1974, Donna Potts had expected to surprise her husband with his favorite supper of spaghetti and meatballs, but instead she was pacing inside her house. She'd start at the kitchen sink and go west across the diamond-patterned vinyl floor through a doorway leading to the compact dining room with its Duncan Phyfe table accommodating six when the leaf was installed, and on most trips she'd peek into the china cabinet and have all sorts of wild thoughts when imagining never celebrating another holiday with her husband and the good crystal they'd collected as wedding gifts, not to mention the new napkin rings she'd only that week ordered from the Lillian Vernon catalog to use for Thanksgiving the next month. It was a set of eight, featuring two each of turkeys, pumpkins, Pilgrims, and Indians. The catalog guaranteed her family would marvel at the festive table setting, but Donna Potts guessed Lillian Vernon couldn't keep such a promise if the head of the family wasn't there.

From the dining room, she'd turn south and move swiftly through the living room where the enlarged portrait of the family taken for the church directory hung over the sofa. The smiles of the family in the picture seemed to mock her each time she passed and even though she vowed not to look up at it again, she somehow couldn't avoid its lure.

Just about every lap included an excursion down the narrow hallway, past the rooms where the two children were ignorantly sleeping, and dead ending at the entrance to the master bedroom. The double bed with its spindle foot posts was neatly made and awaiting the father who was absent from the home.

Due to the modern floor plan of the Potts residence, Donna Potts could continue in her more or less counter-clockwise track through a small paneled den where Mary Richards and Mr. Grant were engaging in a playful repartee on the console television set, and afterward end up back at the sink in the kitchen where she'd stop for a moment, stare into the darkness on the other side of the small uncovered window, look up at the ceiling, and launch once more toward the dining room where the tour and its despair repeated.

Mary Richards eventually gave way to Mr. Bob Newhart who'd at some point become Miss Carol Burnett with special guests Telly Savalas and the Smothers Brothers, and it was late into the evening before Donna Potts finally received the telephone call placed from Dothan, but with no additional detail to suggest where her husband was seemingly holed up.

As fearful as he'd been to dial his number in the first place, Dudley Wayne Potts suspected he'd be able to quickly ascertain the extent of information that had been relayed to his wife since driving away from the church parking lot that afternoon.

"Good Lord, Dudley, what are you doing in Dothan? I've been worried out of my mind ever since Brother Lumpkin left!"

"So Brother Lumpkin was there?"

"Yes! He came here looking for you!"

"What did you tell him?"

"I told him you were at the church practicing the puppets! But he said, no, he didn't believe you were!"

"What else did he say?"

"Just that he needed to talk to you as soon as possible, and that I was to call him if I heard from you! Dudley, what is going on?"

"Donna …"

She was patient, at first, while standing in her kitchen in Buford holding the telephone receiver with both hands. She was completely still, bracing herself for some kind of revelation that would make some sense of the afternoon.

"What? Are you there?"

"Yeah," he said. "I'm still here."

Donna Potts allowed about another ten seconds to elapse before her resolve decidedly changed. Clearly, her husband was not deceased. He was not unconscious in a ditch somewhere amid the wreckage of his truck; he had not fallen victim to foul play and that made her glad she'd not gone ahead and alerted the Litton County Sheriff's Department because, certainly, that cause of death had crossed her mind more than once, too.

"Dudley, I've been so worried I would have already called the law by now if it hadn't been for Brother Lumpkin."

"What do you mean?"

"Well, when I told him I thought you were still at puppet rehearsal he said he believed something had happened at the church—something that might be upsetting to some people—and that he really just needed to talk to you so ya'll could straighten it out."

"That's not gonna happen."

"What?"

She got no immediate reply.

"Dudley!"

"Yeah."

"What do you mean that's not gonna happen? When are you going to be home?"

"I don't know."

"Dudley, what was Brother Lumpkin talking about? What happened at the church this afternoon?"

"It's …" he stalled. "There are some things you'd be better off not knowing, Donna."

"Better off?! I've been going out of my mind wondering where you were and what could have happened, and I think I deserve to know!"

"I'm going back to Florida in the morning."

Donna Potts suddenly freed up one hand that had been gripping the telephone and used it to pull over a chair, into which she promptly sank. The remainder of the conversation with her husband that evening was remarkably brief, as his participation thereafter was devoid of any useful detail. He merely told her he'd be in touch when he got settled, not specifically mentioning where he intended that to be, but assuring her he planned to take care of their children.

It would be a matter of years before Donna or her children saw Dudley Wayne Potts in person again.

Pumpkins, Pilgrims, Poinsettias

Classes resumed at Homer T. Litton Grammar School on the last Monday of August in 1983, one week shy of the Labor Day holiday, and for most everyone else acclimating to another academic year the novelty of Ethel Maywood's passing had expired. Elba Rae's loss, in fact, was only residually mentioned, and then it was in the context of selling Ethel Maywood's house because Irma Young was mildly curious as to whether Elba Rae Van Oaks had at all considered moving into what was generally considered the Maywood family home and leaving her residence on Highway 29 that, by default, was diluted to the status of being considered just the Van Oaks family home. But since there had been no Van Oaks heirs reared at the place and Elba Rae was the only Van Oaks living there—with the exception of Mr. Wiggles who was, by birth, rightfully a Maywood anyhow—it seemed logical for Irma Young to assume Elba Rae might have at least studied the idea.

Elba Rae synopsized an answer to Irma Young regarding the last will and testament of the late Ethel Maywood leaving the real estate equally to Elba Rae and her sister, Lila Fessmire, and that as such the decision was made early on a sale was the most equitable disposition, and that anyway, while they both might have been fraught with sentiment over the home place, Ethel Maywood's house was not at all modern, and it was drafty in the winter and hot as a hen in a wool basket in the summer months; and from strictly a comfort factor, Elba Rae was happy to stay right where she was, and the possibility Lila Fessmire was ever living in Buford again was beyond remote. Elba Rae Van Oaks had always found Irma Young to be a little too inquisitive for her own good. Coupled with the fact that before the monthly faculty potlucks were discontinued in the 1970s Irma used to concoct one of the worst meatloaves to have ever been served in Litton County, there were days Elba Rae didn't have a bit of use for her.

The seasonal heat relinquished to more pleasant days and normalcy was restored, so much so that Elba Rae and her cousin, Hazel Burns, were back to discussing mostly school matters and school people when they'd opt for lunch out at the All Seasons Restaurant after church on Sundays. Two months drifted away as if the summer had never happened.

Elba Rae Van Oaks did not like Halloween. But fifth grade children were just about certain to be predominantly enthusiastic over it, which meant as she'd done for the decades before, she had to endure the day her precious students donned their costumes and their masks to participate in the party held at the Homer T. Litton Grammar School for grades one through six.

Some of the room mothers were charged with baking the cupcakes that Elba Rae Van Oaks knew as sure as she knew her own name would be chocolate and smeared to the heavens with some vile looking shade of orange frosting, and the other room mothers were responsible for concocting a punch that Elba Rae Van Oaks just hoped wouldn't bode a repeat of the unfortunate year a well-intending mother had brought dry ice to effect smoldering. Willadean Hendrix's little grandson, Hoot, who was known to be instinctively curious and popular among his teachers for paying such good attention during science lessons, had apparently not associated danger with the nice mother's warning to avoid any nature of contact with the punch bowl, serving to heighten the element of surprise when he'd rolled up the sleeve of his Six Million Dollar Man costume and plunged his arm into the smoky cauldron all the way up to his elbow. The burns didn't turn out to be as severe as by all rights they should have been, but neither did they do a thing toward softening Elba Rae Van Oaks's disdain for the holiday.

And as if extra commotion at school weren't enough, it was by tradition that the First Avenue United Methodist Church put on the Halloween Youth Party, and Elba Rae Van Oaks knew just as sure as she knew it was inevitable one of her students would arrive at school in some kind of get up making it highly impractical—if not impossible— to go to the restroom, she'd be expected at a minimum to furnish some nature of the refreshments for the church event.

"And they want everybody to bring a covered dish," Elba Rae said to Hazel Burns as they entered the school lounge on the Friday afternoon before Halloween. The final bell had rung and most of the buses were already gone from the campus. "I just need to get my cottage cheese out of the icebox and I'll be ready to go."

"Yeah," Hazel said, "I heard some of them talking about it in Sunday school last week."

"Honestly, I wouldn't mind going places sometime if you didn't have to always take food. It does look like they could have one thing up at that church when you didn't have to drag a dish. Why, when St. Peter calls my name I'll probably have to take a casserole."

"I know it," Hazel agreed. "I told Ulgine I'd bring all the paper plates and the ice."

"Anyway, some of those with little ones ought to be doing the dragging if you ask me."

Elba Rae carefully mined a carton half full of cottage cheese without disturbing the placement of dishes and food and condiments belonging to the other faculty and staff, a talent she'd purposely honed following the near riot that had broken out a couple of years before after Claude Pickle openly accused someone of stealing the leftover deviled eggs he'd brought for lunch.

He'd first been heard grumbling in and about the area of the lounge refrigerator but had apparently become more agitated after the ransacking he'd given every shelf and drawer failed to produce the lone brown paper bag containing the three deviled eggs he was positive he'd stowed on the way to his classroom that morning.

"Where is my sack?!" he'd screamed to the general audience in the lounge that day, and although there had been assorted replies with a common theme of they hadn't seen his sack and which sack was he talking about and what did it have in it, Claude Pickle had just screamed "It was my lunch!" and stormed out of the lounge.

Within minutes, he had returned with Mr. Bailey closely in tow.

"Ask them!" Claude demanded.

The three tables of people theretofore enjoying an otherwise uneventful lunch period had been shocked.

"Excuse me," the principal began. "But Mr. Pickle seems to be missing his lunch from the refrigerator and he—"

"It doesn't *seem* to be missing, it *is* missing! I put it in there this morning, and now it's gone. And unless a student got in here, which I highly doubt, I don't think a sack of deviled eggs got up and walked out of here!"

"Mr. Pickle, please. May I handle this?"

"Yes, sir. I'm sorry. But it's just plain rude for someone to take something out of this refrigerator they know doesn't belong to them! It's—it's stealing!"

Howard Bailey had turned and begun to address his employees.

"Does anyone have any idea of how Mr. Pickle's lunch could have possibly gotten," he paused, "misplaced?"

There'd been complete silence in the lounge.

"Thrown away, perhaps? By accident?"

Mr. Bailey had observed a consensus of head shaking and looked at Claude Pickle.

"And you're absolutely sure you put your lunch in there—today?"

"Yes, I'm sure! I put the sack inside my satchel like I do every morning on my way out the door. And now it's gone!"

"Well, I'm sorry. I'd hate to think a student has somehow pilfered a key to this lounge, but I suppose it's possible. And if something like this happens again, we might need to look into changing the lock."

"Fine!" Claude Pickle said with a pout. "I guess I'll have to go down to the cafeteria and buy my lunch now if I don't want to starve to death," upon which he had done just that.

"Excuse the intrusion," Mr. Bailey had said before following Claude Pickle out of the lounge.

"Of all the nerve," Elba Rae Van Oaks had said as soon as the door closed behind them. "Who would want steal that little fool's old sack of eggs?"

"You know how paranoid he is, Elba Rae," another teacher seated to her left had offered. "He always thinks somebody is after him. I think he's even afraid of some of the students."

"Well, if he's that miserable maybe he just ought to whistle his dogs in home and find something else to do!"

The indignity of the accusation was never erased, especially after into each teacher's mail slot in the school office had been placed a typed memorandum reminding all users of the faculty lounge it was imperative they respect the property of others and not consume anything from the shared refrigerator that they did not put there or otherwise explicitly have permission to consume.

An apology likely would have gone a long way toward diluting the lingering ill will between Claude Pickle and most of the other staff had Claude Pickle apologized. And although it was never told, he had belabored the idea after going to his truck when school let out that afternoon and being nearly overcome by the pungent tang of vinegar and hot mayonnaise that had been radiating from a crumpled up brown paper sack overturned on the floor and partially underneath the seat of the passenger's side.

"Speaking of little ones," Hazel Burns said while Elba Rae placed her carton in the bottom of a tote bag, "it's getting pretty close to Charity's due date, isn't it?"

Elba Rae Van Oaks did not particularly think her grumble about providing food for the church's Halloween party a worthy segue into a subject as potentially awkward as anything to do with the Fessmire family, and Elba Rae wondered if maybe Hazel had just been waiting for an opportunity to ask.

"I'm not really sure, Hazel," she said.

Elba Rae knew Hazel likely considered the lack of confirmation relative to protracted sensitivity surrounding the date of the child's conception and not as much related to a perceived impasse between Elba Rae and Lila, because on that afternoon in October, Hazel let it go.

*   *   *

The children made collapsible turkey centerpieces out of construction paper for their art lesson the week before Thanksgiving holidays, and no sooner had they gotten back to school afterward, they were worrying Elba Rae about putting up the Christmas tree in the corner of the classroom where the globe normally rested on its attached metal stand. Yet no matter the level of worrying she got over the years—and despite the fact Claude Pickle would always decorate the first Monday after Thanksgiving—Elba Rae stood firm on disallowing any sign of a Christmas ornament until after the first full week into December.

A party for the children was held on Friday the sixteenth, the last day of school before a two-week vacation. The long break prompted Elba Rae Van

Oaks to give her desk a more thorough going over before closing it up and heading for home; it was a habit she'd learned the hard way after unwittingly leaving a banana in her second drawer before the 1978 holidays. Hazel Burns strolled in just as the desk check was finalized.

"Hey," she said.

"Hey," Elba Rae said back.

"Mr. Bailey said I could go on home so I guess vacation is officially here."

"Well, I'm ready for it."

"How was the party?"

"I survived it," said Elba Rae, as she took her coat from where it had been hanging off the back of her chair.

"Were the children wild?"

"They weren't too bad," she said, slipping one arm into her coat sleeve. "Except that Richardson boy."

"What'd he do now?"

"Well, I was letting them play musical chairs—which I wouldn't do if it weren't Christmas. They make such a wreck of my room, moving all the desks around, and then I've got to practically threaten them with a yardstick to get everything back in order when we're through."

Hazel Burns took a moment to observe the neatly lined rows of desks. "Yardstick must have done the trick."

"Anyway," Elba Rae Van Oaks said while buttoning her coat, "they're so rambunctious till I know they get hot in here. But when I took the needle up from the record player the last time and looked, that Richardson boy had stripped his shirt all the way off and was running toward a desk barechested."

"For goodness sake."

"I told him to get his shirt back on and I didn't mean maybe. The very idea. Wanting to take his clothes off in here in front of the other children."

"Well," Hazel Burns said, "you know those Richardsons have always had a touch of it in their family."

"I know it. And that little one is going to be just like his grandfather. I wouldn't be surprised if he isn't walking around outside without a stitch on one of these days."

"Me either," Hazel quickly concurred. "His daddy's been wild since the day he was born. His granddaddy was a nut. It just runs in that family."

"And I don't mean to pick on a little boy that probably can't help it," Elba Rae went on. "But you know before he got his shirt back on, I couldn't help but notice he's going to have those same big breasts all the Richardson men have had through the years."

"Well, now, that is a shame," Hazel agreed.

"Anyway," Elba Rae gave the room one last look over. "I guess I'm ready."

"Before we go …"

"What?"

Hazel stared at her for a few seconds, as though it would prompt Elba Rae to initiate the conversation so she wouldn't be forced to introduce it herself.

"You haven't said a word about the baby."

Elba Rae set her pocketbook on top of her desk and stared back, with no response.

"Oh. I'm sorry—I don't mean to bring up any unpleasantness. But I thought you might have at least *mentioned* that Charity had the baby yesterday."

Elba Rae remained stoic.

"There's no unpleasantness, Hazel, I just don't know a lot about it. Bucky called last night and told me, but he was in a hurry and said he had a lot of other people to call, and I haven't talked to any of them again yet."

"Elba Rae?"

Elba Rae continued to stand still behind her pushed-in chair, holding onto the straps of the purse she rested on the desk.

"You know I've never pried about you and Lila."

"Hazel, there's nothing to know."

"Then just listen." It was uncharacteristically bold of Hazel Burns to be so direct with Elba Rae, having as she had for the totality of their lives together historically deferred to Elba Rae's temperament as a conversational guide.

"When you came back from the wedding and snatched up Mr. Wiggles without saying a word to me, I could tell you and Lila had probably had a falling out about something. Now it doesn't matter to me if it was about the wedding or Charity or the fact there was apparently already a baby on the way."

"We didn't have any words about Charity, Hazel, so there's no need to go on about this."

"Well, then I don't care if it was about cleaning out Aunt Ethel's house or sorting out her things. I don't even care if it was about the night Aunt Ethel was dying in the hospital and you didn't call Lila until after she'd passed."

Elba Rae was actually stunned at her cousin's abruptness. "There was nothing Lila could have done in the middle of the night when Dr. Bud said Momma was failing!"

"She could have gotten in the car and come to the hospital and stood at the bedside with you, and I'd bet anything that's just what she would have done—if you had given her the chance."

"Oh, Hazel, you don't know what you're talking about," Elba Rae said while shaking her head.

"Don't I?"

Elba Rae slowly pulled her chair back away from the desk and sat down in it. "I'm not sorry for being alone with my mother when she died."

She said it with the relief of someone making a confession, which only served to confirm what Hazel Burns had theorized since the morning Ethel Maywood passed away.

"Maybe not. But what's done is done. Aunt Ethel is gone and you can't take any of it back."

"Which is why it doesn't matter now, Hazel."

"Does Aunt Ethel's first great-grandchild matter to you, Elba Rae?"

Elba Rae looked up at her but didn't answer.

"This is the first born member of a whole new generation of your family. Do you really want to sever your ties with that?"

"In case you hadn't figured it out, Lila and I haven't spoken since I was there for Charity's wedding in June."

Hazel Burns assumed a seated position in one of the student desks directly in front of Elba Rae. "It's about the hospital, isn't it? You know, I could tell the night at the funeral home Lila was going to have that stuck in her craw for a long time."

Hazel was surprised that Elba Rae laughed a little.

"You know, it doesn't really have anything to do with when Momma died."

"It doesn't?"

Elba Rae Van Oaks looked at her wristwatch and took in a cautious deep breath. For the next twenty minutes, she extolled Hazel Burns with a story about finding a bunch of old photographs in a box when she and Lila were cleaning out their mother's bedroom closet, and about one photograph in particular featuring two teenage girls made up to be what passed for glamorous posing in the storeroom of the VFW Hall, and in part two of the story that took more or less the same amount of minutes to convey, Elba Rae told Hazel Burns about the day she'd come upon the same photograph in Lila's kitchen, and how seeing it again had somehow revived the whole controversy but that the worst part of it was how Lila apparently associated the very period during which the Miss Honeysuckle pageant took place with a time when their relationship was irrevocably broken.

And then she was silent. At last—provoked such as she had been by her cousin's officious questioning about Lila, Charity, and the new little baby—Elba Rae felt an empty sensation from the draining her emotional hopper had just taken. And unburdened, too, if she was being completely straightforward, because she'd finally confided the sequence of quarrels that had begun at Ethel Maywood's house and ended in Lila's kitchen. It was a relief to finally tell her side.

"Elba Rae?" Hazel said with great reserve after a moment of complete digestion.

"What?"

"That's the dumbest thing I ever heard."

"Dumb?!"

"Yes, dumb! The two of you carrying on like that over some old picture of Mary Alice? It hardly sounds important enough to stop speaking to each other!"

"Lila stood right there in her kitchen and just out and out accused me of hating her. *Hating* her, Hazel! That's a terrible thing to accuse me of! It's un-Christian!"

"And what did you say?"

"I told her she was wrong!"

"But you don't think she believed you?"

"Hazel, she's my sister. I could never hate her. We've never had all that much in common—you know that—and maybe I have been a little ... resentful over the years because she was living up there and I was the one in Buford having to always be on call when Momma and Daddy needed something. That doesn't make me hate her."

"No. You and I know that," Hazel said.

"But maybe it did make me feel like I shouldn't have to share Momma's last hour with Lila. Maybe it did make me feel like I deserved to be alone in there. I think I earned that right."

"So what are you going to do now? Are you going to let Charity's baby grow up without knowing she's even got a great aunt down here?"

"I don't know what I can do at this point. You know, Lila's got as much to do with all this as I have. It takes two."

"Elba Rae," Hazel said as she squeezed out of the little desk and stood up, "I've heard you say it too many times yourself."

"Say what?"

"That life can change in the twinkling of an eye."

Hazel Burns, as it turned out, was as near about close to an authority on the full out details of Fettis Van Oaks's last day in the house as anyone was besides Elba Rae, and as impractical a skill as it was to have acquired, felt confident she could do the story equal justice if there was ever anyone who needed a lesson on how friable life could be and, God forbid, the consequences of unscheduled passage in the chariot.

"In the twinkling of an eye, Elba Rae."

Mothers Day

Since the stormy day that Eleanor Mhoon had dropped her sack in the floor at the Buford Baptist Benevolence Boutique, she'd not once slept through an entire night. Consequently, the morning she drove out of Buford in the old Ford truck with the antiquated camper top found her especially fatigued.

The apartment was on the second floor of a long rectangular building with a wrought iron staircase outside at one end. The boundaries of each unit were easily distinguished by its one door and single window to the left but from the ground level parking lot they all looked alike.

Eleanor Mhoon climbed the stairs and slowly strode down the walk until she arrived at the door with the reflective numbers two-zero-six glued on in a diagonal pattern. Her heart raced and she could barely feel her hand against the wooden door when she finally knocked on it.

Their embrace was long and silent until Celeste spoke up first.

"I can't believe you're actually here."

"Me either," Eleanor said. "And I can't believe you've been here all this time. So close by."

"I really thought Aunt Frieda would have told you by now."

"She never did. Never told me anything about you, for that matter."

"I made her promise. I thought the less you knew, the better off you'd be."

"Oh, Celeste," Eleanor sighed. "All these years. But why here?"

"It kind of all just happened, Momma. I didn't really plan for it but I decided it might be a step, you know?"

"Didn't you want me to know?"

"I did, Momma. When I felt like the time was right. Listen, you remember Becky Sue—we were tellers together at the bank. Anyway, I'd heard she moved over here and was working at the mill, so I just called information one day and got her number."

"I imagine she was surprised to hear from you. After so long, I mean."

"Yeah. She was. She even said something about not knowing whether I was still alive or not."

Eleanor Mhoon grimaced at the very thought.

"Anyway, we talked a couple of more times, and one day she said she thought she could get me on if I was willing to move to Alexander City. So, the next thing I knew ..."

"And it's working out?"

"Well, it's not as nice as the bank. But the pay's better and they're good about giving me the schedule I need."

Eleanor surveyed the surroundings for the first time since Celeste answered her knock.

"It's real nice, Celeste."

"It's okay," she said.

"When I got the note you sent me with the address, I wasn't sure I'd be able to find it."

"I wasn't sure you'd try," Celeste replied.

"I never considered staying away."

There passed some seconds where mother and daughter were again satisfied merely to look at one another and take stock of the elapsed years.

"Let's sit down, Momma. You look tired."

"I didn't sleep much last night. I haven't slept much period since I heard you'd been in Buford."

"I didn't want you to find out that way."

"You apparently walked right inside a room full of people at the funeral home. Did you think nobody would recognize you?"

"I figured somebody might. But I didn't really care that night because I wanted to pay my respects."

"That's another thing I couldn't figure. How did you even know that Maywood woman?"

"I didn't especially, but I know Miss Elba Rae."

"Well, I remember you having her for your teacher one year."

"Fifth grade."

"And I recall you being sort of fond of her. I guess it was a nice thing for you to do—to go see her, I mean."

"Do you remember how many times we had to go off to school without a lunch or the money to buy one?"

Eleanor Mhoon had reared her children the absolute best way she knew how under the conditions God had provided, and it hurt to be reminded of the times she'd failed one of them.

"Celeste, you know how hard things were for us back then. I would have never let you miss a meal if I could have helped it."

"I know, Momma. I'm not criticizing you. But when I was in the fifth grade, I never had to miss lunch. Not after Miss Elba Rae figured out there were days I didn't have any money."

"What did she do?"

"She paid for them. Out of her own pocket. And I bet she never said a word to you."

Eleanor Mhoon wiped a tear off of her cheek.

"She took care of me, Momma. I didn't realize what she'd done until I was older. I always wanted to thank her. I thought about writing her a letter one time but I was too embarrassed about waiting so long, plus I wasn't sure she'd even remember me. I told that story to Becky Sue once. She used to go to the Methodist church in Buford, and when she heard about Miss Ethel, she made sure I knew."

Celeste disappeared briefly into the bathroom and came out with a tissue that she handed to her mother.

"Please don't cry, Momma. I didn't tell you that to hurt your feelings."

"I know you didn't."

"And I never would have gotten by all these years without you helping me. I'll never forget it."

"I did what I could, Celeste. I always wanted it to be more."

"I'm surprised he'd ever let you send me money."

Eleanor Mhoon looked away, to the side mainly but focusing on nothing.

"What's the matter? Did he have a fit about it?"

"Your daddy's never known about the money."

"Never known?" gasped Celeste. "How could he not know? He's always kept up with every penny he had."

"He didn't know because it wasn't rightly his money—it was mine."

"I don't understand. Daddy always controlled the money. He handed you an allowance and expected you to make do."

"And I did make do. Sometimes better than he thought I did. And on top of that, I sewed for a lot of folks over the years, Celeste. Some of them were, well, some of them appreciated my work more than others and were generous to show it when the time came. So, I eventually opened my own account at the bank. I asked them to mail the statements to that box at the post office because I didn't want your daddy to ever see them. And that way, I could do with the money how I pleased without worrying over it."

"You mean all this time? You worked, and squirreled away money—just to be able to send it to me?"

"Celeste, I didn't stop worrying about you just because you left home. You didn't stop being my daughter the day you walked down the hill and disappeared."

Celeste Mhoon stepped across the room and looked out the window.

"Momma, I don't know what to say."

"How about thank you?"

Celeste turned around and went to her mother. She didn't thank her by invoking the specific words, but she put her arms around Eleanor and embraced her fiercely before letting go.

"Does Daddy even know you're here?"

"No," said Eleanor. "But I'm going to tell him. And I'm going to talk to him but good about straightening some things out. I want you to come home—not just here, but back to Buford. Where you belong."

"I don't know if I can do it, Momma."

"But you want to, don't you?"

"Every time I think about it all I hear in my head are the things Daddy said. And the way he looked at me when he told me to go."

"That was nine years ago, Celeste. It's time we all healed."

"He told me I wasn't his daughter. What makes you think I can be now?"

"I'm not saying it'll be easy, but he's had a long time to regret what he did. He'd never admit it to me, and I doubt he'll ever admit it to you, but—"

The sound of brakes squeaking as they were applied interrupted her thought.

"What was that?" asked Eleanor.

"The bus. It stops right out front."

Eleanor looked toward the window. "Is he ...?"

"He's home."

*   *   *

Celeste Mhoon had not corresponded with her mother in the nine years since leaving Buford. She had wanted to—many times—but much as she'd procrastinated over a simple thank you letter that would have meant the world to a careered school teacher, she'd put it off and lost her nerve and figured she could always do it the next week or the next month or even wait for a holiday. One year she had bought a birthday card with every intention of mailing it to her mother at the post office number that was always on the return address of the brown envelopes with the fifty dollar bill. And if she had, she was going to enclose the photograph. So that Eleanor Mhoon could actually see what her grandson looked like.

The two women were facing the door when the boy opened it and hurried inside, but the sight of the stranger stopped him mid-step.

"Hi, sweetheart," Celeste said to him.

"Hey, Mom," he said, as he cautiously placed a small book bag on a table in the open kitchen.

"Did you have a good day at school?"

"It was okay."

"Come here and say hello."

The child walked over to his mother, who pulled him toward her and squeezed him until he giggled.

"I want you to meet somebody. Somebody very special."

He looked up at Eleanor Mhoon. "Hello," he said to her.

"This is your grandmother."

"I am so glad ..." and when Eleanor's tears fell that time, they were most certainly not ones generated by grief or sadness, and were not at all ones caused by shame. "I am so glad to meet you," she managed to say.

"Why is she crying, Mom?"

"Because," Celeste Mhoon said through her own sniffle, "she really is happy. We both are."

The little boy with the big brown eyes of his mother but who also bore the unmistakable resemblance to Dudley Wayne Potts did not understand this concept of crying but saying you were happy, but he trusted his mother, and when his grandmother extended her arms, he went to her willingly.

"You know what?" asked Eleanor Mhoon when she finally let go of him. "I don't even know your name."

"My name is Leland," the child said.

The Final Note on Marjorie Whittlehurst

After her mild stroke in the summer of 1975, Miss Marjorie Whittlehurst had been most grateful for the offer of convalescence at the home of her nephew, Mike Whittlehurst. Mike farmed over in Chilton County where he lived in a modest brick house with his pleasant wife but not with his two children who were, mercifully, either attending summer classes at the university in Tuscaloosa in the case of the younger child, or already matriculated and gainfully employed in Meridian in the case of the older one. Those particulars had made for practically no debating at all as far as Miss Marjorie had been concerned since had she accepted the invitation of her other nephew, Miller Whittlehurst, who—from an isolated point of reference factoring only proximity—was co-manager of the Piggly Wiggly in Buford and lived less than one mile from Marjorie Whittlehurst as the crow flew, she'd known she would have been sharing quarters with Miller's always harried wife and their three children who hadn't even gotten through high school yet, and Marjorie Whittlehurst had thought there was nothing about those prospects conducive to an expeditious recuperation.

Her gait was a little slower and the feeling never came back fully to the lower part of her left arm, but Miss Marjorie had no intention of being a burden to her nephew and his wife in Chilton County. And the very idea she'd end up stowed away in the confines of her other nephew's home in Buford had been enough to will a recovery medically satisfying enough to return to her own house less than two weeks after the stroke.

It was fortunate for Marjorie Whittlehurst that her homecoming had coincided with the passing of Ulgine Babcock's mother because that casualty had freed up for new employment a most capable woman named Aileen, who was retired from the cafeteria of the Homer T. Litton Grammar School. As a means of supplementing the monetary bounty of her retirement, Aileen had taken to sitting with the elderly and offering light housekeeping services and would even drive her charges where they needed to go in and around Buford, if they so desired.

Thereafter, Miss Marjorie was rarely seen on Saturday mornings at nine o'clock shuffling into Buford Styles for a rinse and tease and afterward trundling down the aisles of the Piggly Wiggly unless it was on the arm of the devoted Aileen, who finally learned how to maneuver the Dodge just precisely enough to avoid superfluous instruction from her passenger. Miss Marjorie, in turn, had learned to incorporate the John Deere cushion as effectively on the right side of the vehicle as she had in the driver's seat.

It was a pleasant Saturday afternoon in November of 1983 when Marjorie Whittlehurst finally got up the nerve. Either Mabel Moss or Willadean Hendrix was usually good to come by the house on Sunday mornings and then bring her back home after preaching, but every once in a rare while when she felt especially frisky and was sure her right arm was functioning at full capacity, Miss Marjorie would, against all sage advice tendered by those in the community from whom she ever sought counsel, take the key to the Polara and slide her cushion back over to the pilot seat and drive herself right up to the church in defiance of anyone assuming she was overly dependent on hired help.

But there was one thing she'd not had the effrontery to test since the stroke; she'd thought about it a lot—it was one of her first memories in the hospital—but there hadn't been a suitable opportunity with Aileen around on so many Saturday afternoons, and having a spectator on the first try was out of the question. On the days Aileen went home early, Miss Marjorie admitted to herself she'd ultimately opted to stay away because she feared how hurtful it would be to confront the reality she couldn't play the organ at all anymore.

Her right arm was strong and purposeful, and she was at least feeling some tingles in all five fingers of her left hand, so that November afternoon when Aileen finally told her she believed she'd go on to her house if Miss Marjorie didn't need anything else, Marjorie Whittlehurst decided the day of reckoning was upon her. She knew right where to find the music, so she picked it up, backed down the driveway slowly, and pointed the Dodge in the direction of Buford Baptist Church.

There were no other vehicles at the church that afternoon, but she drove around to the kitchen entrance and back just to be sure as she wanted to be positively certain. It was an inspiring sensation to walk up the aisle of the unlocked sanctuary on the approach to the organ because it flooded her with recollections of Saturday afternoons long passed, and it was only once she reached the first step to the choir loft—and even then it didn't last very long—that her pleasant reminiscence was tainted by a flash of depravity when she thought about the tawdry Mhoon girl and the contemptible choir director who'd tucked his tail and ridden out of Buford and had never been heard from since, at least not by anyone who'd ever admitted as such.

She was careful and deliberate about ascending the four steps, holding the rail with the same right hand that clutched the sheet music, and was a little winded by the time she fully landed in the loft proper. Getting winded was a byproduct of being eighty-five years old, she thought, and didn't mean her fingers couldn't still play the organ; at least it didn't mean that yet, anyway. She paused for a moment to look around the empty church and to listen to the hush as well. She was alone.

When she pulled open the organ bench and found the green velveteen pillow with the strings that tied—still put away just like she'd left it the last time she played before the stroke—Marjorie Whittlehurst felt as she had many times in the sanctuary of Buford Baptist Church the presence of God. All was right in the heavens and she was where she was supposed to be.

She had not come, however, without anticipating that her ability might have suffered at least somewhat due to the infirmity and not to mention due to the amount of time that had passed since she'd even sat at the organ last. It was just to be expected, she told herself, and there was no use taking the mulligrubs back home with her if such proved to be the case.

She tied the strings as best she could and climbed on the bench, timidly unfolding the music and smoothing it out with her right hand to flatten the crease. She turned on the mighty instrument. And then she placed both hands in position.

The sound coming from the big pipe organ was as restorative to Marjorie Whittlehurst as any exercise or out-patient therapy at Litton County Memorial Hospital had ever been to her initially following the illness. Somehow she'd known—in the most private and sacred crook of her soul—it would be.

The Holy Spirit was in Litton County, Alabama, and it permeated within the walls of Buford Baptist Church. It came down and flowed right through the compromised body of Marjorie Whittlehurst and out the tips of both her right and left hands. Because on that November afternoon in 1983, Marjorie Whittlehurst performed "For the Beauty of the Earth" as brilliantly as the most accomplished of organists and the most skilled of musicians would ever hope to have the prospect of playing.

She held the last notes of the song, not wanting to remove her hands from the keyboard, and looked into the rafters of the empty church.

"Oh, thank you, Lord," Marjorie Whittlehurst praised. "Thank you!"

*   *   *

Most folks who'd never asked probably assumed Brother Lumpkin was the first one to arrive at Buford Baptist Church on Sunday mornings, him being the preacher and all and probably wanting some time to reflect in the minister's study before taking the pulpit, but that was rarely if ever the case.

As a rule, Mr. Jack Moss was the first to arrive at the church on Sunday mornings because as Sunday School Superintendent, it was his duty to illuminate the hallways of the education building and switch on the lights inside the individual classrooms, and make whatever adjustments were warranted by the season to the three different thermostats controlling the climate of the facility. All those preparations just took time most folks didn't consider. Jack's wife, Florine, was absolutely not prone to accompany her husband that early and always arrived by separate transport only as Sunday school was about to commence and some days as much as ten minutes after.

Because Jack Moss was accustomed to being there first to illuminate and to switch on and to adjust, it was almost alarming when he rode up in his truck on an overcast Sunday morning in November and discovered the white Dodge parked so close to the entrance it was practically obstructing access to the sidewalk.

He heard the music before opening the door of his truck. Odd, he thought. But then it didn't sound so much like music; it sounded simply like one sound. One disagreeable and surely unplanned sound.

Jack Moss maneuvered around the Polara and went up the sidewalk to the double doors. He opened them and leisurely walked inside. The organ sounded much louder with the sanctuary devoid of the usual crowd of people that would otherwise be sitting there to absorb the vibrations.

The scene was certainly bizarre as he walked up the aisle toward the altar and the loft. The organ was on, clearly, and sound was obviously blasting forth from it, but Jack Moss saw no indication of its cause. Whether some type of spontaneous malfunction, he didn't know, but evidently some keys were stuck down in their depressed positions to produce the dissonant noise. And that's all Jack Moss could think to call it—noise—Lord's house or not.

Jack Moss was no organist. He'd never had his fingers on the keys of a piano, and his wife had once implored of him it would be more serving if he'd just hold the hymnbook and move his lips in silence to the music being played rather than actually release into the congregation the sound that came naturally from his throat when he purported to sing along, and she'd made it clear every time he dared to defy her sphere of influence as a music critic it was just a blessing he'd chosen a living in the hardware business and not in the singing field because otherwise they surely would have been on the public assistance years ago.

Jack Moss did, nonetheless and despite Florine's assessment of his crooning talent, believe if he just looked around at the pipe organ long enough he could locate some type of button or lever to disengage it completely and put a temporary stop to the racquet. "Organ failure," he sort of chuckled to himself going up the steps toward it.

And then he finally got close enough to see. It was a sight so shocking and so disturbing to Jack Moss that it was nigh on into the next spring before he could again bring himself to be the first one to arrive at the church on Sunday mornings.

She was face down, so that all he could really make out was the blue and gray helmet of teased up and coned hair. He thought about calling out her name but knew, as his knees buckled underneath his own weight, she wouldn't hear him. He frantically scanned the plethora of controls until he saw the one that read, simply, ON. He pressed it once and the organ began to shut down, wheezing out its last puff of air about a minute later. And finally it was quiet. Dead quiet.

*   *   *

Someone finally thought to call the First Avenue United Methodist Church to get hold of Dr. Bud Millford, who'd just taken the lectern to teach his own Sunday school class, and he arrived in the choir loft at Buford Baptist within fifteen minutes to pronounce Miss Marjorie Whittlehurst. Although services were most definitely cancelled that Sunday, nearly all the arriving members of the congregation remained gathered outside on the lawn, with some spilling out into the parking area—some were standing right next to the Dodge—to observe with reverence and respect the procession of Mr. Charles Robert Tully and his one assistant going into the sanctuary pushing an empty stretcher and eventually coming back out, having picked up their payload of Marjorie Whittlehurst.

Mike Whittlehurst and his pleasant wife, in cooperation with Miller Whittlehurst and his still harried wife, attended to the arrangements for their late aunt. Charles Robert Tully raised no ethical objection to placing the John Deere cushion underneath Miss Marjorie in the casket so she could be (in the words of her nephew Mike) "tall in death," but warned them outright if they insisted on an open viewing at the Buford Memorial Funeral Home they would have to allow the extra preparation time he knew would be required due to the unfortunate spell of time Miss Marjorie had apparently spent in a slumped over position at the organ. And even then—after they consented to delay visitation all the way to Wednesday—Charles Robert Tully was still never completely satisfied with the results of the special putty he employed to camouflage the indention of an F sharp in Marjorie Whittlehurst's right cheek.

The Monumental Spring
of Elba Rae Van Oaks

The Christmas of 1983 was a quiet one in Buford, at least for Elba Rae Van Oaks. She attended the candlelight service at First Avenue United Methodist Church on Christmas Eve, and where historically she had been warmed by the fellowship of all the familiar people who sat in the same spots every time they congregated—holiday service or regular—on that Christmas Eve Elba Rae was gripped by melancholy throughout most of the evening because it was the first candlelight service Ethel Maywood wasn't on the pew beside her.

Hazel Burns traditionally attended Christmas Eve dinner and gift exchange festivities at the home of some Burns kin, who generally rotated hosting duties, leaving Elba Rae to go directly home after church. She ate a chicken pot pie for supper and tried to get interested in the special encore showing of "The Homecoming" on television, but the more she watched the more she regretted it because for some reason that year, Miss Patricia Neal was for all the world reminding Elba Rae of Ethel Maywood, even though she knew good and well Ethel Maywood's temperament wouldn't have been anywhere near as benevolent with seven children tracking snow in the house and wanting to be fed and asking when their daddy was ever going to get home.

Lila Fessmire had not spent Christmas in Buford since the birth of her first child, at which time she'd decreed it was time to forge new traditions with her own family in their own house. Sometimes Ethel Maywood had gone to Birmingham and sometimes, notably after Ethel Maywood's propensity to travel was gone, Lila and the children had visited for a few days after Christmas but before the New Year.

On Christmas day, Elba Rae and Hazel Burns typically shared a meal of a turkey breast and maybe some butter beans if Elba Rae still had any left in the deep freeze, and then they'd sit in the front living room where the small artificial tree was erected and adorned with silver garland and large-bulb colored lights. Their bestowing of gifts to one another was mostly symbolic because they each agreed they neither lacked nor wanted for anything, and afterward they would each remark to the other she had done too much.

Before noon on the day after Christmas, the silver garland was rolled up and the colored lights were wrapped around a piece of cardboard that never seemed to keep them untangled until the next season, and the artificial tree limbs were pulled out of their metal trunk and stuffed back into a big box. Elba Rae Van Oaks was thankful the turkey breast Christmas dinner partaken with Hazel Burns played out in full without mention of Lila, new baby Fessmire, or any other topic likely to have spoiled their otherwise delightful holiday meal.

*   *   *

Mr. Rhinefield at Litton County Monument and Engraving sold monuments and he sold engraving, but he didn't actually do the engraving because engraving monuments took a certain skill he'd never bothered to study on when he bought into the business. And even if he had the skill, he didn't reason he'd be able to be on site selling the monuments and out in the field doing engraving at the same time, and on top of that it just wasn't practical from a fiscal standpoint to employ fulltime an engraver, because every now and again there'd be a bad dry spell in Litton County where a full week would pass without a local citizen obliging by doing the same. He'd spoken about that very topic on more than one occasion with Mr. Charles Robert Tully over at the funeral home. People just didn't understand how perilous it could be to maintain a living when you were relying on folks to die in a reasonable order.

It was for this reason Mr. Rhinefield contracted instead the services of

Mr. Winfred Petersen who knew how to do engraving on monuments and who was in the industry more or less considered an artisan. Mr. Petersen had been known to travel as far north as St. Clair County to do his engraving and as far south as Bullock if they just absolutely couldn't get anyone else to do it, and because the name Winfred Petersen was synonymous with engraving, he wasn't just relying on people going to glory in Buford and the greater Litton County area to generate revenue. His services were pretty much always in demand.

It was the first week of March in 1984 before Mr. Rhinefield at Litton County Monument and Engraving telephoned Elba Rae Van Oaks to notify her that Mr. Petersen had just passed through Buford and had completed his current backlog of orders. Mr. Rhinefield thanked Elba Rae for her business and asked that she please contact him should there be any concerns upon review of the work.

Elba Rae made a fundamental decision that day. She considered discussing the matter with Hazel Burns before executing the plan because it was, after all, Hazel Burns who'd lit the fire under her in the first place, but Elba Rae had recently gotten the impression her cousin was feeling a novel sense of empowerment that didn't need any more encouraging. After a brief holiday suspension, Hazel had taken again to periodically asking Elba Rae if she'd heard from Lila or whether she'd gotten a picture of the baby, and the smugness in her voice was intentionally provoking. She would pick the most inopportune moments to just fling it out there when clearly Elba Rae Van Oaks's natural defenses were off guard, like when they'd first sit down in the Clara Battles Babcock Sunday school class at First Avenue United Methodist Church or when they were sharing a lunch period in the faculty lounge of the Homer T. Litton Grammar School.

Practically since the day school resumed after Christmas break, Hazel Burns had been prone to insinuating the subject of Lila into otherwise ordinary conversations. And every time it happened to her, Elba Rae felt she was being ambushed.

Such a waylay had occurred only a couple of weeks before Mr. Rhinefield called about the engraving when by any possible disinterested party's opinion all Elba Rae Van Oaks had been trying to do was carry out one simple act of compassion. It wasn't as if she'd ever really liked Florine Moss's father in the first place; he was a crotchety old man who most everyone agreed had been plagued with a sour disposition all of his life, and his passing really was a blessing in every sense of the word.

Long before Bufordians had the modern luxury of shopping their well-stocked Piggly Wiggly that since 1979 featured its own deli and in-store bakery counter, Florine Moss's father, Mr. Hawkins, had owned one of only three general merchandise stores in Litton County. Unfortunately as far as Elba Rae was concerned, his store had been the one nearest her childhood home and the one most frequented by the Maywood family. When she was grown and reflected upon it from an adult perspective, it defied all reasoning that Mr. Hawkins had opted for a livelihood in retail sales because he had all the charm of a rattlesnake, that being exactly what Elba Rae recalled her mother saying about him way back in their day anyhow, that he was just mean as a snake.

To a child, he had been intimidating and scary, and the more scared the child, the more he'd seemed to like it. Elba Rae had once been dispatched when she was no more than eight years old to go inside the store alone while her mother, Ethel Maywood, had opted to stay in the car on account of her being near about to deliver Lila at any moment, and it just wasn't proper to be out and about and shopping up and down the aisles of the Hawkins General Mercantile in a gravid condition. All Elba Rae was supposed to have done was select one jar of sweet pickles and take it to the counter where Mr. Hawkins always ran the register himself.

Elba Rae had guessed Mr. Hawkins must have thought she was taking too much time on the other side of the aisle since he hadn't been able to see her from where he'd been standing behind the counter with the register, and that if he had been able to see her he would have perceived clearly she'd merely been exercising appropriate due diligence in her pickle selection. Her momma had been adamant about returning to the vehicle with sweet pickle and for heaven's sake, Elba Rae, don't come out here with dill pickles like you did the last time, because all Elba Rae had been doing was reading the label of the jar just to be sure. Mr. Hawkins, however, had not been able to see Elba Rae and had no patience whatsoever with children who came into his store with their mothers or fathers, much less did he ever have any with children who were unaccompanied. So instead of just leaving the register for one moment and joining her in the pickle aisle, where had Mr. Hawkins not already been mean as a snake he could have conceivably offered assistance, he had instead just yelled, "Hey, Girlie! What are you doing over there?" He'd yelled it so loudly and so gruffly it made Elba Rae drop the jar of pickles she'd finally selected which had, indeed, contained sweet.

She'd begun to cry as soon as she saw him rounding the corner and glaring down at her.

"You're going to pay for those, missy!"

Elba Rae had tried to indicate to Mr. Hawkins that she wanted her momma, but the bawling distorted her plea, so she'd finally just darted past him and out the door. Ethel Maywood—great with child—had ended up having to get out of the car anyway. After tendering currency sufficient for two jars of pickles but getting only one, Ethel had come back, gotten behind the wheel, and said, "hateful ole cuss" as they pulled away.

Elba Rae Van Oaks couldn't help but think about those pickles as she and Hazel Burns had walked into the Buford Memorial Funeral Home together to visit with Florine and the family in the same parlor where they'd had Ethel Maywood on display, and she had to remind herself she was there to support Florine because Elba Rae hadn't wanted to even get close enough to look at the body of old man Hawkins even if he was dead and couldn't yell at her. Florine's mother was already deceased and had been for years, and Ethel Maywood always told it that she sat in a winter's draft and fanned herself to catch pneumonia just to get away from Mr. Hawkins.

"We always hate to give them up, Florine, but you were so fortunate to have him until he was ninety-four."

"I was. But it's just the cycle of life, I reckon."

"That's a good way of thinking about it," Elba Rae said.

"Just like with your momma and the new little one."

Elba Rae Van Oaks stared at Florine as though she didn't know what she was talking about.

"Hazel was telling me just a minute ago about Lila Mae's new grandbaby and you know, it's a shame your momma wasn't able to live long enough to see her first great grandchild."

"Her …" Elba Rae stopped. "Yes, it was."

"I bet she's cute as a button."

Elba Rae smiled at Florine Moss and wanted to respond appropriately while also wishing Hazel Burns would sometimes exercise a bit of decorum and not go around talking about things that didn't need discussing.

"She is," Elba Rae replied to Florine with the intention of saying nothing further on the matter.

By the night a couple of weeks later when Elba Rae Van Oaks sat down in Fettis's chair next to the telephone—after spending the afternoon thinking about what Mr. Rhinefield had said—her heart felt right about what she was doing all on her own; that must surely be a good sign, she thought. Hazel would likely take the credit and think it was all her nudging that did it, but Elba Rae didn't care. She dialed Lila's number in Birmingham and hoped Lila would answer.

Lila could not, plausibly, mask the surprise in her voice when she picked up the receiver and realized it was the sister she'd not talked to in over eight months.

"Am I catching you at a bad time?" asked Elba Rae and it sounded so mannerly, Lila grew mildly suspicious.

"No. I just got the kitchen cleaned up and was about to sit down." She paused. "How are you?"

"I'm fine. How's everybody there?"

"We're all fine. Bucky had the flu right after Christmas and liked to have never gotten over it, but he's finally feeling normal again. Well enough to play golf this morning in forty degree weather, so I guess that means he's cured."

"That's good. And how are Charity and Skippy getting along?"

"Well," Lila said, "they're probably doing better than I expected they would. Skippy's gone to work for Bucky at the agency and Bucky says he might actually have some potential. With a lot of training, that is."

"That's good news. I heard they named the baby Misty."

"They did. Of course, I talked to Charity about using a family name—even if it had to come from his side—but once she and Skippy started looking through one of those baby name books and she saw Misty for the first time, there was never any wavering."

"Misty is a pretty name for a little girl. Misty Grinbar. What about the—"

"I hope Charity remembered to mail a thank you note for the sleeper outfit you sent."

"She did."

"Good."

The flow of conversation then took a pause, and Elba Rae began to feel ill at ease.

"Well, I, uh, the reason I called is I just wanted you to know that Petersen man had finally come through Buford on his rounds and he got the engraving done on Momma's headstone."

"Oh," Lila said, without much feeling. "How does it look?"

"I don't know. I haven't seen it yet."

"Well, you probably should. Before he sends the bill, I mean. Just to make sure everything is right."

"That's what I was thinking, too, but …"

"What?"

"I, uh … I was thinking you should come see it, too." Elba Rae hesitated just briefly, and then, "I mean, I think we should go together to see it for the first time."

"Oh." Lila was then quiet on the other end.

"And," Elba Rae said, "The weatherman on TV said we're going to have a pretty weekend coming up and I was hoping maybe you could get Charity to come down with you. And bring the baby. I'd love to see her. All of you."

"Well, I can ask her and then let you know. Bucky, if you can believe it, has actually been trying to get the boys interested in golf. He gave each of them a set of clubs and they're taking lessons on Saturday mornings. At a public course, obviously, since they're still not allowed at the club. And Skippy spends most Saturdays with his head stuck in a book studying for one of the licensing exams he has to pass."

"Well, okay. Then maybe just you, Charity, and the baby?"

"I'll check with her and let you know."

"All right. Just call me back."

"I will. And, I mean, I don't know why she wouldn't be able to ride down there with me."

"Good," Elba Rae said.

"In fact, Charity will probably jump at the chance to come down with the baby because there's something she's been waiting to tell you anyway—saving for when you finally meet the baby, that is."

"Tell me?"

"Yeah."

"What is it?"

"Oh, it's for her to tell. But I think you'll like it."

*   *   *

Elba Rae stood in the carport door for most of the last fifteen minutes before they arrived, anxious to see the first glimpse of the car coming down the highway so she could be outside to greet them. She was standing in the driveway before Lila turned off the ignition.

Charity Fessmire Grinbar sat in the complementing oyster shale upholstered backseat of Lila's Cadillac, where little Misty was harnessed into a device appropriately protective for transporting infants. Elba Rae opened the car door slowly and leaned in sufficiently to view the child, who was sleeping soundly.

"Hey, baby," Elba Rae whispered collectively to mother and child.

"Hey, Aunt Elba Rae," Charity smiled.

"Hey, Mammaw," Elba Rae said to Lila, with something of a smirk.

Lila rolled her eyes. "That has yet to be determined," she replied while stepping from car. She walked around to the side where Elba Rae was entranced.

"Is she not the prettiest baby you've ever seen?" Lila boasted. She reached inside and tenderly pulled away a hooded top from the baby's head.

"I believe she is and—oh my goodness. Is her hair blonde?"

"Isn't it beautiful?" Lila beamed. "That's apparently a Grinbar trait, since I don't know where it would have come from in our family."

"And it's just as fine as frog's hair," said Elba Rae. "She's precious, Charity."

"Thanks, Aunt Elba Rae," the young mother said.

"I hate to wake the baby up getting her in and out of the car," said Elba Rae. "Do you think while she's sleeping we should go on to the cemetery?"

Lila looked at Charity for a flash of maternal approval.

"I guess we may as well."

Elba Rae was quick to gather a light coat she'd already draped across a chair at the kitchen table, and they were soon en route before the child had a chance to be disturbed.

The three adults courteously conversed along the way about the fortunate warming spell they were experiencing in Buford and how restorative it was to be under a full sun after the gray winter clouds, and Elba Rae even asked Charity about how Skippy was getting along with his insurance lessons. When she mentioned Skippy's name, it didn't seem to Elba Rae that Lila flinched as much as she once had at just the mere mention.

"And Charity," Lila spoke up, "isn't there something you've been saving up to tell Aunt Elba Rae? For when she met the baby for the first time?"

"Oh, yeah!" Charity Grinbar said with excitement. "I can't believe I didn't tell you already!"

The car rolled on down the road toward Glory Hills Cemetery, a place that served as an everlasting reminder of death and loss. Inside Lila Fessmire's car, Elba Rae Van Oaks was all happiness.

*   *   *

No one especially spoke at first while they walked from the narrow road through the graveyard and toward the site where Ethel Maywood was laid to rest. Charity Grinbar stopped once—sidetracked, apparently, by the epitaph she noticed on a marker. She read it aloud softly.

"What's the matter, sweetheart?" Elba Rae asked.

"Oh, nothing, Aunt Elba Rae. I was just looking at this."

"At what? Oh," said Elba Rae, who realized her niece was standing at the months-old plot of Miss Marjorie Whittlehurst that likewise had been recently visited upon by old man Petersen.

"Tall in death. What does that mean, Aunt Elba Rae?"

Elba Rae Van Oaks stared at the marker for a few seconds, shaking her head back and forth.

"I don't know, sweetheart. Because there's no place Marjorie Whittlehurst will ever end up where she'll be tall."

The women resumed their trek. Once they reached the headstone, Elba Rae and Charity stood on one side while Lila took an opposite position. The women looked down at the shiny slab of granite with its newly etched lettering that perfectly and permanently chiseled out the dates Ethel Maywood had been present on earth. The very first sight of it was transfixing.

"He did a good job," Elba Rae finally said.

"Yeah," opined Lila.

And then they stared some more. A few minutes later, the baby squirmed slightly and made the faintest of coo sounds. It was a cheerful distraction from the sobering setting, and Elba Rae was glad to divert her attention to her little grand niece.

"I still can't get over all that blonde hair."

"I know it," Lila smiled widely. "Did you ever see such hair on a baby?"

"No," said Elba Rae. "She's so pretty. She's so pretty she could have won the Miss Honeysuckle contest."

"Miss Honeysuckle contest?" Charity asked, softly, as she gingerly stroked what passed for hairs on the baby's head before repositioning the petite hood around her. "What in the world is that?"

"Oh," Elba Rae sighed, "it's just something they used to have here when we were growing up. Before you were born. It was ..." and when Elba Rae looked over, her eyes immediately met Lila's sudden glance. They grinned at each other across their mother's headstone.

"It was back when Mary Alice was still a blonde," Lila said.

"Who's Mary Alice?" Charity asked.

"She—"

"She," Elba Rae interrupted, "is just somebody from a long time ago."

Elba Rae Van Oaks felt a warming breeze that was meandering through the cemetery. She smiled, and hoped little Misty Rae Grinbar would one day have a sister of her very own.

Appendix

Note: *The following are reprinted with permission of the Ethel Maywood estate, Begina Marie Chittum, and / or other legally interested parties.*

May 26, 1983

Dear Willadean,

We all so appreciated your visit and the food you brought over to the house. Your pecan pies are always the best, and your concern helped us through our difficult time.

Love,
Elba Rae

*   *   *

May 26, 1983

Dear Ulgine,

Thank you so much for bringing the food to the house after Momma died. I had such a crowd in and out over that first few days I don't know how we'd have gotten through it without your potato salad. It was a blessing.

Thank you again,
Elba Rae

*   *   *

May 26, 1983

Dear Florine,

Thank you so much for the delicious Chili Macaroni casserole. You are always so thoughtful and creative with your dishes to come up with something new, and we all enjoyed every bite of it. I want to be sure and get the recipe from you sometime.

Sincerely,
Elba Rae and family

*　　　*　　　*

May 27, 1983

Dear Begina and Aunt Laveetra,

Thank you so much for the beautiful spray of personalized carnations you sent to the funeral home. It meant a lot to us to know you were thinking of Momma. Aunt Laveetra, we're sorry you weren't able to make it over to the service with Begina, but we understand.

Love,
Elba Rae, Lila, and family

*　　　*　　　*

July 23, 1983

Dear Aunt Laveetra and Begina,

Thank you so much for the set of bathtub decals you brought me and Skippy for our wedding. They are very pretty and I'm sure they will keep us from falling. We will put them to good use. You were so thoughtful to remember us.

Love,
Charity & Skippy

*　　　*　　　*

November 28, 1983

Dear Miss Elba Rae,

Thank you so much for the delicious Chicken Florentine casserole you brought over. Your visit and your kindness meant so much to us as we suffered the loss of Aunt Marjorie.

With gratitude,
The Marjorie Whittlehurst family

* * *

January 10, 1980

Dear Miss Ethel,

I know you don't expect any thanks because you are only acting out of the goodness of your heart. But I wanted to say again how generous it was of you to donate the brand new bed jacket to us at the boutique. Some worthy soul will surely be so glad to have it and as you know, all the money paid goes to support our overseas mission.

Sincerely,
Florine Moss

* * *

April 12, 1977

Dear Aunt Ethel Sweetie,

I didn't know what in the world kind of package the mailman was bringing the other day but was just tickled pink to open up the beautiful present. You are so sweet to keep up with my birthday.

The gown is too pretty to wear for every day, but Mother says what's the use of having something nice if you're just gonna save it for the hospital, so I guess I'll have to put it on some time.

Thank you again, Sweetie. Love to Elba Rae and them.

Love you,
Begina
xxx ooo

* * *

January 2, 1975

Dear Ethel Sweetie,

I so appreciate the pair of house slippers for Christmas. Every time I seem to get a new pair, Begina just ends up with them on her big feet so I'm proud to have my own.

Thank you again and you and Elba Rae come see us soon.

Laveetra

*   *   *

March 23, 1969

Dear Laveetra,

Thank you for the new pair of praying hands. You're so thoughtful to always think about me in your ceramics class till I'm almost embarrassed and wish you would stop.

Love,
Ethel

*   *   *

March 30, 1969

Dear Ethel,

I know you told me not to write, but I'm doing it anyway as I thank you for the pretty ceramic hands. You know how I love them so and am always happy to add to my collection. I don't know where you keep finding such unusual ones.

I'm enclosing a picture of them on my nightstand so you can see how nice they look there.

Love,
Wilella

*   *   *

December 18, 1969

Laveetra,

The pretty new pair of hands came in yesterday evening's mail and I didn't want to wait until the 25th to open. Goodness, I just don't know where you find all the different kinds. I don't believe I've ever seen ones holding a baby Jesus before.

Merry Christmas to you and Begina.
Ethel

                    *   *   *

December 27, 1969

Dear Aunt Ethel Sweetie,

Mother and I just love the beautiful crocheted cover you sent us for Christmas. Mother didn't believe you actually made it yourself, but of course I told her I knew good and well you did because I have seen the one covering Elba Rae's plunger and know them to be your work. Where did you ever find a pattern with the praying hands on it?

We have had a mostly good Christmas except for night before last when Mother went wild with the fruitcake and was up with dyspepsia most of the night. I told her she was really going to have to watch herself with that! Ha!

I hope spring will give us a good chance to come to Buford. We're both so lonesome to see you and Elba Rae.

Love you,
Begina
xxx ooo

                    *   *   *

September 2, 1971

Dear Aunt Ethel,

Am back in Denver after another whirlwind trip to Buford last month to finish cleaning out my mother's things. You just have no idea how much stuff somebody can accumulate over the years until you try to pack it all up. Bless her heart, but she still thinks she'll come back from the nursing home some day and will live in her house again. We haven't had the heart yet to tell her it is sold.

Butch and I went through as much as we could, and he took a lot home with him to Montgomery. But I brought a suitcase of odds and ends back with me to Denver and have just recently gotten around to sorting everything out.

As you know, Momma was always the frustrated photographer in the family. I think if she could have left Daddy years ago and gone on the road with her old Brownie camera she'd have lived her dream. You simply can't imagine how many pictures she took and how many were stuffed in drawers, boxes, envelopes, etc.

I was looking through some of them the other day after I got home and came across this old one Momma took of me and Lila Mae when we must have still been in our teens. I'm not certain, but based on our get ups I'm gonna say it was when we competed together in the Miss Honeysuckle pageant. Aren't we a couple of beauties? (HA HA!)

I'm pretty sure I've got a duplicate somewhere so I wanted to send the enclosed on to Lila Mae. But I know they've moved since last Christmas and I can't find their new Mountain Brook address anywhere. I imagine she and the children must be down there in Buford often to visit, so please pass it along to her next time you see them.

Well, I've got about a million things to do and am already late for an appointment to get my hair done, so I'd better finish up. Hope I can stop in to see you next time I'm in Buford.

Love,
Mary Alice

LaVergne, TN USA
09 February 2011
215912LV00002B/45/P

9 781450 267410